Jessica Fletcher Presents...

MURDER, THEY WROTE II

16 All-New Stories From Today's Most Popular Mystery Authors

Featuring:

Deborah Adams · Teri Holbrook · Margaret Maron

Ann Granger · Margaret Lawrence

Veronica Black · Gillian Roberts · P. M. Carlson

Joyce Christmas · Jeanne M. Dams

Leslie O'Kane · Susan Rogers Cooper · Anne Perry

Gallagher Gray · Elizabeth Daniels Squire

Susan Dunlap

MURDER, THEY WROTE II

EDITED BY

Elizabeth Foxwell AND
Martin H. Greenberg

BOULEVARD BOOKS, NEW YORK

MURDER, THEY WROTE II

A Boulevard Book / published by arrangement with
MCA Publishing Rights, a Division of MCA, Inc.

PRINTING HISTORY
Boulevard edition / February 1998

The Putnam Berkley World Wide Web site address is
http://www.berkley.com

ISBN: 1-57297-339-0

BOULEVARD
Boulevard Books are published by The Berkley Publishing Group,
a member of Penguin Putnam Inc.,
200 Madison Avenue, New York, New York 10016.
BOULEVARD and its logo
are trademarks belonging to Berkley Publishing Corporation.

PRINTED IN THE UNITED STATES OF AMERICA

10 9 8 7 6 5 4 3 2 1

Contents

CONTENTS

Introduction

Dear Reader,

It gives me great pleasure to welcome you to another collection of murder mysteries by some of the finest women writers in the field. Even though my career keeps me busy, what with author tours and interviews and all, it's always nice to get back to what I love most—reading and writing mysteries.

The stories in this collection span a wide range of styles, from the classical historical mystery to tales of modern day mischief. Everywhere from nineteenth-century England to South Carolina is visited in the following pages. No matter how much time goes by, it seems that murder is one aspect of life that remains with us, year in and year out. Well, that and the sleuths who solve the cases, of course.

Along with the various locations, the detectives come in all different shapes and sizes as well. From a psychic who assists her local police force to a stand-up comedian to an elderly aunt with a mind like the proverbial steel trap, all of the sleuths in the following pages have one thing in common (besides being female): a knack for solving crime.

Naturally, not all of these stories are from the detective's point of view. We have an unusual gamut of criminals as well, and a few surprises to keep you on your toes.

Interestingly enough, the profession of writing figures prominently in more than one of these stories. I can tell you from long experience, nothing like what you'll read here has ever happened whenever I went on a book tour or sat down to plot my next mystery. These stories almost make mystery writing seem *too* exciting.

Well, be it exciting or not, it has always been great fun, plotting the dastardly crime, planting the red herrings and false alibis, and then solving the case with swift, sure deduction. I hope the authors in this book enjoyed writing these stories; as I read them, it sure seemed that way.

Unlike the first book, I'm afraid my schedule has made it impossible for me to make an appearance, save for writing this introduction. However, I was able to write a few words as a kind of short commentary for each story. I hope you'll enjoy them as much as I did.

One of the most interesting parts of my career is actually going out and meeting my fans. It is wonderful to know that my work is enjoyed by so many people. The fact that an odd accident or two happens to pop up from time to time is a professional hazard, I guess. The pair of detectives in the following story, however, seem to go out of their way to find a crime.

The Cadaver Waltzed at Noon

Deborah Adams

It started during that long, hot summer when I was writing my first mystery novel. I'd already published a half-dozen romances and not one of them had sold more than ten copies. Colleagues insisted that my failure to rake in the big bucks was due largely to my public presence, or lack of same.

You see, writing a book isn't enough these days. One must promote one's work and oneself, hawking the literary wares with inexhaustible energy and enthusiasm. I do not care for what seems to me like good, old-fashioned hucksterism, nor have I the personality to enchant an audience with my wit and perky charm. I am a writer, and that is all I wish to be.

I realized, of course, that the same silly requisite would

1

apply to the mystery genre, and this dilemma hung over me on that humid afternoon when my neighbor Jennifer Fischer popped in to deliver a plate of freshly baked brownies. Jennifer had taught home ec at Coble Court High School for years but had recently retired, just weeks before the sudden death of her beloved husband, Francis. Without a job or a dependent male to absorb her, she'd invested her considerable energy in hovering like a mother hen around the residents of Coble Court, our picturesque seaside village.

"Oh, Lydia," she had said to me on more than one occasion, "there's so much time in my life now! And I do so love baking and serving and hosting the occasional soiree. Humor me, dear. Let me whip up a meal for you. Cornish hen? Or some of my famous clam chowder?"

Jennifer *is* the domestic goddess, cleaning and scrubbing and polishing everything from bedknobs to broomsticks. Always impeccably groomed, she seems to have been born with full understanding of the social graces. This was a great help to Francis and his career, but with him dead and buried . . . well, Jennie's art was wasted.

Jennifer Fischer was exactly what an author ought to be in public—she could small talk for hours on end, exhibited saintly patience with tiresome people, and she never, never put her foot in her smiling mouth. Her greatest handicap was that she simply couldn't bear to be alone—due in part, I am sure, to the fact that there is so little activity in her brain that she could easily drop into a coma without external stimulation. What a pity, I thought, that we couldn't toss ourselves into a blender and come out neatly balanced.

And then it hit me. Why couldn't Jennie be me? She could go on tour to promote the books, stand for hours at cocktail parties carrying on inane conversations with total strangers, and smile without embarrassment when fans praised the latest book or respond civilly to reviewers who trashed it. It was the perfect solution. Jennie would get the life she was suited for, and I could stay home and write.

The hardest part was not convincing Jennie to go along with the plan, but making her understand it. As I've mentioned, she isn't a terribly clever woman. I had to explain several times, stressing the importance of secrecy, before she caught on. "Oh!" she exclaimed at last, clapping her manicured hands. "It's almost like being a spy. How glamorous!"

Once that was settled, it was simply a matter of typing her name—J. B. Fischer—on the manuscript. That first mystery novel was an instant best-seller, and while I feel that it was a well-written book, I must give credit where credit is due. Jennifer played her part so well that my editor (who spoke condescendingly to me over the phone in his firm belief that I was merely drab little Lydia Vickers, Jennie's secretary) actually became somewhat infatuated with her upon their first meeting.

Best-seller followed best-seller and book tour followed book tour. Jennie sparkled before audiences, live and televised. I feared that someone would question her ability to write all those books when she was constantly away from the typewriter on promotional tours or frolicking on holidays with her endless supply of relations. Luckily most people believe that a novel can be written during the odd weekend, and after a few years, when no one noticed the discrepancy, I relaxed and admitted that we had hit upon the ideal way in which to manage a writing career.

Jennie's successful personal appearances would have been enough to keep her in the public eye, but there soon developed an unusual, even spooky, side effect to her tours. Wherever Jennie went, murder followed. What's more, she began to fancy herself a sleuth and made well-intentioned, if muddled, efforts to solve the murders that surrounded her.

This is why I eventually took to wearing a pager. Jennie's reputation (and therefore, my sales) grew more and more dependent upon her ability to keep herself in the news by solving these murders. Since she is quite hopeless at untangling clues or following a thread of logic, it is necessary for us to remain in almost constant contact so that I can steer her in the right direction when she undertakes her detecting. Naturally this sort of consultation took time and energy I'd have preferred to devote to writing, but I could see no way to avoid it.

While I'd gained some freedom from the promotional activities, I hadn't been able to untangle myself from the social whirl of Coble Court. Friends and neighbors, perceiving me as a lonely and pathetic woman because of my reclusive ways, were intent upon drawing me out of my shell. No less than six busybodies had cajoled, harassed, and nagged until I'd agreed to attend the annual Halloween ball. Held at the historic Bellvue Mansion, the party is traditionally dull, but for reasons I don't understand the entire town attends year after boring year.

Jennie and I arrived together, she dressed as Cinderella's fairy godmother and I in my usual working costume. "You're going as a bag lady?" Jennie had said with disapproval. I chose not to enlighten her.

The Halloween ball is always held in the middle of the day to free up our citizens for their candy-dispensing duties in the evening. This, of course, makes the party-goers look even more ridiculous as they parade about in vampire teeth and werewolf masks in the early hours. An effort had been made to give the scene an eerie atmosphere—candles burned in strategic nooks and corners, angel hair spider webs and crepe-paper ghosts dangled from the doorways, and a life-size plastic cadaver was suspended from the chandelier in the foyer. It was exquisitely tacky and I meant to say so to Jennie, but she was immediately surrounded by adoring fans and friends, all of whom wanted to know when her next book would be out.

"You know, I've got a standing order at the bookstore. The minute a new J. B. Fischer mystery comes out, they just put it on my tab and send it on over," said one.

"Same here," said another.

Jennie smiled and chuckled. "What dear, dear friends you all are," she said sincerely.

Having been thoroughly ignored by the literati, I made my way across the room to where the Harvey girls were in command of refreshments. *Girls* is hardly an accurate description of the sixty-something twins, but their behavior belies their age. Still giggling and flirting and wearing matching taffeta gowns with beaded and feathered masks, they must have believed themselves to be belles of the ball. I myself was a reluctant debutante at best and I both envy and despise their coquettish behavior.

Just as I reached the table, Sylvia Harvey eagerly thrust an overflowing cup of punch into the hands of our gruff but lovable town doctor who had dressed, appropriately, in a white lab coat. A man after my own heart! "Here you are, Doc," she giggled. "I poured this just for you."

"Why, thank you, kind lady," Doc said graciously, but with a leery glance at the sisters. A confirmed bachelor, he's been on the run from their artless advances for as long as any of us can remember, but Sylvia and her sister Sybil never give up. Sylvia even attempted to grab Doc for a dance, but he sidestepped the grasping hand with gallant and long-suffering ease.

I held out my hand for a cup of what Jennie calls "the Harveys' vile brew" and was rewarded with a few drops of Sybil's secret recipe punch. Seeing my dismay, Sybil explained, "Don't want to run out too soon, do we?"

There was no point in reminding her that Doc had received his share and three others. I understood the politics of besotment. Speaking of politics, I thought, and looked around for an escape route as Jerry Manchuria appeared out of nowhere. He was dressed as George Washington, complete with powdered wig.

"Doc! Lydia!" Jerry tried to capture both of us in his beefy arms, but quick reflexes saved us from his grasp. Unperturbed, Jerry launched into his spiel. "I hope I can count on your support in the upcoming election!" he boomed.

I could sense the sharp retort building in Doc and did my best to ward off hostilities. "Isn't that your cadaver, Doc?" I asked, pointing to the gruesome chandelier decoration.

"Drumming up business, Doc? Or is that one of your patients after treatment? Ha ha!" Jerry's guffaw shook the room.

"Now, see here, you—" Doc sputtered.

Thick as ever, Jerry babbled on. "Dick Arnold was supposed to be here with one of my campaign posters. Clever idea my mother had. It's a cardboard door with the slogan *The door to the future is open*. Now where could Arnold be?"

"A few minutes ago," the doctor said through tight lips, "Arnold raced out. Of the door, I have no knowledge."

"You can't find good help these days," Jerry grumbled.

Muttering under his breath, Doc eased into the crowd attempting to escape, but Jerry Manchuria stayed with him. "Now, Doc," I heard him say, "about your campaign contribution . . ."

Finding myself alone with the tittering Harveys, I held out my near-empty cup. Still dazed by her nearness to Doc, Sylvia absentmindedly ladled out a second tiny helping.

"He's such a nice man, isn't he?" she sighed.

Before I could snap out a nasty retort, I felt myself lurch forward, propelled by a solid blow from behind.

"Oh, gosh, Miss Vickers!" exclaimed Brady Fischer. "I'm so sorry! I didn't even see you!"

Jennie's bumbling nephew stepped all over me in his attempt to apologize. It is possible, I suppose, that he will someday overcome the family curse and actually develop a functioning brain, but that remains to be seen. For now he is simply a chronically unemployed adult living off the generosity of his aunt.

"Never mind, Brady," I said wearily. "No harm done."

"I've caused you to spill your punch," he pointed out. Sure enough, the cup had dribbled its contents all over the floor. "Let me get you another."

"It might be better to wipe up the floor before someone steps in it," I pointed out.

"Oh, sure," he said, still flustered. He pulled a handkerchief from his pocket and wiped ineffectually at the sticky spot. "Just let me be sure you're all right." Brady carried on as if he thought I might have a broken bone or two I hadn't noticed.

"Forget it, Brady. If any lumps develop, I'll have the doctor check me out."

"That old coot couldn't spot an extra arm growing out of your ear!"

Brady's comment contained more anger than you might imagine. Dim as the boy is, it hasn't escaped his notice that Doc has been spending an unusually large portion of his time with Jennifer lately. No doubt Brady is worried that the relationship might develop into something permanent. Something, say, that would roust Brady from his comfy position as Jennie's live-in caretaker, thus forcing him to make his own way in the world.

Feeling a twinge of sympathy for the boy, I made an effort to assuage his fear. "Don't worry, Brady. Jennie isn't likely to take on a new husband at this stage in her life. Why, she's busy enough with her travel and, uh, writing."

"I certainly hope you're right," he said plaintively. "Aunt Jen only sees the best in people. She hasn't got a clue what's really going on with—" he stopped suddenly, as if he'd let slip a secret, then continued with false cheer. "Well, I think I'm ready for some of that delicious punch!"

I watched Brady whispering with the Harvey girls. Then he left the table abruptly, heading across the crowded room. If it was punch he wanted, he certainly was taking the long way around. I wondered where on earth he might be headed, but before he reached his destination, I was distracted by a tap on the shoulder.

"Have you seen Jerry?" Dick Arnold asked. Dick is one of those unfortunate men with shifty eyes and a pointed chin that make him look like the weasel-faced crook in a bad movie. One can't help but suspect him of being up to *something*, even though his reputation, so far as I knew, had always been without blemish.

"He just left," I said helpfully. "He was chasing after Doc and looking for you. Something about a door."

"Oh, no! The door!" Dick's hands flew up to his mouth and he seemed to be chewing all his fingernails at once.

"Did you forget to bring the door, Dick?" I asked.

He nodded nervously.

"Then why don't you run out and get it while Jerry's occupied?" I suggested.

Poor Dick scurried away, a nervous collapse waiting to happen. Deciding that I had fulfilled my social commitment for the month, I darted into the kitchen in search of a quiet place to jot down notes. Dick's door would make a fine clue in the book I was outlining and I wanted to get my thoughts on paper right away.

Thirty minutes later I had finished mapping out my plot and deemed it an appropriate time to take my leave. Surely I had suffered enough social chitchat! Unfortunately, I bumped right into Jennie as I was exiting the kitchen.

"Dear heart," Jennie said. "You are supposed to be enjoying yourself. There's food, music, good company—why, there's something for everyone, even an old stick in the mud like you. So why are you standing in the corner?"

"I was just chatting with Dick Arnold. And before that, with Brady," I told her. "He's—"

"Yes, dear, I know. He's a court jester, awkward and worthless. But I adore him and he does keep the grass cut, so let's not dwell on it."

"I was going to say—"

"You know," Jennie went on, "this room is entirely too bright. It would be so much more evocative with candlelight. Or even gaslight. I wish someone had asked my opinion." She put her empty punch cup on a nearby table after first rounding up a coaster for it, then smiled hypocritically at Sylvia Harvey. In a not-so-discreet whisper she hissed, "I see Sylvia is still wallowing in her season of passion. The poor woman . . ."

There was no point in trying to talk to her. Jennie's mind seldom sticks to a subject for more than two minutes, but I wasn't about to stand there discussing party decor or unrequited love for even that length of time.

"I'm getting a terrible headache," I told her. "I'll just go on home now. Come by in the morning and I'll tell you the plot of the new book. You've got that phone interview tomorrow afternoon, you know."

"Oh, Lydia," she sighed. "You know I never remember all those details. Jot down a few notes and I'll refer to them. I don't know how anyone can tell these books apart anyway.

They're all the same: someone dies, someone investigates, someone gets arrested."

My retort was lost in the clang of a grandfather clock announcing midday. At exactly the same time, a piercing scream cut through the room and echoed until the last bong had tolled. The cadaver above us danced as heavy footsteps thudded across the second floor.

"What on earth?" Jennie asked. She marched boldly across the room and up the wide steps, where she met a screaming Sybil Harvey in the dark at the top of the stairs.

"Oh, Jennie!" Sybil sobbed. "I just went to powder my nose and I found . . . I found . . ." Sybil threw herself into Jennie's arms, screeching and howling like an enraged banshee.

By the time the sheriff arrived, the party-goers had separated into clumps of four to five people eying each other suspiciously. Jennie and I were guarding the guest bedroom where Doc's body lay cooling on the plush-pile carpet. This had been my idea. Knowing that the famous J. B. Fischer would be expected to investigate, I thought some coaching was imperative before the authorities arrived.

"Keep it simple," I instructed. "You heard Sybil scream. You peeked into the room, saw that Doc was beyond help, and then ordered everyone away from the crime scene. Since then we've been right here."

"But shouldn't I look for clues?" Jennie asked.

"Leave that for the police, Jennie. Don't even try to think."

It seemed like a workable plan. So long as Jennie offered no comment, she couldn't put her foot in her mouth and she would appear modest and ladylike. I thought I'd covered all the bases. Unfortunately her reputation for detection had preceded us.

From the sheriff's shallow examination of the body, one might have assumed the doctor's corpse was nothing more than litter on a sidewalk. With a puzzled expression our primary law enforcement officer looked up at Jennie. "Now, Miz Fischer," he said, "what do *you* think happened here?"

Jennie was accustomed to being on stage, and with the flair of the consummate performer, she jumped in on cue. "It appears, sheriff, that the doctor has been murdered. Stabbed in the back with a pair of scissors. Unless, of course, he stumbled and fell backward, impaling himself on those scissors."

"Ha, ha," the sheriff chuckled. "I've always admired your sense of humor, Miz Fischer."

"Yes, Jennie," I flashed her a warning glance. "It's very thoughtful of you to try and lighten our sense of loss. Maybe the sheriff would be interested in what you told me earlier. You know, when you suggested tracing the doctor's movements throughout the morning?"

For a moment Jennie's face registered pure bewilderment, and I feared she'd blow our cover right there. Luckily the sheriff picked up the ball.

"That's a good idea, Miz Fischer!" he beamed. "Uh . . . where do you think I should start?"

Jennie turned to me for help. "Lydia?"

"Yes, that's right," I said quickly. "I saw him at the punch bowl just after we got here. The doctor and I spoke briefly and then he excused himself."

"Did you see anybody else talking to him?"

"I believe Jerry Manchuria was trying to start a conversation. I'm not sure how successful he was. Doc has never been one to mince words, and Jerry was particularly irritating today."

"Then I guess I'd better have a talk with candidate

Manchuria," the sheriff said. "Sure would appreciate it, Miz
Fischer, if you'd come along."

"Why, certainly!" Jennie chirped graciously. "I'll do all I
can to help."

Left alone with the corpse, I began my investigation in
earnest. Doc's pockets yielded nothing of particular interest—wallet, pocketknife, a few pieces of loose change. I
crawled slowly around the body, scanning the area for any
stray clue such as a button from the killer's clothing, but
nothing had been left behind. Just inches from his right
hand, however, I felt a damp spot on the carpet and ran my
fingers across it. It appeared that someone had washed away
something, but what? There was blood enough everywhere
else, and certainly no effort had been made to conceal the
cause of death.

I rose to my feet, speculating on the meaning of this one
enigma as I continued to search for information. The bed-
covers were rumpled, and there was a sticky ring on the
table nearby, but by far the most mysterious discovery was
the moist carpet. By the time the suspects gathered in the
room with me, I had formulated a theory.

Jennie and the sheriff had brought with them Jerry
Manchuria, Dick Arnold, and Brady Fischer, all of whom
resembled frightened rabbits. Jerry, of course, still managed
to get in part of his campaign speech, insisting that such a
heinous crime would never have happened under his admin-
istration.

"You three," the sheriff said sternly to the twitching assembled males, "were the last ones to see Doc alive. It
stands to reason that one of you must be the killer."

"Does anyone have a motive?" I asked cheerfully.

Dick Arnold broke down immediately. "I'd never kill

anybody!" he insisted. "Not even Doc, not even after what he did to me!"

"And just what might that have been?" The sheriff was reaching for his handcuffs, certain that he had the murderer.

"Oh, I may as well tell you," Dick said. "The Doc knew about something I did. But it was only once! I kept telling him that, but he wouldn't—"

"What did you do that was so horrible?" I asked gently.

Dick dropped his head and mumbled into his chest, "I took a magazine."

"A magazine?"

"One with those pictures. You know, the dirty ones." His face flushed a brighter red than boiled lobster as we all waited to hear why this was of any interest at all to the dead man. "Well, I couldn't very well buy it, could I? Then the store clerk would've known I had it! Doc saw me, though, and he wouldn't let me forget. He made me do things—mow his yard, clean his windows! I was a slave to him, but I swear I didn't kill him."

"It's not much of a motive," I agreed, and even the sheriff nodded.

"How about the rest of you?" I asked. "Brady, when you said you were going for punch, I noticed that you actually left the room. Did you follow Doc?"

"No, no!" Brady cried. "It was Sybil! She'd asked me to meet her in the back hall. She said she wanted to talk to me privately, about getting Doc's affections back from Aunt Jen."

"And Sybil will back up your story?" I asked.

Brady nodded firmly. "You bet she will."

"Well, Mr. Manchuria, I guess that just leaves you, doesn't it?" The sheriff, now convinced that his deductive reasoning had paid off, removed the handcuffs from his belt.

"Now, now," Jerry said in his smooth, slimy manner. "It's

true that Doc had jested with me about a boyish stunt. Why, it's certainly nothing to kill for. Everybody does it. I ask you, what senior class president hasn't pulled a few strings to get elected?"

Well, this was a fine mess. The sheriff looked at his prime suspects and sighed. "So all of you were being blackmailed by Doc. This seems to be goin' nowhere." Turning to Jennie, he added, "Unless you've got an idea, Miz Fischer!" He gazed at her, faith shining in his eyes.

"Wel-l-l-l . . ." Jennie said hesitantly.

"Did you show him this?" I pointed to the table beside me, and the ring of punch that marred its surface.

Jennie stepped forward for a closer look. "Travesty," she declared with a shudder.

"Jennie noticed this right away," I explained to the sheriff. "See? There's a sticky ring, most likely made when someone put a cup of punch here. Notice, too, this damp area on the floor—where someone obviously cleaned up a spill. The killer came to this room expecting not to kill the doctor, but merely to talk to him. Isn't that what you said, Jennie?"

She replied tentatively, "Why . . . yes."

"Jennie thinks the conversation took a bad turn, and the murder was committed on impulse," I went on. "The killer dropped his punch during the struggle, then tried to clean away the evidence on the carpet but overlooked this ring on the table."

"Do tell." The sheriff gazed at Jennie with undisguised awe. "So who did it? Who killed the Doc?"

Jennie turned to me with that deer-in-the-headlights look. "It's—"

"You're right, of course, Jennie," I said quickly. "there's only one explanation. Brady," I looked him straight in the eye, "you remember bumping into me. You caused me to spill my punch. Didn't the cup leave a ring just like this one when I set it down?"

"I didn't do it!" Brady shouted. "I didn't kill anybody!"

"Of course you didn't commit the murder, Brady. I saw it myself—you never took a cup of punch before leaving to meet with Sybil."

Jennie's eyes were wide. "Lydia," she said quietly.

"Yes, yes! I confess!" I screamed. "I killed the doctor. I came here to seduce him, but he spurned my advances!"

At this point in the narrative, I began to sob.

Jennie was the first person to visit me in the tiny jail cell, arriving almost before the sheriff had booked me. "Lydia," she sighed. "What on earth are you doing? The doctor didn't spurn your advances! Why, you wouldn't know *how* to seduce a man. You had no reason to kill him."

"So long as you keep quiet, though, no one will ever figure that out. And you *will* keep it to yourself, Jennie," I warned.

She took a step back.

"If you don't back up my story—that I loved Doc and killed him in a jealous rage—then the truth will have to come out."

Jennie blanched. "You mean—?"

"That's right," I said. "I couldn't help noticing, Jennie, that you had an empty punch cup later. Just before Sybil screamed. And since you have often expressed your opinion of the Harvey girls' punch, I can't believe you'd have gulped down so much as a drop."

"You're right, of course, Lydia," she said quietly. "I had hoped I could get away with it. I thought I'd learned enough from you to commit the perfect crime, but I see I was wrong. Oh, who would have believed that good housekeeping habits would be my downfall? I only wanted to rinse out that darned cup before the punch dried in it. I suppose just this once it would have been better to leave the dirty dishes." She sighed heavily. "There's nothing to do but tell the sheriff the truth and get you out of this horrible place right away."

"And how would you like to spend *your* life behind bars, wearing prison drabs and eating clam chowder from a can?" I could see that the very thought terrified her. "No, Jennie. You aren't going to say a word to contradict my confession. I shall take full blame for the murder, and you—you will follow my instructions to the letter. Won't you?"

Jennie nodded miserably. "Whatever you say, Lydia," she whispered.

"One thing, though. Tell me why you killed him. Surely Doc wasn't blackmailing you, too. What could there be in your pristine life that would put you at his mercy?"

"Francis," she said, so quietly I almost didn't hear.

"Francis?"

Jennie collapsed onto the lumpy cell cot and pulled a starched, hand-embroidered handkerchief from her purse. "After forty-five years of marriage, I woke up one morning and realized that Francis had sucked me dry. I'd cooked, I'd cleaned, I'd thrown dinner parties for his boss on a moment's notice—everything I did, I did for that husband of mine. And do you know, Lydia, he never once thanked me. He never washed a dish or even lifted his feet when I vacuumed. The man was a slug, and I was sick of him. I thought retirement would give me time for relaxation and hobbies I'd always wanted to try, but Francis absorbed every minute. 'Now that you don't have anything else to do,' he'd say, 'come and sit by me while I read.'"

Her description of this forced togetherness made me cringe. No wonder she'd had to do away with her husband.

Under the circumstances, what woman wouldn't have done the same?

"And so I killed him," she said simply. "It's very easy to poison someone who gobbles down every bite of food you put in front of him without even tasting it. If only he'd complimented me once or twice. If only he'd stopped to smell the chowder."

I let her shed a few dainty tears before I asked, "And was Doc blackmailing you, too?"

"Oh, yes," she admitted. "I thought we were friends. Very close friends, of course. He'd mentioned marriage once or twice, but I convinced him that I could never replace Francis. And then today, when I met him in the bedroom for— well, for a little romance—he wouldn't take no for an answer. He told me that if I didn't marry him, he'd spill the beans. Oh, Lydia! All these years, he's been keeping the results of tests he did on Francis's body. Doc *knew*."

I suppose even Jennie's dull mind must have understood that her confession gave me a great deal of power over her— every bit as much as Doc had wielded. She listened intently as I explained that I would keep quiet about her crimes and that she would be able to keep her share of future royalties, just the way we'd originally planned. After all, I wouldn't be needing much where I was headed. I also reminded her that it was more important than ever that she keep our arrangement secret.

"Oh, yes, Lydia," she said tearfully. "But I feel dreadful about this. You're a saint to take the blame for me. Isn't there something I can do to ease your load?"

"Yes," I told her. "Bring me paper and pens while I'm in prison. Finally I'll have the time and privacy to write all the books that are in me, and no one will expect me to go on a book tour. At least not until after my parole."

Although there's something to be said for friendly competition, every once in a while people just go too far. And whether it's playing music or murder, there can only be one winner. Best not to think about what happens to the loser. Maybe someone should have told that to the two women you're about to meet.

Both Feet

Teri Holbrook

The best thing Olive Bless ever said about Marla Parcels was that she thought her hair a conceivable shade of orange. "Not that it'd be found atop anyone's head," she always added. "It's conceivable if you happen to be in the life jacket section of Kmart." She would insert a pause for the giggles and the *Law, Olive, how you go on,* then turn from the mirror and stalk away. Olive never made comments about Marla in public; that would be tacky, and even without hairspray Marla had enough tack for everybody.

For forty years Olive and Marla had faced each other across the sanctuary of the tiny Methodist church in Kirkins, Alabama—Olive to the right of the altar rail on the piano, Marla to the left on the organ. From that position they held weekly duels, firing gospel songs at each other and lobbing processionals like grenades. At least, that was how Olive

saw it. For her part Marla seemed oblivious to the war, gazing beatifically at the preacher, her fingers never missing a
key. Like she didn't despise Olive. Like she didn't know
Olive was banging on the cracked piano ivory like it was
Marla's own white skin.

Olive couldn't pinpoint the exact moment she realized
she detested Marla Parcels. It had been gradual, a slow understanding that the face across the sanctuary was an unset-
tling thing, then an unlikable thing, then finally a despicable
thing. Part of the problem was Marla's lipstick, which in her
youth had been pink and inside the lines but by her fifties resembled a toothed and dented stop sign. Part of the problem
was Marla's earrings, which knocked against her jaw and
drew attention away from the mozzarella chin that grew
longer each year despite the tape stuck behind her ears to lift
the sag. But the main problem was her instrument. Olive's
piano was as straight an arrow as an instrument could be:
press a key and a felt hammer hit a string. On occasion a single foot tapped the damper pedal. The organ, however, was
something else entirely—mysterious, groaning, driven by
air and pipes and a floor of bones. It required all limbs,
which Marla gave it, her legs far apart and rising, her dress
pushed free of her knees. That, Olive knew, was the reason
the front pew was never empty of men. It also explained
why Marla had been married and divorced five times.

So when she saw Marla running up the drive to her house,
the wind pushing her hair and flattening her dress, Olive had
to argue with herself before opening the door. She'd seen
the woman Wednesday night at choir practice; she'd see her
in the morning at church. She didn't need to disrupt a quiet
autumnal Saturday afternoon listening to babble. At the window, however, she paused. There was something in the
wildness of the other woman's eyes as she mounted the
porch, something about the slack mouth, the blanched lips,

that filled Olive with excitement. No, that wasn't right. It filled her with superiority.

Marla was near panic as Olive opened the screen door.

"You've got to help me," she said. "I killed Luther."

Olive eyed Marla critically. "You killed Luther? Whatever for?"

"What do you mean, whatever for? He was seeing a woman over in Huntsville. He said awful words to me, Olive, just awful. It all got out of hand. I hit him with my hoe."

"What makes you think he's dead?"

"I hit him twice."

Olive bit back the comment that it was probably the first time Marla had ever done the same thing twice to a man. She leaned against the door frame, the screen propped open with her elbow, and studied her nemesis. Marla certainly looked as if she could have done murder. Her hair, usually cotton-candy stiff, listed to one side of her head. Her left knee poked out of a large hole in her pantyhose. She wore no makeup, motive enough, Olive thought, for killing a witness. With a surge of contempt, she noted that without cosmetics, Marla looked much younger than fifty-four. How ironic that a woman who had pursued youth and sex so ferociously could have had both with a simple jar of Ponds.

Then she glanced down at Marla's hands. Her fingernails were encrusted with red grime.

"Marla," she whispered. "What have you been up to?"

"I told you." Marla's voice was frantic. "I killed Luther Barns."

Luther Barns was an unmarried, small-time cattle farmer who owned land west of Kirkins. By Kirkins standards he was well off, although the bulk of his fortune lay, as he readily explained to everyone, in the future when the growth that had hit Huntsville and Decatur drifted south and he could sell his property for a country club development. He had it all worked out: The rolling valley land that fed his cattle was golf ball nirvana, and he could already point out the imaginary paths where golf carts and their executive cargo would purr and curse in the early mornings. "And I'm going to be one of them," he would beam, even though he had never hit a ball in his life. "I'm going to be out there in my clean golfer's cap and my shiny clubs, and I'll have to beat lonely women off with a stick."

This last part Olive had overheard in the Kwik Stop, when she was in the toothpaste aisle and he had been talking with Jasper Claybourne at the counter. She had slipped from the store without buying anything, knowing she had not been meant to hear.

Well, she thought, staring at Marla, it wasn't Luther doing the stick beating after all. She cringed at the thought of the hoe biting into the softness of his neck. It would be the neck, wouldn't it? If not the first blow, then surely the second . . .

"Where is he, Marla? Where did you leave him?"

Marla started to cry. "In the shed behind my house. He was in there looking for the trug he gave me—said his mother brought it over from England and it was supposed to go in the house, not the shed, that I was trash for putting it in the shed, and I said, but it's just a stupid basket, not even a whole basket, flowers won't stand up in it, and he said he didn't know what he was thinking when he gave it . . ."

Olive held up her hand. "Okay, Marla, calm down." She looked around her yard and down the road. "How'd you get here? I don't see your car."

"I parked it over by the church. Nobody's there Saturday afternoons. I didn't want anyone to see me come here."

Olive bit the side of her lip, her fingers tightening around the hook on the screen door. "Why me, Marla? Why did you come here?"

Marla's pale green eyes widened. "You're my closest friend, Olive. I've known you all my life. If I couldn't come to you, what would I do?"

The tip of the metal hook bit into Olive's hand. Her closest friend? Balls. They had never been friends. True, they had been together for at least twice a week for four decades, but it had always been behind their boxed barricades—Marla's golden oak, Olive's deep mahogany. Olive couldn't even say that the music had bonded them together. They had developed a certain synchronicity, each playing to match the other's rhythm, but the organ always ruled. No matter that Olive was the better musician on the piano with her cupped palms and precise fingering. The breath of the organ was absorbing. It drew in the congregation like a call girl.

The green eyes were impossibly wide now, a layer of water magnifying the irises. When most people cried, their eyes grew small like nuts, Olive thought. Leave it to Marla . . . Still, they were the only women from the county Comprehensive High School class of 1960 to remain in Kirkins. And Marla, while a harvester of husbands, had never taken to women friends. Perhaps in her limited world of matrimony and divorce lawyers Olive did constitute her closest friend. How odd. What a damned peculiar thing.

"Come in, then," Olive said. "You wash up while I get the keys to my truck. We'll go out the back way so no one will see us." She paused. "Use the guest towel in the bathroom, wipe out the sink real good and then bring the towel with you."

The truck was a 1982 black Chevrolet, bought because of her late father's insistence that a single woman with a mere car was a ninny. "What if you have to haul a hot water heater? What if the tractor breaks and you have to take it in for repairs? You gonna go prissing over to some man to help you? No, lady-girl, you do it yourself."

Of course, the first time the hot water heater broke, she had to call Jasper Claybourne to help her load the thing for the dump. And when the tractor—a small vehicle that was little more than a glorified riding lawn mower—did finally need attention, it took Jasper, Luther and two McClanahan boys to get it on the truck. Nevertheless, she knew her father had been right. No one was ever going to call her a ninny.

She threw two blankets and a box of large plastic trash bags into the bed of the truck. She had no idea what she was going to do, but she figured blankets and bags would figure into it.

At the door to the cab she hesitated. Marla shivered in the passenger seat, the dirty towel wrapped around her arms. For a second Olive wondered if she was doing the right thing, if it wasn't in her best interest to slam the door shut, run to the house and call the sheriff's office. *Marla Parcels is in my truck with Luther Barns's blood on her. I always told folks too much hair dye could seep into your scalp and make a mess of your brain. . . .* Then she looked through the truck window at Marla, who sat staring at the dashboard, her fingers plucking at the towel's brown cotton piles. Not exactly the organ, is it? she thought. No line of men waiting for you to lose yourself in the chorus of "Standing in the Need of Prayer." And no man you can run to, is there? Marla Parcels the Man Killer ain't likely to find herself walking down the aisle anymore. If anyone finds out. Olive grabbed hold of the door and hauled herself up behind the wheel.

The geographical layout of Kirkins was conducive to murder and secrecy. Olive lived on a five-acre plot of land on the outskirts of town. Her nearest neighbors were three teenagers who lived in a trailer located on the other side of a thick stand of cedar trees; she was aware of them only on Friday nights when they drank too much and she had always possessed the good sense to never call them on it. As she followed the dirt drive along the tree line to the back of her property, she was grateful for their urbanlike anonymity. The drive ended at an asphalt road that, had she turned right, would lead to the heart of Kirkins, past the church, the post office, the volunteer fire department, and city hall. Olive turned left and followed the asphalt road as it meandered westward through the outlying farms and piney woods before eventually curling in on itself and heading toward Marla's simple frame house.

Beside her Marla made hiccupping sounds.

"He said awful words to me, Olive. Told me I was stupid, how no man would want someone as old and stupid as me. Said he found a smarter woman over in Huntsville. Can you believe that? Said he'd been seeing her for nearly six months. Six months! He'd been seeing me for seven. To think that only a month after we started dating, he had taken up with someone else."

She lifted her arm and wiped her face with the dirty towel. Olive started to tell her to stop but then kept quiet. Marla blew her nose.

"He was a liar. You know what he used to tell me? He said, 'Marla, a man who's just using a woman sleeps with one foot in the bed and one on the floor. When he loves her, he commits with both feet.' He even left his nasty old bedroom slippers under my bed—both of them—to make his point. And to think all that time . . ." She blew her nose again and turned her red eyes to Olive. "You work in Huntsville. You ever see him out with a woman?"

"No," Olive said. "But then I never saw him out with you. Not very observant, I guess."

"We were careful. It bothered me some, but he said it was because of my marriages. 'Everyone'll say you're just looking for number six,' he said. 'It'd be a strain on the relationship. Better we get things firm between us and then

we'll let people know.' I am such a fool and everybody
knows it. But you're not, Olive. You never have been.
That's why I came to you."

Olive was silent, her eyes focused on the blacktop. Marla
had always reminded her of what the silhouetted naked girls
on truck mudflaps would look like when they reached middle-
age—breasts and fanny lifted and separated with construc-
tions of elastic and nylon. When she dressed up, she wore
pink lace that stretched tight over her belly. People thought
she was a fool because she looked like one. Olive wouldn't
have traded bodies with her for the world. Her own sinewy
looks pleased her. Her body announced that she was a reli-
able woman. She was a woman of sense. Nobody would
mistake her for a fool.

The November afternoon was passing into twilight, and
the horizon was a fiery realm of scarlet and gold. She
checked her watch. Twenty minutes at Marla's, ten minutes
to get to Luther's. It would be after six before they reached
their final stop. Good and dark by then.

"I'm assuming Luther's Toyota's at your house, right?"
she asked.

"That's right. Parked in the back. He always parked there
behind the azaleas so no one would see."

"Good. Now, I'm going to give you a choice, Marla. You
can drive Luther's car or you can drive my truck. Which is
it?"

"I can't drive a truck."

"Okay, then, you'll have to drive the car. This is what
we're going to do. We'll put Luther in the car . . ."

Marla let out a wail. "I'm not driving with Luther in the
car . . ."

"All right." Olive fought to keep her voice calm. "We'll
put Luther in the back of the truck and then you follow me

in the Toyota. Marla, you got to keep your head clear. You keep yourself thinking clearly and we'll be okay."

"You're right," Marla answered. "I knew I could turn to you, Olive. I knew you were my best friend."

As Olive pulled the truck to a stop in Marla's yard, she could barely make out the fender of the yellow Toyota hidden behind the massive screen of denuded azalea bushes. About fifteen paces away sat the wooden shed, the door padlocked. On the far side of the bushes was Marla's house, lights off, obviously deserted in the gathering dusk.

From the passenger seat Marla inhaled sharply.

"I can't go in the shed, Olive. You're going to have to go in alone."

"I can go in alone, Marla, but you're going to have to help me move the body. Scrawny as he is, I can't lift Luther by myself." Olive stared at the darkened house. "Besides the bedroom slippers, what else you got in there that's Luther's?"

Marla shook her head. "That's all he ever gave me. Said he'd make up for it when we came out." She laughed, a rude sound that made Olive jerk her head. "That's what he called it. Like we were debutantes. Or something else."

"Listen carefully to me, Marla. I'm going into the shed. You go into the house and get those slippers. Put them under your seat there. Then come into the shed and help me."

"I can't," Marla whispered.

"You damn well can."

Marla started at the profanity, her eyes wide. Then she nodded and quietly opened the truck door.

"You're right, I can. What you're doing, you're doing for me, Olive. How will I ever pay you back?"

"I'm not worried about payback. I want to get that man out of here. Now, give me the key to the padlock and go do what I said."

She waited until Marla had slipped in through the back door of the house before climbing from the truck. The sky had turned lavender; a chill nipped her skin. She faced the shed, an unassuming construction of tin and splintering pine. A solitary window, blurred with old paint and dust, was partially obscured by a nailed, weathered plank. Below the window aging cans of latex paint sat stacked against the exterior wall. Olive stepped gingerly to the window and placed her foot on a can. With little pressure the stack fell apart. Even if folks had come onto Marla's property, it didn't appear they had approached the window.

Satisfied, Olive walked to the shed door and fitted the key into the padlock. The door swung easily on its hinges, then stopped as it nudged something soft. Olive shoved harder and, fighting a sudden nausea, pushed Luther's legs across the shed's dirt floor.

She reached up and pulled the white string of the over-head bulb. She had sometimes pondered what it would be like to stumble across a dead body, to be one of those people walking along a woodsy path, calling to their dogs and wondering what on earth they were sniffing at. She had always assumed the shock would be in the surprise. She was wrong—the shock was in the stillness. She stared at Luther's back, his red flannel shirt pulled over his head to reveal a white T-shirt tucked into a pair of baggy green work pants. His left arm was folded beneath his body and his right arm was flung to the side. Resting in the palm of his hand was the broken handle of the trug, the basket's flat bottom smashed against the wheel of a fertilizer spreader. The hoe lay across his backside.

"Luther . . ." she started, but the word never formed. She was amazed at how quickly she could objectify flesh. This wasn't Luther. This was a problem, and she had about an hour and a half to take care of it. She bent down and patted the pants pockets until she found the keys to the Toyota.

Outside, the leaves on the ground stirred, and Marla stood in the doorway.

"Here," she said. She held out a pair of brown corduroy slippers. "They're the only thing of his I could find."

"Good. Now, go to the truck and get the blankets and the box of plastic bags. Put those shoes under the driver's seat." Olive lifted the hoe. "While you're at it, wipe this off real good with the towel and throw it in the back of the truck. Then come back in here and help me."

Marla took the hoe silently and left the shed. In less than a minute she was back, the blankets and plastic bags in her arms.

"You're gonna cover him, aren't you?" she asked softly. "You won't make me look at him, will you?"

"You won't have to look," Olive said, "but you will have to touch. I'll let you decide which is worse."

Olive worked quickly, first wrapping the head and then the rest of the body. She found no visible wounds, but blood had dripped into the packed dirt floor and soon soiled the blankets. Without a word, she and Marla lifted the body— eerily light in death—hauled it to the truck, and rolled it into the bed.

The muscles in Marla's face had loosened.

"Now what?" she whispered.

"Now you take these keys and follow me in the Toyota. When we get to Luther's place, I'm going to park by the end of his driveway and I want you to drive to his house, pull into the garage, then back out just like you were Luther leaving. I don't know nothing about tire tracks or whatnot, but if the sheriff comes looking around, I want the tracks to say that Luther Barns did not come to your house tonight—or if

he did, he went somewhere else later. Do you understand?
When you get to the end of his drive, just follow me."

It was fully dark by the time Olive turned onto the grass
beside Luther's mailbox and watched Marla slowly bump
the Toyota down the gravel drive. The drive was long and
curvy—Luther's house wasn't visible from the highway,
surrounded as it was by a stand of pines and 200 acres of
grazing land. Several minutes passed in total blackness before Olive saw the gleam of headlights and the Toyota
reemerge at the road. She waved to the car, then pulled her
truck onto the highway and headed south.

The place she was thinking of had been part of a proposed
development on the Tennessee River in the 1970s—her father had once considered buying property there, building an
A-frame and retiring to the fish and seclusion. He had taken
her there several times to walk over his chosen plot, but in
the end he had forgotten it, as his illness had caused him to
gradually forget her. Providential, as it turned out. The development had gone bottom up before the first house was
constructed. All that remained now was a dilapidated
wooden signpost and some dirt roads leading to the river's
edge, all hung with silvery vines.

It was an hour before she slowed, searching for the sign
that, when she last saw it four years earlier, was already
veiled by overgrowth. At first she was afraid she had passed
it, that the development wasn't as far removed from civi-
lization as she remembered. But then the truck headlights lit
a pale sandy delta and swept over the broken uprights of the
sign. She turned on the blinker.

She drove about a hundred yards up the road and parked
on the side. The Toyota pulled up next to her. Olive reached
across to the glove compartment and retrieved her flashlight
before motioning Marla to the front of the car.

"All right, Marla. Help me get the body into the passenger seat of the Toyota. Then you wait in the truck. I don't know how long it will take me—I'm going to walk back on foot—but you wait, you hear? Go to sleep if you want, I don't care, but don't turn on the radio and don't leave. You understand?"

In the blackness she could barely discern the tilting of Marla's head.

"I understand. I'm so grateful, Olive. The repayment— it's going to be enormous."

Olive's watch read 8:10 P.M. when her flashlight finally illuminated the black nose of the truck, hunkered silent against the tangle of vines on the roadside. She breathed heavily, partly from fatigue, partly from dismay. It had gone so smoothly: the ignition, the brakes, a sure-footed push. The fat waters of the Tennessee had closed over the car like arms. Not a bad burial; she would have to remember it for herself when the time came.

Marla was awake and trembling when Olive slid into the driver's side of the truck.

"Is it over?" Marla asked. "You took care of it?"

"I took care of it. Let's go home."

"Something's been bothering me."

"What's that?"

"Did you check him to make sure?"

"Make sure what?"

"That he was dead. Did you check to make sure he was dead?"

Olive laughed. "Well, of course he was dead, Marla. You hit him twice, remember?"

Marla's clamped hands shook uncontrollably in her lap. "But I never checked. I hit him once, he turned on me, I hit him twice, he fell. He was real still, but I never checked. He could have been in a coma, he could have just been badly hurt."

"Quit talking nonsense."

Marla's voice rose. "Why didn't you check him, Olive? You did everything else tonight. What if he was still alive?"

"Shut up!" Olive backhanded Marla across the face. "He was dead. I touched him. I wrapped his body. You've got the damn blood in the dirt of your shed to prove it. You murdered him, Marla."

Marla slowly brought her hand to her cheek and rubbed the place where Olive had struck her. "Maybe. But then, I'm a fool, Olive. What are you going to tell folks is your excuse?"

They took only one detour on the way back to Kirkins, stopping at a bridge three miles downstream to throw the hoe into the Tennessee. Olive dropped Marla off at the church, where she stayed for a while to practice the organ, just in case someone had noticed her car in the parking lot. Olive drove home, clenching and unclenching her grip on the steering wheel the entire way.

Once home, she took the bedroom slippers from beneath the truck seat and carried them into the house. The temperature had dipped cold enough that smoke from her chimney would arouse no suspicions, even if the teenagers next door had cared.

She placed the bedroom slippers on her mattress and lowered herself to her knees. Slowly, she reached beneath her bed and pulled out an identical, although slightly newer, pair of men's brown corduroy slippers. She waited until the fire was roaring before tossing all four into the flames.

The next morning at church Olive sat at the piano, her fingers listlessly running up and down the keys. No one had missed Luther yet; it probably would be the afternoon before anyone started wondering. The cry wouldn't go out until tomorrow. She thought of the river—so receiving, so accepting—and Luther, his eyes shooting open with shock, then fear, as the black water poured into his mouth. *Ohgodohgodohgod. What have I done?* She began to pound on the keys, tears streaming down her face.

Across the sanctuary, Marla played the organ with all her body. Her stop-sign red lips were pinched in a closeted smile. She gazed at Olive beatifically. No, that wasn't right. She gazed at Olive with superiority.

Kittens are such delightful creatures to watch at play. It's when they get the idea that your favorite wingback is their personal scratching post that the delight lessens a bit. Still, they have their good points. And some of those points can be very surprising indeed.

The Stupid Pet Trick

Margaret Maron

When Dr. A. Forrest Robinson, B.A., M.A., Ph.D., unlocked the door of her Georgetown house that chilly March evening, it felt almost like stepping into one of those old domestic sitcoms—the Breadwinner Returns Home scene.

Time: 7:30 Sunday night.

Action: After a weekend business trip, enter Weary Traveler screen left. Pause to savor return and assess household. Washing machine chugs away quietly in its closet under the stairs, the smell of something savory wafts from the kitchen, the domestic sound of the vacuum cleaner aloft. Drop garment bag on 19th-century deacon's bench in the hall, put briefcase on slate-topped Queen Anne side table, step to foot of stairs and call up, "Hello, honey. I'm home!"

But she wasn't Dick Van Dyke and Kevin certainly wasn't Mary Tyler Moore and he didn't come running to greet her with a radiant smile and soft murmurs of how much he'd missed her this weekend, hateful old business conference— or, in this case, academic conference—that took her away for three whole days. Nor was there a child to rush down-stairs and demand to be told if she'd brought him a present.

The only one who noted her return was Mittens, a little black cat with neat white paws, who came out into the entry hall, thrupped a perfunctory welcome, watched as Amelia took off her coat and stuffed her gloves in the pocket, and then went back to whatever she was doing behind the couch in the den.

Upstairs, the vacuum cleaner continued its back-and-forth roar and now that she thought about it, Amelia looked around the ground floor in surprise.

Kevin?

Domestic?

Usually when she went away for the weekend, to a con-ference in Chicago or Philadelphia or to visit her only daughter in New York, she would return to find the lovely old two-story town house cluttered with three days' worth of dirty plates and glasses and take-out cartons, clothes strewn all over their bedroom, damp towels on the bathroom floor, Mittens's litter box reeking to high heaven. Although they had been married almost four years, she wasn't aware that Kevin even knew how to turn on the washer, much less how to program the dishwasher or run the vacuum. He was al-ways perfectly happy to let her do it or tell her to leave it for Mrs. Ortega, their weekly cleaning woman.

Tonight the house shone as if Mrs. Ortega had just left. Fresh candles and flowers were on the dining room table, where two places were set with her best china and silver. Except for a couple of mixing bowls in the sink, the kitchen was immaculate. In the den beyond, more candles sat on the Pennsylvania Dutch dower chest that served as a coffee

table and two sparkling crystal goblets waited for the un-
corking of a nearby bottle. He had even lit the gas logs, and
the flickering flames gave the room a sensuous ambiance.

She lifted the bottle in her hands and read the label of her
favorite wine, feeling now like a character in *Dynasty* or the
video version of a Danielle Steele novel.

Kevin's footstep sounded on the stairs and Amelia suddenly wished she'd taken time to run a comb through her
graying hair and freshen her lipstick before getting out of
the car. She turned almost shyly as her husband entered the
den.

"Amelia! Hey, you're home early. I didn't expect you for
at least another hour."

"I got away earlier and traffic was lighter than I expected," she began to explain, but he took her in his arms
and kissed her long and deeply.

She hadn't realized how perfunctory their kisses had become lately until the rising passion of this one almost took
her breath away.

"Ummm. Nice," she said when they came up for air. "But
what's all this in aid of?"

"All what?"

"House Beautiful. Martha Stewart."

"Nothing," he said, tenderly nuzzling her neck. "You
think I'm such a slob, I thought I'd surprise you for a
change. If you'd waited another half hour or so, the wine
would be chilled, the candles would be lit, Rachmaninoff
would be playing on the CD—"

"You'd be draped on the couch in a black lace negligee?"
she teased.

"Something like that," he grinned, turning her to him for
another kiss.

She met his lips eagerly and with such hunger that he finally said, "Whoa! Wine and dinner first, dessert after."

• • •

Dinner was like a rerun of their first weeks together when every glance, every innocuous scrap of conversation, had erotic overtones.

A tenured professor of modern philosophy at the university, Amelia had been asked to set up an interdisciplinary seminar on popular culture and one of her graduate assistants had mentioned that there was a dishy part-time poet in the English Department who could relate Byron and Cummings through the Beatles to LL Cool J.

Amelia had never developed a taste for rap—too misogynistic for her tastes, but she recognized its significance in pop culture, and a poet who could dish the subject sounded like a good addition to her team. That he himself might be "dishy" hadn't been a factor.

Not at first, anyhow.

That was later.

After the seminar was successfully completed.

After the grad assistant became discouraged.

After he'd persuaded her that the seven-year difference in their ages didn't matter.

"You wouldn't give it a second thought if you were thirty-six and I were forty-three," he'd said. "Why are you clinging to an outmoded double standard, Dr. Forrest?"

And so, to the displeasure of her daughter, Elizabeth, who thought Kevin was a gold-digging bimbo ("hedonistic opportunist" were her actual words), they were married, and so he had moved into the gracious old Georgetown house she once shared with her late husband. Despite Elizabeth's assessment, he worked hard on his poetry—three chapbooks in four years. So what if he only got paid in copies of the books? So what if he still taught part-time on a nontenured line?

"It's not as if we need the money," she told Elizabeth.

"Well, clearly, *he* doesn't," Elizabeth said. "Not with you supporting him."

"I don't support him. He never takes a penny from me."

"No, but does he give a penny? Does he pay anything for utilities? Taxes? Car insurance?"

"Those bills are practically the same as before we married," Amelia argued uncomfortably. "He brings me yellow roses—"

"Which he loves, too."

"—champagne and brie—"

"Which he helps you drink and eat. Face it, Mother: the only reason Kevin can afford roses and champagne and imported cheese is because he doesn't have to pay mundane living expenses."

"You could take a lesson from him," Amelia said sharply.

"Live for today? Let tomorrow take care of itself? Oh, honestly, Mother. You're starting to sound like one of those kvetching mamas on a TV sitcom, always nattering about when's the career girl going to give her grandchildren."

"I just don't want you to look up from your work someday and realize you're too old to have children."

"*You* may be sorry you didn't have a houseful, but that doesn't mean Tom and I will have any regrets."

The wine, the flickering candles, the utter relaxation of being home with Kevin after four hours behind the steering wheel were getting to Amelia. She smiled to herself as Mittens went past the doorway carrying a dark limp shape in her mouth.

Poor Mittens. Sublimating her frustrated maternal instincts by pretending that one of Kevin's socks was a kitten.

Kevin poured the last of the wine into her glass and she was just muzzy enough to smile into his eyes and say, "Are you ever sorry we didn't try to have a child together?"

For one nanosecond, there flashed across his face a look of horror identical to Elizabeth's.

"Good God, no! Whatever made you think that?"

She wasn't sure whether to feel pleased that he was satisfied with their life just as it was, or whether it was sad that he'd never experience the deep and selfless sense of completion that came when you held your own child in your arms.

"Diapers? Two A.M. feedings? Colicky crying? We're too old for that routine."

"You're not," she said quietly.

"Oh, yes, I am, my darling, even if you aren't. What I'm *not* too old for—"

He stood and blew out the candles, then took her hand and led her upstairs.

The doorbell rang while she was still marveling at the fresh linens on their bed.

"Maybe if we ignore it, they'll go away," Kevin said hopefully, as he slipped his hand inside her sweater.

The doorbell rang again with a steady insistence.

Sighing, Kevin headed downstairs.

Amelia followed to the head of the steps.

"Mr. Kevin Robinson?" asked an authoritative male voice.

"Yes?"

"Sorry to bother you, sir, but—"

"Marc?" Amelia came all the way downstairs so that she could get a clearer look at the taller of the two men in gray topcoats, who filled the doorway. "Marcus Galloway?"

"Dr. Forrest?" A genuine smile spread over the newcomer's warm brown face. "I *thought* this was where you used to live, but they told me Robinson."

"That's my name, now," she said, gesturing to Kevin. "Darling, this is one of my old students. It must be what,

Marc? Nine or ten years since you took my Philosophy 4.1 seminar?"

"At least. Good to see you again, Doctor. And this is my partner." He nodded toward the white man who appeared to be a couple of years older than he. "Detective Frank Boland."

They murmured pleasantries and shook hands all around, and Amelia drew them in out of the cold night and into the warm and cozy den. She put the empty wineglasses on a nearby sideboard and relit the candles.

"Partner?" she asked, when everyone was comfortable. "You're with the District Police Department? I thought you majored in modern lit."

Detective Galloway grinned. "I did. And believe it or not, Kafka and Beckett and Solzhenitsyn give me a lot of insight into this job."

"A literate police officer," said Kevin. "Now there's a play against type. And what did you major in, Detective Boland?"

"*Kevin!*"

"Sorry, darling." He looked at the two detectives and gave a rueful shrug. "I apologize, gentlemen, but my wife's has been gone since Thursday and—" He broke off with another shrug and headed for the kitchen.

"Why don't I make a pot of coffee while you two catch up with old times?"

"We're the ones who should apologize," said Galloway. "Coming over late like this, interrupting your evening."

"Nonsense," Amelia said. "It's only nine-thirty and I think coffee's a great idea."

"Actually, it was Mr. Robinson we came to see," said Boland.

"Me?" Kevin turned in his tracks and came back into the den.

"Yes, sir. I'm afraid I have some bad news. One of your colleagues was killed Friday night."

"*What?* Who?"

"A Roseanne Chapman. We understand that you shared an office with her?"

Kevin nodded. "Along with three other part-timers."

"Roseanne Chapman?" asked Amelia. "*Pinkie?*"

Galloway cocked his head. "Pinkie?"

"I'm afraid that was our not very nice nickname for her," Amelia confessed. "After that famous pair of frothy English paintings. You know—*Blue Boy* and *Pinkie*? Rather insipid picture actually, and Roseanne Chapman took it a step further. She dyed her hair strawberry blond and wore nothing but pink: dusty rose in winter, pastel pink in summer. By now you must have been told that everything she owned was pink. Pink shoes, pink suits, pink coats, even pink note pads and ballpoint pens."

"Pink was her 'look,' " said Kevin.

Despite the horror of hearing that someone they knew had been murdered, Amelia couldn't help smiling at the memory she and Kevin were sharing at that moment.

They had gone up to New York to see Terrence McNally's *Master Class* on Broadway last summer. At the lines, "Everyone needs a look. You have no look. Get a look," they had turned to each other and silently mouthed, "Pinkie!"

Guiltily, Amelia pushed that unkind memory away and said, "What happened, Marc? How did she die?"

"Head wound." He spoke succinctly, as if they were caught up in an episode of *NYPD Blue*. "Someone smashed her hard and then dumped her in the Potomac, over near Roosevelt Island. Couple of joggers spotted her pink coat at the edge of the water yesterday morning. We've been questioning her friends, colleagues, the usual routine. When did you last see her, Dr. Robinson?"

Amelia looked to Kevin for help. "I can't remember if I've even seen her this semester. She was never there when I popped in to meet you."

"That's because I'm teaching a Tuesday–Thursday this semester and I think she has—*had* a Monday–Wednesday schedule," Kevin told her.

"What about you, Mr. Robinson?"

"I'm trying to remember. I did go in for a department meeting last Monday and I think she was there then, but it's such a big department and we're both part-timers, so I couldn't swear to it."

"You didn't see her since then?"

Kevin shook his head.

"Ma'am," said Boland, "if you don't mind me asking, what's that cat doing?"

Amelia leaned across Kevin to look over the end of the couch. In the open space between the couch and Boland's chair, Mittens had curled her abdomen around several cloth blobs which she alternately patted and licked.

"Damn it, Amelia!" said Kevin. "She's got my best pair of argyles again."

Automatically, Amelia leaped to Mittens's defense. "If you'd put them in the hamper instead of leaving them on the floor—"

She heard the snap in her voice and broke off with a smile at Boland. "She's playing mommy. Like a little girl playing with dolls. She steals socks and things and carries them around in her mouth as if they were kittens. She's really quite imaginative."

Kevin retrieved his argyles and gave a sour laugh. "We're thinking of trying to get her on *Dave Letterman*."

Marcus Galloway smiled. "The stupid pet trick segment?"

Kevin nodded. "Except that she's too stupid to do it on command."

"Or too smart," Amelia said lightly.

"You could videotape her," Boland suggested. "Maybe get it on *America's Funniest Home Videos*?"

Annoyed at having two of her "babies" snatched away, Mittens trotted from the room with an ancient catnip mouse in her mouth and headed for the dining room. A moment later she sneaked back for one of Amelia's old black wool socks.

"Now she's pretending to move her kittens so we won't know where they are," said Amelia.

"My mom used to have a cat that moved her kittens every week," said Galloway. "We never knew where they were going to show up next."

He watched the little cat disappear through the doorway, then turned back to the routine questions at hand. "What about boyfriends, Mr. Robinson? Ms. Chapman was young and pretty. Did she have anything going with somebody at the university?"

"I really couldn't say. We didn't talk much, especially this semester, and when we did talk, it was about schedules or desk space, nothing personal."

"Too bad," said Boland, " 'cause she had a bun in the oven and nobody seems to know who the baker is."

"Two lives taken?" Amelia felt her heart tighten with sadness at the little pink life snuffed out before it could begin. Before it—

Sadness turned to shock as Mittens crossed her line of vision.

Instantly recognizing it for what it was, Amelia willed herself not to gasp, but she was too late. Marcus Galloway had seen it, too, and he made an awkward grab for the thing that dangled from the cat's mouth. Mittens easily eluded him and scampered through the doorway.

Galloway jumped to his feet but Amelia slipped past him. "Let me," she said. "You'll only scare her."

The little cat had heaped her "babies" beneath the heart pine hunt board Amelia had inherited from her grandmother, but there was no resistance when Amelia fished out the dusty rose glove.

Numbly, Amelia found herself trying to remember the name of an old black-and-white *Twilight Zone* episode. By Ambrose Bierce, she thought. "An Occurrence at Owl Creek Bridge"? Where dozens of incidents zip through the person's mind in a single brief second before the rope snaps his neck?

In that instant, with the faint smell of rose perfume arising from Roseanne Chapman's glove, Amelia saw again a tube of pink lipstick that had mysteriously fallen out of their medicine cabinet after one of her weekend conferences last autumn. Kevin told her it was a grad student and he swore it was nothing more than a casual one-night stand. Unimportant. Almost anonymous. That it would never happen again. That he didn't want to lose her.

("Didn't want to lose his comfortable life." The thought was hers, but the voice was Elizabeth's.)

So this is denouement, she thought bleakly, the dramatic moment of untying all the knots that comes just before they roll the credits of a Perry Mason or a Matlock or any of a dozen Grade B detective movies. Only this wasn't a movie or television program or even a clichéd he-done-me-wrong Patsy Cline song.

She thought she had made it very clear that while she might teach an occasional class in pop culture, she had no intention of living a life governed by pop values. Who would think that Kevin was such a slow learner? Or that he would flunk the most important test in his life?

Although it felt like a hundred years since she'd followed Mittens into the dining room, the men had barely moved when she returned.

She came no further than the doorway and she spoke only to Marcus Galloway.

"He's spent the weekend cleaning, so I don't know how much evidence you'll find in situ. But the washer has a lint filter that he probably didn't think to clean and you have my permission to take the bag that's in the vacuum cleaner. There's bound to be pink hair, pink threads, pink something."

She handed Galloway the glove and turned to go upstairs. Almost as an afterthought, she paused and added, "Oh, yes. I'd appreciate it if you would take him with you, too."

"Amelia, please!" Kevin begged. "Don't do this! I love you!"

She halted on the staircase and gave him an ironic smile. It was a *Gone With the Wind* ending and Rhett Butler's words were on her lips, but she'd be damned if she'd say them.

Besides. They wouldn't be true.

*Every so often I come across one of those handbooks on man-
ners they keep publishing now and again. Personally, I've
never gone in for all those rules and regulations. A little
common sense goes a long way when it comes to minding
your manners. But sometimes, there are exceptions to the
rule, as the sleuth in our next story discovers.*

A Lady Should Avoid Murder

Ann Granger

Amongst Jane Pritchard's childhood memories was a
book. It'd belonged to her grandmother and been entitled
Everything a Lady Should Know. Everyone can recall semi-
nal reading of long ago, and the venerable handbook had
fascinated young Jane. Embellished with pictures of a
smirking Lady writing little notes or embarking on a visit in
hat and gloves, it advised the reader on the correct response
to every conceivable situation in which the unsuspecting female might find herself. Armed with rules as rigid as the
corsets worn by the illustrated examples, the Lady could
sally forth, fearing no man and no social pitfall, to knock
'em dead with her impeccable grasp of etiquette.

Ah, yes, dead . . . Unfortunately, as far as Jane could recall at the present moment, the wonderful book hadn't offered any handy hints on dealing with a murderer. Surely an

oversight. Allowing herself a moment's daydreaming, Jane mentally composed a letter of inquiry,

> *Dear Editor,*
>   *I have recently made the acquaintance of a gentle-man of homicidal tendencies . . . Please advise . . .*

Catching herself out in this lapse of concentration, she wriggled on her chair and smiled nervously at the young man sitting opposite her in her tiny living room. He was rather younger than she was, by about eight years, she judged. She was thirty-seven. He was pleasant in appearance except for a sharp look about the eyes and wore a neat sports jacket and well-pressed slacks. She was momentarily inspired to wish she wasn't wearing cut-off jeans and a washed-out sweatshirt.

A Lady who has taken Trouble with her Toilette will always be at her Ease.

"Shall I make us some more tea?" Jane asked, seizing a chance to get out of the room for five minutes and pull herself together. It was a stressful situation and she ought to be keeping her mind on matters, not indulging in eccentric fancies.

"Thanks very much," he said, picking up the pottery mug she'd handed him earlier. "Need a hand?"

"No, thanks!" she replied rather too forcefully and bolted into the kitchen to switch on the kettle.

Tea is taken between four and five o'clock. A selection of plain and fancy cakes should be offered. Napkins are essential.

Jane opened a tin and stared in dismay at the one crushed cracker lying forlornly in the bottom. She dunked the teabag in boiled water and hurried back to her visitor.

"Sorry, no cake or anything . . ." she apologized.

"Never eat it," he said. He sipped from the mug which had been hand-decorated by Jane with comical cats and glanced out of the French windows leading to the back lawn.

"Nice little garden you've got here. I'm a bit of a gardener myself."

He was prompting her nicely. She took the hint. "I bought this cottage just about a year ago, after my divorce. I'd been living in London. But, you see, most of our friends—my ex-husband's and mine—had been joint friends and—well, I wanted to get right away and start over with no ties. I'm a writer. All I need really is my computer and a stack of paper."

She had a horrible feeling she'd told him this before. Like a child who has rehearsed a piece for a school concert, once interrupted she could only resume by going back to the beginning and starting again.

"I know the cottage is isolated but I didn't—I don't—mind that. I also realised there was a house next door, behind all those trees, but I didn't give a thought to who might live there. I think I imagined at first it was empty. There was no sign of life . . ."

She stopped, wondering if that had been a simple turn of phrase or a Freudian slip. "I mean," she went on firmly, "I hadn't seen anyone going in or out. So it was a real surprise when Mr. Warren put in an appearance about a week after I moved in."

She'd been out in the garden, trying to fix a rotary washing line. The metal post was heavy and it needed someone else to hold it while she wedged it. Otherwise, once it had laundry pegged to it, a good wind would carry the whole lot away like a ship under sail.

There was a rustle from the further side of the nearby hedge, between her property and the next, and without warning, a head popped up like a puppet's from behind a curtain. It belonged to a man of about her own age or slightly older, perhaps forty-one or two. He had straight flat mousy hair and a small neat moustache.

"Can I help?" he asked. Of course, he could.

When he'd arrived in the garden and she'd been able to see him top to toe, the rest of his appearance had also been mousy. Small, a little tubby, wearing brownish trousers and a beige sweater. A dark maroon tie was knotted neatly below his Adam's apple. He'd scurried around fixing the washing line with nimble fingers and smiling all the while at her, showing slightly prominent front teeth.

"It's nice to have neighbors again," he said. "My name is Harold Warren. I live with my mother."

Jane replied with a brief word about herself.

"A writer, eh?" said Mr. Warren, eyes sparkling. "I'm a great one for books. I love a good book. I read all kinds, anything I can get my hands on."

He went on to explain he was unmarried and his mother, with whom he shared the house, was elderly and infirm. She required constant attendance so he didn't work. Jane gathered there was some family money, enough to live on. She supposed his mother must have a pension as well. She thanked him for his help with the clothesline and offered him a cup of tea.

He refused. "Can't leave Mother for long!"

With that, he went back to his own side of the hedge.

A silence fell in Jane's living room. Her visitor sipped his tea. Jane picked up her own mug.

"See much of him after that?" asked her visitor conversationally.

She shook her head. "Hardly anything. Their garden's completely overgrown and you can't see their house from here because of the trees. The exit from their drive is around the curve in the road and so I wouldn't normally see anyone go in or out, either. I heard the car occasionally and saw it sometimes when I was walking along the road. I supposed he was going shopping or something. He had to leave the place sometimes. He always waved to me and sometimes lowered the window to call out a greeting. We'd exchange a brief word. I felt sorry for him and that he must be an exemplary son. The next time I had any real conversation with him was when he brought me some apples."

She'd been outside in her back garden, hoeing weeds from a flowerbed. There'd been a rustle on the other side of the hedge and Mr. Warren's head popped up as before, surprising her into letting out a yelp and nearly dropping the hoe. He'd apologised for giving her a fright and held out a plastic carrier bag.

"Thought you might use some apples. They're only fallers, so you'll have to use them at once. They won't keep. But they're very good cookers, Bramleys. We have more than Mother and I can use."

"How is your mother?" Jane asked.

"Oh, much as usual." He sighed. "Nothing can be done. She's a bit of a trial, poor old darling, but we manage."

With that, he'd scurried away.

It had been the second time he'd shown neighborly kindness. Jane felt impelled to respond in some way.

A return Visit should not be made too soon, neither should it be left too long!

She used the apples to make a batch of pies. She froze all but two of them, put one aside for her own immediate use, and set off for the Warren house, bearing the remaining pie as a thank-you gift. After all, he probably didn't do much cooking, not if he had to wait hand-and-foot on his mother.

When visiting the Housebound, some little home-baked Delicacy is always welcome.

Jane walked up the long, weed-strewn drive to the house. The lofty old trees to either side almost met overhead, blocking out the daylight. It was chilly and damp. Fallen leaves had formed a slippery mulch. Everywhere was silent. There was even a curious absence of birdsong.

The house itself appeared ahead of her with the disconcerting suddenness Mr. Warren himself had shown when his head appeared over the hedge. Jane, still holding the pie before her in both hands like a religious offering, stood studying the scene. Had she not known better, she would have believed it deserted. The tall narrow windows were covered with a film of dust. The place clearly hadn't been painted in years. There was a detached garage standing among the trees to her right. Indents in the soft soil showed where a car had passed in and out, the only sign of life. The garage door was shut.

As she approached the front door to the house, she saw that garden débris had piled around and across the steps and clogged the cobwebby cellar windows. She climbed the stone slabs, her feet disturbing the leaf cover which gave a soft shur-shurring sound, and put out her hand to the unpolished brass torque which formed the knocker. The sound echoed throughout the house like a distant clap of thunder.

After a moment she heard footsteps approaching the door. It was tugged open with some effort. It must have swollen shut. A form was dimly discernible on the far side, through the crack. Then it was pulled open wider and Mr. Warren stood there in his mouse-brown trousers, beige pullover and maroon tie. He wore slippers.

"Oh," he said, blinking at her. "Mrs. Pritchard!"

Jane held out the pie. "I brought this. I thought, as you

were so kind and gave me the apples. I made a whole lot of pies, perhaps you'd like—"

"Thank you, yes, you really shouldn't—" he interrupted her. He seemed agitated and reached out to take the dish.

Before his hands closed on it, a door opened in the depths of the dark hallway to the rear of Warren. A female form appeared, silhouetted against light from the room beyond.

The woman, whom at first Jane couldn't make out clearly at all, began to move quietly towards them. She had a curious, uneven gait and put out her hand to steady herself against the wall. Now Jane could see that she wore a dowdy print dress and rather dirty cardigan. Her hair was grey but abundant and fell loose to her shoulders in long, tangled strands. She had large pale blue eyes which were fixed on the visitor with puzzled wonder. It was impossible to judge her age, but her skin appeared fine and remarkably unlined.

Then the smell hit Jane. An insidious stench of soiled underwear, sweat and grime-stiffened clothing, unbathed skin. The woman's feet were bare—that was why she moved so quietly—and the unclipped toenails had grown to curl over like the talons of a bird of prey.

Jane's expression betrayed what had happened to Mr. Warren, or possibly he'd sensed that someone stood behind him. He whirled round and gave an exclamation which sounded part surprise, part dismay or embarrassment and part anger.

He bustled towards the dishevelled apparition at once and took her arm in a firm grip.

"Now, dear," he said. "You shouldn't be out here."

"Who is this?" the woman asked, staring at Jane over his shoulder with the same kind of wonder. Jane could see now that the pupils of the pale blue eyes were dilated and curiously unfocused.

Raising her voice, Jane replied, "I'm Jane Pritchard from

the cottage, Mrs. Warren. I expect your son has told you about me—"

"I haven't got—" the woman began in a peeved tone.

Warren had moved to place himself more fully between the two women. He looked over his shoulder to Jane and said irritably, "She doesn't understand. It's dementia." He began to push his mother ahead of him towards the rear room.

"Come on, dear, back to the warm kitchen. You'll catch cold."

"You've taken away my shoes," said the old woman, sounding even more sulky.

"No, I haven't," he retorted with crisp authority. "You keep taking them off yourself."

He propelled her through the door at the back of the hall, shut it and scurried back to Jane.

"You see how it is, Mrs. Pritchard," he began hurriedly. "It's dementia and nothing at all to be done."

"I understand," faltered Jane. She didn't know quite how to phrase this, but the woman was filthy and ought at least to be bathed and her toenails clipped. "Do you have any help with your mother, Mr. Warren? The district nurse could call, say, once a week and—lend a hand."

"No!" he said sharply. "There's no need!" He made an effort. "I don't want to sound ungrateful, Mrs. Pritchard. It's kind of you to ask. But I can look after Mother perfectly well. Besides, strangers worry her. I'm the only person she'll let do anything for her."

He made to close the door in Jane's face. She was still holding the pie dish and, anxious that he should take it, pushed it forward. The result was that it caught in the closing gap and she almost dropped it. Mr. Warren grabbed it in the nick of time.

"I'm sorry," he stammered. "I didn't expect—it's not one

of her good days. You shouldn't bother. We can manage quite well, Mother and I. I'm something of a cook, if I say so myself!" With a flash of his rodent's teeth, he was gone.

"I felt so embarrassed and frankly rather foolish," Jane told her visitor.

He sat, cupping his empty mug between his palms and watching her intently.

"I hadn't meant to intrude," she went on. "Goodness, a nosy neighbor can make life miserable! I had no wish to interfere. But I thought, how dreadful for him. How awful to be shut in there all day long—and all night too—with someone in that state. Of course, it was clear to me he needed outside help, but he would refuse any offer. He was determined to look after her himself.

"You see . . ." Jane hesitated. "I felt a sort of responsibility for them both. In one way it wasn't my business. But in another, if someone's in need, you don't ignore her, do you? Sooner or later, as I saw it, he was going to have to get some help and the sooner, the better, for them both. I decided to leave it for a week and then call again."

During the following week she saw nothing of Mr. Warren. On Saturday afternoon, the sun shone so brightly after several overcast days that Jane decided to go out for a walk. Her book, on which she'd been trying to work, had reached an awkward stage. She needed a break.

Returning to the cottage, she passed the Warrens' drive and on impulse, turned in.

This time, she decided, she wouldn't knock at the front door. Obviously it wasn't in daily use and on the previous occasion, she'd disturbed the old lady. It was customary, in country areas, to use the back door. She'd forgotten that.

She would make her way to the back of the house and tap discreetly at the kitchen door.

The rear of the property was as overgrown as the frontage. Here, years ago, had been a productive orchard, but now the trees—source of the apples she'd given her—were unpruned and grass grew high between then. A shrubbery close by the house had turned into a veritable jungle.

There was a window open near the back door and a movement on the other side of it caught her eye. It was Mr. Warren but as she made to signal to him, he turned aside without seeing her and went back into the room, out of sight.

Jane went up to the window and peeped in. Her hand was raised to tap on the glass, but she stilled the gesture.

It was the kitchen, all right, large, old-fashioned and untidy. Mrs. Warren was sitting in a rickety overstuffed armchair near an antiquated kitchen range. She wore the same dirty print dress, but a different, though no cleaner, cardigan. Her face gleamed with sweat and her tangled hair clung to her shiny skin. Her large blue eyes were wide open and held such an expression of dread that Jane had to clap a hand to her own mouth to stifle a cry.

Warren himself leaned over his mother and held a glass of water or some other liquid to her mouth.

She shook her head, cowering back.

"Come on!" he ordered roughly. "Get it down you!"

"I don't want it, Harold . . ." whimpered the old lady.

"You'll do as you're told. I've got to go into the village, right? I'm not having you wandering about while I'm gone."

"I won't, Harold, I promise!"

He merely pressed the glass to her mouth. "If you don't drink it," he said, "I won't give you any dinner tonight, nor tomorrow, nor even, perhaps, the day after."

There was no doubt in Jane's mind that he meant it and that this punishment had been employed before. The tone of his voice was unlike anything she'd ever heard in any voice. It wasn't only threatening. It hummed with a barely concealed quiver of exultation, taking pleasure in the prospect of cruelty.

The woman believed it too. Jane watched as she gulped down the contents of the glass, some of it spilling and dribbling down her chin, spotting the print bodice.

Warren turned back towards the window. Jane just had time to duck down under the sill. She heard the sound of running water, the metallic groan of metal. The sink unit must be under this window. She waited for two or three minutes and when she ventured to take another look, she couldn't seen Warren. Mrs. Warren was in the chair, eyes closed. She was mumbling faintly to herself.

Jane ran back to the shrubbery and concealed herself amongst the bushes. After a while she heard the scrape of the garage door being pulled open and then the throb of an engine. Warren drove out, down the drive, and was gone. All was quiet.

Jane came out of hiding and hurried towards the house. The kitchen door was locked, but the window, thank goodness, was still ajar. She didn't know how long he'd be away in the village, but she wouldn't get another chance to get into the house.

She pulled the window wide open and scrambled up on to the sill.

"Mrs. Warren? Don't be scared, please! It's only Jane, from the cottage . . ."

But Mrs. Warren was slumped in the chair, apparently asleep.

Jane managed to get over the sink unit and drop down on to the floor. She hurried to the chair and its immobile occupant. Her nostrils were assailed by a sour odor, but she was prepared for it this time and not put off. Gently Jane shook

the woman's shoulder but Mrs. Warren slumbered on. So
close and in repose, she looked younger, her skin little lined.
The grey hair, though dirty, grew thickly. Trimmed and
clean it would be quite an asset. Jane frowned and tentatively touched one of the sleeper's eyelids, raising it.

"Drugged . . ." Jane muttered. She straightened up and
turned. The glass still stood on the draining board and beside
it was a small bottle such as pharmacists use when making
up prescriptions. She picked it up. It contained a white, crys-
talline substance. Its label, which looked as if it had been
stuck on some time ago, read Chloral Hydrate.

So Warren had made up and forced his mother to drink an
old-fashioned but undeniably effective sleeping draught. It
seemed a drastic action. Prolonged use of choral hydrate had
depressive, debilitating effects. If the woman couldn't safely
be left alone he had to do something, but this was out of all
proportion to any need.

Jane moved across the kitchen and looked into the hall. It
was as she'd seen it from the front door on her previous
visit, dingy, the carpet worn. A clock ticked quietly but not
here—the sound came through the half-open door to a room
on the other side of the hallway. Jane crossed the narrow
passage and went in.

It seemed to be an all-purpose living room and study used
by Warren. It was warmer and tidier in here than elsewhere
in the house. The gas fire in the hearth must have been in use
earlier. There were a few books, but not as many as his
claim to be a dedicated reader might lead one to expect.
There was, however, a large television set and a new CD
player. The other furniture comprised mostly solid, quite
valuable pieces, including a large Victorian rolltop desk. It
was open, showing the ranked pigeonholes and flat writing
surface. Warren must have been working on it before he

found he had to go to the village. Jane could see that various papers were laid out neatly.

She ought not to be doing this, she knew. But in extreme circumstances, one could only take extreme action. Jane went to the desk and glanced quickly at the papers. They were bank statements and the amounts listed made her blink. A little family money? A lot of family money! But there was only one name printed at the top of each sheet: Harold Warren. Everything, then, was in the son's name.

A prickle ran up Jane's spine, and what had been a growing suspicion hardened into chill certainty. But how to prove it? The bank statements didn't do that. If the old woman was senile, than naturally, control of all financial matters had to lie with the son. He probably had power of attorney.

But there were other papers stuffed into the pigeonholes and with luck, one or more of them might provide more clear-cut evidence. She didn't know how long she had to work before Warren returned. Feverishly Jane pulled out a handful of assorted paperwork and began to riffle through it. Domestic bills for gas and electricity. Others from a village garage for repairs to the car.

An envelope slipped from the middle of the bundle in her hand and fell to the ground, spilling its contents. Jane gave a gasp of dismay and knelt to gather them up.

They were photographs. She spread them on the carpet. They were a mixed bunch but here was one, not so very old, which showed a couple. The woman wore a smart two-piece outfit and a corsage of flowers. She was smiling happily at the camera. The man beside her also had a carnation pinned to the lapel of his suit. Small flecks of colour dotted the ground around the couple's feet. Confetti.

•   •   •

The young man in Jane's sitting room stirred. He put his mug carefully on the table. "So," he said. "That's when you twigged what it was all about!"

"Yes, they were wedding pictures. The man was Warren and the woman—even given the awful state she was now in—was the same one he was passing off to me as his mother. But she wasn't his mother. She was his wife!"

"And that's when you contacted the police." Detective Sergeant Sullivan smiled at long last. "You acted in the nick of time to prevent a very nasty crime, Mrs. Pritchard."

"Yes, but I can't honestly say I understand all of it, even now. How was he going to work it?"

"Oh," Sullivan made a wide gesture with his hands. "It was simple enough. Clever crooks make simple plans. It's a mistake to make 'em too complicated. Warren worked on the assumption that most people believe what you tell them. After all, why should they disbelieve you? He told you she was his mother and you had no reason to suppose otherwise, or that she wasn't, as he claimed, in an advanced state of senility.

"He was a pharmacist in a seaside town when they met. Mrs. Beryl Darcy, as she was at the time, was a widow. Her husband's death had left her financially comfortable but lonely. She had no family and frankly, was in that holiday resort looking for companionship. She found it in Warren.

"He was some years younger than she was. But she'd looked after herself and could afford nice clothes. She didn't see why a younger man shouldn't find her attractive. They married. He probably started feeding her drugs little by little almost at once. She fell completely under his sway. He was able to get her to sign away money and property. Once she'd done that, it only remained for him to get rid of her.

"He bought a lonely house, moved her in, began to dose

her regularly so that she didn't know half the time what was going on. He told anyone who inquired that she was his mother who never went out.

"If he'd said 'wife,' people might have been more curious, wondered why he didn't seek some help. But an elderly parent—well, people accepted a sad situation and that he was a devoted son. In due course, after a suitable time, he'd have told you that she'd been taken into a nursing home and shortly after that, he'd have reported she'd died. He'd probably have claimed her body had been taken for burial miles away—to her birthplace, perhaps. You would have believed it, why not?"

Jane shivered. Sullivan got up and went to the French window through which they could see Jane's garden and the hedge beyond which lay the tangled vegetation and trees of the Warrens' property.

"He probably intended to bury her out there in the grounds somewhere," the sergeant said. "Or under the cellar floor. Somewhere safe. Then, well? He might have just slipped away, gone abroad and started again. Or if he felt secure enough, even cleaned the place up and gone on living there."

Sullivan glanced over his shoulder to where Jane sat, pale-faced.

"You can be sure you prevented a murder, Mrs. Pritchard. We got to Mrs. Warren in the nick of time."

"How is the poor woman now?" Jane whispered.

"Poorly but making a good recovery. She knows what happened and is most anxious to meet you properly and thank you."

"I don't need thanks," Jane said. "But I will go and see her. I'm so glad she's all right. What—what will happen to him? I hope they lock him up and never let him out!"

Detective Sergeant Sullivan pulled a wry grimace.

"That's too much to hope for! He'll serve his sentence and then, who knows? Perhaps just disappear, never to be heard of again? But once a con man, always one. They nearly always return to their old tricks. He may decide he knows where he went wrong this time and next time, aim to get it right!"

Sullivan gave Jane a shrewd look. "Personally, I think that if he'd got away with it, he would have stayed here and looked about for another victim. There are plenty of women on their own, with a little money, living in quiet spots, lonely . . ."

His voice died away and he looked expressively around the room.

"You mean," Jane said dully, "that the murder I prevented may ultimately have been my own!"

"You're smarter than poor Beryl Darcy Warren," her visitor assured her kindly. "But probably, yes, he intended you to be next."

Sergeant Sullivan returned his gaze to the view from the windows and gave an appreciative nod. "Yes, you've got a very nice garden here, Mrs. Pritchard. Very nice little place altogether, in fact. Don't worry about being here on your own." He turned back and smiled at her. He was a good-looking young man. "We'll keep an eye on you!"

"Huh!" thought Jane. She scooped up the empty mugs and marched out into the kitchen.

Everything a Lady Should Know, Grandma's old book, had done its best but it had left out the most important rule of all:

LADY, WATCH OUT!

There are more than a few stories in here using a historical backdrop as their setting. The past can be many things, educational, entertaining, and sometimes tragic. But there are some parts of history, like the fate of a young man in this next story, that are better left forgotten.

The Ghost Who Died Dancing

Margaret Lawrence

"Blast you, Thomas Swallow! I didn't come all the way to London from darkest Wales just to watch you pick the currants out of your scone, thank you very much!"

Amaryllis Desmond drew a deep breath and clenched her remarkably regular teeth. They were her best feature, actually, along with eyes of a startling peacock green and a dangerous penchant for minding other people's business far better than she minded her own.

"Sorry, Moll," said Thomas absently. He was *Sir* Thomas, really, now that his father was dead. But he detested titles.

It was June, 1927. The twenty-first of June, in fact. Their annual tea dance in the Palm Court of the Hotel Superbe on the Strand was always a kind of mad cross between a celebration and a wake. But this year it was turning into a funeral.

Molly—for so she was usually called, thank God!—was looking fairly splendid in a claret-colored gown that bared significant and tantalizing bits of her in the most stylish manner. But Swallow had hardly noticed. Instead, he seemed unable to take his eyes off a couple down on the dance floor, a tall, slender pair about his own age, which was nearly thirty-six.

Molly sniffed and selected a cream bun from the passing tea cart. The white-gloved waiter laid it clumsily on her plate with golden serving tongs, inclined his thick torso in what was meant to be a bow, and moved on to the next table.

Definitely not Palm Court standard, she thought ruefully. Things had gone downhill badly since the war, even at the Hotel Superbe. Unconsciously, Molly shifted the pastry to bring it into perfect alignment with a large pink rose on the china.

"Look, Tom," she said, "I do wish you'd make an effort to remember I'm here. It's our wedding anniversary. Or it would have been, if you hadn't got the heebie-jeebies and decided you preferred Scotland Yard to me."

His soft, dark eyes grew a shade darker, his brows narrowed. "I'd have made a rotten husband, and I made a pretty fair policeman, though."

"For a while." He'd left the Force recently. It was a sore subject between them.

Thomas studied her bare shoulders without seeming to notice who was attached to them. "You didn't actually mind not getting married. Did you?"

Molly Desmond's determined chin tilted up another quarter inch. "Speaking as the daughter of a proud line of pickle bottlers, I'd say I had a fortunate escape." She stabbed a piece of bun with her dessert fork. "All I asked was that you meet me here once a year for the tea dance. Now here we are, and all you do is stare at *them*." Molly frowned at the couple on the dance floor. "Dreadful orange dress, what a common color! Do you know her?"

"No," he said gruffly, and looked away. "I don't know anybody in these posh places anymore."

The slender ladies in ankle-length chiffon and the young men with pomaded hair moved like puppets across the polished oak. The band was playing "Three O'Clock in the Morning," but Thomas Swallow didn't ask Molly to waltz. He only took a sip of his rapidly cooling Earl Grey and looked at her cautiously over the edge of the cup.

She's thinner, he thought, *and her skin's too white. She was never cut out for a schoolmistress. She might've been anything. Anything. You only have to look at her to see she's bloody bored.*

Involuntarily, Swallow's gaze travelled back to the couple on the dance floor, the tall, blonde girl in shrimp-colored chiffon and the man, slightly shorter than she, with soft dark hair that fell over his eyes as he waltzed and had to be brushed away with the back of his hand. The gesture followed the pace of the dance as though it were itself a step.

Swallow closed his eyes and forced himself to keep them shut for a count of twenty-five. How was he to explain to Molly that he was seeing a ghost?

He's thicker, she thought, studying him through the black veil of her velvet hat. *And his moustache is going grey already. He should never have left the police force. He was a damn fine copper. You only have to look at him to know he's bloody bored.*

"I've been absolutely faithful to you, you know," said Amaryllis Desmond suddenly. "All these years since the war. There, now. I've got your attention at last."

On the floor, the fair girl and the dark man swirled away and Swallow had to crane his neck to keep them in view.

Surely it couldn't be Hazleton, he told himself. Ian Hazleton had died on the Somme.

"But it's nearly ten years, Moll," he said softly. "Surely . . ."

His voice trailed away, as it always did when he allowed himself to speak of their abortive dash toward matrimony. They had met in a Red Cross hospital in Rouen three days after the Armistice. In a week, they were engaged. Neither of them had wanted to go home. For two months after, they were lovers. It had been the best time of Molly Desmond's life.

As she had said, it was Swallow who ended it. The war did something to everyone; it left you with at least one piece of yourself that flew out of control at the oddest moments. Molly's piece was sorting and straightening as she had done in the dispensary at Rouen; even now she had unconsciously arranged the sticky crumbs of her cream bun into a tidy row in order of size.

Tom Swallow's piece, the thing he couldn't seem to grasp, was settling down and coming to rest on any one kind of life or any one person. Nothing and no one could be relied on—especially himself. He had not been faithful to anything. It was stupid, but there it was. His feet got cold with disheartening regularity.

And he saw ghosts. For Thomas Swallow, the dead were everywhere.

After he stumbled into that business of the Masterton kidnapping and found he did rather well at skulking and sleuthing, the ghosts had stopped coming for a while—years, in fact. He had almost begun to hope that he and Molly might settle into a comfortable arrangement, marriage or no marriage. That he might be settled at last, and healed.

But then his father had died—rather miserably, poor old

gaffer. Another hopeless war, a tiny, inoperable cancer. The delusion of possibility crashed about Tom's wide, hunched shoulders. There was no beating war; it was the only permanent fact, and it changed its shape and came and found you, and took things away that you might've loved.

So he'd left the Force, too, just as he was about to make chief inspector. Well, he'd never have known, would he, whether they were only doing it because he'd come into a title? He got cold feet, again the old malady.

And now that dark young man on the dance floor, the ghost who would not let him go. Ian Hazleton, whose dead body he had seen lying beside him, half-buried in a sodden, shelled-out trench.

"Are we going to bloody-dance, Tom, or are we going to not-bloody-dance?" Her voice was shrill and nervous. She knew something was wrong. Why could he not simply tell her?

The five-piece band behind the lustrous potted jungle of the Palm Court struck up a tango.

"Not," Swallow said and gazed out across the dance floor. "Sorry. Can't tango worth stink."

But the ghost of Ian Hazleton could.

The late afternoon light came through the high windows—as London light will often do—not in golden shafts, but in a sheer mist of bewildering pewter that burnished the russet carpets of terraces and stairs, turned battenberg tea-clothes to old ivory, and lay upon the soft, powdered shoulders of the ladies and the expressionless faces of their dancing partners like a magician's spell. They seemed to move beyond their own control, suspended, not choosing whether to dance or not dance, to waltz or Charleston or fox-trot, to live or to take life away.

"It's an institution, really, isn't it?" said Swallow thoughtfully. Hazleton's ghost was dancing his partner closer, almost to the edge of the railed Terrace where Thomas and Molly were sitting. "The tea dance at the Superbe, I mean. *It's* permanent, at least. It'll go on long after we're all dead."

Molly reached across the table and grasped his hand. The cup it held was shaking and the cold split tea had made a mud-colored puddle on the creamy cloth. The dancing ghost looked up at Thomas and smiled.

"Christ," said Thomas softly. "I'm mad. It can't be him. But it is."

She looked down at the couple. "*Who*, Tom, for God's sake? Some crook you snaffled? Let's bash him! What's his name?"

"Ian Hazleton. My lieutenant at Auvergne-le-bas." He paused, studying her face. His fingernails were digging into the palm of her hand. "We were dug in by a little wood along the Somme. 1916, in the autumn. He'd got a letter from home that morning, first mail we'd had in weeks. Some girl or other. He still had her letter in his hand when the shelling started. Whole bloody trench came down on us. He was hit. I *saw* him die, Molly. I had him in my arms, and I *felt* him die. Do you understand?" He looked away. "No, of course you don't. How could you?"

Molly watched the dancers swirl away, but she didn't let go of Swallow's hand. The shaking was not so bad now, but still she held him.

"Obviously, you old goof," she said, her voice very calm and soft, "the man didn't really die. When they dug him free, you were unconscious. You thought him dead, but he never was."

"Yes, he was, damn it!" Swallow was shouting, and people stared. "Ian was dead and now—"

"My God!" cried Molly. "Look!"

Down on the dance floor, the fair-haired girl in the shrimp-colored tea gown screamed. The other couples stopped, drew away from the girl and her ghostly partner. Ian Hazleton—if so he was—stumbled a few steps into the empty center of the room and turned to look up at the table where they sat. His handsome face was convulsed, his dark eyes under their heavy brows staring. His hands gripped the brass railing at Swallow's elbow.

The band was playing "Tea for Two."

"Tom," gasped Hazleton. His neck and cheeks were suffused with deep pink, as though he were blushing. A scent drifted toward Molly, and she was surprised that death could smell like flowers. "I'm a dead man, Thomas," said the dancing ghost. "By God, I am."

Swallow rushed for the terrace steps, with Molly no more than a pace behind him, but before they reached him, he had fallen. Another woman screamed. The blond girl in shrimp-color had disappeared.

Thomas Swallow took his dying friend in his arms for the second time. "Ian!" he cried, a long, wailing cry, as though the world were caving in on them again.

Hazleton was overwhelmed by a convulsion, and Molly Desmond looked away. He would be dead in a minute, she knew.

Thomas had his face very close to his friend's, listening.

"Melford," said Hazleton's lips, without making any audible sound. "Dear God. Old Melford."

Then the last convulsion claimed him. The ghost was dead.

"Cyanide, of course. Smell of almond, plain as day." Detective Sergeant Augustus Spooner reached a scrawny arm across and handed the teacup to Thomas Swallow for inspection.

It was the sweet smell Molly had caught as Ian Hazleton came near them. The aunt who had raised her had a bush of flowering almond by the parlor window. She felt suddenly cold.

"We've taken the photos, of course," intoned Spooner mournfully. "For all the good they'll do. And the finger-prints, all this newfangled claptrap. I rely on common sense, myself. When I can find it."

"There was a girl with him," said Thomas, letting his eyes rake the serried ranks of hotel manager, head waiter, and guests. "Surely some of you saw her? A fair-haired girl, rather tall. Nice looking."

Nobody spoke. What had they to do with murder? The hotel manager studied his lavender spats. The head waiter tapped his fingers on the tabletop.

"She was wearing a sleeveless orange dress," said Molly, eyebrows arched. "By the time we got down to the dance floor, she'd done a bolt."

"There's your murderer, all right. No more than common sense, is it? Anyway, poison's a woman's weapon," said Spooner. Then he remembered Molly. "Oh, ah. Begging your pardon, Miss."

The tip of Molly's tongue came out between her lips. She bit it and took a deep breath. *God help the girl,* she thought. *He's got her in the dock already.* "She didn't look like London," she told him. "I'd say a county family."

"Now, why's that, Miss?" asked Sergeant Gant, who had just finished taking useless statements from the last of the staff and guests. As they filed out, he nabbed a handful of *petits-fours* from a nearby tea tray. He popped one thought-fully into the wide mouth that lurked beneath his jovial moustache. "Shouldn't think there'd be much to choose be-tween London girls and the other sort."

"She was tanned," Molly went on, "but not deeply, not like the beach at Cannes or Antibes or anywhere. Her arms were tanned, and the back of her neck, but not her face. She wore a wide hat, you see. That's a gardener's tan." Molly set her chin, not to be gainsaid. "And she had a bosom. London girls don't, not nowadays. They're all shaped like ruddy clarinets. No, she was county, all right."

Gant and Spooner exchanged glances, impressed. They also, it must be said, did not fail to notice that Molly herself was most certainly *not* a clarinet.

"Deceased's identification, sir," said Spooner, handing Ian Hazleton's pocketbook to Swallow. "Louis Rocher, 21 Bright Street, Maida Vale."

"His name wasn't Rocher, Sergeant Spooner. It was Ian Hazleton. He was my lieutenant on the Somme. I thought he was dead till this afternoon. He may have been living in Maida Vale, but his home was down in Devon. His father's estate. Melford Hall, near Hatherleigh."

"M-E-L-F-O-R-D, are you spelling that, Inspector Swallow, sir?"

Gant was making notes. Thomas spun round on his heel and came toe-to-toe with him. "Bloody hell, Gant. I'm not in the Force any longer."

"Oh, I know that, Sir Thomas. Only—"

"This is a murder case. Where is your commander, Chief Mellors?"

Probably playing golf with the Home Secretary, thought Swallow, answering his own question.

"Well, now, we thought, being as it was you that rang us, sir," said Spooner, "and now we know he was a particular friend of yours . . ."

"I want nothing to do with it, Sergeant. If you're finished, Miss Desmond and I will be going now."

Thomas slipped an arm through Molly's and she could feel a kind of electrical charge in him, not of death perhaps, but certainly of resistance to life. She had felt the same tension when they made love, the spark of death the war had planted pulling him away from her.

"Tom," she said clearly. "What did Ian say to you just before he died?"

Swallow frowned down at her and took his arm away. "He said, 'I'm a dead man, Tommy. By God, I am.' Then, just at the last, he said 'Melford. Dear God. Poor old Melford.' "

Spooner frowned at Gant. Gant scowled at Spooner and shoved a jam roll under the moustache.

"So," he said, chewing thoughtfully, "p'rhaps he knew you'd be here, sir. P'rhaps he'd come hoping to see you."

"Or hoping *you'd* see him!" cried Molly. "Of course he could've known. We come here every year on this date. You've been in the papers often enough, and he might've followed you. He was living under a fake name, there must've been some reason he didn't dare to surface. If he knew you'd be here, and wanted to ask for help—"

"Don't be ridiculous!" Thomas had begun to pace round and round the body, which still lay on the ballroom floor, discreetly covered with one of the battenberg tablecloths. "If Ian had wanted to speak to me, all he need do was walk across the ballroom. But he didn't. He didn't."

"Not till he realized he'd been poisoned," said Molly softly. "Then he made a beeline for you."

Spooner sighed. "You thought he was dead, you say, sir?"

"Yes. We were shelled, our fellows lost most of the company. I saw Ian die. I'd have sworn it. Obviously, I was wrong."

"No chance he had a twin brother, sir, anything like that?"

"No, of course not. That only happens in Shakespeare." Thomas stopped pacing, knelt again beside the body. "I went home with him once on leave. To Melford. Lovely place. Happy, even then. The war might not have existed, so long as we were there." *Like the Palm Court,* he thought. *Like the dance that goes on for all the dead.* "Ian had no brothers, but he had one sister, I think. Evelyn, or—No. Eleanor. That was her name. Eleanor."

"Could she have been the young lady in orange, sir?" asked Gant.

"That girl was fair, and Miss Hazleton was dark-haired, like Ian. And not so tall." Thomas drew back the cloth for a moment. Hazleton's handsome face had found no peace in death. The deep pink that sometimes comes with cyanide poisoning gave him, as before, a look of terrible chagrin. *Died of shame,* thought Swallow. That was what people said of themselves. *I could have died of shame.* He jerked the cloth back over his friend's face and stood up, swaying slightly. "Anyway, his sister was very fond of him; there's no reason she should've poisoned him."

"Not ten years ago. But you don't know about now, Thomas, do you?" Molly dug her heels in. He had cold feet again; she knew the signs. Well, he wasn't to get away with it this time. "And you know damn-all about girls. Everyone's using peroxide these days. It might even have been a wig!"

He was angry; she knew it. He gripped her arm too hard.

"Come on, then, Molly," said ex-Inspector Sir Thomas Swallow. "You'll miss your train. If there are any further questions, Spooner, you know where to reach me."

When they'd gone, Gant turned to Spooner.

"He'll be down in Devon by nightfall," he said, chuckling. "Give you eleven to five. *She'll* see he gets there. Regular bull pup, that one."

"Nightfall?" Spooner scoffed. "If he's not there in an hour, I'm a monkey's bootblack."

•   •   •

Thomas drove a Morgan, conspicuously shabby and notoriously hard to start. He helped Molly into the passenger's seat, got in himself, and after a few moments' grinding, the engine turned over and caught.

"Don't take me to the station. I'm not going back to Wales," said Molly. "I'm going to Devon. With you."

Thomas Swallow couldn't help smiling. *She's like a little steam train when she gets running,* he thought. *Straight down the track, all passengers have tickets ready. I must've hurt her badly, to leave her there alone in France. It interrupted the schedule.*

"I really do love you, Moll," he said gently. "Always did."

"I know. Nothing to do with love." She took his hand and kissed it, then laid it back onto the steering wheel. "Now drive, blast you!"

He did, without stopping or even slowing down, for if he had, the temperamental Morgan might not have started up again. They arrived at Melford Hall just before dusk, bouncing up the long, rutted avenue of lime trees, whose unpruned boughs reached out and scraped the car at each turn.

"Place has gone to seed," muttered Swallow. "The Hazletons may not even own it anymore."

He parked in the gravel circle before what was once the grand entrance to Melford Hall. It was clearly eighteenth century, a domed Palladian central section flanked by two wings, a double curve of steps leading from both sides to the huge double doors. Perfect in every proportion, built of silvery granite with here and there a pinkish or even a lavender cast in the failing sunlight. A beautiful thing, now gone to seed.

As they climbed the west staircase, Molly caught her shoe on one of the loose blocks and fell. Grass grew through the cracks. The double doors at which they knocked were peeling badly, and a hinge was loose. The door sagged as it creaked open.

"You're late." The man who stood there was tall and heavily built, with black hair that grew in tufts on his thick neck and peeped out from underneath his shirt cuffs. "Estate agent told me you'd be here at three. Bloody ass." He glanced at Molly. "Sorry. Irritating chappie, though. Never gets things right."

He opened the door and led them into the hall. It was almost empty of real furniture, only a few unwieldy pieces of no particular period. A stack of portraits and paintings leaned against a marble pillar, their picture wires dangling musically in the draught. Packing cases were strewn everywhere.

The man led them down a passage and into a great room. "Salon, of course," he said. "Rest's the usual guff. Morning room through there. Library. Music room. All the family clobber's been sold. If you're seriously interested, naturally, I can clear the rest of the stuff out within the week. Though I'd prefer a bit more time. Wedding, you see. Tomorrow, fortnight."

"Congratulations," said Swallow. "But we're not buying."

The hairy man's fact turned brick red. "Now, look here, Wyndham! That ass Padget told me—"

"Sorry. Not Wyndham. My name's Amaryllis Desmond," said Molly. "And this is Sir Thomas Swallow."

The brick red turned purple. "Oh, I say. Awfully sorry. Took you for the new owners. Well, prospective owners. Sir Thomas—"

"Just Swallow." Thomas offered a hand. "Mr. . . . ?"

"Colonel, actually. Colonel Holland. Soames Holland."

He shook Swallow's hand a bit too heartily, held it a bit too long.

"Holland Silver?" Molly beamed at him.

"Yes," he said, and smiled. Leered, perhaps, would be more the word. It was the only sort of smile his face was constructed to manage. "My old governor's business, but I run it now."

" 'Save for silver. No bride should be without it,' " said Molly.

"Oh, right-oh!" Holland laughed. "Jolly successful campaign, that."

It was the hottest advertising gimmick of the decade. You got coupons for spoons and knives and creamers and such on everything from washing powder to cigarette packets. *Electroplated tin,* thought Molly. *And they sell the rubbish like hotcakes. Lucky if you get through the wedding breakfast before it turns black. At least my father's pickles were good pickles.*

"How lucky, Colonel Holland," she said out loud. "Eleanor can have all the spoons she wants. You *are* marrying Eleanor, of course. Ian's sister?"

"Indeed he is."

Her voice came through the empty room like silk unreeling itself, soft and contained and with a richness that put back all the looted furniture, hung the portraits again upon their nails, laid down the thick Aubusson carpets Thomas remembered, replaced the hundreds of books upon their dusty shelves.

He turned to face her.

Eleanor Hazleton was indeed the fair-haired girl from the Palm Court, but now her hair was as dark as her brother's. She had his pale, fair skin, too, and his heavy brows, and she wore them unplucked, counter to the fashion. She had changed the shrimp-colored gown—burned it, probably, like the blonde wig, Thomas concluded—and she was wearing a long white dress, simple, open at the neck. She looked very young.

Swallow could see the large vein along her throat pounding. *She's afraid of the bastard,* he thought.

"I think we should talk about your brother's murder, Miss Hazleton," he said softly.

Soames Hazleton laughed. "Murder? Ian died at the Somme, Sir Thomas." He tried to lead them toward the entry hall, but Swallow didn't move. "Really, this is a bit awkward, you know. I hate to rush you, but I'm expecting buyers at any minute."

"Soames, dear," said Eleanor. "Sir Thomas was Ian's friend. I'd like very much to speak to him. Perhaps if we three walked a bit, in the garden?"

"Very well." Holland's face was grim and furious. "I'll get my stick and come with you."

"No, no. Your buyers, my dear. You wouldn't want to wander off and miss them." Eleanor smiled at Molly and slipped her hand through the crook of Swallow's arm. "My roses are perfect in June," she said and led them out through the French windows onto the gravel path.

If the house and drive had seemed rundown, the garden was a wilderness. The boxwood hedges of the knot-garden were overgrown and shaggy; the scented clumps of lavender, rosemary and lemon balm and the mat of creeping thyme had all but overwhelmed the brick walk to the rose arbor.

There alone things were as Thomas remembered them—perfectly mown grass swathe underfoot, at each end a white-washed wicker swing, and overhead, masses of pale, blush-pink roses. They were an ancient variety, centuries older than the house; in the sinking darkness, with the scent of the flowers heavy around them, a thousand years, a thousand wars might never have happened at all. Swallow breathed deep, his eyes closed for a moment.

"This is the only thing I shall really miss," said Eleanor Hazleton, "if Soames sells the place."

Sitting in one of the wicker swings, she laid her long hands flat in the lap of her dress, and Molly could see the facets of her engagement ring winking in the dusky light.

Might as well give her a dog collar and keep her on a leash, she thought, *or paint her a sign that says:* PROPERTY OF SOAMES HOLLAND, ESQUIRE.

Thomas sat down beside Eleanor. "It *was* you at the Palm Court this afternoon. Wasn't it?"

"Yes. I'm afraid I panicked when he—" She broke off, but there was no hint of tears in the quiet, steady voice. People register grief in different ways, and Eleanor Hazleton seemed to drift in it, will-less and beyond hope. "We'd argued, you see. I thought, if guests at the other tables had heard us—"

"That you'd be thought guilty."

"Yes. I loved Ian dearly, but he could be terribly pig-headed. I almost think there were times when I *could* have killed him. He wanted—" She stopped, drew a breath of the rose-perfumed air. "He wanted everything *his* way, that's all. It's very hard to explain. It's all been such a shock, and he had so little patience with things as they are. But, you see, I thought Ian was dead myself until about six weeks ago. My mother died thinking so, poor love."

"It's been nine years since the war ended, and almost eleven since the Somme." Tom stared into the darkness. "How did you happen to find him, after so long?"

"He found me. Here, in the arbor. God, I thought I'd seen a ghost." Swallow offered her a cigarette and Eleanor took it gratefully. She drew the smoke in and breathed it slowly out again before she went on. "As you know, Ian was left for dead that day. They took you and the other wounded away, but they had to wait to recover the casualties until the Germans stopped shelling. It was nearly two days, but there were lulls in the firing, he said. He clawed his way out and began to crawl, then lay still when it started again, or dug into a trench or a shell hole. He had no idea how long it took, or when he was found. He stumbled into what was left of a farm, and they took him in. An old couple. They nursed him. Afterward, he simply couldn't support going back to the war. He became their son. That's what he told me."

"He became a deserter, you mean?" Thomas frowned.

It was an idea that had crossed his own mind in that shell hole, not from cowardice so much as from Spooner's beloved common sense. Only a fool, he had always believed, never considered the wisdom of running away from insanity, no matter how noble the sermons it preached.

"It's hard to think of it that way. But I suppose so. Of course he was listed as missing-in-action," Eleanor said, "and the army presumed him dead. Then, after the war, he was trapped. How could he explain where he'd been?"

"So he took a false name and bought a French passport." Swallow knew at least four men in Boulogne alone who could forge undetectable British papers. "And became Louis Rocher of Maida Vale."

"I wish he'd never come back! He'd still be alive, and I—" Eleanor stood up and stamped out the cigarette on the grass. "I blame myself, you see. Why did he ever have to see that photo of me in the *Times*?"

"Your engagement photo?" asked Molly. "Didn't he care for the idea of you marrying old Soames?"

"I don't think he minded who I married. It was Melford," Eleanor replied. "He couldn't bear the idea of Soames owning the place."

Much less Soames selling it and copping a tidy profit, thought Swallow.

"Ian wired me yesterday to meet him at the Palm Court tea dance. The closer my wedding day, the more frantic he got. He actually meant to confront Soames." Eleanor laughed softly. "You must think me daft. The blonde wig, and everything. But Soames is very jealous, the old darling, and he follows me sometimes. It's really rather flattering. Only I couldn't let Ian come face-to-face with him, there'd have been the most awful row."

"It's been eleven years. Ian was legally dead, so Melford Hall's yours, unless he surfaced and reclaimed his inheritance. And if he did, there might have been a court martial," said Molly. "He might've been charged with desertion."

She remembered Soames Holland's heavy-jowled face, and the brick-red flush that had suffused it at even the slight embarrassment of mistaking them for house-hunters. A court martial would mean public scandal, and Colonel Holland would not take kindly to having a deserter for his brother-in-law.

He wouldn't have married her, thought Molly Desmond. *He'd have dropped her like a hot brick. "Bad for business, old girl. Sure you understand."*

"What did Ian say to you this afternoon?" Swallow got up from the bench and grasped Eleanor's shoulders. "Why did you put cyanide in his tea cup?"

"I didn't!" she cried, pulling herself free. "It's all wrong! It's been wrong ever since he went to France! God, how I hate men, going off strutting around in uniforms, and then coming back expecting to find things just as they left them! It was all *my* fault, according to him. The woodworm and the rising damp and the weeds and—" Eleanor took a few steps away from them, stood with her back to Swallow. "May I have another cigarette, please?"

He gave her one, but it fell from her fingers, which seemed to have lost all control over themselves. Thomas took another from his case, put it delicately between her parted lips, and lighted it.

"You really didn't kill him," he asked her softly. "Did you?"

"No," whispered the girl. "How could I?"

"Was Soames in the Palm Court this afternoon? Did he follow you?"

"No. No. He was at his solicitor's. Germyn and Finsfield. I rang his office before I left for London, just to make sure he'd gone. I'd have seen him, if he had followed me. He's not very subtle, you know." She was silent for a moment in the rose-scented darkness. "You said it was cyanide?"

"Yes."

"Terrible." Her voice was almost inaudible. "Terrible."

"Yes," said Molly. Her voice was angry and shrill and very cold, so cold that Thomas hardly knew it. "But then, it was the sort of death men often have. Men who go off and strut around in uniforms."

She marched past them and out of the arbor. In a moment, Thomas was beside her.

"Where are you going?" he said.

"Don't know." Suddenly Molly spun round on her heel and caught his lapels and held him, her arms tight around his chest. "I don't like her, that's all. She's not real. She and Soames Holland deserve each other, if you ask me. Phony as flatware, the pair of them." She paused, still holding onto him. "I'm sick of this. Can't we go back to London now?"

"Not yet," he said. "Go and wait for me in the Morgan."

But she followed him into the house. There was a telephone in the front hall, and he picked up the receiver.

"Are you calling Spooner and Gant?"

"No. Go wait in the car. Please."

"*He* did it, of course. Soames, he must've done! She's a frigid little bitch, but she's no poisoner."

Swallow spoke so quietly into the mouthpiece that Molly caught only the words "electroplating" and "Wednesday." Then he hung up.

"Well?" she said.

Thomas didn't answer, only dialed again. "Telegram, June 20," he said. "Yesterday, that's right. Miss Hazleton, at Melford Hall? I see. Thanks."

He hung up and walked to the foot of the staircase, and stood there in silence for a moment before he shouted.

"Holland!"

His deep voice entered all the open doors and forced its way into all the rooms where nobody would ever live again except the dead.

"Soames Holland! Where the hell are you?"

The first bullet struck him before he could shout again, and Swallow fell heavily, bleeding at the temple. He moved slightly, groaned. A second bullet came, and struck his chest. He lay still.

Dead, thought Molly Desmond, and went to kneel beside him.

There was blood everywhere, his chest and the side of his face. Her bones remembered the shape and the warm living weight of him, and grief flared up in them as though her bones themselves were burning. When she touched his arm, it was still warm through the coat, and she tried to remember how long a body stayed warm after it was dead. She would be with him that long, at least. Even if Soames Holland shot her and she was dead, too, she would stay there with her hand on Swallow's arm.

Holland had come down the stairs now and stood above her, the gun in his hand. He was wearing gloves, and suddenly she knew him.

"It was you!" she said, almost laughing. "The waiter at the Palm Court! You wore white gloves to hide the hair on your hands. You served us our tea and cakes."

"You're a clever little cow, I'll give you that." Soames smiled and lowered the gun.

I'm no threat to him, that's what he thinks. Thinks? He can't think, he hasn't got the equipment.

"You use cyanide, don't you?" she said. "To make those trashy silverplated spoons you sell? You spied on Eleanor, found out where she was going to meet her brother. Perhaps you found the telegram and read it. You knew he could take Melford away from you, court martial or not. He didn't mind what happened to him. After all, Ian was a ghost, wasn't he?"

She stood up and took a step or two to see if her body would obey her. Then she went on. "People get wise to trash eventually, no matter how many coupons you give away. Business was bad, wasn't it? You couldn't afford to lose Melford, and you couldn't risk a scandal. So you got some cyanide from your workroom or your laboratory or something, and you kitted yourself out as a waiter and poisoned Ian."

Molly heard a door close and footsteps coming through the empty morning room, but she didn't care who it was, nor if Holland's gun exploded against her temple. Suddenly she understood Swallow, why he had not been able to stick with her or with his work or with anything. Why he went on, but not toward anything, nor because of anything.

Oh, Tom, she thought, *we are all ghosts now. All the living and all the dead.*

"Tell me," she asked Holland suddenly, "how do you intend to get rid of Eleanor, once you've sold Melford? I really wouldn't suggest using the cyanide again."

Holland grabbed her arm and dragged her into the pitch

dark of the salon. There was a flare of light from a struck match, and Molly could see the girl's long, pale face as Eleanor lit an old alcohol lamp on one of the packing crates that littered the room.

"What in the name of God have you done, Soames?" she said coldly.

"Exactly what you told him to," said the ghost of Thomas Swallow from the doorway.

Molly felt the darkness sway around her, and though she would never have fainted—for it was hardly her style—she might have fallen from sheer relief if Holland's fingers hadn't been clamped so hard around her wrist.

"A large flask of hydrocyanic acid turned up missing from the lab at Colonel Holland's factory after you paid them a visit on Wednesday. Very interested in the new process of electroplating, you said. And of course you knew what cyanide could do, you've used it to keep the greenfly off your roses, haven't you?"

"I don't know what you're talking about!" Eleanor moved toward him. "I had no idea—"

"Yes. You planned everything. There was no telegram from Ian, yesterday or any other day. *He* suggested the Palm Court, perhaps he really did know I would be there. But it was you who invited him. A letter, on your monogrammed stationery. A telephone call. He looked so happy at first. Did you tell him you'd decided to break your engagement? Did you tell him he could come home to Melford and become himself again?"

Swallow's voice seemed to fade, and Molly took up the thread to finish the knot.

"You planned the whole thing with darling Soames, didn't you? Did you give him that ridiculous waiter's outfit, too? Terrible fit. Then you told us he was at his solicitor's. When we checked and found out he wasn't, he'd look guilty as sin." She looked up at Soames Holland's staring eyes. "Oh you poor old goop. Don't you understand? She poisoned her brother, but she didn't mean to hang for it. That honor was meant to be yours, my dear old sport. Why do you think she chose cyanide? You had access to it, of course."

"It's a lie! Eleanor loves me!" Holland's voice was a wail, like a small boy's tantrum.

"Oh, she'd have married you," Molly went on. "Got a nice marriage settlement, her share of Holland Holloware. Bet *she* picked out that rock on her finger, didn't she? The money from that alone would keep the wolf away from Melford for a good while, once you were done for."

"Look at her, Holland!" Thomas's voice was a hoarse bark. "Look at her face! You shot me to protect her. Do you see gratitude there? Concern? *Anything* you might mistake for love?" Swallow's body slid inexorably down the door frame until he sat on the floor. "There's only one thing she loves. This house. Melford."

"And none of you will take it from me now," said Eleanor quietly. "Give me the gun, Soames."

He looked from one of them to the other, dazed and frightened—of himself, of this new Eleanor, of consequences. But they didn't matter. Soames Holland had joined the ranks of the ghosts, and nothing mattered any longer. He gave her the gun.

"You idiot!" shrieked Molly Desmond and kicked over the packing crate that held the alcohol lamp.

After that, chaos exploded. The wood slats of the packing crate caught instantly and blazed up bright, and sparks caught the long skirt of Eleanor's white dress. She screamed, and the gun fell clattering to the floor. Then she ran for the French windows, screaming, screaming, a train of flame behind her, burning into the darkness. Holland didn't go after her. He let go of Molly's arm, took off his jacket and began to beat out the rest of the fire.

From outside they heard men's voices. Then the woman's screaming stopped.

In another minute, Spooner was with them, and then Gant, stamping out the last of the flames. A pair of constables led Soames Holland away.

"What in the name of God are you doing here, Spooner?" gasped Thomas. "How did you know we were here?"

"Well, sir," intoned the detective sergeant. "Followed you, didn't we? Thought we'd let you have your innings, before we meddled in. Knew you'd sort things out, so we just had a nice plate of chops and a pint in the village first. Good beer hereabouts. Worth the drive and all."

Thomas Swallow could only groan.

Molly was once again kneeling beside him. "Really, Tom," she said, putting pressure on a compress. The chest wound was more blood than damage, it turned out. "You're not safe to be let out alone! If Holland weren't as rotten a shot as he is a silversmith, you'd be bloody dead right now."

"Mark my words, Spoony. She'll have him back on the Force by the first of July," muttered Gant.

"Nine to five, odds-on," said Spooner.

"I make it eleven to three," replied Gant.

"*Will* you marry me, Moll?" said Thomas Swallow.

"Oh, probably. Some time or other," she replied. "But you owe me a bit more penance first. And quite a bit of pain."

She bore down on the compress again, and Swallow yelped.

"Bull pup," said Spooner.

"Odds-on," said Gant.

It's said that the Lord works in mysterious ways. While people interpret that however they wish, the nun in this story is certainly a godsend for a woman she's never even met. Mysterious ways or not, this sleuth practices her own form of "divine intervention."

Daughter of Compassion

Veronica Black

"Do you think," Mother Dorothy had enquired, the faintest trace of sarcasm in her voice, "that you can possibly go into town without finding a dead body?"

"I don't stumble over them on purpose, Mother Prioress," Sister Joan had answered meekly.

Mother Dorothy had sighed slightly, handed over the money, and dismissed her with the customary, "Dominus vobiscum."

"Et cum spiritu sancto," Sister Joan had knelt briefly and gone out to where the taxi waited.

Taxis were rare sights at the Convent of the Daughters of Compassion, but the convent van had developed a fault that required garage attention and since it was five miles from the gracious old home on the moor to the railway station a taxi had been ordered.

Waving to Sister Hilaria, who was drifting across the

lawn with her novice in tow, Sister Joan reminded herself
not to loll against the cushioned back seat and fastened her
seat belt conscientiously. The driving mirror had given her
a rare glimpse of her own face, round and pink cheeked with
an inch of curling black hair showing beneath her short
black veil, the eyes darkly blue and long lashed. At thirty-
eight she didn't look too bad, she decided.

The bundle of notes in her wallet weighed heavily on her.
Normally underwear for the Community was bought locally, but the announcement of a sale in the next town had
brightened Mother Dorothy's eyes behind her steel-rimmed
spectacles. Money was always tight in the Order even
though the sisters, being only semi-enclosed, were permitted
to take work that didn't infringe upon their religious duties.
Sister David undertook translations for the universities; Sister Martha sold produce from the garden in the local market;
Sister Catherine made bridal and First Communion dresses.
Nobody earned very much.

The train journey was a treat to be savoured. Taking a
corner seat Sister Joan studied the other occupants of the
carriage with covert interest. People imagined that living in
a convent somehow distanced one from the rest of the
world. Sister Joan had always found that it sharpened her
perceptions of human nature. What she couldn't deduce she
could imagine.

An elderly gentleman in the opposite corner was reading
the advertisement section of the local paper. Forced into
early retirement by his firm and looking for a nice little part-
time job that would get him out from under his wife's feet,
Sister Joan guessed. Next to him a young couple sat primly
side by side, not touching, their mutual glowing glances
telling Sister Joan what they didn't want others to guess. She
spotted a ring on the girl's hand and hoped they were married to each other.

A middle-aged woman who looked as if she counted calories too rigorously got in at the next station. Silver grey hair was swept up at the back of her head and secured by small diamante combs; sharp features were masked by subtly applied cosmetics; a well cut dark green suit was complemented by a pair of dark brown court shoes that matched her handbag. She looked like the kind of woman who would normally travel by car.

Seating herself next to Sister Joan, she gave her the faintly self-conscious nod and smile with which so many people acknowledged the presence of a nun, and said brightly, "It's so long since I was in a train. It's quite clean, isn't it?"

A neat way of letting people know she was merely slumming. Sister Joan said politely, "There are not many of these closed carriages left now."

"With parking so difficult I decided to give myself a treat," the woman said.

"A shopping trip?" Sister Joan thought that it would prove rather difficult to find a Harrods in the little market town.

"I'm visiting my aunt," the woman said. "Poor dear! she's in a nursing home. Very well run and the carers are absolutely dedicated, but one feels for her. Of course we'd love to have Auntie Bea with us but there's the garden, you see."

"Yes, of course," Sister Joan wondered if Auntie Bea dashed out in the middle of the night and uprooted the roses or something.

"Not that we've able to do very much with it this year," the woman was continuing. "Hodge said to me that it was useless doing much until we'd had a good shower of rain. You must feel it—the heat, I mean."

Sister Joan glanced down briefly at her light grey habit, ankle-length and belted at the waist.

"The modern habit is more comfortable," she said.

"And grey is so much nicer than black," the woman said. "I can't wear black. So drab!"

Sister Joan smiled, her glance straying to the window. They were almost at their destination now, the moors giving place to long rows of houses and the occasional block of high rise apartments. The long platform slid into view and the elderly man folded his newspaper and placed it in his briefcase.

"After you, Sister." He leaned to open the door as the train stopped with a shudder, spilling its passengers out as if they were indigestible.

Sister Joan alighted and walked briskly to where the tickets were checked. The woman in dark green had gone ahead of her, slim legs hurrying.

The large store on the corner of the main road had its windows plastered over with brightly coloured stickers tempting people to step inside for the bargain of the year. Prices that would never have been paid in the first place had been slashed by fifty percent. Anyone who spent more than fifty pounds was entitled to a free coffee and cake in the cafe on the top floor. Sister Joan dived into the crowd melling about within the open doors.

"One dozen of everything, Sister," Mother Dorothy had instructed. "Plain black. No frills or flounces and no uplift bras!"

Sister Joan had surreptitiously noted down approximate measurements, feeling justified because little Sister Martha would look ridiculous in the voluminous black knickers that would fit plump Sister Mary Concepta, and Sister Hilaria would find any slip which fitted Sister David as inadequate as a miniskirt on her own gaunt frame. Mother Dorothy was not in the least concerned with proper sizing or fit, which could be interpreted as meaning that she relied on Sister Joan to see to all that. Or so Sister Joan told herself, holding a pair of briefs at waist height and trying to imagine Sister Teresa in them.

Beyond the jumbled piles of underwear suits hung on racks, each with a large metal tag on. A slim woman in dark green was rapidly sliding the garments along the rack, her expression concentrated. She chose a garment, held it against herself for a moment, nodded, and with the suit over her arm headed for the cash desk.

There wouldn't be time for that free cup of coffee and cake now, Sister Joan thought with regret, quickly making her final selection and taking the pile of underwear to the checkout.

By the time she had paid and, two large carrier bags clutched in her hands, left the store, the woman in green had gone. Sister Joan bit her lip, looking up and down the street.

It was, of course, none of her business. Almost certainly it meant nothing at all. What she ought to do was head for the railway station and leave events to follow their course. There probably wouldn't be any events anyway.

"My trouble," she scolded herself silently, "is a constitutional inability to trust my fellow men and mind my own business."

"What on earth are you doing here!?"

A tall man with rugged good looks and grey streaking, enviably thick black hair had stopped in front of her and was staring.

Sister Joan came back to earth with a bump and a frisson of pleasure.

"Detective Sergeant Mill!" She transferred one of the bags to the other side and held out her hand. "They've not transferred you, I hope?"

"Regional meeting to pool information about known criminals. Happily it didn't last as long as I was led to expect. And you?"

"Buying knickers," Sister Joan said with a grin.

"Good Lord! one never thinks of nuns as wearing—well, you know!"

"Oh, we do." Her blue eyes glinted with mischief. "You're a bit behind the times, you know! Nowadays they're called undies and can be mentioned in polite society. Are you going to the sale?"

"No, thanks." He grimaced as he shook his head. "I don't believe in hell, Sister, but if I did it would contain large notices announcing prices off and hordes of females trying to grab the cheapest bargains. My car's round the corner. May I give you a lift home?"

When she had determined on the right course of action, the devil always provided temptation, Sister Joan thought, picturing a comfortable trip back to the convent with a civilised man who never permitted his admiration for her to topple over into embarrassing familiarity. On the other hand, the fact that temptation had presented itself was a pretty strong hint that the course of action she was contemplating was the right one. The devil could be more helpful than he knew.

"I've not quite finished my business here," she said. "Anyway I've a return ticket."

"Then I'll not deprive you of the pleasures of travelling by British Rail," he said. "I can take your shopping in the car if you like, and you can pick it up at the station later. No sense in lugging it around with you."

"Thank you, that's very kind."

She handed over the two heavy carrier bags gratefully.

"Take care, Sister." He nodded at her and turned with some reluctance away.

There was one nursing home in the town where an elderly woman whose means were handsome might choose to end her days. Sister Joan had never visited the place but knew where it was situated and went in her usual brisk fashion down the street, crossed the road, and negotiated the maze of narrow streets that radiated into the surrounding country-side, houses becoming larger the further they were from the centre of town. As she walked she found herself conducting a silent argument with herself.

"You're an idiot to go haring off simply because your in-stincts are jangling! If you had less imagination you'd stay out of trouble.

"If you don't check this out you might be reading about it in the newspaper and then your conscience will trouble you."

She had argued herself to the outskirts of town, the red brick facade of St Swithin's Nursing Home for the Elderly rising before her. Someone was emerging from the main door. Sister Joan ducked her head and whisked around the next corner barely in time to avoid the woman in green who, carrier bag in hand, came down the path and crossed the road without a backward look.

She'd hit on the right nursing home then. Cheered by this, she walked back to the gates, pushed one open and went in-side. At each side of the curving drive a lawn yellowed by the summer heat was bordered with brightly coloured stocks. A large tub of geraniums stood on the top step by the front door.

Nursing homes smelt of polish and lavender air freshener and boiled cabbage with a faint but unmistakable odour of clean but ageing flesh. The floor was carpeted, a stairlift was fixed to the bottom of the staircase that rose up to the land-ing above, a shiny desk half blocked the passage along which an old lady with a zimmer frame was making her way. A door at the end opened and the *chunner chunner* of a television set was briefly heard.

"May I help you?"

The girl seated behind the desk looked young and healthy, somehow out of place here. Her hair was shiny, her eyes brightly enquiring. Sister Joan had the feeling that were she a few years older, the girl would be calling her "dear" and speaking very slowly.

"I called in to see how Aunt Bea was," she said.

"Oh, are you a friend of hers?" The girl looked surprised. "She doesn't get any visitors, except Mrs Wainwright of course."

"I'm just passing through," Sister Joan said. "Did Mrs Wainwright call today?"

"You only just missed her," the girl said. "She never stays very long. Of course her husband being a solicitor means they have lots of functions to attend."

"And how is the old lady?" Sister Joan asked.

"Rather difficult today, I'm afraid," the girl said. "They can be awkward sometimes, you know, but one has to make allowances, I suppose. It can't be much fun to be in your eighties and know that you haven't got many years left."

"She's not ill?" Sister Joan felt a stab of alarm.

"No, not at all. She's been having a few tummy upsets recently. Nothing to speak of but Mrs Wainwright was quite worried. I said to her, 'Honestly, your digestion can't be as good when you're eighty as when you were twenty. I'll give your auntie her cake just as soon as she's on speaking terms with everybody again.' Mrs Wainwright worries a lot."

"And Aunt Bea likes cake, of course." Sister Joan nodded as if she knew all about it.

She wasn't surprised not to have been asked her name. Some people assumed that nuns didn't actually have individual names but went through the world as faceless, anonymous vessels of God.

"Actually she's rather greedy about it," the girl confided disapprovingly. "I mean there's always plenty to eat for everybody. Cook goes to a lot of trouble with the menus. This being a private home, the budget's more generous than it would be on the National Health, but Aunt Bea will cherish her bits of cake and her biscuits and when Mrs Wainwright brings her a homemade one, she won't share a crumb of it. Funny how people get, isn't it?"

"Very funny," said Sister Joan.

Out of the corner of her eye she could see a small square package wrapped in pink paper reposing at the girl's elbow. A light biscuity sort of cake, she guessed, that would fit neatly into a flat dark brown handbag.

Somewhere in the depths of the building a bell rang. The girl jerked to attention, looking animated.

"I'm off duty now," she said. "Were you collecting for anything?"

Some people also assumed that nuns were only let out to go begging. Sister Joan said, "Not today. Look, don't let me keep you!"

"Well, Ken gets annoyed if I hang around too long," the girl said. "Shall I tell Aunt Bea that you came?"

"She probably wouldn't be able to place me," Sister Joan said truthfully. So the old lady was Aunt Bea even to the staff. It implied they were all one happy family, but she suspected the old lady had reached the age when, like nuns, few people cared to dignify her existence by remembering her individual name.

"See you then," the girl said, smiling as she gathered up her things. Her eyes were already dreaming ahead to the evening.

To Sister Joan's relief she whisked out from behind the

desk without waiting for her replacement and ran lightly up the stairs. There was no time to argue with her conscience. Reminding herself of the convenient maxim that the end justifies the means, Sister Joan leaned over, picked up the pink-wrapped package which had, she saw, Aunt Bea printed on it in heavy black characters, shoved it into her capacious pocket and left.

She ought to have expected it but the train had gone and, with it, she presumed the lady in green. She thought of whiling away time before the next one by buying herself a cup of tea but decided against it. The change in her pocket might be needed for an extra journey.

The woman had boarded the train at the midway stop, a station that had been threatened with closure by successive governments but had somehow survived. The village it served was a tiny one, hidden in a fold of the moor. It was highly unlikely that Mr Wainwright practised as a solicitor there, but he did probably commute from one of the large villas that stood on the outskirts, their gardens neatly trimmed, their white walls and red roofs imitating Mediterranean dwellings.

When the train arrived she boarded it with a feeling neatly poised between excitement and apprehension. If she was wrong then at least she could expect to be castigated as a fool who had brought disrepute on her Order, but if she was right—on balance she decided she was probably right.

She was the only passenger who got out at the pretty, flower-decorated station. No doubt one of the reasons it had been spared was because it pleased the tourists who looked out at the picture postcard view and decided this was the real Cornwall.

A man who looked as if he'd been planted along with the flowers that bordered the narrow platform shambled towards her, took her ticket and squinted at it doubtfully for a moment before informing her with a certain relish in his tone,

"You got off a stop too soon, Sister."

"Yes, I know. I have to visit Mrs Wainwright," Sister Joan said.

"We can't have people breaking their journeys wherever they please," he reproached.

"I'm terribly sorry," Sister Joan said placatingly. "This is something of an emergency."

"Not her auntie, is it?" He brightened up considerably. "They've been waiting for her to go this past couple of years. Very well heeled the old lady is, you see, and Mrs Wainwright offered her a home with them but the old girl's awkward—prefers to spend her money on a posh nursing home, so of course it's going down, isn't it? Very selfish some of those old biddies are!"

Selfish enough to want to live out their full span of years in safety, Sister Joan thought nodding smilingly as she enquired, "Would there be a short cut to the house?"

"Over the bridge and up the lane. You can't miss it. Her laburnum's a real treat. I gave her some cuttings from this one here."

"You made the garden here?"

"Can't get anybody else these days to take a pride in the place," he said gloomily.

"It looks beautiful," she said sincerely.

"So you want to break your journey?" He'd reverted to the earlier problem. "Well, seeing at it's a nun—I've a lot of respect for nuns—there'd be no harm in your slipping up to see Mrs Wainwright. There's another train along in forty minutes, so you'd need to get your skates on!"

"I will!" Sister Joan sped across the bridge and up the lane.

It was impossible to miss the handsome villa with its

vivid yellow laburnum dropping its deadly little seeds over the manicured lawn. There was no car in the drive but the woman in green, her jacket removed to reveal a simple and expensive cream blouse, was watering a poinsettia on the glassed-in porch.

"Mrs Wainwright?" Sister Joan gained the porch, panting slightly.

"I'm sorry but we already make contributions to several national and local charities," the woman said.

Sister Joan stifled a sigh. Mrs Wainwright clearly never looked at nuns' faces.

"I'm not collecting for anything," she said patiently. "I've come about your aunt."

Odd how cosmetics and carefully styled hair couldn't disguise greed and satisfaction. Both these emotions flashed across the artificially smooth face before Mrs Wainwright set down the watering can and said in a tone of carefully modulated regret, "Poor Aunt Bea! Well, she'd had quite a lot of stomach trouble recently so it was to be expected. It was very good of them to send someone personally."

"She's not dead yet," said Sister Joan.

"Not dead?" Mrs Wainwright stared at her for a moment. "Then I don't see how—"

"We shared a compartment earlier today."

"Did—? Yes, I believe we did. Your voice sounds vaguely familiar." Mrs Wainwright was still staring at her. "I had rather a lot on my mind."

"The death of your aunt, I daresay?"

"Yes, I—no, of course not!" Mrs Wainwright bent and picked up the watering can again, holding it in front of her like a shield. "If Aunt Bea's all right then I really don't know what it is you want. My husband and I are both agnostics so if this is a conversion drive or something like that—we wouldn't be interested, really we wouldn't."

"Actually we're still living down the Borgias," Sister Joan said. "They used mercury and arsenic, I believe. Various combinations in various dishes. I've always thought that dining out with them must've been rather adventurous."

"I don't know what you're talking about," Mrs Wainwright said with an attempt at hauteur that was both threatening and pathetic.

"I'm talking about a homemade cake you left for Aunt Bea," Sister Joan said steadily. "A flat, biscuity kind of cake, full of seeds?"

It was a shot in the dark but the barb had found its mark. The other woman had blanched beneath her blusher. Her face looked curiously stiff, only the eyes bright and aware.

"She didn't share it with anybody, did she?" she said. "Aunt Bea never shares anything."

"She hasn't eaten the cake yet," Sister Joan said.

"Then where? How?"

"The cake's in a very safe place," Sister Joan said. "Very safe." Her blue eyes were guileless as she looked at the older woman, her hands neatly clasped before her. Not an eyelash flicked towards her capacious pocket.

"Is it money you want?" Mrs Wainwright spoke in a series of jerking gasps. "You're always short of money, aren't you? I don't have very much. The house is mortgaged and we've had to give up one of the cars. My husband—he doesn't know—he's a very moral person. What is it you want?"

"A promise there'll be no more cakes," Sister Joan said.

"I only—that is, I never meant to do anything," Mrs Wainwright said, holding onto the can as if it were her last refuge in an uncertain universe. "It was only—every week having to trek over to that damned Home and half the time she refused to see me! We offered her a nice home here with us but she wanted to be with other old people, she said. That was just an excuse! She's a selfish old woman, hasn't any friends. Won't join in the activities! I don't always take her anything, just now and then. A bar of chocolate, some pastilles, a little cake. She's very fond of my homemade cakes!"

"And recently she's been having quite a lot of stomach trouble."

"That wasn't all the cake!" Mrs Wainwright said defensively. "There are some things she can't digest properly! That was what made me think of it. I didn't put many seeds in, just one or two ground up very fine. They looked like cinnamon. I didn't do it every time either, only now and then. But now the money's so tight and we're going to have to sell the silver."

"Tough," said Sister Joan.

"If I promise—" The watering can clattered down and two hands were joined in a grotesque parody of prayer. "Please, Sister, if you can—aren't you bound by the confessional or something?"

"I'm not a priest," Sister Joan said.

"If I swear—I won't ever, ever—?" Her voice broke on a harsh sob.

"I shall expect Aunt Bea to live for a good many years and die of something like—well, not stomach trouble anyway," Sister Joan said. "You'd never get away with it, you know. The police always check out the obvious."

"I swear," Mrs Wainwright said again.

She evidently believed that nuns could read minds and ascertain motives simply by looking at people. Sister Joan hadn't the slightest desire to enlighten her.

"I hope we don't meet again, Mrs Wainwright," she said coldly and turned away, walking steadily down the steps.

She could feel the bright, desperate eyes boring into her back and felt a tremor of relief that Mrs Wainwright hadn't been using a pair of shears.

"You've been a long time," Detective Sergeant Mill said when she arrived at the police station to pick up her shopping. "You must've missed a couple of trains. Is everything all right?"

His glance had sharpened.

"It is now," Sister Joan said.

"Jump in and I'll give you a lift back." He held open the door.

"I ought not," Sister Joan said, getting in anyway.

"What have you been up to?" He slid behind the driving wheel and slanted a look towards her.

"Playing God," Sister Joan said sombrely. "I hope I've done the right thing."

She'd taken a risk, she thought now, going off on her own to set things right. And all she'd had to go on had been the uneasy feeling inside her when she'd seen a woman who hated black buying a black suit for herself at a sale. Women like Mrs Wainwright wore sales garments once if at all. And not many people bought mourning before the death had occurred.

"Anything I need to know?" Detective Sergeant Mill asked.

"Nothing, honestly." She relaxed for the first time in hours, reminding herself that her first task on reaching the convent must be to burn the pink parcel in the incinerator. And perhaps preventing a crime would earn her a few points to set against her other transgressions. It was a pity she couldn't tell Mother Dorothy the real reason why this time she hadn't found a body!

I've met my fair share of fellow mystery writers in my time. And, to my delight, they've all been very kind and gracious. It's strange, and perhaps for the better, that I don't recall ever hearing of the woman in this next story, however. I'm sure I would have remembered it . . .

Murder, She Did

Gillian Roberts

I was having a bad day. Or maybe a bad decade. Either way, it was not a good time for Cookie Meyers to chirp into my life.

As the final trial of this hideous, exhausting day, I was trying to survive a flight on Sadist Airlines during which I'd been forced to be entirely too intimate with a toe-tapping, gum-snapping, knee-juggling behemoth in the seat next to me. My special meal had been misplaced and they ran out of vodka before they reached my row. My blood pressure reading looked like the national debt, and I was not at all happy. And that was before we began a descent that felt like being dragged headfirst down a flight of stairs.

Definitely the wrongest possible time to encounter Cookie Meyers.

My name is Jessica Branch. You've probably heard of me. I write mysteries. Yes, like that *other* Jessica. For years

I have suffered ill treatment because of my first name, but I've said nothing. Smiled, in fact. Damned graciously, too, the way I was supposed to. But today, six arduous days into my book tour, the muscles of my mouth had refused to continue the charade, to grin and imply that it was fine for strangers to publicly mock my very existence. Today, when I was once again introduced as "the *other* Jessica" I quit pretending that such words were tolerable.

Instead, after a long and considered pause, I spoke the truth to the interviewer. I spoke from my heart. "*She's* the other Jessica!" I cried out. "I started writing years before she did! I have more titles—what books does she have, anyway? But how would a dimwit TV chatterer know? Have you ready anything, ever, besides a prompt card?"

The TV personality didn't know what to say. There was no prepackaged response on the monitor. So she laughed nervously and pretended I was joking.

I made my farewells.

She burst into tears, the TV station cut to a commercial and when they returned to the air, I'd been replaced by a pie-baking demonstration.

Apparently, even though I work—I in fact slave—for him and the other Jessica does not, my Judas of a publisher was peeved by my attempt to share my pain. Also by the fact that my farewells to the TV lady included the words, "That's it, you silicone-augmented bitch!" And he was really miffed that the entire exchange happened to be broadcast on national TV.

The bimbo-interviewer had called me names, too. I heard "crone," "witch" and "harpy" before I was out of earshot. But that didn't strike my publisher as a problem. As if it was fine for a television personality to be vulgarly rude, but wrong when her victim attempts to defend herself.

By late afternoon, my publisher was making oblique threats about my future. He said I was "difficult."

I am not difficult. Ask anyone—except, of course, boorish louts who have no idea how to treat a sensitive artist such as I. It is true that I am not a dishrag, that I have a backbone, but of course, that isn't acceptable from a woman of a certain age. We are supposed to be mild little grannies. Crone, indeed!

The plane lurched and bumped onto the tarmac. My seatmate's beefy forearm occupied every inch of the armrest, as it had most of the flight, despite my attempts to use the half that is mine by rights. My bad day was not getting one whit better. I aimed for the spot near his elbow we called the "funny bone" as children, although why funny, except maybe as "odd," I can't say—the place that sends hot wires of pain down to the wrist, and I whirred into it with the corner of my book—my own, newest title—hard as I could. His arm shot out straight and the papers it had held fell to the floor. "Sorry," I murmured, but I smiled while I said it.

That small strike for equality made me feel better, although only because I didn't yet know that still ahead waited Cookie Meyers.

I took out my compact and tried to redo my face. I may be "the other" to TV airheads, but as Jessica Branch I have a public of my own, after all. My works enjoy a modest measure of fame.

Modest. Right there is the problem. I suffer from an insufficiency of fame. Or perhaps, from misdirected fame, all of mine sidetracked to feed hers. A real and painful identity crisis.

The thing is, Jessica Branch is not a household word. The *other* Jessica, the Fletcher one, is. This terrible and unfair disparity nowhere becomes as apparent as during my annual Trail of Tears—my author tour. From one assigned city to another go I, wrenching my shoulder as I drag my suitcase plus a tour bag of emergency supplies—makeup and clothing changes and hairspray—banging the drums for my latest mystery, just as I was doing today before the unfortunate tete-à-tete with the idiot TV girl.

Touring is exhausting work which I would gladly forego if my publisher would allow me to. I still believe that in providing my readership with exciting and interesting puzzlers, I have completed the terms of my contract, and there is no reason for me to be subjected to those needy eyes, tedious stories, damp handshakes, insincere conversations. Let alone the planes and the dreadful people with whom one is forced to share them, the wretched food, the cold comforts of hotel rooms, the prattle of the hired drivers. Everything.

The last publicist assigned to me was a nitwit who said, just before she quit, that I had a bad attitude and she'd rather plan Satan's book tour than mine. This is patently ridiculous. I have the correct attitude, which is that it is my job to write the books and the publisher's job to sell them, and if selling means dragging from one city to the next like a migrant worker, answering the same questions the same way each time, then let *them* do it. Or send a programmed robot, for all I care.

But in my case, those indignities pale beside what inevitably awaits me, once I have dutifully delivered myself into the hands of The Media, whose generic TV, newspaper and radio interviewers—and too many booksellers—twinkle and say, as if the idea had just been invented, "And here we have The Other Jessica."

As if I were second-rate, an afterthought. Not completely real. A shadow. An imitation.

The Other Jessica. Oh, how I detest the other Jessica. The famous one. The victims in my last four mysteries have all been thinly disguised variations on the theme of That Jessica. First time, I made her an opera singer, then in the next book, a soap star, then a plagiarizing songwriter and finally, in this newest book, a hellishly evil, though superficially sweet, magazine freelancer. Despite all my creative input, the critics have implied that there is a sameness to the books, and now my career is endangered. It's not my fault that I'm obsessed with the injuries that woman has caused me. It's That Jessica's fault.

Why am I doomed to share my pitiable share of the lime-light with her? She doesn't drag her high heels across the country. I do. Why the jokes, the confusion? We have noth-ing in common except a not-astoundingly unusual first name and the fact that we are women of a similar age. Neither of us is a member of Gen X. Perhaps not even of Generation Y or even Z. But blending us together because of that is bla-tant ageism, an outrage. All old women look the same to them?

I understand that we also share the profession of mystery writing. Or, more accurately, I write. She claims to. She says she writes, she's famous all of the world for it—but I've searched my library shelves under "Fletcher" and found books about but not by her. Frankly, if her life is even vaguely like that TV show about her, then no wonder I can't find her books. When would she find time to write a word? She's too busy rushing away from her lovely seaside town to visit one doomed friend after another. The Typhoid Mary of Murder. And why hasn't anyone, anywhere realized the obvious? *She* isn't a writer at all—she's a murderer—a ser-ial killer operating week after week. I think she kills for hire, does it for money. How else would she pay the rent on oceanside real estate? She should be locked up. Nonethe-less, even if we were both writers—would that be enough to bundle us together as a package? There are other duplica-tions of mystery-writing women's first names—Sue Grafton and Sue Dunlap, Margaret Truman and Margaret Maron, Linda Grant and Linda Barnes, to name but a few, and are they treated like pale echoes of one another?

It's my parents' fault. Their warped sensibilities put me in a situation where I had to rename myself. I was originally Olive. Well, you might say, so what? Sure, it's the name of a bitter fruit that needs curing and salting before it's edible. Not an inspired name, but the plus side is that no other mystery-writing Olive comes to mind. There'd be no duplication, no humiliating interviews, no prime-time TV fiascos, no threats from publishers. And my books might have more variety and critical praise since I wouldn't need to kill the same person, over and over.

But my parents named me, their only child, Olive, despite the family surname, and I emerged, Olive Branch. "We named you for the symbol of peace," they said. But as it worked out, they named me Target A, the butt of schoolyard jokes, fair prey. My taste for elaborate fantasies of murder began back then, on the schoolyard.

So in order to not put a fool's name on a book's title page, I was forced to look elsewhere, and I picked Jessica instead of something exotic and writerly, instead of a unique moniker no one shared. I had my reasons, but all the same, think of the alternate possibilities. I could have been Hypatia. Or Mississippi. Cleopatra, Sassafras, Her Royal Highness. Anything at all.

If I'd only chosen a name that would let me have my own identity, as if I were whole, singular, sufficient. I had the chance to become anyone and I very deliberately and for good reasons chose Jessica because there seemed to be no other choice. Jessica was who I'd wanted to be for the better part of the twelve years of public school. More precisely, Jessica Smith, the class beauty. Most popular. Who, with her pert features and safe solid last name, laughed at my name, at me. Who never once included me in anything she and her friends did. Who stole the one and only boy who'd ever paid real attention to me and did it without a backward glance, without caring particularly about him and without caring at all about me.

Jessica Smith. Who hadn't one hundredth of my brains but had all the love and adulation I craved.

If I'd lived in another culture, I would have made a voodoo doll of her and pincushioned it. But all I could do, when given the opportunity, was steal her label, unmake her. I took her name. I took what was in it, her aura. I changed my attitude, my approach, my style. I became a Jessica. That Jessica. I left the Smith to her. Branch was more interesting.

It was my bad luck that I wasn't prescient. I couldn't predict that years later, well into my career, a middle-aged upstart from Cabot Cove, nobody I'd ever have wanted to be, would suddenly seize both the torch and my Jessicahood. Seize my life, in fact.

When the onerous Jessica connections began, I tried to change my name again, to drop the Jessica altogether, but my publisher squelched the idea. He said my readers would become confused.

The truth is, they adore me and they would seek me out and find me. I don't confuse them. *She* does. Once, I saw someone in a bookstore pick up my newest Jessica Branch and say to her friend, "Darn. I think I've probably read this already, I'm such a fan." And she then described the plot of The Other Jessica's latest TV show. "It wasn't all that good," she said, and she walked off while I stood there, fuming.

She has deliberately and without remorse stolen my name and my audience. Jessica-Come-Lately should have changed *her* name.

But despite everything, here I was, bravely struggling on,

landing fifty-three minutes late, my skirt wrinkled, my hair sagging, my spirits crushed. And it was only day six of the fourteen-day, thirteen-city tour I was still condemned to complete. Even though I had been humiliated nationwide by Ms. Personality and then locally by my publisher, I wasn't permitted to nurse my wounds in private. The show, and I, had to go on.

I stood below the overhead storage, waiting for the mastodon in the seat next to mine to help me retrieve my luggage. He did not. Instead, he rubbed his elbow and looked at me resentfully, and I was obliged to climb up on my empty seat and do it all myself. The bag hit me hard on the side of my head as it emerged from the bin. I gave it a push so that it crash-landed on Mr. Unhelpful, and when he groaned, I looked away. Served him right.

I slowly retrieved the suitcase, plus my emergency tour bag, which was stashed under the seat, set them both in the aisle, then opened up the luggage carrier and strapped the luggage onto it. The people behind me were grossly inconsiderate, refusing to wait their turn, calling me names under their breath—suggesting that I was a senile old bat. I'm not deaf, though—I heard them. And they pushed at me as if I were a barrier they wanted lowered. There is no respect for age in this country. None. I thought about a mystery in which an entire line of airline passengers were wired, so that if they pushed at a woman simply taking care of her luggage, she could push a button, set off a charge and detonate every one of them.

By the time I left the plane, I had a bruise on the side of my face, a blouse pulled half out, a run in my stockings and a desperate need for a cigarette which, of course, I couldn't have until I was out on the street. I nearly slapped the flight attendant when she smiled and said "Buh-bye!"

So it really, truly wasn't a good time to be faced with the

broad and smiling face of a plump middle-aged woman, not at all well-preserved, waving the latest Jessica Branch. "Yes, yes," I said. "Hello." I waited for her to take my luggage. It took her quite a while to even notice it, she was so intent on me.

I disliked her—make that loathed her—immediately. I have tried, for the sake of my writing, to comprehend such instantaneous aversions, but they remain mysterious. Associations, people say, but I couldn't pinpoint this one. It wasn't the rushed and sloppy look of her makeup and hair. It wasn't her abysmal taste in clothes. Even a few decades ago when the gigantic hoop earrings, pedal pushers, golden ballet slippers and V-necked sweater might have been in style, they had been in poor style.

It wasn't any of those externals. They were surface, and I felt as if I were reacting to her essence as revealed by the way she held her lips, the specific flare of her nostrils, the hyped-up energy in her voice and the shape of the fingers taking hold of my luggage.

And all that was before she opened her mouth. "I recognize you from your jacket photo!" she burbled. "You look just *like* it! You know, some authors use ancient photos, or touched up ones, but you—you're as pretty as your picture! I'm so excited to meet you—I'm such a fan!"

She had toxic levels of perkiness and needed her system drained. The idea of being locked inside a car with this chatterbox for twenty-four hours made me tremble and yearn still more intensely for a cigarette. I was sure my angry publisher had arranged to have this particular pest drive me as additional punishment.

"I need a cigarette," I said.

Her eyes widened. "Not in here, although there's a special lounge if you must—"

"I'll wait till I'm in the car," I said.

Her eyes widened still more She looked near a stroke. "Oh, gee, I hate to be picky about anything, but I'm really allergic, and I definitely have to keep my car smoke-free and—"

I had submitted a list of my tour requirements headed specifically with "Smoking-friendly cars and drivers." And in second place, "No talkative perky escorts, please!" My very bad day was in further decline. I looked at my itinerary. "You're Estelle McCann?" I asked.

She waggled her head and giggled, as if that were just the biggest joke ever. "Estelle is sick," she said. "I'm filling in for her."

Now I was positive plans had been altered to further torment me. They'd given me a novice who would get lost, deliver me to appointments too late and dying for a smoke and wreak havoc with the schedule.

"Hope you don't mind about the smoking thing," she said. "I drive for Estelle a lot," she said, "but I wasn't going to this time because I was just bushed."

Okay, so she wasn't a novice. She was still repugnant.

"The truth is, when Estelle said who needed picking up, I *begged* for the chance. You know why?"

I shook my head, but I knew. I could taste what was coming, could feel it inside my veins, like metal shavings coursing through my bloodstream.

"Because I'm such a fan of your TV show!"

I, of course, have no TV show. Except the one I stormed off of this morning. I might have had a TV show if That Jessica hadn't gotten there first. But now, what was left for me to be? The *Other* Jessica's Show?

"You're prettier than the actress who plays you, to tell you the truth."

Idiot. I was entrusting myself to a woman who couldn't distinguish between the names Branch and Fletcher. Besides, I knew she was lying for politeness' sake. It's been my experience that people who repeatedly say "to tell you the truth" are inveterate liars.

En route to the parking lot I learned that I also hated the tempo of her speech and the rhythm of her walk. I felt a nervous tremor, almost a small seizure, a physical condition I hadn't felt since high school. Given the gut-flopping aversion her features inspired, their sickening familiarity, if she were seventy pounds lighter, prettier, if her hair weren't bleached an unnatural strawberry blonde, she might look just like . . . "I know that your name isn't Estelle, but I don't know what it is," I said. I had to know. Because it couldn't be . . . We were nowhere near the wretched town I'd lived in until the day after high school graduation. Nowhere near Jessica Smith.

"Oh, gee, I'm sorry," she said. "How rude of me! In such a rush to meet you, so excited, you know, I didn't even— golly, you must think I'm a real—"

"Your name?"

"Oh, sorry again! It's Cookie," she said. "Cookie Meyers."

I was able to exhale. A stranger. Nobody in my high school class had been named after baked goods.

The hotel room was cramped and room service sluggish, and my morning coffee arrived one minute before Cookie did. I was able to burn my mouth with a single sip before the concierge rang up to say my media escort was here.

Today she wore long jet earrings better suited for an evening gown, tight black jeans and a frilly white blouse. It might have been a striking ensemble on a stunning twig of a young woman, but Cookie was more of an ancient Giant Redwood, and the effect was alarming. Had she looked in a mirror in the last fifty years?

And then we were off, with Cookie's overenergized voice drilling through my eardrum directly into the center of my brain. No matter my lack of response, she was determined to be both my driver and guide. I reminded her that this was a book, not a sight-seeing tour, and she laughed and told me I was so hilarious it was no wonder I was such a success.

My books aren't funny at all. My self-declared big fan hadn't ever read them. A liar, as I suspected. Although maybe she meant The Other Jessica's books, if they existed.

She pointed out her favorite supermarket, the local high school—which had just won the regional basketball finals, mind you—the new highway overpass, the "best" department store in town. She was a compulsive pointer outer. "I want you to get your full dime's worth," she said. "Be here now and all that jazz. I feel so sorry for the people who whisk into town, do their interviews and whisk out. They miss so much!"

I didn't miss a single architectural, historical or social item. And that cloud still encircled her, that miasma that agitated me every time I saw or heard her. I was physically allergic to her, and I felt dizzy, weak and helpless, as if trapped in a nightmare.

"And this!" she said with a touch to my arm—"this is our brand new Civic Center. Isn't it something? It took six entire years to build, what with union quarrels and zoning laws and over there is just my favorite Indian restaurant, to tell the truth. When I first moved here, that'd be during my first marriage to Mr. Stebbins—Hank Stebbins, the no-good—but that's another story—there was absolutely nothing out there, but the development since then has been nothing short of . . ."

She stored a quantity of stultifying noninformation, as if she swept up and hoarded the droppings of other people's minds, the ideas and facts they discarded as being too trivial. This was a woman with nothing of value to offer. Nature had not been kind to her. She had probably once been attractive. But she'd let herself go and whatever she'd once had was lost to blubber, sag, gravity and bad taste. It is even possible that while she was young, her looks compensated for her brainlessness. But at this point, the absence of both mind and body was appalling.

I closed my eyes, put my head against the window and tried to ignore her. My actions had no effect. I would have moved to the backseat, but it was covered with fabric and wallpaper sample books. There was barely room enough to stash my tour bag. Since her divorce from Mr. Meyers—her second or third divorce, by my calculations, she juggled several jobs. "No real career, the way you have," she said. One of her several noncareers was as a decorator. Judging by the design sense ruling her wardrobe choices, I shuddered to think about entire rooms she might put together.

Silence apparently frightened her. She stuffed words into every airpocket between interviews. Words about the landscape, words about color-coordinating somebody's family room.

Even when I asked her to pull over so that I could have a cigarette, she herself also got out of the car, stood nearby and continued her monologue, sprinkling it with anti-smoking warnings.

Back in the car, I told her I was tired, and she nodded sympathetically and told me to rest up. She'd take care of everything. Which she did, via a monologue explaining where we were going and what the interviewer was like and what other jobs she'd had before this newspaper and where her son had gone to college and why smoking was bad for you.

Eventually, after I'd given up the attempt to rest and I was more tired than ever, but sitting up straight, she flashed a smile and posed the inevitable question. "So. Tell me. Where do you get your ideas?" she asked, perkily, wide eyes not on the road but on me.

I pointed to the highway and she faced forward. Good thing, too, so she couldn't see that my eyes were labelling her: IDEA. KILL ME! It would be a switch from That Jessica, at least.

"I use the annoyances of life," I said with deliberation. "For example, if somebody drives me out of my mind—"

"Oh, my!" she interrupted. "For a second there, you scared me!" she said with a nervous laugh. "I thought you were saying you got your murderous ideas 'if somebody drives me.' And here I was, the somebody driving you!"

And driving me out of my mind. She had become an idea. "Umm," I said, and returned to silent fantasies of how I'd do her in in my next novel. If for no other reason than simply to silence her.

Over lunch, while Cookie blessedly took herself off somewhere, the reporter from the *Globe* smiled and told me—proudly, I swear it—that her profile was going to be called "The Other Jessica."

I got her back, though. I didn't answer one question truthfully, starting with my birth, which I relocated to Sri Lanka and a mix between an exiled Russian princess and an Untouchable. I said I received my plots from voices I heard at seances. Let her look like a fool. I'd claim journalistic irresponsibility. I'd say she had been drinking straight through lunch.

And where do I get my ideas? Places and moments like this. I planned how, in my next book, there'd be a ferret-faced reporter whose own obituary, after her untimely death, would be an insulting headline.

She didn't add to my general goodwill toward men, nor did another car-session with Cookie. More boring scenery

explained, more stops for simpering interviews and sign-
ings.

She brought me a dry and withered sandwich to eat en
route to the final interview of the day, a stupid few minutes
on a second-rate station on which the interviewer openly
said he'd never heard of me at all—only of The Other Jessica, and he actually asked me questions about her.

The only pleasure in this stop was that it was my last in
this town. I would leave first thing tomorrow morning. Cold
comfort, indeed, given that I still had two rides left with
Cookie—the one back to my hotel and tomorrow's ride to
the airport. Cookie, that silly-named woman, had taken on
almost demonic shape in my mind. She was now linked to
the accumulated miseries of the past twenty-four hours and
in addition, she carried her own nightmare quality of half-
remembered misery. Something lethal. I tried to deflect her,
hoist her on her own petard. I grabbed three fabric-sample
books out of the backseat—they were damned heavy, too—
and pretended to be engrossed with examining squares of
cloth.

My ploy failed miserably.

"I have this friend who writes," she said. I knew she'd say
that sooner or later. We were headed toward the hotel, but
unfortunately, the interview had been on the opposite side of
the city, so I'd have a long time to hear about this friend of
hers. Ultimately, everybody either had written a book,
planned to do so "when they had the time" or had a friend
who already had. And everybody thought I cared.

"The reason I mention it is that she's written a mystery
and the detective is a parrot."

And why should I be surprised that Cookie's friend's
mystery was an even worse concept than the general run of
stupid ideas?

"Unusual, huh?" she said. "Of course there are human beings in it, too, but it's the parrot who figures things out. And of course, she—it's a female sleuth parrot—I hear female detectives are hot—and she can talk, so she can even explain what she finds out—and she can fly, too! Think what an asset that is for getting out of trouble!" She actually paused for a reaction.

I said nothing. I considered it a kindness.

"I thought you could give her some advice on how to market it and all. And don't you think it'd make a great movie?"

"It's . . . I don't know what to say."

"Overcome, huh? Great idea, isn't it? Very high concept. And know what? The parrot's name is *Jessica*!"

Another Jessica. Just what the mystery world needed. Although this, of course, would never sell, and the least I could do was be properly grateful. "Homage, eh?" I said. "To . . . me? Or to . . . ?" Of course, Cookie was the one who didn't quite comprehend that there were two of us. To whom I, in essence, even sitting beside her, was invisible.

Cookie was the one who'd written the parrot-trash. I was so sure of it I didn't even need to ask her.

"I don't get what you mean," she said.

"The name, Jessica. That's after . . ."

"Me," she said.

She forgot that "a friend" had written the book. She'd also forgotten her own name. "I thought you were . . . you said your name was—"

"Cookie. Sure. It's like automatic now. It's what people have called me for so long, since I left home, that I never even think about my real name, except in banks and things like that."

My head turned red inside. Really. Red and raging and full. All the obnoxiously familiar traits, the fleeting sense of features long-ago burned onto my retina returned and flashed. All that I'd denied because she called herself

Cookie now. But that sick feeling upon sighting her. My gut had know all along. Of course it was she.

"Jessica," I said softly.

"Just like you! I didn't want to say it, didn't want to appear to be . . . I don't know, kind of seeking favor with you or something. Besides, nobody calls me that anymore."

So I'd stolen nothing of value when I'd taken her name. Nothing more than something she shed like outgrown snakeskin before she moved on. It felt a replay of high school. A bright unthinking betrayal. Another one. The sort of thing the Most Popular Girl in class might do, toss something outgrown to a nobody, and the nobody named Olive would seize it out of desperation and a lack of other options.

So Olive had wound up with Jessica, a name that came to be no more than an echo or a shadow of somebody else, somebody more important, in the larger world.

And it didn't matter what the former Jessica-turned-Cookie had become, that everything bright and compelling about her had deserted her. It didn't make anything better. "Jessica," I repeated out loud. "Jessica . . . Meyers, right?"

She shook her head. "Meyers was my second husband. There was a third, but it lasted such a short time it seemed wrong to keep anything of his so I—"

How was I to establish the truth subtly. "All the way back, when people called you Jessica, your last name wasn't Branch, was it. Like mine?"

She removed a hand from the steering wheel to wave away the very suggestion. "Wouldn't that have been a kick though?" she said.

"It's not a common last name," I said.

"Guess not. Never have met anybody else with it," she answered.

Then maybe it wasn't her. She couldn't have forgotten me so completely. As if she'd never even noticed me?

"No," she said, nattering on as usual. "My name was as ordinary as you get. It was Smith."

Jessica Smith. It was. *It was.* Here in the night in the car. Jessica Smith who had created the misery I lived in, had obliterated me in school and had managed to do the same in perpetuity by making her name a used hand-me-down I had to wear for the rest of my life. Jessica Smith, who didn't even remember the girl she'd ignored and scorned. Jessica Smith had done this to me. All of it—the TV interviewer who called me a crone, the newspaper reporter and her derivative profile, the spirit-draining daily round. She'd done it. On purpose.

It was time for me to stop being such a nice person. It was time for revenge.

Where do I get my ideas, indeed. This was barely an idea at all. This was impulse, history, the delayed arrival of wishes dormant for decades.

I looked around. We were in the quiet tree-lined recesses of a residential area, but I'd seen a cabstand two or three blocks back. I'd plotted enough stories to think this through. I had my bad-hair-day turban in the big bag. Plus makeup and emergency changes. I'd paint on dark eyebrows, pop the glass out of my sunglasses, add an enormous scarf that covered a multitude of sins and jewelry, every piece of it, all at once, become an eccentric turbanned, bespectacled, crone. And I wouldn't have the cab take me to my hotel. I'd get a second cab midway. Say I stopped for a midnight snack, if anybody asks. And they wouldn't. Crones are invisible. and when they become garish, people want them out of their eyesight, simply want to get away from them.

I pulled my bag up front with me and extracted the scarf. I slid two of the books off my lap and held onto the third, a collection of greens. Including olives. That felt appropriate. "I need a cigarette," I said.

"Now? Really?"

"Now."

She sighed and pulled over. Spare me the tobacco lecture, I silently pleaded, and I'll make this as painless as possible. Even though you don't deserve leniency.

"You shouldn't smoke, you know," she said as she opened her car door and swivelled around so that her feet were on the ground even though she still sat in the driver's seat.

She didn't spare me, so I didn't spare her.

"The Surgeon General says that smoking is bad for—"

Being bopped on the head with a scarf-wrapped olive fabric-sample book is even worse for your health than a smoke. Several bops can be fatal. And were. Barely a grunt and it was all over.

You might not expect a decorator's sample book to be that heavy, so chock-full of fabric that they have to bind it with rock-hard boards and long grommets, but it appeared demonstrably lethal.

I had to be certain. I reached into my always-helpful emergency travel bag and pulled out my compact for the old familiar mirror to the mouth business. First time I'd tried it outside of my fiction, and it worked. The mirror was clear. I used it to apply crimson lipstick and to check the effect of the turban, glasses and jewelry I put on.

I left Jessica-Cookie that way, half-in, half-out of the car. Let the jogging surburbanite who'd find her speculate about who and how and why on earth.

Not surprisingly, things went pretty well as planned. After all, thinking through a killer's pitfalls and snares is my business.

I caught two separate cabs, one from an all-night restaurant not far from where I'd left Jessica Smith, and where I had a quick snack. Neither cabby ever connected me or my route with the dead woman in Kings Commons. I was questioned, of course, by the police about my media escort and my whereabouts the evening before, but when I explained about being dropped off at the restaurant, opting to take a cab home from there, they thanked me and that was that.

The next morning, I called the publicist. "My driver has not shown up," I said. "I'll miss my plane if I wait any longer, so I'm taking a cab to the airport. Get me someone competent next time!" And I slammed down the phone.

Incidentally, I included the receipt for those two taxi rides—from the restaurant to the hotel as well as the one to the airport—along with my other out-of-pocket expenses for tour necessities and was promptly reimbursed by the publisher.

Cookie's demise remains a mystery to this day. Except to me, the real Jessica. Crime writer and unraveller of mysteries.

Fact is, as I said, I think this is precisely the method whereby the other Jessica has come to seem like such a whiz. She stumbled on the formula first. First you commit the crime, then you solve it. You finally have complete control over your material. And there's so many deserving victims out there, waiting, you never have to worry about where you'll get ideas.

Pure genius. I have to hand it to her.

Maybe I've been too hostile to her too long, thereby overlooking a good thing. My new philosophy is: if you can't conquer the other Jessica, join her.

My publisher says my attitude's improved.

I see better days ahead.

Oh, to have half the pluck of the protagonist in this next story, a tale of politics, perjury and plotting, all set against Ireland's fight for independence in the late nineteenth century. But of course I don't go around toppling governments and such; the politicians do a good enough job of that themselves.

The Uncrowned King of Ireland; or, A Most Toad-Spotted Traitor

P. M. Carlson

Lordie, no! I never meant to bring down the British government! And you know that I love Ireland. But you must understand that sometimes a young lady, temporarily penurious, is in need of a new bustled dress in the latest fashion in order to win a role in a play, so that she may acquire the funds necessary to repair the leaking roof of her dear little niece's house. Now suppose that the said young lady suddenly encounters Father Christmas in New York City—to be precise, in the dining-room of the highly respectable Metropolitan Hotel. Hang it, you wouldn't expect her to turn away from the proffered good fortune! On the contrary, I found myself whispering the Bard's words to myself: "Down on thy knees, thank the holy gods!"

The gentleman bore a striking resemblance to St. Nicholas, his bald head fringed with curly silver hair, his round face adorned with bushy whiskers of the same hue. He was neatly attired in a black jacket and brown striped trousers, and a monocle sparkled in one eye. Other observations, however, were less satisfactory. His nose was rather too fleshy and red, his expression rather too mournful, and his Irish brogue rather too slurred as he called for more port wine.

Nevertheless, a quick survey of the dining room offered me no better prospect. I glanced at the pier mirror nearby to make certain that my auburn hair peeked prettily from beneath my little plumed hat and adjusted the lilac-flowered cream flounces of my skirt in order to hide the worn velvet trim and an unfortunate wine stain. Then I approached the bewhiskered gentleman with all the elegance I could muster and said, "Sir, I beg your pardon, but I fear that I left my fan behind when I sat at this table earlier today. Have you seen it, perchance?"

I know, I know, my Aunt Mollie would agree with you. She always told me that proper ladies do not mislead gentlemen—and of course the fan was nonexistent. But I have found that gentlemen are usually quite pleased to assist ladies, whether the problem truly exists or not, and that pleasing a gentleman is more profitable on the whole than ignoring him. Even Aunt Mollie approved of profits, for she was an excellent businesswoman.

"I have not seen your fan, dearest madam," my soon-to-be benefactor replied, bouncing eagerly to his feet, though the gallant effect of his action was marred by his having to grasp the back of his chair in order to avoid toppling over. "But may I help you search?"

We spent a moment or two searching under the table for the fan—trimmed with crimped lace, I told him, like the edging of my neckline. Although he did not find the fan, he had certainly memorized my neckline by the time we gave up the search.

"Dear madam," he said with an adoring glance, "might I console you on the loss of your fan by offering you a glass of port wine?"

"That would indeed be most welcome," I declared, sinking into a chair before he could reconsider. "You sound so like my dear papa, sir! He lives here in America now, but he was born in Dublin."

His small, wide-set eyes brightened. "I reside in Dublin. So you are Irish, madam!"

"Irish-American, yes sir. My name is Bridget Mooney. May I inquire to whom I have the pleasure of speaking?"

"I am, uh, Roland Ponsonby, at your service, Miss Mooney." He leaned forward as far as his round belly permitted, adjusted his eyeglass to peer nervously about the dining-room, and murmured, "Are you, or your good father, members of Clan-na-Gael?"

I hesitated. Clan-na-Gael was the Irish-American society that supported the violent Fenians in Ireland, those men of extreme views who fought most outrageously against the British yoke. Only four years earlier they had assassinated the young British Chief Secretary for Ireland, Lord Frederick Cavendish, and his aide as they walked in Dublin's Phoenix Park. The murders had been committed with twelve-inch-long surgical knives smuggled in by an Irish-American.

I knew it would be unwise for me to admit to belonging to Clan-na-Gael if Mr. Ponsonby were a spy in the service of the British government. It would be equally unwise to claim to oppose it if he were himself a violent Fenian. I said, "No, sir, but some of my friends are sympathetic."

He pinched his lip nervously. "Tell me, lovely Miss

Mooney, would any of your sympathetic friends have a position for an experienced journalist?"

My heart sank. "Are you an immigrant, then, Mr. Ponsonby?" Hang it, a British spy or even a Fenian assassin would be preferable to a penniless newcomer.

His Father Christmas face grew mournful. "If only I could find a position! I came to this land of splendid opportunity, but have found no way out of my pecuniary difficulties, except for unsuitable manual labor on the docks."

I was puzzled by my new acquaintance. Despite his complaints of poverty, I could not give up hope that he might yet provide the funds for a new roof for my little niece. Yet he had given me a false name. Yes, of course I had noticed his hesitation. Roland Ponsonby—I was willing to wager that was not his true name.

"Mr. Ponsonby," I began, for Aunt Mollie always said that it is prudent to appear to take people at their word if one does not yet fully understand a situation, "I can see from your bearing and excellent turn of phrase that you have achieved success in your profession. Pray tell me, what misfortunate leads you to seek a position in America?"

"It was that preening blackguard Parnell!"

"Charley Parnell?" I blurted, astonished. Any Irishman would be astonished to hear the hero of the nation so maligned.

"You know him?" Fear flickered in his wine-dimmed eyes.

Know him? Lordie yes! Sweet memories crowded into my head of the Fifth Avenue Hotel on a chilly night just after the New Year in 1880, when some Irish friends introduced me to the tall, slender, regal man known as the Uncrowned King of Ireland. Parnell's hair and beard were dark, though his complexion was so pale that one was anxious for his health. In public his manner was reserved and intelligent, even aloof, except for the dark eyes that blazed with inner fire. In private—well, we'd got on quite well, yes indeed. At the time I thought him the most intriguing man I had ever met, and the most heroic except for President Grant.

Unfortunately, Charley had left New York almost immediately for a tour of the United States to raise funds for the Irish cause, and then he'd returned to England to serve as an Irish member of Parliament. Although he had sent me appreciative notes, even those had ceased in July of 1880.

So I regarded the self-styled Roland Ponsonby with added interest. He clearly knew the Irish hero, because although most people pronounced his name PaRNELL, Charley himself preferred PARnell, and Ponsonby had pronounced it correctly. But how could anyone regard dear Charley as a blackguard? I exclaimed, "I cannot claim a close acquaintance with Mr. Parnell. But surely such a famous man would never offend a gentleman like yourself!"

"Offend? Ah, Miss Mooney, 'tis far worse than that! I was at one time the editor of the finest newspapers in Ireland, the *Irishman*, the *Flag of Ireland*, and the *Shamrock*. At the end of 1880 I found myself in very needy circumstances, and thus when Mr. Parnell offered to buy the newspapers from me I naturally entered into negotiations with him."

"He bought your papers?"

"Yes, and at a scandalously low price, because I naturally assumed that I would continue in the post of editor. After all, I have fought long and hard against the British yoke!"

"I have no doubt of that, Mr. Ponsonby. But surely it was one of Mr. Parnell's underlings who erred!"

"No, it was himself! I have proof!" my Father Christmas declared indignantly, fumbling in his portmanteau. I could see a revolver within, and stealthily drew mine from my bustle pocket. But in a moment he straightened, holding only a pair of letters. "You see, Miss Mooney, in his own hand!"

The first letter, dated June 13, 1881, was addressed to "Richard Pigott." The name Richard Pigott suited my new acquaintance far better than Roland Ponsonby, don't you agree?

I slid my revolver back into its pocket and read the letter, which indeed said in part, "We cannot undertake to provide you with permanent employment on the paper; but, on the other hand, we shall want you to undertake for at least two years not to publish any other paper in England or Ireland."

I looked up at Pigott/Ponsonby. "Lordie, two years is a long time!"

"Yes it is." Morosely, he swallowed some more port.

The second letter, dated three days later, refused a further plea for employment. Both letters were certainly from Charley. His letters to me had been signed, "With numerous kisses to my American princess, C.S.P." Pigott's two were signed more formally, "Chas. S. Parnell," but there was no mistaking the distinctive flourish of the initials. I asked, "But sir, why did you not refuse to sell the papers, if the conditions were so cruel?"

"There was illness in my family." His small eyes were sorrowful. "I had no choice. Parnell destroyed my livelihood and left my children destitute!"

"Why, then he is a blackguard indeed!" I murmured.

I know, I know, the uncrowned king should not be called a blackguard. It's also true that the illness Pigott mentioned doubtless had more to do with his bottle than with his family, and Charley surely had had good reasons for his refusal to employ the man. I soothed poor Pigott as best I could and asked, "Did you use the money from the sale to come to America?"

"No, no, that's long gone."

"Why then, you have cleverly discovered another way to earn your passage here!"

He fumbled in his pocket and showed me a ticket to Ireland on tomorrow's Cunard. "They pay my passage, yes, and my expenses. But unless I find evidence, they will never pay me again."

"What evidence, sir?"

"Oh, it is quite confidential," he said doubtfully.

I signalled the waiter to bring him more port. He accepted the bottle and poured himself another glass. "Perhaps one of my friends can help," I said. "It may require money—"

He looked at me hopefully. "Yes, Mr. Houston—uh, they expect it to cost money."

"Well, sir, if you tell me what is required, I will direct you to it." I gave him the earnest winning look I use when I play Lady Macbeth welcoming King Duncan to her castle. "But you must tell me what we are searching for."

Eager now, he said, "Many gentlemen who oppose Irish home rule believe that Parnell inspired the Phoenix Park murders."

I was shocked. "Why, Mr. Parnell had finally convinced Gladstone himself to back the Irish Home Rule bill! Those murders set back progress on the bill for years!"

He was glum again. "Yes, it is hopeless. I know he was not involved, and he was distressed by the murders. And yet Captain O'Shea and—uh, my employers believe that I can find incriminating letters, perhaps on this side of the Atlantic."

He'd pronounced it O'Shee. I said, "And you led the gentlemen to believe you could?"

"Oh, Miss Mooney, I am in great distress for want of money to support myself and my large family. My son is ill. I knew that finding such letters was not likely, but claiming to search for them gave me the opportunity to look for a position in America. But I have failed in that as well. Oh, do not think ill of me!"

"Think ill of you? On the contrary, Mr. Ponsonby! As for incriminating letters—yes, I can find incriminating letters."

He could hardly believe his ears. "Letters that link Parnell with the murders in Phoenix Park?"

"Precisely," I said. "The existence of such letters is well known in certain circles on this side of the Atlantic."

Well, yes, I must admit that the circles in question were quite limited; limited, in fact, to myself. But sometimes a young lady must stretch the truth a bit if she is ever to get her little niece's roof repaired.

Pigott appeared to be impressed. He said nervously, "Certain circles? Clan-na-Gael? Your friends must be extremely violent men, Miss Mooney!" His little eyes shifted about the dining room, as though my ferocious friends might be hiding in the carved mahogany buffet or among the tasseled draperies.

I reassured him, "My friends will be quite reasonable if you can offer them, let us say, three hundred dollars for their incriminating letters. Can you obtain that?"

"Yes, of course," he said, so readily that I wished I had asked for five hundred. Then he aimed his eyeglass at the crimped lace at my neckline and added nervously, "But I don't wish you to endanger yourself, Miss Mooney! I have become extremely fond of you in our short acquaintance. Perhaps I can accompany you, to keep you safe from these violent men."

"Why, thank you, sir, but I assure you, it is quite unnecessary. I need only a note from you to my friends."

"Why should I say?"

"Say that they must furnish the letters to you without delay. Say hesitancy is inexcusable."

He nodded and dashed off the note. Spelling was not his strong point, but it would do. I stood, arranged my lilac-flowered flounces, and bowed to him. "Please occupy yourself with obtaining the money. My friend will be at this address after two hours. Don't arrive too early, Mr. Ponsonby."

I hurried from the hotel, caught the Broadway omnibus, and in a short time was in my lodging house in Water Street, pounding at my neighbor Tim McCarthy's door.

"Bridget, duckie, whatever is the matter?" Tim asked as he opened the door. He was a short, wiry fellow with freckles spattered from chin to bald pate. He was a long-time actor and an excellent dancer, but like myself, unemployed at the moment.

"Loan me money for paper and ink, Tim, and get ready to play a Clan-na-Gael man."

"Clan-na-Gael? No, no, Bridget! Those hotheads have no sense of humor, and might not take kindly to impersonation!"

"True, but there's no need for them to know, and you shall have fifty dollars before the day is done."

"Fifty dollars? Let's begin!" Tim gave a little celebratory hop.

In a few moments we were hard at work, I at my table and he before my mirror, rehearsing ferocious grimaces.

Imagine my surprise half an hour later when there was a great crashing about in the hall outside. I peered through the keyhole. "Lordie, Tim, it's Pigott, come too early! Hide everything! Are you ready? He mustn't see me." I dove under the bed.

Tim put on a Simon Legree sneer and opened the door, growling, "I'm Tim McCarthy. Are you here about the letters?"

Then he jetéed aside with great alacrity. I understood the

reason when Mr. Pigott burst into the room, drunkenly waving his revolver in the air.

Pigott plunged toward the bronze plush window curtains and ripped one down as he looked behind them. "Where is Miss Mooney? Have you done away with her, you blackguard?"

To see Father Christmas wearing such a scowl was terrifying, and to see his drunken finger trembling on the trigger was worse. Tim attempted to soothe him while jigging about the room like a rabbit pursued by a hound. "All is well, Mr. Pigott!"

Pigott whirled from the window, his revolver surprisingly steady on Tim. "Pigott? Pigott? Who told you that name?"

Tim paled under his freckles and ducked behind an easy chair. Fortunately, when Pigott moved to keep him in range, one striped trouser leg landed next to the bed. With a quick tug on his ankle I pulled the corpulent fellow off balance and snatched the revolver from his hand as he fell. While Pigott struggled to right himself and find his monocle, I removed the bullets, then pushed the gun back out from under the bed with a sign to Tim that all was well. Tim nodded, crossed his arms, and resumed his Clan-na-Gael scowl, though he stayed behind the chair.

Pigott regained his feet, picked up his revolver, and pointed it again at Tim. "Answer me, scoundrel! Who told you that name?"

Tim sneered. Pigott squeezed the trigger, to no avail. Tim said, "We have our ways. Now, do you want the letters or not?"

Pigott stared at the useless revolver and pinched his lip nervously as Tim's words slowly penetrated his port-fogged mind. "Letters?"

"On the table," Tim said.

Pigott glanced at the table. Then he leaned forward, adjusted his eyeglass, and read it out loud: " 'January 9, 1882.' "

"Shortly before the Phoenix Park murders," Tim interjected.

Pigott read, " 'What are these fellows waiting for? This inaction is inexcuseable; our best men are in prison and nothing is being done. Let there be an end to this hesitency.' And signed 'Chas. S. Parnell.' " Pigott picked up the letter, squinted at it, sniffed it, and looked at Tim with joy on his face. "I can hardly believe it! The gentlemen who hired me are right! Why, this letter could hardly be better if someone had—"

And suddenly his scowl was back. Tim had not had time to hide everything. Now Pigott reached for the nearby sheet of delicate tissue paper and inspected the "Chas. S. Parnell" traced on it. Then he looked at the "Chas. S. Parnell" signature on the letter. "Is it—it is genuine, isn't it? It looks genuine."

Well, of course it did! How could he even question it? My Aunt Mollie had taught me well. As I have noted already, she was an excellent businesswoman, and while doing copy work for a bank had learned that a few additional copies of financial papers were often convenient to have. She had imparted the skill to me. Working from the letters Charley had sent me as well as the two I'd hooked from Pigott, it had been simple to create letters that indicated Charley's instigation and approval of the Phoenix Park assassinations.

Tim said, "I am sure your employers will pay handsomely for the letter. Do you have the three hundred dollars?"

Pigott was not as foolish as I thought. He looked carefully at the tissue paper and said, "I cannot pay that much for a forgery."

Tim shrugged. "Then we will sell them directly to Captain O'Shea and Mr. Houston."

"Wait, wait!" Pigott pinched his lip, inspecting the letter.

"Look at the others," Tim suggested.

Pigott looked. They were, of course, as excellent as the first.

"Five hundred for the lot," said Tim. I nudged him from under the bed. "Oh, yes, one other thing. If the letters are questioned, you must claim first that they are genuine, obtained through the secret societies. We like to publicize our strength. If that fails, you must confess that you forged them. If you connect our name to a forgery, our assassins will find you."

It was Pigott's turn to become pale. But what could he do in the face of the violent Clan-na-Gael? He soon agreed to our terms and departed with the letters. As soon as the door closed Tim and I danced a jig and divided the money. I immediately sent the roof-repair money to my friend Hattie Floyd, who cared for my little niece, and hurried to the dressmaker's for the new frock I required for my *Twelfth-Night* audition.

The next day, I saw Mr. Pigott off on the great Cunard steamship, innocently inquiring if he'd got on well with my friend and expressing pleasure that he had. Our leavetaking required more time than I had anticipated, for a combination of gratitude for helping him obtain the letters and admiration for my fetching neckline had made him quite amorous. Finally, after promising to write, I stood on the Cunard pier, fluttering my handkerchief in what I thought was good-bye to Mr. Pigott forever.

Oh, you are concerned about Charley? No, no, he was a clever fellow, and who would believe Pigott's word over his? I was sure Charley would suffer only mild inconvenience. And don't you agree that he deserved mild inconvenience for dropping off correspondence with an excellent young lady? Yes indeed.

So I believed we had reached the happy ending: clumsy Mr. Pigott had departed to collect his money from the mysterious Mr. Houston and Captain O'Shea, the young lady was rejoicing in a beautiful new striped silk visiting dress, and the little niece was rejoicing in a new roof. At the final curtain the audience would go home contented.

But, hang it, life is not so orderly. On my way back to Water Street from the Cunard pier, I noticed a throng of excited people. I joined them and saw with horror that a poor bleeding corpse lay in the shadows of an alleyway near my lodging.

It was Tim McCarthy.

I turned away aghast, but not before I had noted that Tim had been shot at close range in the middle of his freckled forehead.

Clan-na-Gael struck swiftly indeed at those who borrowed their dread name without their consent. I had warned Tim to keep our adventure to himself, but he loved to tell a good story and was as unreliable in his cups as Pigott himself. As I packed my trunks to move to a safer address, I remembered my friend's cheerful capering and vowed to find the scoundrel who had so cruelly cut him down.

There were few clues, however, and even the newspapers took no notice of Tim McCarthy's death, as he was a mere unemployed actor. Because I feared asking too many questions of Clan-na-Gael, my own investigation languished too. A year later, I was none the wiser. Then, while touring in the West, I read the news that no less a paper than *The Times* of London had printed a facsimile of a letter that purported to show that Charles Stewart Parnell had approved of the Phoenix Park murders. It was one of my letters!

The Times, of course, was a more formidable opponent than Pigott. Reminded of dear Tim's misfortune and hoping that Charley would not suffer too much, I followed the papers anxiously for the next few weeks. Clever Charley merely laughed at the letter, and he did not even take action against *The Times* for libel. I hoped nothing would come of the matter.

Mr. Pigott had proven much better than Charley at maintaining a correspondence and in August unexpectedly began to propose marriage to me. Now that his wife had finally died, he explained, he would observe a decent mourning, but then he was prepared to offer me his heart, his ready-made family, and his worldly possessions. Naturally I declined, as kindly as I could, because poor Mr. Pigott did not seem to realize that his heart and his family were decided drawbacks to any thought of union, and his worldly possessions, which included more than a few debts, were hardly more attractive. But, with fond memories of his five hundred dollars and of my niece's sound roof, I declined very politely each time he asked, explaining that I was occupied with my stage appearances and could not yet come to England.

Then Charley's situation took a turn for the worse. Despite his contempt for the letters, *The Times* was unrelenting in its accusations. More of the forged letters were published, and the affair became serious when Charley's enemies in Parliament appointed a Special Commission to investigate his connections with the Phoenix Park murders and with other crimes. The handsome hero had already been jailed once, and I was sorry to be the cause of further persecution. So when our fine production of *Camille* closed because of unfair competition from Buffalo Bill's Wild West show, and I returned to my room to find yet another letter from Pigott, I was ready to consider it. Pigott renewed the offer of his hand, stated that his motherless children would adore me, and added that he would be delighted for me to continue my interest in the stage. In fact, he said, he knew the manager of the Alhambra and could easily arrange an engagement for me there. And he had saved up fifty pounds to help me with expenses if I came.

He also enclosed a steamship ticket to London.

I sat for a long time, tapping the ticket against my teeth.

I had never been to London, but it seemed to me a delightful prospect to play Shakespeare in the land of my illustrious tutor Mrs. Fanny Kemble and of my dear friend Mrs. Langtry.

And surely in London plays did not have to close because of competition from Wild West shows.

My friend Hattie in St. Louis was envious, but I told her I was sure I would prosper and could soon send for her and my little niece. I packed my best frocks and costumes and boarded the great ship, visions of applause from posh British audiences and guineas from posh British managers dancing in my head.

We disembarked at the splendid new Tilbury Docks, and I took a hansom cab to the address in Wardour Street that Pigott had sent. When the driver announced that we had arrived, I began to have misgivings, for the address was that of a public house. But as it appeared to be of the better class, I paid the driver and entered.

A quantity of cigar smoke enhanced the genteel twilight character of the establishment. A servant appeared, a lively-eyed woman with broadening hips and neatly coiffed hair, who, in answer to my enquiry, said, "Mr. Pigott is dining with Captain O'Shea, mum." She gestured toward a table in the far corner where I could dimly make out a handsome swell. His companion had his back to me, but even in the haze of smoke I recognized Mr. Pigott's silvery hair and rotund figure. I followed the servant to the table.

"Why, Caroline, whom have you brought us?" asked the handsome dandy in an elegant British accent. Caroline bobbed a curtsy to him with a simper that told me the two knew each other well.

Pigott exclaimed, "Miss Mooney!" He bounded up to welcome me, and I had to deflect his embrace with my parasol. Full of enthusiasm, he introduced me to handsome Captain O'Shea, a member of Parliament for Ireland. The captain was of middle age, with fine clothing, a fine mustache, and a discontented air. Then Pigott hurried after Caroline to bring me something to drink.

Captain O'Shea said, "My dear Miss Mooney, how pleasant that you are visiting our sceptered isle."

"I am honored to be visiting the land of Shakespeare," I replied. "But is it true that you are a member of Parliament for Ireland?"

"Indeed it is true. I may add that I have the ear of Gladstone himself."

"And naturally you have the ear of Mr. Parnell?"

His handsome visage darkened. "Ah, Parnell, that swine!"

"Why, sir, I thought that Mr. Parnell was your leader!"

"A leader about to go down in ignominy, because of the letters your friends found for us." Captain O'Shea looked gleeful at the prospect. "The newspapers are full of revelations about the Phoenix Park crimes, and a Special Commission of Parliament will begin examining witnesses next month."

I was alarmed. "Sir, I will not be required to give evidence, will I?"

"No, no, don't fret," said the captain benevolently. "Mr. Pigott will give any necessary evidence, correct, Pigott?"

"But sir, Mr. Houston promised me I would never be questioned," said Pigott, putting down our drinks.

"Well, Mr. Houston is too young to realize how much evidence is needed to bring down a scoundrel like Parnell!" said O'Shea.

Pigott nodded morosely. "He is young indeed. Captain O'Shea, don't you agree that, if I must give evidence before a Special Commission, I am justified in requesting additional remuneration?"

O'Shea laughed. "Come, Pigott, old fellow! You are a man of the world. You know that if one does something politically useful, one may have to give evidence."

I was becoming apprehensive about Pigott's request for money. "Mr. Pigott," I said, "it would be very agreeable if you would give me the money for expenses that you promised me, as I will soon need it."

Pigott pinched his lip. "Well, ah, that is—dear creature, I am short of funds just now. But Captain O'Shea has agreed to provide us with a meal, and I have made arrangements for you to stay the night in the Anderton Hotel in Fleet Street."

"And the funds you promised me?"

"I will not rest easy until they are in your pretty hands!"

Well, this was not heartening news, but I consoled myself with thoughts of my upcoming London debut on the stage of the Alhambra Theatre and turned to other topics. "Captain O'Shea, Mr. Pigott has told me that your aunt is a kind lady of considerable means. I trust that she is in good health?"

"Yes!" snapped O'Shea. "Who's been telling your otherwise?" He glared at Pigott.

"Why, no one, sir! I am only just arrived from America!"

He relaxed but retained his discontented air. "The old lady is living quite a long time, you see," he said. "She has always favored my wife, Katie, who has lived near her in Eltham and cared for her for many years. But my wife's relatives are jealous, and attempt to drive wedges between Aunt Ben and Katie."

"That is sad news indeed," I said. "Bitterness within families is always unfortunate."

He shot me a suspicious glance before he continued. "When Aunt Ben understood their evil plans, she changed her will to favor Katie. So the relatives began to petition the Masters in Lunacy to commit her to an asylum."

"Oh dear!" My hand flew to my mouth in dismay. Could it be that Captain O'Shea's wealth was in jeopardy, and therefore Pigott's, and therefore mine? I said, "If she is judged a lunatic, I suppose the family may overturn the will and Katie will lose the money?"

"Quite." Captain O'Shea leaned back with a satisfied air. "But you see, dear Miss Mooney, as a member of Parliament I have come to know Gladstone well, and Gladstone's personal physician has certified that, while elderly, Aunt Ben is of sound mind."

"Why, that is excellent news!" I exclaimed.

Captain O'Shea waved at the servant. "Caroline, you minx, bring us some beef stew!"

"Yes sir!" She took down some bowls.

He said, "Excellent woman. Caroline was once our cook in West Brighton," said Captain O'Shea. "Now, Miss Mooney, I look forward to seeing you at the Alhambra. What is your specialty?"

"My specialty?"

"On the stage."

"Why, as I said before, I admire Shakespeare. I play Viola, Lady Macbeth, Rosalind—"

I broke off because Captain O'Shea was shaking his head with amusement. "No, no, my dear! We are talking about the Alhambra! It's a music hall!"

"A music hall!" I gasped in horror.

"Can you sing, or dance? I suppose you might recite Lady

Macbeth if you make it comical. What do you think, Pigott?"

I was glaring at my would-be Saint Nicholas. He said nervously, "The Alhambra does excellent shows, Miss Mooney!"

Just then Caroline arrived with our steaming bowls of beef stew. "For the handsomest of MP's," she said fetchingly.

O'Shea kissed her rough hand. "Thank you, my mouse."

Caroline turned away, tucking a pound note into her bodice, and her well-feigned look of affection gave way to one of weariness. I liked her better, yes indeed.

Captain O'Shea had turned back to my problem. "Miss Mooney, surely you understand England has a sufficient number of Shakespearean actresses. You couldn't have thought that Mr. Pigott here has enough influence to promise you a role in Shakespeare, in London!"

"Whyever not?" I said, casting a disdainful glance at the squirming Pigott. "He had enough influence to find letters that incriminate Mr. Parnell, didn't he? At great cost to those who provided the letters!"

"Oh, dear Miss Mooney, it is terrible indeed, the end that came to our mutual friend Tim McCarthy!" Pigott said with a stricken look. "Clan-na-Gael are extreme men, and it is difficult to do business with them."

Not half as difficult as it was to do business with Mr. Pigott, don't you agree? Performing in a music hall, indeed! And no expense money in sight! I realized how foolish I had been to trust a man who would betray the hero of the Irish nation. Wise old Shakespeare had a phrase for Pigott: a most toad-spotted traitor! I wanted to toss the bowl of boiling stew right into that Father Christmas face.

But in my head, Aunt Mollie the businesswoman was yammering away, telling me that I shouldn't burn my bridges, that I must at least scoop up the crumbs that were offered. So I ate the stew instead of hurling it, slipped a chunk of bread into my bustle pocket for supper, and accepted the room in the Anderton Hotel.

I allowed Pigott to bring my trunks there, then, pleading exhaustion, dismissed him. When he had gone I slipped out and found my way to the Alhambra Music Hall.

It was a splendid theatre, yes indeed. Situated on Leicester Square, it was built in the Saracenic fashion, with a great dome and Moorish arches ringing the vast auditorium. It was built of the best fireproof materials, because of the conflagration it had suffered in 1882. The crowd was large and enthusiastic, due in part to the bars fitted into many snug corners of the building. If Pigott's taste ran to music halls rather than Shakespeare, he had indeed offered me an excellent opportunity.

But as I watched the performance my heart sank. The artistes were highly skilled. What could I do that was not already being performed on this stage? The poetic turns were excellent, so my Shakespeare would not be needed. There were skilled step-dancers, singers of jolly political songs and of risqué songs, tumblers, equestrians. I had hopes of doing an Irish song, but there were two Irish turns already. I do a most amusing impersonation of Lillie Langtry trying to play Rosalind; but as I feared I might have to apply to dear Lillie for funds, it seemed advisable to avoid any actions that might upset her.

I returned to the Anderton Hotel, having much to consider that night.

One thing I considered was that Mr. Pigott had been quite lavish in his sympathy for dear Tim's death. Now, I had never mentioned Tim's death in my letters to Pigott, thinking it too depressing a subject for a man already fearful of Clan-na-Gael. I did not wish him to hesitate if I needed to sell him another letter. And of course the newspapers that recorded every cough of the wealthy and powerful had ignored my friend's demise. How, then, could Pigott have known of it?

I remembered Pigott's revolver and realized I had been searching for dear Tim's murderer on the wrong side of the ocean.

The next morning I rose full of resolve, donned my fine new visiting dress striped in rose, green, and brown and trimmed with Irish guipure lace, and walked forth into the warm August day. It took some time to find Charley, but I learned at last that he was lunching at the Cannon Street Hotel. I lurked outside and when he emerged and climbed into a carriage, I leaped into the next hansom and asked the driver to follow him. We whirled through crowded Holborn and Oxford Streets to Portland Place and Marylebone Road. He alighted at last in a quiet street of old-fashioned Georgian houses known as York Terrace. I paid my driver and followed.

There was no butler. The parlormaid seemed surprised to see a caller, but after a brief hesitation took my card and disappeared, closing a thick door behind her and leaving me to sit in the hall looking at the egg-and-dart moldings of the ceiling. The parlormaid's voice sounded lower through the door, and I could not make out her words. I thought I heard a door slam. At last the parlormaid returned to show me into the room.

As always, Charley was delightful to look upon. He was tall, lean, and pale as ever, but his smile was contented as he greeted me. Then suddenly his brown eyes flashed and he stared at me with burning intensity. "Why—why, it's Bridget!"

"Yes, Charley," I said demurely, and was surprised to see him step back in confusion. I explained, "In view of our long friendship, I come with news about the letters published in *The Times*."

"Yes, yes, so you said in the note." He tapped it with his long, well-shaped fingers. "But however did you find me?"

"I followed you from the Cannon Street Hotel."

"Ah." He nodded. "You Americans are quite resourceful. Do others know I am here?"

Well, when a famed and handsome man is taking pains to discover if he is alone with a lady, she cannot help but be pleased at her prospects. I said, "I came alone, and told no one, because what I have to impart to you is a very private matter."

"Excellent!" He was clearly pleased. "And are you in good health, Bridget?"

"Why, yes, thank you, although I find myself in pecuniary difficulties at the moment."

"I see. Well, here's ten pounds. I hope you enjoy your stay in London." And he reached for the bellpull to call the maid.

I took the proffered note but held up my hand in protest. "Charley, wait! I must tell you about the letters!"

"Oh, yes. What about them?" he asked kindly.

"Well, they are forgeries."

"Of course! I know I didn't write them. But there is no sense fighting it. It will only fan the controversy."

"But isn't your career in danger?"

"Yes, but how can we prove they are forgeries before a Special Commission of Parliament? They have accumulated so much false information that our Irish Home Rule bill is threatened, as is Mr. Gladstone's government, because he has backed our bill."

"Why, I am pleased that my information may help save you, and the Home Rule bill, and Mr. Gladstone's government. But you must promise never to mention my name."

"Secrecy will be observed," he said, so easily I suspected that he thought my information would be worthless.

"First, you should subpoena Mr. Richard Pigott, for he forged the letters," I said.

"Pigott? That poor old drunkard? Come, Bridget, it must be someone of higher rank!"

"No sir, it is Pigott. It might be that he is in someone's employ, but I can say nothing of that."

I know, I know, perhaps I should have mentioned Mr. Houston or Captain O'Shea, but I find it more profitable on the whole to avoid offending gentlemen whose wives have rich aunts. Besides, neither of them had shot dear Tim McCarthy.

Charley appeared to be worried about another problem. "But even if it is Pigott, we still cannot prove it."

"Charley, you purchased his newspapers a few years ago."

"Yes. What of it?"

"Well, if you look at the letters you wrote to him at the time, you will see phrases that are repeated in the forged letters."

"Indeed!" Charley's delightful eyes lit up. "I will look at my copies! You are right, that would go far to prove that they are forgeries. But how do you know all this?"

"An American I know, who must remain nameless, assisted him in this work. Charley, there is more."

"More?"

"Mr. Pigott is not very skilled at spelling."

"What of it? He is not very skilled at anything."

"Consider asking him to write the words 'hesitancy' and 'inexcusable' before the Special Commission, and then compare his misspellings to the misspellings in the forged letter."

The door to the back room burst open and a small woman

with dark Italian good looks, large passionate eyes, and a rose in her bodice hurried in. For an instant I thought she was a tart, but her elegant silk faille dress and her well-bred voice spoke of the upper classes. One of Charley's sisters, perhaps. With a pretty smile, she exclaimed, "Charley, this is splendid! I must thank this delightful lady, who has come from America to help you."

I realized that the voice I had earlier taken for the parlor-maid's had in fact been this lady's, who had left the room and hidden before my entrance. I wondered why.

Charley smiled, caught her hand in his and said, "Katie, this is Miss Bridget Mooney, a kind American friend. Bridget, this is—yes, let me say my true wife, Katharine."

"Oh, Charley, you shouldn't!" she exclaimed, looking at him in distress.

"Bridget will keep our secret, Queenie," he said fondly, patting her hand, which he still held. "And she has helped me find a defense against the lies in *The Times*..'

"Oh, that is true! Thank you! And do call me Katie!"

"I shall," I replied, hiding my indignation behind my sweetest smile. "And you must call me Bridget. But I had not heard of your marriage! May I congratulate you?"

"Thank you," said Charley, exchanging a merry glance with Katie. "But there is good reason you have not heard, Bridget. We beg you to keep silence. Our hearts are pledged, but there are many reasons that we cannot yet become man and wife in public."

"Of course. I won't speak of it," I promised.

"Thank you," Katie said with her charming smile. "It is very difficult. For eight years, we have kept our secret. But it is so good of you to give us weapons to use against the forger and *The Times*. Dear Mr. Gladstone will be pleased as well!"

She and Charley beamed at each other. Having seen

enough of these turtledoves, I took my leave. They heaped
more gratitude upon me and then called for the parlormaid,
who showed me to the door and handed me my parasol.

"Thank you," I said, handing her a coin. "Tell me, have
you worked here many years?"

"Why, no, mum, Mrs. O'Shea only rented this house in
March of last year. And they have other houses, in Eltham
and Brockley."

I stood thunderstruck. Eltham. And she'd said 'O'Shee.'
I murmured, "I see. Yes, I see. Thank you."

Well, did you ever hear of such a cad as Charley? It was
truly reprehensible to tantalize a young lady with a delightful evening at the Fifth Avenue Hotel, and to write her
lovely sweet notes, and then to forget it all when a dark-
haired temptress with a rose in her bodice, a husband, and a
rich aunt appeared! He'd called me a princess; he called her
"Queenie"! A most toad-spotted traitor, was Charley!

Worst of all, when I kindly reappeared with the information that would save his career, the Irish cause, and the
British government from the attacks of *The Times*, he had
cut me off with a mere ten pounds!

What a cad!

I turned into the verdant acres of nearby Regent's Park, as
furious as a hornet trapped in a jar.

Should I forge another letter, one without the telltale
handwriting and misspellings that pointed to Pigott? No,
that would not succeed now. With the information I had
foolishly given Charley, even genuine letters would be suspect, and Pigott's career would be destroyed; and when I
thought of dear Tim's dead freckled face, I remembered
how much I wanted to destroy Pigott.

But how could I bring down Charley too?

I crossed a bridge over an arm of a pretty lake.

Should I tell Captain O'Shea that Charley and Mrs.

O'Shea were living as man and wife? No; on reflection I realized that he already knew. His bitterness against the leader
of his own party and his delight in the thought that Charley's
career was about to be ruined indicated that he knew. But
why didn't the captain divorce his adulterous wife, naming
Parnell as the guilty party, and ruin Charley's career in that
manner? I realized that the captain would happily be rid of
Katie, but not of her rich aunt. Captain O'Shea had to remain married or suffer financial ruin.

A well-tended garden filled with late-summer blooms at-
tracted me. A sign said it was in the care of the Royal
Botanic Society.

Should I tell the rich aunt about Katie's sinful ways? No;
I realized that it would be difficult to make her believe me.
Her own relatives, jealous of Katie, had been unable to convince the aunt that her favorite niece did not deserve her
support. And even if I succeeded in proving it to her, a rup-
ture with the aunt would hurt not only Katie and Charley,
but also Captain O'Shea and all those he supported, such as
Pigott and myself.

It seemed hopeless; but at last, amid the fragrant breezes
of the Royal Botanic Society's rose garden, I worked out the
answer.

It took me a month to arrange everything, and a difficult
month it was, because Pigott had no money, dear Lillie
Langtry was not available, my illustrious but aged tutor Mrs.
Fanny Kemble saw no one, and even the generous Captain
O'Shea was home suffering from gout. I soon had to leave
the hotel in Fleet Street and take up cheap lodgings in
Whitechapel, a particularly unpleasant place that September, very nearly worse than Pigott's suggestion that I go
with him to Ireland.

I told Pigott, "No, dear sir, things are far too unsettled for
me to consider marriage to you. But I would like to make

one observation, and that is that Captain O'Shea is a true gentleman, worth three of your other employers."

"But he won't even be seen with me, only in dark corners of that public house. And he said I must give evidence, while the others promised it would not be necessary!"

"And who told the truth?" I asked.

Pigott looked unhappily at the subpoena with which he had just been served. "The captain was right," he admitted. "Oh, do marry me, Miss Mooney! My life is in need of some joy!"

"That is not possible just now," I said kindly. "Now, of course the captain was right. He is as true a man as I have ever seen, Mr. Pigott, and if you ever need assistance, turn to him."

"But if I give evidence, they may require me to mention the captain's name! He will be angry with me then!"

"Do be sensible, Mr. Pigott! To begin with, they cannot prove that the letters are forgeries. Could you prove it?"

"No. Only your friend Tim McCarthy could have proven it," he said, cheering up.

"And poor Tim is gone, rest his soul," I reminded him— as though he needed reminding. "So there is no difficulty. And even if difficulties arise, your course of action is clear."

"It is?"

"Of course it is! You will explain how Mr. Houston and *The Times* paid you, but do not mention good Captain O'Shea. Gratitude will then bind him to you, and he will arrange a way out of the dilemma for you."

"Yes, yes, he would do that for me!" Pigott exclaimed. "One way or the other, it will come right."

He little knew how truly he spoke.

I made further arrangements. When Captain O'Shea's gout improved, he reappeared at the public house in Wardour Street. He was surprised when the lively Caroline led me to his table. "Why, how delightful to see you, Miss Mooney! It has been some time, because I have been ill, and there have been demands on my time from my business in Madrid. But pray, where is your fiancé?"

"Sir, we are not engaged. Mr. Pigott tends to exaggerate."

"That he does. Caroline, my minx, bring us some ale," said the good captain. With his mustache and twinkling eyes, he was a most appealing fellow, even if a bit gouty. I didn't see why the greedy Katie O'Shea needed Charley as well.

But when he turned back with that discontented air, I could see that a lady might weary of him. For now, however, I hoped he would be my ally. I said, "Mr. Pigott has gone to Ireland. I must admit, sir, I am sorely disappointed in him."

"What has the rascal done now?" He was twinkling at me now. As Caroline set down our ale, she gave me a considering glance.

"Nothing as yet, sir, but this subpoena has made the man mad."

Captain O'Shea looked alarmed. "He carries a revolver, I know. Is he dangerous?"

"Yes, because he is a coward at heart. The danger now is not from his revolver; it is from what he may tell the Special Commission."

"Why, all he has to do is tell how he obtained the letters," said the captain. "They are so incriminating that Parnell will fall."

"Yes, but you see, Captain, I fear that Mr. Pigott is so weak that under cross-examination he may attempt to shift the attack to his betters."

Captain O'Shea looked worried. "Well, it's true I would prefer not to be mentioned," he said.

"Of course. You have done well to keep the scandal from your wife's aunt. But if it comes out that you helped pay for evidence that could ruin Mr. Parnell, you can no longer expect the newspapers to remain quiet. Katie's aunt will be sure to hear."

Captain O'Shea glared at his ale and said, "It's true. But we must let him testify! The Special Commission needs his proof that the charges against Parnell are sound."

"Why don't you promise Pigott you'll help him escape if necessary? Then if he appears distressed enough to betray anyone, it won't be you, and you can spirit him away before he does too much damage."

O'Shea nodded slowly. "He could be silenced."

Well, I couldn't have phrased it better myself. I nodded. "He could, but not until he has helped expose Mr. Parnell's perfidy."

"True. Oh, how I wish there were an easier way to bring down Parnell! Mr. Gladstone and I favor Home Rule for Ireland, you know. But Parnell's fall carries some risk to the Home Rule bill, and thus to Gladstone and me."

"I trust that Mr. Gladstone will keep Parnell at arm's length. As for bringing him down—well, sir, I realize that it is your kind consideration for your wife's dear aunt that stays you from divorcing the faithless Katie and bringing down Mr. Parnell in that manner. It is an eternal credit to you."

"Yes." O'Shea succeeded in looking both melancholy and proud at the same time. "After Aunt Ben dies, I can divorce Katie. But I fear I will lose the case even so. You see, Parnell is such a weasel, he will claim I abandoned Katie long before he began his perfidious visits to her, and that we were wed in name only. Then Katie will win the action."

"Even so, sir, you can ensure that whether you win or not, Mr. Parnell will lose."

"How?" he asked eagerly.

"You say that Caroline was your cook once?"

"Yes, in West Brighton. She was one who told me that Mr. Parnell was visiting Katie in secret."

"Excellent. Call her to the table, and I will explain."

When things were arranged, Captain O'Shea gratefully gave me enough money for my passage home.

Back in America, I followed the newspapers with great interest. Perhaps you recall how things fell out. In February of 1889, the Special Commission at last called for testimony from Mr. Richard Pigott, who stated that the letters had been owned by an unnamed source in America and spun quite an interesting tale of secret societies in Paris and New York. The Special Commission was impressed, until Parnell's counsel rose to cross-examine Pigott, and before beginning, asked him to write the words "hesitancy" and "inexcusable." Of course he misspelled them "hesitency" and "inexcuseable." As the testimony went on, and phrases from *The Times*'s letters were seen to be copied from phrases Charley has written to Pigott when buying the papers, the forgeries became glaringly apparent, as did Pigott's guilt.

After the second day of cross-examination, the poor old fellow disappeared from his hotel room. His flight removed all doubt. Charley was innocent.

A week later, news came from Madrid that a traveler staying at the Hotel des Ambassadeurs had died while police were trying to arrest him. The traveler had given the name Roland Ponsonby.

The Madrid police said he had taken a revolver from his portmanteau and shot himself; but I knew that Captain O'Shea, still eager to keep his name out of the affair, was in Madrid on business that same day.

When Ponsonby was identified as Pigott, Charley returned to Parliament for the most triumphant year of his career. Gladstone embraced him, and the Home Rule bill seemed assured.

Then, in May, rich Aunt Ben died at last. There was much dispute about the will in the courts, and O'Shea finally brought a divorce action against his wife and Charley. The two did not bother to contest it, partly because Aunt Ben was now dead, and partly, I'm sure, because Charley thought O'Shea would not call witnesses if unopposed, and the divorce would be granted quietly and unobtrusively, thus reducing the damage to his soaring career.

But to Charley's surprise, O'Shea did call witnesses— chiefly the servants I myself had instructed. The best was Caroline, who said that while she was the O'Sheas' cook in West Brighton, Parnell frequently slept at the house when the captain was away. Several times, when Captain O'Shea arrived home unexpectedly, Charley had slipped out onto the balcony, slid down the rope fire escape (that was my invention), and then a few minutes later had rung the front doorbell and asked to see Captain O'Shea.

Just as I'd expected, the absurd idea of dignified, aloof Charley scrambling monkeylike down the rope convulsed British and Irish alike. Columnists joked about him, cartoonists ridiculed him. Very soon, a little toy model of a Brighton house was on sale in the market stalls, complete with a tiny Parnell dangling from the fire escape. And those in my profession reenacted it gleefully in music halls like the Alhambra.

The Uncrowned King of Ireland had been shot at, jailed by his enemies, insulted, and accused of the Phoenix Park crimes. From these vicissitudes, he had emerged stronger than ever. But now he could not conquer the waves of malicious laughter about a nonexistent fire escape.

Charley fell. Gladstone's government fell. The Irish people did not get their own nation for another thirty years.

I was sorry about that. But don't you think it was partly their own fault for electing a most toad-spotted traitor? Yes indeed.

I've always found the library to be a pleasant respite from the pressures of life. But it's far too easy for me to try to look up just one more reference book for my latest novel. I often end up with a stack of books as tall as I am. Anyway, the library is an excellent place to research committing a murder. Or to start solving one.

Up the Garden Path

Joyce Christmas

Wednesdays didn't trouble Betty Trenka at all. On Wednesdays, she had something to do, the kind of routine responsibility that reminded her of the old days, before she had been asked to retire from Edwards and Son with no right of refusal. She was out of the place just like that after thirty-seven years and into the small house she'd bought in East Moulton, Connecticut, several miles downstate from her old apartment near Hartford.

Since she didn't care to cook, scrape and paint or perform other tiresome domestic chores, and never had in all of her sixty-three years, and there was little opportunity to exercise her undeniable skills as an office manager except for occasional temporary typing jobs, the last six months had found her frequently restless and at sea. She liked routine, responsibility, a meaningful pattern. A real life, to be honest.

But on Wednesdays, at least, she volunteered at the East
Moulton Public Library. Despite slight friction with the
somewhat dictatorial librarian, Harriet Fuller, she enjoyed
her volunteer chores. She had a definite job to do.

She liked seeing the regulars who came in at midweek to
replenish their supply of books for the weekend. Not everybody had succumbed to passive addiction to the TV screen.
Old Mrs. Broome always got her books on Wednesdays and
explained that she still had time to exchange them before the
weekend if none of them appealed to her. Mrs. Broome was
a fan of cozy mysteries and once said she'd read all of
Agatha Christie four times. They didn't make them like
Christie any more, did they? Certainly the small, upright old
lady with fluffy white hair, floppy hat and dingy smock (she
usually came directly from her garden) could easily have
passed for Miss Jane Marple herself.

Clarisse Broome always brought her grandmother in,
since the old lady wasn't up to walking the short distance
from her home on one of the tree-shaded streets near the
center of town, and she certainly wasn't allowed to drive.
Indeed, Betty couldn't imagine the sweet old thing behind
the wheel of a car. A truly frightening thought. Mrs.
Broome, harmless as she appeared, had brief explosive moments when matters were not to her liking. Clarisse usually
bore the brunt of her outbursts, but patiently. Consider the
driver who might cut Mrs. Broome off in traffic. And then,
too, she often complained of her "spells." Clarisse said they
were nothing serious, a way of getting at Clarisse, which
naturally brought a vehement denial from Mrs. Broome.

Clarisse interested Betty. She reminded her of her own
younger self. Shy and somehow yearning, although she was
prettier than Betty had ever been, that's for sure, but at least
Betty had never had to live with a demanding, aging relative
and care for her. It must be a lonely and frustrating life for a

young woman in her late twenties, trapped in a small town and trapped in a life that tied her to Grandmother Broome. That probably explained why Clarisse invariably picked up a couple of torrid romance novels while Mrs. Broome looked over the latest warm and fuzzy murder tales. Still, Clarisse struck Betty as determined. She'd find her own way eventually.

Herb Graff was usually in on Wednesdays as well. He was into Westerns, do-it-yourself home repair, and the occasional Tom Clancy. Herb was into middle age, but what her mother would have called "a fine figure of a man," with an unruly shock of gray hair, bright blue eyes, and a jaunty walk. He always had a funny story about his battle with the new kitchen cabinets he was installing for the Missus—that would be Eleanor, his rather domineering wife. Betty had served on a committee with her for a children's holiday party, the preceding Christmas, and had formed her own opinion of her. Then there were the problems he'd had figuring out the right proportions for the mortar for the barbecue he was building.

Also interesting to Betty was the fact that Harriet found him appealing. He was about the only person she warmed to. Maybe it was because he was a flirt and liked to tease her. Harriet always softened and turned coy and girlish when he spoke to her. She watched the clock and fluffed her hair when his Wednesday arrival was imminent.

Herb didn't flirt much with Betty, who generally struck people as a no-nonsense person, rather tall, slightly awkward, somewhat intimidating. But he always twinkled at Clarisse and made her blush becomingly. Herb's library visits usually coincided with Clarisse's, and Betty rather wonder about that. She was making unfounded assumptions, of course, but the subtle messages beneath the surface of small-town life intrigued Betty. She'd grown up in just such a place. Too, it was all rather like the office life she knew so well. The mutual attraction between the handsome executive and the pretty young file clerk, and the resulting coincidental encounters at the water cooler. Then the sad conclusion when the office romance was halted by an irate spouse. The petty jealousies, the deep possessiveness that arose when one employee felt that another was usurping the attentions and favors of a favorite supervisor.

The teenagers were a different story, six or seven of them, mostly girls and a couple of studious boys, who had a book review group that met on Wednesdays after school. Harriet had grudgingly granted them the little side reading room, and one of Betty's tasks was to remind them periodically that this was a library, not a sports stadium, and their loud, allegedly literary disputes disturbed the other patrons in spite of the closed door. They seemed to listen to her more readily than to Harriet, who had a way of implying that the books, the tables, the very building were her property and they were intruders.

Betty would have bitten her tongue before she'd suggest to Harriet that the library was the property of the taxpayers of East Moulton, and besides they were just kids eager to learn. Still, despite minor conflicts, Harriet ran an efficient ship; books were returned on time; the shelves were regularly stocked with new titles even given the library's budget constraints. Once when Betty had timidly tried to express her approval of Harriet's good work, Harriet had simply pointed to the sign on her desk: "Harriet Fuller, MLS," and said, "I am a trained librarian."

Harriet was a widow of middle years, plumpish, but with fine features and a stylish way of dressing. She was also a dedicated dieter. Molly Perkins, the pharmacist's wife and a world-class gossip, had told Betty that "poor Harriet" had been the town beauty in her youth but had been left at the church years before by an itinerant tap dancer who passed through East Moulton and won her heart only to break it. According to Molly, Harriet had refused to cringe before the town's inevitable delight in her misfortune and said she was damned if she'd let a bit of romantic folly blight her life.

"Then she married Bradley Fuller, of all people. And she was no chicken when she hauled him in, but she was still a lovely thing. No wonder that tap dancer fell for her. Bradley sure was something too. The handsomest man in town. I'd just met Perk, and we were courting, so I didn't envy her. The other girls did though."

Bradley Fuller, however, was taken from Harriet by the Korean War. "It turned her kind of sour," Molly said, "and she tried to sweeten up with a few too many hot fudge sundaes, if you ask me. Good thing she had an occupation to fall back on. Studied library up at some college in Boston after Bradley's ship went down during the Inchon landing. Then Agnes, the old librarian, up and died just about when Harriet needed a job."

Molly was a veritable font of information on the town's inhabitants and had plenty to contribute to Betty's view of the library's patrons. "Herb Graff's only been in town ten years. He's still an outsider." Betty wondered what her mere six months in East Moulton made her. A real alien, perhaps. "He's a handful, let me tell you. Pinched my bottom once, he did. I thought Perk would punch him out. He's always joking around with the ladies at the pot luck suppers. They say Harriet was sweet on him when he first moved to East Moulton, but Eleanor Graff won't stand for any foolery with the ladies, any more than Harriet does with the kids at the library."

"'They'? Who are 'they'?" Betty was curious, but of course she knew the answer. The eyes and ears of a small town.

"You know. People. People notice the little things that go on. I know I do, and when I saw her cozying up to Herb, I mentioned it to her, more than once. Not that she listened to me, but you have to be careful in a place like this. And careful of men who promise to fulfill your dreams. Well, we were much younger then and not so wise. I know that Eleanor Graff had to tell her off once, and then there were no more giggles in the corner at Town Meeting."

Whatever her history, Betty decided that Harriet was basically all right. It was just that Betty was accustomed to being in charge, so she had to learn to keep her mouth shut and attend to checking books in and out, helping to shelve the returns and sometimes recommending a favorite title to Mrs. Broome and Clarisse, and even Eleanor Graff who often accompanied Herb, probably to keep an eye on him. She generally headed straight for the latest Mary Higgins Clark. Not much flirting when Eleanor was around. Betty had never had much time to read while she was working at Edwards and Son, but she'd always read the *New York Times Book Review* on Sunday, to keep current on what was new, although Harriet seldom paid much heed to her opinions.

The library opened at ten, and Betty was on duty from noon until six, although she sometimes stayed later if her help was needed. Elizabeth Trenka was not one to leave a task unfinished at day's end.

Tina, the difficult cat who had taken up residence with her, watched sullenly as Betty stuck her nose out the back door to discover that it continued mild and springlike, although her backyard was a disaster, drab and forlorn. A few flowers would help. All that remained from the previous owner were a few weedy crocuses. She thought she knew how to remedy that. The problems of the past winter seemed insignificant now, and suddenly Betty was looking forward to a nice chat with Mrs. Broome about gardening. Mrs. Broome was an avid—indeed legendary—pruner, weeder and cultivator. She made gardening sound almost exciting. It was a topic she frequently mentioned, and Betty imagined her shuffling around her beds of iris (prize-winning!) and roses (likewise!), pausing to greet the frog who lived in her lily pond, then tottering off to a comfortable chair under the maple tree for a soothing cup of tea brewed up by the long-suffering Clarisse. Surely she could guide Betty in sprucing up the back yard. A few colorful blossoms at the foot of the old evergreen, daffodils and tulips out front.

No! It was a toad that lived in the damp shade at the edge of Mrs. Broome's pond. Whatever, Mrs. Broome often expressed her conviction that when she scratched its back with a twig, the toad responded to her voice and "almost understood" everything she said. Mrs. Broome was so taken with her toad that a couple of weeks ago, Herb had offered to build a brick wall around the pond to keep it from eroding and give the toad a nice vantage point from which to view the garden.

Mrs. Broome had said quite seriously that she wasn't sure the toad would like that. She'd have to ask it. Betty noticed that Clarisse had winced at her grandmother's comment. Herb had merely winked at Clarisse and elicited a shy smile. Then she'd gone off to locate the well-worn copy of Anya Seton's passion-filled historical novel, *Katherine*, about John of Gaunt and his beloved. Betty had loved it years ago and had enthusiastically recommended it.

"Tina, kindly leave the couch alone," Betty said sternly. Tina desisted reluctantly and examined the guilty paw that had been ravishing the sofa leg. "You have a hundred trees outside. Go molest them." She opened the door and nudged Tina out into the sunshine. Tina looked back over her shoulder contemptuously. She certainly did understand almost everything, albeit ungraciously. Cats were surely smarter than toads. Betty watched Tina stalk through the tall grass— time to get someone to mow—and thought how nice a big patch of white daisies would look, some of those tall red things—salvia? And bright yellow marigolds. She wasn't up to prize-winning roses and likely never would be.

At quarter to twelve, Betty got into her trusty Buick and headed for the center of East Moulton. It wouldn't take her more than a couple of minutes to drive the mile along Timberhill Road to town, and she liked to be prompt. More important, Harriet expected her to be prompt. She went home for her low-calorie lunch at twelve on the dot.

Harriet was alone in the library when Betty arrived. Midmornings were never busy. She was sitting behind the main desk checking off new titles reviewed in *Library Journal* for possible purchase. A book sale to benefit the library was coming up shortly and would bring in a few dollars to add to the meager book-buying budget. Harriet was spending the money before it even reached the cash box. "Ah, Betty. Right on time."

"Lovely day, isn't it?" Betty said. "Makes me wish I were a gardener like Mrs. Broome. Get out there and put my hands in the dirt." Maybe she'd been thinking too much about a garden. Ted Kelso, her neighbor across Timberhill Road, had a fine garden which he maintained for his bees, but she'd asked so many favors of him that she didn't want him to feel he had to instruct her on the finer points of growing a patch of petunias. Besides, she was almost embarrassed to ask. She'd made such a point of being totally disinterested in house and garden activities, and more important, it would be difficult for him to get to her yard in his wheelchair. His little stone house and the grounds had all been remodeled to make every part accessible, but her place was virtually inaccessible.

Harriet sniffed. "Martha Broome never deigns to get her hands dirty. She has some boy who does the heavy work, and Herb comes around to help out from time to time, since he's practically next door, but if you ask me, it's not out of love for Martha Broome, rather . . ." She shuffled papers on her desk. "It's not for me to gossip. I'll leave that to Molly Perkins. Although he's actually started to build that brick wall for her stupid toad. And Clarisse works like a slave over those damned irises and the roses. Trust me, all Martha does is point to the spot where something should be planted and somebody does it. Look at the time! I'll be off for lunch. You can get going on shelving the books that came back yesterday."

The book trolley was loaded with volumes. Betty suspected they represented two days' worth of returns. The Tuesday volunteer, Mrs. Cable, had arthritis, so shelving books was not her favorite task.

Harriet said, "Poor Mrs. Cable didn't get around to finishing up yesterday." She marked her place in *Library Journal* and completed tidying up the desk.

"Have the Broomes been in today?" Betty asked. Even if Mrs. Broome wasn't the hands-on gardener she pretended to be, she certainly knew enough to advise Betty on what to plant in the shade out near where the old garage used to stand.

"It's a little early for them," Harriet said. "Martha likes her nap after lunch. She isn't as strong as she used to be. We'll be seeing them before five. Martha has a big stack of books due today, and you know she doesn't like to pay fines." Harriet stood up. "I have a couple of errands to run after lunch. Just keep those wild Indians under control until I get back."

Betty thought the mild spring weather would cause most teens to forget their devotion to literature, especially the boys who played baseball and the girls who loved them. "I can handle them," Betty said.

After Harriet walked out the door, Betty looked over the books on the top shelf of the trolley. All fiction, a few children's books. A simple alphabetical task, and she'd get it out of the way right now. She looked up at the shafts of sunlight streaming through the row of small windows near the ceiling of the little one-floor library. Dust particles danced in sun. She waited until she was sure that Harriet had driven away, then opened the door to let the fresh air stream into the room.

For the next half hour she dutifully replaced the returned books in their proper places on the shelves. Someone was reading a lot of tried and true mystery classics: Christie, Sayers, Allingham, along with the newer practitioners of the art of mystery: Susan Rogers Cooper, Polly Whitney, Elizabeth Daniels Squire. Stephen King and R. L. Stine for thrill lovers of various ages. Grisham for those who favored legal settings or wanted to be a part of the best-seller crowd. Danielle Steele for the romantics. Older historical novels in heavy library bindings.

When the fiction titles had been replaced, she started on the books that had to be shelved according to subject, taking care that they were put in exactly the right spot. The East Moulton Public Library didn't have a huge collection, but Harriet had it firmly organized on recognized Dewey decimal principals and was easily provoked if something was misshelved. There were a surprisingly large number of books on medieval subjects today. You could always tell when a teacher at the high school assigned a report on a specific topic. The public library was a better information source than the meager school library, although she understood from the teens that cyberspace offered a lot of information nowadays. The high school had computers, as did many of the students, and they were all linked to the Internet. Not a substitute for books, but nothing is.

Surprisingly, Harriet hadn't returned by two, but Missy Caldwell showed up with her five-year-old Maggie, who knew exactly where the picture books were kept on a shelf near floor level.

"I suppose I should be happy she's interested in books," Missy said. "They're better for her than cartoons on TV. Dan wanted me to find something about sailboats. What do you have?"

"I don't imagine there's too much. East Moulton is pretty far from Long Island Sound. Have a look." She pointed Missy toward the card catalog. Harriet was obsessed with computerizing the catalog, but the funds simply weren't there. "Is Dan taking up sailing?"

"He's going to build a sailboat," Missy said wearily. "In the garage. I hope Herb will help him out. Maggie honey, be careful of the books. They belong to the library." Maggie dropped the picture book she was examining and hung her head, but only for a moment. Then she was on the floor turning the pages. "I was hoping to run into Clarisse," Missy said. "Doesn't she usually bring the old lady in on Wednesdays? She said she needed to talk to me about something. I'm kind of worried about her. She's been edgy lately."

"After Mrs. Broome's nap," Betty said.

"What a life, running around after that old tyrant. It must be worse than having a toddler. Clarisse was always so popular and active in high school. She's older than I am. All of us little kids used to look up to her. She was real smart, and everybody expected her to get a scholarship to the university. But it never happened. Both her mother and her father died, and there was nobody to take care of Mrs. Broome. They say Mrs. Broome has enough money to go to a retirement home or hire a companion, but it had to be Clarisse."

"She seems happy enough," Betty said, "and really quite devoted to her grandmother."

Missy shrugged. "It's a roof over her head and three squares, but she's not happy. We've gotten to be friends, sort of. Our yards back up on their garden, and we talk over the fence when Mrs. Broome allows her a minute of rest from digging up flower beds and pulling weeds. It's nice to have someone to talk to who has more to say than what their kids are up to. She reads and everything. I don't know why she couldn't say what she had to say over the fence."

Betty remembered how office life meant that confidences had to be shared away from casual eavesdroppers, especially if the confidence brought on a few tears. "Maybe it's something difficult, and she didn't want her grandmother to hear."

"It might be about some guy," Missy said cheerfully. "Clarisse is a real pretty girl, and the old lady wouldn't like the idea of losing her unpaid servant." Missy checked on Maggie, then looked around the library. "I don't read as much as I should, mostly I watch TV, but I do like that Judith Krantz. And *People* magazine."

"Clarisse likes romances," Betty said.

"I guess you would, if you don't have any. Of course, now that she's found a guy . . . If she has . . ." Missy spun around to halt Maggie from dumping a couple of fat, encyclopedia volumes on the floor. "I'd better look for that sailboat book before the kid destroys the place. Clarisse is probably at home in the garden."

Missy actually found a book about sailboat construction and checked it out, along with some picture books for Maggie. And she did have a library card. Betty relaxed in the now empty and silent library. Harriet was taking her own sweet time getting back; not that there was a lot to do. Betty looked through the cards for the books due. Mrs. Broome had six, Clarisse three. Herb Graff was due to return three yesterday, but he never minded paying fines. In fact, he often sweet-talked Harriet out of charging him. But if his books were due yesterday, he must have come in on a Tuesday last week or the week before. Maybe he was dropping by just to see Harriet.

Harriet finally showed up around four, just as three teens raced in to confess that they wouldn't be using the reading room today. Too nice to stay indoors.

"Too nice to stay indoors," boomed Herb, who slapped his books on the desk in front of Harriet. "Good-looking woman like you should be out enjoying the sunshine."

Betty knew he wasn't talking to her. Harriet almost giggled behind her hand. "Get along with you, Herb," she said.

"I will be getting along," he said. "I've got some cement hardening, and I want to keep an eye on it."

"Are Mrs. Broome and Clarisse coming in, do you know?" Betty asked.

"Well . . . they're in the garden," Herb said. "I just saw them. I'm doing that thing with the bricks for her pond. Clarisse is digging up a bed to plant some tulip bulbs. You'll be seeing them sooner or later."

Herb sat on the corner of the desk and began talking in a low voice to Harriet. Betty decided she was not wanted and went off to straighten the books Maggie had disturbed. But she felt uneasy. The failure of Mrs. Broome to appear on schedule. Surely she'd had her nap by now. Missy's comments about Clarisse's possible "guy" and her edginess. She watched Herb and Harriet for a moment. And something else was nagging at her. She remembered visiting Ted in his garden across the street, quite soon after she'd made his acquaintance. It had been late fall. He was doing chores to help his bees survive the winter. And he was doing some planting for the spring. Since she wasn't interested in gardening then, she barely paid attention. But Elizabeth Trenka didn't forget much. All at once, she felt a rush of anxiety.

"Harriet, I need to go out for a few minutes. I won't be long."

"I hope not," Harriet said. "Herb's asked me to take a ride with him out to the mall."

"Whoa," Herb said. "I said I had to get out to the mall to pick up some paint at that big hardware place. Eleanor's been cranky lately. Won't come with me."

"You said you needed a lady's eye to pick out the right colors." Harriet sounded disappointed.

"I did," Herb said, "and I have one. Clarisse is meeting me there to aid me in my time of desperate need."

Harriet reddened in her disappointment that she hadn't been the chosen one. As if a trip to the big mall out on the highway was in a league with dining and dancing at a romantic hideaway.

"I'll only be fifteen or twenty minutes," Betty said. "I really need to check something."

"All right," Harriet said. "Just don't be too long. I don't want to be stuck here by myself."

"Miz Trenka needs a break, after all the time you took for lunch," Herb said. Betty looked at him sharply. How did he know how long Harriet was at lunch?

Not unlike Mrs. Broome's toad, or Betty's cat, for that matter, Herb seemed to understand. "I ran into Harriet in town," he said. "It was well past the lunch hour."

Pondering that chance meeting by the hypothetical water cooler, Betty hurried out to the Buick and drove slowly to the center of town. She was pretty sure she knew where the Broomes lived, on a quiet street lined with lots of big trees. A white house with a green door. Mrs. Broome had once asked her to deliver some books when Clarisse had the flu. The Graffs lived two houses away. Missy Caldwell was on the parallel street behind this one. Betty parked in front of the Broome house.

No one answered her ring. She was very nervous now. Had Clarisse done something unwise to free herself from her grandmother? So many young women who had worked under Betty at Edwards and Son had taken obvious but ill-conceived steps to resolve personal problems. And she didn't really trust Herb Graff, the harmless town charmer of lonely women. She walked around the side of the house, but a tall redwood fence blocked the view of what was probably the garden. There was no gate, and no chinks in the fence.

A few minutes later, she was at Missy Caldwell's door. She could hear television sounds, and shortly Missy appeared.

"Don't ask why," Betty said, "but I'd like to look over your fence into Mrs. Broome's garden. I don't have much time."

"Well, sure," Missy said, clearly puzzled and greatly intrigued. "Come this way." She led Betty through the house out into a big backyard with swings, a slide and a sandbox. "We haven't done much out here. I've been trying to get Clarisse to help me do a garden. Dan would love fresh tomatoes. But I guess she gets enough gardening with the old lady."

Betty reached the low fence at the end of the yard and peered over cautiously. Although it was still early spring, Mrs. Broome's garden was a wonder. The iris were in bloom, looking like a mass of orchids. Purple, white, and yellow blossoms on tall stalks in stately rows. Betty remembered her mother telling her as a child that iris bloomed by Memorial Day, and that was only a couple of weeks away. She saw the little silvery patch of the lily pond and the beginning of Herb's brick wall around it. There was a wheelbarrow nearby, which he probably used to mix the cement, and a pile of heavy garden tools. At the far end of the garden there was a bed of freshly turned dirt. And on the flagstone path that led to the pond, she could see a crumpled pile of . . . something.

"Oh no!" Missy shrieked. "It's Mrs. Broome, isn't it? We've got to help her."

It certainly was Mrs. Broome. The fluffy white hair and the gardening smock alone identified her.

"There's a gate into the garden," Missy said, almost breathless with fear and anxiety. "It used to be wired closed because Mrs. Broome didn't want people tramping around her property, but Dan opened it up so Herb could bring things through our yard into the garden without going through Mrs. Broome's house." Missy's hands were trembling as she undid the latch that held the gate shut. "I'd better call the ambulance."

"Yes, and, I think, the police. Officer Bob, the resident state trooper. I know him."

"Was Herb around today?" Betty called after Missy, who was hurrying to her house. She stopped and turned back to Betty.

"Well, sure. He brought his wheelbarrow through. To work on something for Mrs. Broome. Eleanor was with him."

"Anybody else?"

"Who else would there be?"

"Harriet Fuller. Around lunchtime."

"No, never."

"And Clarisse?"

"Well," Missy said hesitantly, "when I got back from the library, she and Herb were out there and . . . well . . . I'd better call the ambulance. I think there's something going on. Eleanor wasn't around, so I guess they thought they were safe." She was frowning as she dashed into the house.

Betty hurried to the body of Mrs. Broome. She didn't see any signs of violence, and indeed it appeared that Mrs. Broome was still breathing. She looked as though she were merely sleeping in the warm sun. In a moment, her eyes fluttered open.

"I . . . I felt dizzy," she managed to murmur, "and then I fell. Where's Clarisse? She said . . . she said she was leaving. It upset me, made me dizzy. I'd just come out of the house and asked her why she'd dug up the south bed."

"We've called for the ambulance," Betty said. "It's best you don't try to sit up now."

Mrs. Broome gave up her attempt to rise.

"And what did she tell you about the south bed?" Betty asked.

"She wanted . . . wanted to plant something. I told her it was my garden, and I decided what got planted."

"Maybe she wanted to plant tulip bulbs," Betty said.

"At this time of year? They go in in the fall."

At least, Betty thought, I retained that much from Ted's talk about planting. Tulips and daffodils and hyacinths were planted in the fall. She heard a faint siren. The ambulance.

"And what was Eleanor Graff doing all this time?"

"Eleanor wasn't here when I came out to see what Clarisse was up to. Herb was here, but Eleanor wasn't in the garden," Mrs. Broome said. "Then Clarisse came to me and said she'd decided to leave. I got so dizzy when I heard that. She went into the house and Herb went with her. I guess that's when I fainted."

The ambulance crew led by Missy came through the gate, and soon Mrs. Broome was carried off to be examined.

"I don't know where Clarisse is at a time like this," Missy said. "The car is gone. She must be grocery shopping."

More likely, Betty thought, she was up at the mall, waiting for Herb Graff to take her away. A romantic escape from an unhappy life. But it wasn't going to be easy. There were obstacles. The biggest obstacle was Eleanor Graff. Betty looked around the garden, and then she knew.

Bob, the resident state police trooper, appeared, looking faintly displeased. "Mrs. Broome seems to be okay, Betty," he said. "What's the problem that needed me?"

"I may be crazy," Betty said, "but I think there *is* a problem that needs you." She pointed to the fresh bed of earth. "I think the problem may be there."

Eleanor Graff was, after all, in the garden. Officer Bob found her body hastily buried beneath the rich soil. Someone had hit her on the head with a heavy object, if the blood in her matted hair was any clue. Bob looked at the tools near Herb's wheelbarrow.

"Who did this?" he asked. "The husband? Although given Herb's reputation, I would have thought she'd have done *him* in first."

"You're the policeman," Betty said, "you figure it out." Then she hung her head. "Sorry. I think I do know what must have happened. Herb was part of it, but you'll have to find Clarisse Broome, as well as Herb. At first I thought that Harriet Fuller had decided to make Herb Graff her own by disposing of Eleanor, but it seems likely that Clarisse had the same idea. She had to get rid of an obstacle to her happiness. Herb's wife. Since Herb was here, it might have been a joint venture. I think you'll find that Herb and Clarisse met at the hardware store at the mall and went off together. The only person who could have noticed something going on in the garden was Missy, and she was at the library when the deed was probably done." But she had noticed something: Herb and Clarisse in some compromising situation. "Of course, Harriet Fuller was away from the library for a very long time, and she had her eye on Herb too."

"He's something, isn't he?" Bob scratched his head.

"These little towns are scary. I've got to call some people to handle this."

Betty walked along the garden path to the lily pond. She was saddened by what she imagined had happened and the reasons for it. Poor Clarisse. She'd chosen the worst option. Or Herb had.

But now Betty wasn't going to lose her only opportunity to see the legendary toad.

The water lilies weren't in bloom yet, but the surface of the pond was dotted with round, shiny leaves and a few buds. Too bad, Betty thought, that Mrs. Broome didn't have a resident frog instead of a toad. Clarisse might have kissed it into a prince, and there would have been no need to murder Eleanor Graff.

She saw the toad, sitting comfortably in the shade at the edge of the pond, an ugly little thing with a throbbing throat and big staring eyes.

"Everyone was in the garden, being led along the garden path," she said aloud. "And no one would have thought to look here so soon if it hadn't been for claiming to plant bulbs at the wrong time of year." The toad blinked, flicked its tongue and captured a fly. "It is just like the office," she said. "Fooling around at the water cooler." It seemed to Betty that the toad nodded its head in agreement, closed its eyes and appeared to doze with a look of contempt for the follies of the human race, so easily led up the garden path.

Maybe toads are as smart as cats, after all.

I've always had a fond spot in my heart for the villages of England. That's probably why I live in Cabot Cove. You can always meet the most interesting people in small towns. I've never had the experience our next sleuth had, but I can almost guarantee that it would never have happened if she hadn't been in a small town.

The Miser of Michely Hall

Jeanne M. Dams

Little Denholm is one of the pleasantest villages in England, amongst a lot of competition. Not only is it peaceful and picturesque, pure sixteenth-century, but the local pub brews its own ale, and if you can get the locals to talking, they may tell you the entertaining story of the Miser of Michely Hall. But I can tell it better. I was there.

The only good-sized town anywhere near is the cathedral town of Sherebury, where I was living at the time, renting a house, trying to make up my mind whether to settle down in England for good. My name is Dorothy Martin. I'm American, a widow, a little older than I like to think I look, and a rabid Anglophile. So when I found myself with some leisure time, I started taking little local buses around to neighboring villages, drinking in atmosphere. Little Denholm captivated me so completely I booked a room for a couple of weeks at the only pub, the Lady in Battle (with its delectable inn sign of Boadicea in full battle cry, and somewhat less than full dress), and moved in.

That's where I met Emily. She came into the pub the first night, just before dinner time, a sweet-faced little lady with fluffy white hair and a fluffy white dog. She settled primly on a bar stool with the dog on the next stool and sipped genteelly at the glass that Mr. Weekes, the barman, had put in front of her without question. I enjoyed the scene for a moment, trying (unsuccessfully) to think of any establishment in America where a pair like that would be regulars. Then I followed my curiosity to the bar, ostensibly for a refill of ale. Mr. Weekes, who had begun to know me already (after the manner of good bartenders all over the world) took his time about filling my glass, and I took the chance to pet the furry little white head. "What a pretty little dog," I said, making sure my American accent came through loud and clear.

"He's a very fine dog indeed, aren't you, Rex?" Rex responded suitably and his mistress went on, as I knew she would, "You're American, aren't you? Rather an out-of-the-way place for visitors, Little Denholm."

Before my ale was half gone we'd settled my life history and started on hers. Her name was Emily Winthorpe (I'd already met Rex). She was a nearly lifelong resident of Little Denholm, having moved in with her uncle and aunt at Michely (rhymes with richly) Hall upon the death of her parents when she was only six. "And that was not yesterday, I'm afraid. Of course I didn't spend a lot of time there when I was a child. I was sent to school at eight, and didn't come back until I was fifteen."

"You must have been a child prodigy."

"Oh, no, I wasn't at all clever. No, I wasn't ready to leave school, but you see Auntie died, and Uncle Simon didn't be-

lieve in education for girls. He brought me straight home to
look after him. And I've been there ever since."

She sounded so forlorn I hardly knew what to say. "It's
certainly a remarkable old house." Architecture seemed a
safer subject than crotchety uncles. "I saw it this afternoon
when I went for a walk."

"I've always rather liked it, though people round here call
it hideous. Of course Uncle neglected it shamefully. After
Aunt Alice died, he began letting the servants go, a few at a
time. At the end I was doing all the work myself. And of
course I'm not as young as I once was, and it was too much
for me."

"The end? Your uncle is—um—gone, then?"

"He died last week. You'll think me heartless, I'm sure,
going out to a pub like this . . ."

"Not at all!" I assured her hastily. Frankly, from the
sound of Uncle Simon, I would have been toasting his
demise in the best champagne, but I could hardly say so.
"You need to get out—do you good."

"That's what the vicar says. And after all I've always
dropped in to the Lady after organ practice. Every day for—
oh, it must be quite forty years now."

"Right you are, Miss Emily," said my host, who had been
listening attentively. "Wouldn't 'ave known 'ow to open up
the place at six o'clock, me father wouldn't, without you
first in the door. And me following in 'is footsteps, as you
might say. Not that we 'as to close down in the middle of the
day, now they've passed the new law, but it still don't seem
like the evening's right started till you've 'ad your drop 'n'
skedaddled back to the 'All. Not as you 'as to skedaddle,
now that 'ee's gone—savin' 'is memory, o' course. So 'ow
about another, on the 'ouse?"

"Oh, no, I couldn't!" Emily looked quite alarmed. "It
wouldn't seem right. Uncle wouldn't have liked it. Of

course," she said, turning confidentially to me, "he never did like my coming here at all, but I have a little money of my own, just a little, from my mother, and I felt I had to stand up to him now and again. So I would come down to practice the organ, every day. I play the organ at St. Stephen's, you know, and he didn't like that either. I'm afraid he wasn't *very* good about going to church."

"Never darkened the door," muttered Mr. Weekes, wiping the bar unnecessarily and staying in the conversation.

"And he didn't believe in wasting money on drink. But it was my money, after all, and I never neglected him, indeed I never did, even at the end when he wouldn't buy food and I had to buy it myself."

"Oh, dear," I said inadequately. "I gather your uncle was of the impoverished nobility we hear so much about? Family fortune eaten up by death duties, that sort of thing?" I was trying to be delicate about it, but the effect was spoiled by Mr. Weekes's roar of laughter.

"Impoverished? Not 'im! 'Ee could've bought 'arf the county and 'ad change comin' to 'im. Rich as old what's-'is-name, Crocus or that, was old Mr. Michely."

Emily was concerned about another of my misconceptions. "We're not a noble family, you know, Mrs. Martin. No, indeed. My grandfather bought the Hall and renamed it when Lord Randal's family died out and there was no one left to inherit. He was a fine man, Grandfather, and my mother took after him, but Uncle Simon . . ." Her voice trailed off, and I nodded to Mr. Weekes, who produced a second gin and tonic with the swiftness of conjury. Emily sipped it absentmindedly, and I decided to abandon delicacy and come right out with a question.

"Then why wouldn't your uncle spend anything on the house, or servants, or your education, or anything?"

"Because 'ee was a miser, that's why!" chimed in the

Greek chorus from behind the bar. "'Ee never spent a far-thing without pinching it first, and 'ee got worse the older 'ee got. I 'eld my tongue when 'e was alive, Miss Emily, to spare your feelin's, like, but tell the truth and shame the devil, as they say. 'Ee used to treat 'is servants somethin' shameful, too, when 'ee had any. Tell spiteful jokes, and set 'em against each other, and kick their dogs and then say they 'ad to go because they barked too much. You know you 'ad to board your dogs with the vicar all these years, Miss Emily, and though I shouldn't say it I'm glad you're rid of 'im!" Mr. Weekes gave the bar a vicious swipe to relieve his feelings and moved away to tend to other customers who had just come in.

"Well, really, Miss Winthorpe, it does seem as if your life will be easier without him."

"Oh, call me Emily, do. You do seem to understand. Of course Fred Weekes is too outspoken, but most of what he says is true, I'm afraid. I've managed to have a bit of my own life, what with the church, and my dogs, but I hadn't much money, and Uncle would never let me get any train-ing. It will be easier now, with plenty of money and all."

"He left you his money, then, Emily? And I'm Dorothy, by the way."

"There was no one else. He didn't want to; he told me so. He said if there was anyone else, he'd see that they got it. But there wasn't, and he didn't believe in charities, or the church, or anything like that. Truth to tell," she giggled a lit-tle, "I truly believe he wanted to take it with him. But the so-licitor is coming down from London tomorrow, and I should know then just where I am."

"Well, I hope you don't mind my saying so, but he sounds a most unpleasant old man, and I personally am glad he's where he can't hurt anybody now."

•   •   •

In which I was entirely wrong. The next day Emily appeared on the stroke of six, as usual, but her face was as long as the drink Fred set in front of her after one look. There was no one else in the place, so I went over to talk to her. I was afraid she might be standoffish; confidences with a stranger have a way of being regretted next day. But her grievance was great and had to come out.

"Oh, Dorothy, the most awful thing has happened!" she began with preliminary. "The money's gone!"

"Oh, *no*! The usual story, I suppose—invested in some plausible scam. Why is it that those who love money the most are the most easily taken in—?"

"No, you don't understand at all," Emily interrupted frantically. "We don't *know* what happened to it! He didn't buy anything, or invest in anything—it just disappeared!"

"But—how much are we talking about, Emily?"

"Nearly ten million, the solicitor says." Her voice was a wail.

I had to hold onto the bar. "Great heavenly days, ten million! *Pounds!* Emily, that kind of money doesn't vanish without a trace. The man just means he doesn't know what Uncle Simon did—"

"No, he knows, but it makes no sense. I simply don't know what to do. I'll have to leave the Hall, and I've nowhere to go, and no money to speak of." She picked up Rex, who was whining anxiously at her distress, and buried her face in his fluffy white fur.

"My dear, if it comes to that you can come stay with me for a bit. But I'm sure it won't. Pull yourself together and tell me what you know."

Emily obediently took a sip of her gin and blew her nose. "Very well. Perhaps you can think of something. I can't seem to think at all."

"Of course you can't. What a terrible shock! Now tell me."

"Well, Mr. Grey came down this morning, the solicitor. He told me the most extraordinary story. You see, I thought—we all thought, the lawyers and I—that the money was invested safely. Uncle used to get checks every day from this company or that company, and I don't know how much they were but I think they were quite large, from the way I used to see him gloating over them. There at the end he didn't get any, the last few weeks, I mean, but he said he had told the companies to send the money straight to his bank, that he didn't trust me any more to give him his mail! Well, that hurt, of course, but he was getting so strange anyway I didn't really think about it. And then he got really ill and I didn't have time to think about anything, because he wouldn't let me hire anyone to help nurse him or bring in a doctor or anyone; said it was throwing away his money and he'd be all right if I'd feed him decent food. And me spending my pittance on whatever I thought he'd fancy! It was really a mercy when he went off his head and I could send him to hospital, but by that time it was too late to do anything and he died. And Mr. Grey came down and read me the will, and it seemed everything was going to be all right and there was plenty of money, and I was so relieved I cried, because say what you will about the Hall, it's been my home since I was six and I'd hate to leave it. And then today he came down again, Mr. Grey, I mean, and told me the awful news!"

She paused dramatically, finished her gin, hiccupped, and set her glass down with a bang. "The money's gone! A few months before he died, Uncle went up to London and went to a lawyer, one of the new men in Mr. Grey's firm, and made him cash in every single one of the investments. He took the money, in *notes*, Dorothy, Mr. Grey said Uncle insisted on that, and they don't know what he did with it! Mr.

Grey wasn't there at the time, he said he never would have allowed it, but the young man did try to talk Uncle out of it and couldn't. And he said, the young man I mean, that Uncle said he was going to buy shares in the French Bureau of Mines. And Mr. Grey looked into it and there is no such company, and nobody knows where the money is!"

"Unbelievable! They've searched, of course?"

She nodded. "Well, Mr. Grey looked everywhere he could think of. Uncle didn't keep anything at the Bank, of course, stock certificates or anything; safety deposits cost money. But Mr. Grey checked anyway, and there's only ten pounds odd in the account. He's going to check around and see if he can trace any big purchases of bonds or something. But we don't think it will do any good, because of—this!" She handed me an envelope, a cheap white dime-store envelope, with her name scrawled on it in a shaky old man's hand, and a flimsy enclosure. "It was with the will. Read it."

There was no date and no salutation. It began abruptly: "If you're reading this it means I'm dead. I have no doubt you're delighted. You never treated me as a niece should, and now you can have your way in this house as you always wanted. You'll have a wonderful time throwing out all my things, but be careful you don't outsmart yourself. Some day you may find out that my collections were valuable, as I always told you, and you'll be sorry. But it will be too late. If you'd take my advice you'd keep Aunt Blanche's pen, at least, against a rainy day. But you always were a fool."

That was all. No signature. Not a note that I would have cared to receive from a fond uncle, and it cast a cruelly bright light on his character. I shuddered and gave it back.

"What a dreadful old man he must have been. I don't see how you put up with him at all. And I think you're quite right; this is definitely a hint that he did something odd with the money. Bought something, most likely, and hid it somewhere in the house. Does it tell you anything? What on earth does he mean by collections? And did your Aunt Blanche have a special pen?"

"But that's just it, you see," said Emily, near tears again with exasperation. "I never had an Aunt Blanche. Uncle Simon's wife was Aunt Alice, and a dear sweet lady she was, too, until he worried her into her grave. But Aunt Blanche! I don't have any idea what he's talking about.

"And as for his collections, well, that could mean anything. He collected everything you could possibly get without money. Sheet music, there are stacks of it all over the place. Songs you never heard of. Picture frames. Just the frames, mind you, with nothing in them. Rocks. He fancied himself a mineralogist, and near the end he was even picking up pieces of gravel from people's drives. It was embarrassing! You've never been in the Hall, of course, but it has fourteen bedrooms and you can't move in any of them for the rubbish! Glass jars, old newspapers, rusty bits of iron he called artifacts, old clothes—oh, he kept everything. It's a wonder the place didn't burn down years ago. He hated it when I tried to tidy up, said there'd come a time when I'd appreciate his thrift. Thrift, that's what he called it, keeping every scrap of paper and sliver of wood that came in the door. I tell you, it's hopeless trying to look for anything. And I don't even know what I'd be looking *for*! I'd have to clean the place before I could even begin to search, and I might throw away the very thing that mattered, not knowing."

"Well, but look here, we can't just give up without even trying. Let's have Fred give us some dinner and then go take a look at the problem. I have a few ideas. Maybe we're looking for some sort of white pen—*blanche* is French for white. Or something like that. That is, if you don't mind my helping?"

• • •

I should have given the matter more thought. I had, of course, seen the Hall from the outside and thought it a rather remarkably ugly, but definitely interesting, late Victorian pile of brick. It had all the turrets and gables and chimneys and other excrescences of its day, as well as a striped roof, decorative brickwork, wrought-iron work, and an enormous weather vane. I had longed to see the inside, but even warned by Emily's description, I was not prepared for what I saw.

My first impression was of paper. Tottery piles of newspapers and magazines filled the large, dark foyer, leaving only narrow aisles to the stairway and the doors on either side. The dark paneling was hidden by pictures. Photographs, lithographs, and bad paintings competed with calendars, pictures torn out of magazines, and empty frames. The huge tomb of a dining room was even worse, for the enormous table was covered with more papers in mad disarray.

"Well," I said rather flatly as we wandered aimlessly from one cavernous room to another. "I do see what you mean. This could take months. But there must be some place we can start. What about his desk?"

"Mr. Grey already looked. But you can too, if you like."

I looked. We both looked. There was nothing there. Oh, there was everything, but definitely no secret drawers, no hidden stock certificates, no hollowed-out legs. No fortune.

"Well, we didn't expect to strike gold in ten minutes," I said brightly, trying to keep our spirits up. "We'd better begin to work systematically, organizing things in categories. You start on the picture frames; I'll tackle the papers. In the dining room," I added, trying to pretend the task was manageable.

We worked for an hour in dispirited silence. The work

was discouraging enough in itself, and for some reason a silly tune kept jiggling about in my head, and I couldn't get it out. You know how maddening that can be. I tried concentrating on my work. I tried deliberately humming something else. Bach succeeded Mozart, followed by John Denver and the Beatles and even "The Star-Spangled Banner." "O-oh say, can you see?" I warbled, as I sorted through a stack of papers on the dining room table.

Really I was inclined to agree with Emily. This was truly hopeless. A complete search of the house would take several months to accomplish, and even then, with no idea what we were looking for . . . I sighed, and a cascade of old magazines slid to the floor. Emily plodded into the room, swept a pile of newspapers off a chair, and dropped into it.

"You must be ready for a cup of tea," she said with a sigh. "I know I am. Dorothy, I don't believe there really is anything in this house. Or if there is, we'll never find it."

"I know. I think all your uncle's papers are going to be the death of me." I stopped suddenly. The tune in my head acquired words. "*La plume de ma tante . . .*" I jumped up, propelling yet more paper to the floor. "Emily, that's it! The pen of my aunt . . . does your uncle, did he, I mean, have another desk? A big one?"

"No. We've *looked* in his desk." Her tone was beginning to be resentful.

"Oh. Well, then . . . but I'm right, I know I am. Look, where did he keep his collection of pens?"

"But they're none of them any good. I already looked at them, truly, and they're just cheap things he used to pick up when people dropped them or Biros that have gone dry."

"Yes, of course, but where did he keep them?"

"Well, all over the house, really, but most of them in his bedroom chest of drawers. It's for clothes, really, of course, but he put nearly everything in there in the last year or two, because he couldn't go downstairs very easily."

"Listen, Emily," I said, grabbing her by the hands. "What did he call it, your uncle?"

"What do you mean? What did he call what?"

"This piece of furniture you're going to show me. What did Uncle Simon call it?"

"Oh, that was another one of his oddities. He spent some time in America, you know, and he picked up some funny terms there. He always called it his bureau."

"Eureka!" I shouted. "Lead me to it!"

Ladies of my age and figure are not meant to race up uneven, dimly lit flights of stairs, but I made it to the top in record time, with Emily well in the rear. "Come *on*," I panted. "I don't know which way to go."

"This way—in here. Dorothy, what *is* it?"

I found the big white-painted chest and rummaged furiously, pulling out drawers. There were the pens. Old pill bottles in another drawer, stacks of paper napkins in another. The bottom rattled as I pulled it out.

"Part of his rock collection, you see," said Emily. "I told you he was picking up gravel at the end."

"Yes." I sat back on my heels, relishing the moment. "Yes, he probably did, to throw you off the scent. I don't like your Uncle Simon, Emily. But, in fact, most of this isn't gravel, my dear." I ran the dingy-looking pebbles lovingly through my hands. "I'm no expert, but I have a good friend who's a jeweler, and I've seen things like this before. Unless I'm very much mistaken, what you have here is a fair-sized fortune in uncut diamonds."

"But how did you know?" said Emily. It was the next day, and she was treating me to a sumptuous tea at the Ritz. We had taken the stones to a famous London jeweler, who had refused to commit himself to an estimation of their value before studying them thoroughly. His look of awed astonishment, however, spoke volumes.

"My subconscious knew before I did. You know that annoying song I kept humming? I couldn't get rid of it, and it was the key to the whole thing." I helped myself to another cucumber sandwich and went on.

"You remember French exercises, of course. You had to translate idiotic things like, 'My sister's book is in my brother's room.' Well, there was a silly song, oh many years ago now, that was really nothing but a French exercise. *'La plume de ma tante est sur le bureau de mon oncle.'* " My cracked soprano caused heads to turn in our direction. I lowered my voice. "And then it went on in English, but translated literally: 'The pen of my aunt is . . .' "

" '. . . is on the bureau of my uncle,' " finished Emily. "Of course! That's what he meant by Aunt Blanche's pen!"

"Yes! It was a clue both to 'white' and to 'French.' And the song went on with something about the paper of my uncle, and when I was in the dining room and said something about your uncle's papers, I remembered the 'French Bureau of Mines,' and it all just sort of clicked."

Emily was silent for a moment, and then said, sadly, "You know, he never did really mean for me to find it. He always told me as a girl that learning French was useless, and I know he never thought I would make the connection. And of course I didn't. I can't thank you enough, you know."

"Don't be silly. It's the most fun I've had in ages. I hope you're going to do something with the money that Uncle would have disapproved of? It really was mean of him to try to do you out of it."

Emily started to laugh. "Well, I hadn't thought of it that way, but now that you mention it—I did rather have an idea or two. I want to have the Hall put to rights, of course, and the telephone put in, and the gardens seen to. But then I thought it would be nice to give the vicar enough to restore St. Stephen's bell tower. Poor Uncle! He did hate the bells so. And then—oh, it's wicked of me, but I think I'll give most of the rest to the RSPCA!"

"Well, then," I said, lifting a tea cup, "here's confusion to Uncle Simon, and long life and success to the French Bureau of Mines!"

It's always important to remember one's health, I always say. Unfortunately, there are those who take a too active interest in the welfare of others. When this happens, they often have more sinister motives in mind. As the villain in this next story finds out, plotting a murder can be hazardous to one's own health as well.

Tipping the Scales

Leslie O'Kane

Richard Dornbell loathed being called Dickie D. Yet he'd told his wife to use that as her pet name for him. Each time she did, the memories that name evoked kept him focused. In his mind's eye, schoolmates would eternally circle him on crooked, gray sidewalks, taunting him with jeers of "Dickie D! Little Dickie Dumbell!"

The name reminded him to hate his wife.

He'd married her because she fit the profile for the next Mrs. Dornbell perfectly—fifteen years his senior, sky-high blood pressure, sky-high bank accounts. The woman's ticker was a walking time bomb and yet was still going strong two years later.

He opened his front door noiselessly, sinking his stocking feet into the plush white carpeting. With equal stealth, he closed the door behind him and crept toward the kitchen

189

with catlike tread. There she was, humming some old show tune as she rinsed a glass. Despite her advancing years, she was gorgeous from the back—long legs, delicately curved hips, tapered waist, thick, Clairol-enhanced auburn hair that shimmered in the soft lighting from the nearby bay window.

He took three long, silent strides across the hand-painted Mexican-tile floor. Pausing, he weighed the idea of clapping an unannounced hand on her shoulder but opted instead to cry, "I'm home, Celeste!"

Celeste gasped and jumped, dropping the glass in her hand. It shattered with a crash that made him salivate.

She whirled toward him. In that instant, her beauty was gone, and all he could see was that coat hanger she called a nose. Her hands flew to her flat chest. "Oh, Dickie D!"

Richard inwardly winced at the name fit for a fast-food mascot, but he maintained his practiced grin.

Celeste finally—darn it all!—caught her breath. "I wish you would quit sneaking up on me like that! One of these days, you're going to give me a heart attack!"

I might ever be so lucky, Richard thought, but he flashed what he knew to be his most sexy smile, topped with his patented deep, resonant laugh. "I'm sorry, sweet cakes." Yet another carefully planned pet name. He'd hoped the tag would make her crave fat-laden cake.

"Don't take another step," Celeste warned, holding up her palm. "You're going to cut your feet." She tiptoed through the glass shards and began sweeping them into a dustpan.

"I brought you a present," he said and brought his hand out from behind his back with a flourish. Technically that was a lie, he told himself, for he had shoplifted the gift. "I saw this in a store window, and I had to get it for you."

"Oh, that's so cute," Celeste said, pausing from her cleaning long enough to look at the little plastic duck.

He sidestepped the mess on the floor and filled a juice

glass with water. "Watch," he said, as he tilted the duck's nose, coated with absorbent red fuzz, into the water glass. The weight of the absorbed water set the toy off balance on its fulcrum legs. The fuzz would soon dry, which again altered the duck's balance point, causing the head to drop into the water. And on it went. Richard had swiped the toy because he regarded it as the perfect metaphor for his marriage.

"Thank you, Dickie," his wife cooed, rising with a dustpan full of shards to watch her symbolic self suck him dry. "I love it. You must be the most thoughtful husband in the world."

"You got that right," he replied, responding to her upturned lips with a quick kiss. He *was* thoughtful. Once, though, he had slipped up. During their honeymoon two years ago, he'd asked her why, with all of her money, she didn't have some cosmetic surgery and shuffle things around a bit—take some weight off her face and put it on her chest where it belonged. He'd considered that a very reasonable question. Yet she'd cried so many tears that night, he just knew she'd be low on salt for weeks. That was dreadfully counterproductive.

The incident had, however, inspired his first plan of attack. To raise her blood pressure even higher, he needed to build up her salt intake. He bought her a new brand of salt substitute, then swapped its contents with actual salt. He always urged her to use it liberally. He'd also taken over the cooking duties for the household and served nothing but fatty, salty foods. And he vowed to get her heart pumping hard in bed—every night, if that's what it took. But did she have a heart attack? No way. Apparently, it was only men who died while having sex.

As the end result of all of his Herculean efforts, her blood pressure dropped three points. His rose five points. Plus, he gained seven pounds. It wasn't fair!

Now, however, he was well into Plan B—quite a bit riskier, but sooner or later, success was inevitable.

The doorbell rang. Celeste grinned and touched his arm. "That's Sarah."

"Your sister?" Richard asked, struggling to fight down the expression of horror that threatened to overtake his features.

Celeste nodded, heading for the door. "Her flight had a layover in Denver, so I . . ." She paused, altered her course back toward the kitchen counter and snatched up a tissue just in time for a hellacious sneeze. "I invited her to stay the night," she said rapidly, then sneezed a second time.

"Bless you," Richard said, now fighting back a smile. His heart was pounding. Finally. Finally! This was it, he knew it!

"Oh, goodness," Celeste said, her voice wonderfully, magically hoarse. "I seem to be coming down with a cold."

"That's too bad." He waited until he could hear the two sisters yakking away at each other in the living room to whisper, "Yes!" Richard shook his fists and turned his face heavenward.

Celeste's honking sneezes were music to his ears. While he had always suspected that with her huge nose a head cold could prove fatal, he had tipped the scales in his favor. Provided, he silently considered, dear old Sister Sarah didn't find yet another way to foil his plan. Foil. He grinned. He'd made a pun.

"Dickie, come say hello to Sarah," Celeste called.

He mentally used every four-letter word he knew, but managed to answer kindly, "Be there in a moment. Sarah? Can I get you anything to drink?"

"No," came her abrupt reply.

He searched the refrigerator and grabbed a long-neck bottle of beer. Checking his watch, he hesitated, this early-afternoon hour giving the appearance of impropriety, but he could use the reinforcements.

Whenever he as much as thought about his sister-in-law, the memory of his wedding overtook him. There he was, at his most dashing and gallant self, asking Sarah to dance. A waltz, for Chrissake.

They'd only taken a few swirling steps when she growled in his ear, "I see through you so clearly you may as well be made of plastic wrap! I'm warning you right now, if my sister dies before her time, I'll see to it you're behind bars, cursing those pretty-boy features of yours for the rest of your life!"

He had chalked those words up to one of the earliest lessons he'd learned about life: Ugly people were jealous of him. Yet he couldn't forgive her for what happened last year, when she'd managed to destroy his Murder-by-Rich-and-Salty-Diet plan. Sarah had arrived on another of those damned visits—her spouse let her use his frequent-flyer miles to travel to Denver far too often. On that particular occasion, Celeste had been bubbling away about how terrific the "salt substitute that Dickie got me" was.

Sarah had whisked up the container, poured some into her palm, and tasted it. "Well, no wonder this tastes just like salt," she'd announced. "It *is* salt!" Then she glared at him, her lips pursed so tight they looked like the knotted end of a balloon.

He'd explained it all away quite masterfully—manufacturer's mistake, happens all the time—but she refused to believe him. The witch.

Now, in his living room, the chattering noise of the two sisters grew louder as they neared. He took a couple of deep swigs of beer and set the bottle on the stove, catching sight of his reflection on the stainless steel hood. His strong chin was smooth. His blond, curly mane had just the right hint of disarray. He had movie-star good looks, and it was time for another Oscar-caliber performance.

He stepped toward the younger, meaner version of his wife and held out his arms. "Hi ya, Sis. How was your flight?"

"Don't call me that! I'm Celeste's sister, not yours," she snarled. To make matters worse, that damned poodle of hers was in her arms. The stupid dog growled and yipped at him—an exact canine replica of Sarah's voice.

Richard let his jaw drop. A soulful, wounded expression flickered across his features.

The routine hit its intended target, as his wife cried, "Sarah! Dickie is always so nice to you. If you can't get along with him, maybe you shouldn't stay in our home."

"Fine. I won't even ask the lazy lout if he's gotten a job yet or is still sponging off your inheritance."

"Sarah!"

She held up her hands. "Like I said. I won't even ask him that question."

Ignoring her, he swept up his bottle and gulped his beer, wishing he could belch in her face. She thought he was lazy. Ha! She had no idea how diligently he'd worked to pry off and then reseal the tamper-protective foil backing on all those cold medicine packets! He'd spent countless hours with razor blades, glue guns, and tweezers.

"I do hope you don't mind having my Percy here," Sarah said to Celeste. Burying her nose in the overgrown cotton swab's fur, Sarah said in a baby voice, "I just couldn't stand to leave my fluffy puffy!"

"Oh, I know," Celeste said wistfully. "I still miss Missy Pinkerton so."

"Me, too," Richard said, lowering his eyes. That damned

Pekinese had come with the marriage. Took him six months to finally coax her out onto the road in front of an oncoming car. Six months and a good pound or so of hamburger. If only Celeste were as food-obsessed.

He heard a sneeze and looked up hopefully.

"Bless you," Celeste said. "I do hope you're not catching a cold, too."

"I probably am," Sarah grumbled. "You know how those airplanes are—dry, recycled air. I catch a cold almost every time I fly."

Damn! Why hadn't he thought of taking Celeste on a plane!

Originally, he had wanted to poison some over-the-counter medication that Celeste was more likely to use, such as aspirin, which she took daily for her heart. But try finding aspirin in capsule form *these* days. Drug manufacturers were so paranoid, cold medicine was the only gelcap product he could find.

And so, a year ago, he'd gotten five boxes of cold capsules. To make this look like random poisonings, he'd filched them all from different stores, each with the same lot number. Originally, he'd intended to play it safe and fill every single pill with poison, but once he discovered how painstaking and time-consuming it was to defeat the tamper protection, he'd settled on one poison pill per packet, then returned four of them to the stores.

As his rotten luck would have it, two of his four jury-rigged medicine packets had killed men. He'd hoped his sacrificial victims would be women. The other two packets had been located when the stores pulled the product. But that had been months ago. The scare was long past, and he'd assured Celeste not to worry—that these cold pills were far too current to have been contaminated.

In the meantime, he'd systematically set out to assist Celeste in catching cold. This had proved a mission in which a lesser man would have crumbled. He'd taken drastic measures—deliberately getting the two of them far from shelter just before imminent rainstorms, fetching used tissues out of public trash containers and holding them up to Celeste's face while she slept.

Until now, Celeste had stayed in perfect health. Richard had since caught three colds so severe that he'd been forced to use all but the corner pills. He had always been careful to poison the capsule in the bottom right packet compartment. However, so much time had passed he couldn't remember for sure which corner was which, and he was taking no chances.

Celeste caught his eye and smiled lovingly at him. Watching them, Sarah rolled her eyes and shook her head.

Richard cranked up the air conditioner and waited.

By dinnertime, things had progressed quite nicely. Sarah was sneezing even worse than Celeste, but Celeste couldn't hold out too much longer. She'd take a cold pill soon. She wasn't one for living with discomfort.

He had wanted to not touch the pills himself—make sure her fingerprints were all over that particular pill compartment—but now, with Sarah here and sneezing herself, he was growing tense. If Sarah took the poisoned pill, he would have to start all over, find a whole new plan.

As dinner grew near—he'd concocted a wonderful beef Stroganoff with loads of sour cream that he'd passed off as low-fat yogurt—Sarah had settled in at the dining table, guzzling wine. Celeste had come in to the kitchen to help serve and put on the finishing touches. She sneezed.

Richard rubbed her back and said, his voice rife with concern, "You'd better take a cold pill, sweet cakes. You don't want to spread germs into our food."

"I guess you're right," she said, wiping her hands on her apron.

Oh, glorious night! This was it! But he couldn't take any chances. The odds were still three to four that she'd get the wrong pill. "I'll go get them for you," he said, calculating he could at least hand it to her such that he could encourage her to select the right corner.

He raced upstairs, threw open the master bathroom cabinet, swept up his magic pills, and stared at the foil backing. He could barely make out some scratch marks on one edge. Yes, this was the right pill, he was quite certain. If she started to go for the wrong one, he could always create a distraction, then help her get this one.

He forced himself into a regal pace as he descended, mustering a look of spousal concern. Damn! Celeste was now sitting next to Sarah! Sarah was always muddling everything. He couldn't take the chance of her examining the pill packet. He'd have to keep custody of it himself. "Here you go, sweet cakes," he said, pushing the poisoned pill out of its compartment and handing it to his wife.

"What is that?" Sarah asked, fastening the beady eyes of her hawklike face on the tablet.

"Just a cold pill," Celeste answered.

Richard could feel his teeth drying out as he maintained his stupid smile, but he couldn't seem to move.

"Don't you remember hearing about the poisonings in your city?" Sarah screeched. "Cold pills! They were cold pills!"

Celeste gave her sister a friendly pat on the forearm but still hadn't swallowed the pill. "Don't be silly. These were brought way after those incidents. There's no chance that there's anything wrong with these. Right, Dickie D?"

"Right, sweet cakes," he said, feeling set to puke. Sarah's

damned poodle was circling him now, yipping and growling at his ankles. He longed to give the mutt one good drop kick.

Sarah sneezed again and snatched the pill out of her sister's hand. "So then, there's no reason why I shouldn't take this particular pill? Right, Richard?"

"Right, Sarah," he answered with unmistakable venom.

She studied his face, then her sister's, and tossed the pill in her mouth, swallowing it.

Celeste rose. "Well, I'm going to get Dickie's wonderful meal on the table." Sarah started to rise, but Celeste gestured for her to stay seated. "That's all right, my dear, I'll get it."

Richard slumped into his seat chucking the pill packet onto the table in despair. He met his sister-in-law's eyes. She was staring at him. All that planning. Two years of waiting. All gone. He lifted his chin. At least Sister Sarah would die. That was a worthy consolation prize.

Celeste swept back into the room, not with the meal, but with the toy duck and its glass. "Look, Sarah. Dickie got this for me today. Isn't it just the cutest thing you ever did see?"

She set it onto the table and they watched its perpetual motion in silence. Richard wondered how many head bobs he would witness until the poison started to take effect. He stared at it long after his plate was in front of him, and he ate what he had hoped would be the last meal he would ever have to prepare for Celeste.

To his amazement, nothing happened. Sarah and Celeste chatted away. The duck pecked away. Nothing changed. Either the expiration date on the poison had passed, he had selected the wrong pill, or Sarah had faked taking the pill and spat it into her napkin. Her cold symptoms didn't seem to be lessening. All the more reason to suspect the latter.

Celeste passed on dessert, as did Sarah. Celeste's cold had clearly worsened, and she grabbed the packet of cold capsules, saying in nasal tones, "I've held out as long as I care to."

Sarah smiled, "I will say that mine is finally kicking in. Though I'm starting to feel a little groggy."

Celeste swallowed the pill that was kitty-corner to the one Sarah had taken.

Richard brightened. If he had given Sarah an unspiked bottom-corner pill, Celeste had to have selected the right capsule! It was almost over now!

The poodle increased its incessant yips and now whined and scratched at the door. Sarah rose and left the room. When she returned, she carried a sequined leash. "Time for me to walk Percy."

Richard bolted up from the table so fast his seat nearly tipped over. He didn't want to be alone with Celeste when the symptoms struck. "I'll do it," he said. "You two stay here and get caught up."

Sarah raised an eyebrow, but Celeste gushed, "You're such a sweetheart. I don't know how I ever got along without you. Thank you."

Percy snarled and yapped at him. In the corner of his vision, Richard could see Sarah grinning at the dog. Richard tapped his thigh and whistled, inwardly cursing. Hurry up, you little mutant! He faked a move to the left, and as Percy tried to dodge past him, Richard snapped the leash onto his collar. He put on his shoes and glanced again at his sister-in-law, who was stifling a laugh at his expense. Wait. It would never do to have Sarah here—too risky that she might administer life-saving CPR on Celeste.

"Sarah, can you come, too? Celeste has to stay and do the dishes, and Percy seems hesitant to leave you."

Sarah stood up and murmured, "It's just that he can't stand *you*." Then her expression softened and she said to Celeste, "I need to have a chat with Richard. We'll be back

soon." They headed out the door, Percy growling and nip-
ping at Richard's heels. Walking yet another overgrown rodent, he thought. Once Celeste kicked the bucket he was
getting himself a respectable dog—a pit bull.

"Bye, honey," Celeste called after him.

Wordlessly, Sarah snatched the leash from him. They
walked side by side for four blocks to the park. The street
lights illuminated the well-maintained sidewalks, and the
air was brisk and clear. Finally Sarah said, "It has occurred to me that there is no point in my continuing to
treat you like the devil incarnate."

"Excuse me?" Richard said.

"In the past two years, my sister has had nothing but
good things to say about you."

"Of course. I love Celeste." What, he wondered, had
caused Sarah's change of her shriveled heart? Was she
trying to suck up to him so he'd relax his guard? In any
case, she was too late. He searched his mind for more
words—the longer he kept her talking, the more time the
poison had to do its work. He drew a blank, too anxious
for idle conversation.

"I love her, too," Sarah said. "You understand I want
only the best for my sister."

"I'll do my best to take care of her for you."

They were now in a dimly lit section of the park, and
he couldn't see her face, but he heard her click her tongue
disapprovingly. "Well, from now on, Richard, I'll do my
best to be more civil to you. Regardless of my personal
opinion regarding you, I can see my remarks are hurting
Celeste. So I have to put a stop to them."

How was he supposed to respond? Thank her? "I'm
sure you mean well," he muttered noncommittally.

The poodle had done its thing. He tried to coax Sarah

home the long way, but she wouldn't hear of it. All too soon they were walking up the steps.

He opened the door, holding his breath. The house was silent. She was no longer at the dining room table.

"Celeste," Sarah called.

No answer.

Please, let her be dead! "Celeste," Richard echoed, "We're home." The dog darted ahead of them into the kitchen, dragging his leash. Richard followed.

Celeste lay on the kitchen floor. Her hand touched the handset, which dangled from the phone.

Sarah was right on his heels. "Celeste! Oh my God!"

She shoved him out of the way and turned Celeste over onto her back. Her eyes were open, unseeing.

"Oh, dear Lord," Sarah sobbed. "Call nine-one-one!"

Percy whined and licked at Celeste's face. "Uh—don't let him do that!" Richard was afraid the dog slobber might revive her. Sarah was too busy sobbing over her sister's body to respond. Richard grabbed the leash, threw Percy into the guest room, and slammed the door. When he returned to the kitchen, Sarah was calling 911.

Richard Dornbell paced in the living room, making an occasional sobbing sound for the benefit of the policemen and the medical examiner in the nearby kitchen. Sarah was in the master bedroom, talking to one of the officers—probably telling him all about the salt substitute and God knows what else. His only hope was for one of the officers to recognize this as the work of The Phantom Cold Caps Killer.

A ruddy-cheeked officer who looked all of twenty was seated on the love seat. Richard took a seat on the couch.

"Well," said the young officer. "I guess we've got all

the information we need. As soon as Sarge is finished with your sister-in-law, we'll be out of your way."

Richard clenched his teeth. The police had asked him questions about his whereabouts and what had happened. Nothing about the cold pills, even though he'd told them she'd taken a capsule when he left the house. If these turkeys didn't get the connection, he'd be a sitting duck—staring at a murder rap. The packet was right on the dining room table. They couldn't possibly miss it.

"I can imagine how hard this is on you, Mr. Dornball."

"Bell. Dornbell. Yeah. It's terrible. I can't even think. I have such a bad cold." He got to his feet, and announced, "Maybe Celeste's *cold medicine* is around here someplace." Richard went to the dining room and swept up the pills. He dropped them on the coffee table, right in front of the officer. No reaction.

"Achoo!" he cried. "Darn. I seem to be getting my wife's cold."

The officer still seemed oblivious, scanning his notes.

"I wouldn't be ruining your evidence if I took one of my wife's cold pills, would I?"

"No, no," the officer said, "Go right ahead."

Richard stormed into the downstairs quarter bathroom and poured a glass of water. When he returned, the officer was looking downright bored. Richard popped out a capsule and swigged it down with a gulp of water. He set the packet down with the label facing the policeman. Come on, you idiot! Look at the capsules!

The officer gave him a small smile. "Sorry about the delay. I don't know what's taking Sarge so long."

"That's all right." Richard drummed on the table, making the packet shake. The officer sat in silence, staring at the floor, turning his cap round and round in his hands.

What kind of an idiot is this? Richard wondered.

After what seemed like several minutes, the officer looked at the container of pills and pointed. "Hey, I hope you checked the lot number on that box."

Finally! "Why, no. I didn't. Oh, my God. You don't think . . . My poor Celeste. Poor Heavenly Celeste!" He hid his face in his hands. He straightened, stared into the policeman's eyes, and said, "She might be another victim of that maniacal poisoner!"

The policeman shook his head. "Naw. Sarge and I got called in to investigate both of those murder scenes. Experienced 'em first hand. And, let me tell you, all it takes is once and you know what to look for. It's horrible. Vomit all over the place . . . bright-red faces of the victims." He paused and shuddered. "Rest assured, your wife's death was quick. Nothing as painful as those poor souls. The medical examiner told me your wife probably had a plain ol' heart attack."

Richard fought to control his rising panic. Had Celeste put everything together at the last before her symptoms grew too severe—her heart unable to withstand the shock? What if she called the police before she died?

His throat hurt. Oh my God! The pill! He touched his cheek. It felt red hot. "I think—" Richard stopped and clutched his neck. His throat and mouth burned. He doubled over in pain, his insides aching and burning.

"You all right, there, Mr. Dornbell?"

Richard looked up at him, trying to speak. His throat was on fire, he felt burning bile building up. He swept the glass of water up from the table, sending the toy duck flying in the process and tried to drink, but he could barely even force a smile.

The young officer's eyes widened as he looked at Richard's face. "Uh-oh. This could be trouble."

"Help me," Richard said, his voice almost a croak. He

retched. The pain was agonizing. He dropped to his knees. He reached out, desperate. His vision swam. He could barely make out the policeman, staring at him in horror.

"Hey, Sarge! Come take a look at this!"

*For the record, I don't believe in ghosts, although there are
a fair number of people out there who do. Usually the
"haunting" can be easily explained by the application of a
little patience, logic, and deduction. In the end, more often
than not the ghost is as flesh-and-blood as the rest of us.*

Ghost Busted

Susan Rogers Cooper

*T*he following is an exact transcript of telephone conversations recorded between Friday A.M., 14 April, and
Monday A.M., 17 April. Said recordings were the result of
surveillance by an unnamed government agency on the
home and office of one Phoebe R. Love, attorney-at-law,
Austin, Texas, in an attempt to ascertain certain information
concerning an unnamed client represented by Attorney
Love. The voices on this tape are identified as Phoebe R.
Love, attorney-at-law, and her tenant and longtime associ-
ate, Kimberly Anne Kruse, aka Kimmey Kruse, a professional comedian. These calls were to and from the city of
Baltimore to the city of Austin. It has been ascertained that
these telephone calls at this time are considered to be in no
way related to the subject under surveillance and therefore
of no particular interest to the unnamed government agency
which initiated the surveillance.

FRIDAY, 3 A.M. EST (INCOMING—HOME)

"Hello?"

"Hey! I got here safe and sound!"

"Kimmey?"

"Who else?"

"What time is it?"

"I dunno. Wait. Around three here. Did I wake you?"

"What do you think?"

"Well, I thought you might be worried about me. Driving all the way from Pittsburgh to Baltimore in a raging thunderstorm—"

"How would I know it was raining in Pittsburgh?"

"I thought your concern for me might have you watching The Weather Channel, but don't feel guilty. I'm okay."

"I'm glad to hear it. Can I go back to sleep now?"

"Phoebe, you really have to do something about this conservative streak you've been getting lately."

"Did you rent a car?"

"No. Didn't have to. I rode in with Marilyn Miranda."

"Marilyn Miranda? You're kidding. That can't be her real name."

"You're right, it's not. Her parents named her Carmen. She says they thought it was funny."

"God, what people do to their children in the name of laughs."

"Excuse me, Ms. Phoebe *Rainbow* Love—"

"That wasn't for fun. It was a political statement."

"Right. Anyway, believe it or not, the club's put us up in this really nice townhouse in Fells Point. Within walking distance of the club. It's got furniture and everything."

"Beds?"

"I think you have a one-track mind."

"I *was* sleeping."

"You're always sleeping."

"That's because you always call me in the middle of the freaking night!"

"Well, if you're gonna get testy, good-bye."

"Yeah, right."

DISCONNECT

FRIDAY, 3 P.M. EST (INCOMING—OFFICE)

"Phoebe Love."

"Hello, Ms. Love. My name is Ernestine Humperdinck—"

"Kimmey, I'm working. Or attempting to. I didn't get a lot of sleep last night."

"You know you're getting old before your time, don't you?"

"It's the company I keep."

"The coolest thing—"

"What?"

"This townhouse we're in is haunted."

"That's nice."

"No, seriously. Pay attention."

"I have to be in court in three days and I do have work—"

"Phoebe, this place is haunted! Aren't you listening?"

"Yes, I'm listening. The townhouse is haunted."

"Could you be more bored?"

"Probably not."

"Would you be at all interested in hearing why I say the townhouse is haunted, or would you just rather get back to your little briefs and stuff?"

"I don't call twenty-seven pounds of paper 'little'."

"Is that really the salient point here?"

"Why do you think the townhouse is haunted?"

"Okay. Listen. Six months ago, the couple that lived here

died in a murder/suicide thing. Yuppicide. Real up and com-
ers, these two. He's from an old Virginia horse family; she's
the daughter of a New England congressman. He was a
stockbroker, she was a lawyer. Serious yuppies."

"Not all lawyers are yuppies."

"Name me three."

"Get back to your story."

"Okay, he kills her and then himself. Tragic. Right?"

"Um hum."

"Are you listening?"

"Yes!"

"The gunshots were heard by neighbors at exactly 1:06
A.M."

"One oh six A.M."

"Right. Ever since then, at least two or three and sometimes more times per week, at exactly 1:06 A.M.—"

"What?"

"The neighbors see movement and light in the house."

"So? *You're* staying there. Surely other people stay
there."

"Not until the club owner bought the place three weeks
ago! For a steal, I might add."

"So you're saying the place is haunted because people see
movement and light."

"At exactly 1:06 A.M.!"

"Did you see anything last night?"

"We didn't get here until after two."

"So you haven't seen anything?"

"I said we didn't even get to the townhouse until after two
A.M., Phoebe. The crucial time is 1:06 A.M. Not after two.
Have you been paying attention?"

"So where did you get the information?"

"Oh, there's this really cool bar, an Irish pub type of
thing, on the corner. We walked by it coming back from re-

hearsal, so Carmen, I mean Marilyn, and I went in. There was only this one woman in there, and the bartender, and turns out the woman, her name's Nancy, lives right next door to us and she knew the couple. And she's seen the lights like dozens of times. And the bartender—Kevin, who's really cute by the way. Gorgeous blue eyes—anyway, he says he's seen it several times. The bar's across the street and down a couple of houses from ours, and he says it's become one of those 'things' at the bar for the patrons to run out at a little after one and see the show. He says dozens of people have witnessed it."

"And you believe this?"

"What's not to believe?"

"The entire story for starters."

"Why would they lie?"

"Why wouldn't they?"

"Jeez, sometimes you are *such* a lawyer!"

"And sometimes, Kimmey, you are the most gullible person in the world. Okay, say the murder part is true. Did the club owner verify this?"

"Yeah, he's the first one who mentioned it! So there!"

"Okay, so say that part's true. Can you think of a better joke to play on a bunch of comedians than to tell them they're staying in a haunted house?"

"I don't think that's much of a joke."

"Some people would."

"Phoebe, you're losing your zest."

"I left it in my other suit."

DISCONNECT

SATURDAY, 12:06 A.M. CST (OUTGOING—HOME)

"Hello?"

"Well?"

"It's supposed to be happening right this second! You could have waited to call!"

"Is it happening?"

"I'll call you back!"

DISCONNECT

SATURDAY, 1:15 A.M., EST (INCOMING—HOME)

"Hello?"

"The phone ringing scared it!"

"I'm sure that must be true. I take it, then, that there were no lights nor movement in or around your townhouse tonight at precisely 1:06 A.M.?"

"You know, if you ever decide to give up law, you could become a professional pain in the ass."

"The pay's not nearly as good."

"It could be because we're here."

"Why are you there? You usually don't get out of a club until three or later."

"Marilyn and I took off as soon as our sets were over. We left the junkman to do his headliner thing."

"The junkman. I don't think I've heard of him."

"That's not his stage name or anything. Cleve Martell?"

"Oh, yeah, I saw him on Leno."

"Isn't that nice? Anyway, we, Marilyn and I, call him junkman because he has that fabulous new, ultra-chic junky look that's so *in* right now."

"Is he a junky?"

"I have no idea."

"So the two of you are just being mean."

"Hey, he's the headliner. It's our right."

"Have you told him about your ghost?"

"We haven't established as yet, Phoebe, that it *is* a ghost.

It could be a poltergeist or any number of other psychic disturbances. We're just not sure."

"Who's we?"

"Marilyn and Nancy and I."

"Nancy?"

"The next-door neighbor. We invited her to meet us over here to see if we could catch it. So far, so bad."

"Did you answer my question?"

"What question?"

"Good night, Kimberly."

DISCONNECT

SATURDAY, 4:06 A.M. EST (INCOMING—HOME)

"What?"

"There's someone in the house!"

"Kimmey? Why are you whispering?"

"There's someone in the house!"

"Then why did you call me? Call 911 for God's sake!"

"Oh."

DISCONNECT

SATURDAY, 3:35 A.M. CST (OUTGOING—HOME)

"Hello?"

"Did you call the police?"

"Yes."

"Why are you still whispering?"

"They're not here yet!"

"And you picked up the phone!?!"

"Don't scream. They might hear you."

"You think they might have heard the phone ringing?"

"Not now, Phoebe. Okay. Not now."

"What's going on?"

"Somebody's downstairs."

"Could it be the yardman?"

"Who?"

"The headliner!"

"Oh. The junkman. No, he's here with us now."

"Who's that talking?"

"Cleve. He doesn't like his nickname."

"Told you."

"Phoebe, I think I really should hang up now."

"Can you still hear them down there?"

"Yes."

"What are they doing?"

"Moving things around. Oh, God—"

"What is it?"

"They're on the stairs!"

"Kimmey—"

DISCONNECT

SATURDAY, 5:15 A.M. EST (INCOMING—HOME)

"Hello?"

"Hi."

"Oh, God, Kimmey, are you okay?"

"Yeah. Whoever it was was on the stairs when the cops started banging on the front door. We heard them scrambling down the stairs, but by the time the police got in, there was no one here."

"Is there a backdoor?"

"Yes. But these townhouses have high walls around them in the back and locked gates."

"Well, a high wall to you is not necessarily a high wall to a normal person."

"Do you really think this is the time to take pot shots at my height?"

"Anytime is a good time to take pot shots at you about anything. You scared me to death last night."

"This morning."

"Whatever."

"What I'm trying to tell you is, I think it was the ghost."

"What was the ghost?"

"Whatever was on the stairs!"

"Why do you think it was the ghost? Although we have not yet established there *is* a ghost!"

"Because it just disappeared! We heard the footsteps—"

"Do ghosts have footsteps, Kimmey? Do ghosts even have feet?"

"God, sometimes you are so, so—"

"Logical? Rational? Right?"

"Unimaginative."

"Unimaginative?"

"Yes."

"Oh, really? Well, imagine *this*."

DISCONNECT

SATURDAY, 3:46 P.M. EST (INCOMING—HOME)

"Hello?"

"I'm sorry I called you unimaginative."

"I'm sorry you're such a gullible idiot."

"Phoebs, have I ever mentioned how bad you are at this accepting apologies stuff?"

"You're right. I accept your apology."

"Now apologize for calling me names."

"I didn't call you names."

"Maybe not to my face."

"I apologize for calling you names in my mind. How's that?"

"What did you call me?"

"Are we really going to go there?"

"You're right. But, let's face it, Phoebe, something strange is going on in this townhouse."

"You had a break-in. Fells Point's a beautiful spot, Kimmey, but it's not the safest in Baltimore."

"Which is why there are burglar bars on the doors and the windows. And in the courtyards. So how did our 'burglar' get *in*, much less *out*?"

"The police will figure that out."

"And how do you know Fells Point?"

"Um."

"Um what?"

"Well, I spent a lovely weekend in Baltimore once."

"With whom?"

"Never mind."

"Oh, God. When you were clerking for the senator, right? Had to be Ernest. Yuck."

"Ernest had his moments."

"Please don't elaborate. I'd rather not know."

"Let's talk about your ghost."

"Oh, really? You're willing to admit there's a ghost just so you don't have to admit to Ernest, huh?"

"I admitted to Ernest years ago. I've grown beyond that now. Let's talk about the break-in. What did the cops say?"

"That we're three kooks with overdeveloped imaginations."

"You *didn't* tell them about the ghost?"

"Well, it *might* have come up in conversation."

"You need to get out of the house. Go for a walk."

"I already did. Did I tell you we're only about four blocks from where they film *Homicide*?"

"What's that?"

"It's a TV show."

"Oh."

"But they're on hiatus. I was going to work on getting a walk-on, but nobody's there."

"Sorry. Take a nap."

"I did."

"Stop whining."

"Why?"

"Bye, Kimmey. Be careful."

"Um."

DISCONNECT

SUNDAY, 1:06 A.M. EST (INCOMING—HOME)

"Hello?"

"It's here!"

"You're whispering again!"

"It's here! The ghost! It's 1:06 A.M. for God's sake!"

"No it's not, it's 12:06 A.M.—oh, never mind. What do you mean it's there? What's there?"

"The lights! The movement!"

"You see something moving around?"

"No, but we hear it."

"What is it?"

"I don't know!"

"Where are you?"

"In the living room."

"Where is *it*?"

"In the hall outside the living room."

"And you don't see it?"

"No."

"Go out in the hall!"

"We can't. The door's locked from the outside."

"Oh, my God."

"Give me a boost and I'll look through the transom—"

"Who are you talking to?"

"Marilyn. There's a transom over the door into the hall. She's going to boost me up—"

"Don't hang up!"

"No, I'm on my cell phone. I'll take you with me. Umpth. Okay, we're going up. Ouch. Yeah, got it. Don't jiggle me! Jeez. No, I can't see diddly."

"Kimmey, what's going on?"

"The hall's dark. I can't see anything— What the hell?"

"What is it? What's going on? Oh, God, are you all right?"

"No, there's something written here on top of the door jamb— Ahh."

LOUD NOISE FOLLOWED BY UNINTELLIGIBLE VOICES

"Kimmey!?! Kimmey!"

"Ouch, are you still there?"

"What happened?"

"Carmen dropped me."

"What time is it?"

"Way past 1:06 A.M., I'll tell you that much."

"Are the lights and movement still going on?"

"How would I know? We've been making so damn much noise. Yes, it is too your fault!"

"Who are you talking to?"

"Carmen! Well, then you shouldn't have told me, should you? I'll damn well call you Carmen if I want to! It's your legal name!"

"Kimberly!"

"What?"

"You realize you can badger Carmen or Marilyn or whatever the hell her name is for free, right? You don't have to be charging it to your cell phone."

"Right. Anyway, it's gone now."

"The ghost?"

"Aha! I knew you believed!"

"I'm just calling it that for want of something more con-
crete. Is the door still locked?"

"Check the door. See if it's locked. It's not locked. Go
look. No, you go, I'm on the phone. Okay, jeez. We're going
to look, Phoebe. Wanna come?"

"Wouldn't miss it for the world."

"Turn on the lights. Right there next to your hand, dufus.
Nothing."

"What was that you were saying about something written
on the top of the door jamb?"

"Oh, yeah. Weirdest thing. I couldn't really read it. The
light was bad, but there was something written up there."

"Well, get a flashlight and go see."

"I'm not letting her lift me up there again!"

"How about a chair?"

"These ceilings are twelve feet high in here."

"A ladder?"

"We don't have a ladder or we would have used it before,
duh."

"Then you lift Marilyn—"

"You are *out* of your mind."

"Kimberly, it could be a clue."

"What could be a clue?"

"Whatever's written on top of the door jamb!"

"Oh, yeah, Nancy Drew. Golly gee, I bet it's a clue."

"I'm hanging up now. Don't call me again, please."

"Jeez. All right. Marilyn, where's the flashlight? I don't
know what flashlight! Don't we have a flashlight? You
should always travel with a flashlight! Do as I say, not as I
do. Get that lamp. No! God. The small one, dumb ass. Because you are lifting me back up here so I can see what is
written on the door jamb. Because the lawyer on the other

end of this line thinks it might be a clue. Yeah, I know. But we should humor her."

"I'm really ready to hang up here."

"Oh, just hold your water, as my pawpaw's fond of saying. Okay, I can't juggle the phone and the lamp. I'm giving you to Marilyn."

"Hello?"

"Marilyn?"

"Yes?"

"This is Phoebe."

"Hi, Phoebe."

"Hi."

"Okay, augh, I'm lifting her up now. God, you weigh a ton! Ninety-eight pounds my ass. Phoebe, you there?"

"I don't believe that ninety-eight-pound business either, Marilyn."

"If you ever had to lift her you'd know for sure she was lying. Yes, Kimmey. You're lying. You're at least a hundred and twenty! Wait. She's got it. Okay. Read it. Okay. It says, 'Mid-East Cryo, 84W93J7.' What the hell does that mean?"

"Beats me."

"Ouch. Well, get down. Hold on, Phoebe."

"Phoebe?"

"Yes, Kimmey. Mid-east Cryo. What's that?"

"Marilyn, get a phone book!"

"Cryogenics?"

"Like freezing dead bodies? Lovely. Wait, here's the phone book. Mid-East Applied Freight, Mid-East Boiler Makers, Mid-East Cabinet Makers . . . Here it is. You were right. Mid-East Cryogenics. Gross."

"Wait, now. They do more with cryogenics than dead bodies. Actually, very little is actually being done with dead bodies. Or dying bodies. What they use cryogenics for most is sperm and eggs and the like for reproductive purposes."

"No kidding? Marilyn, use the house phone and call them!"

"At 1:30 in the morning?"

"Damn, you're right. And there probably won't be anybody there until Monday! Shit!"

"Kimmey, just get some sleep. Did you write it down?"

"What?"

"The number."

"Damn. Marilyn, boost me back up."

"I think I'll pass on this trip."

"Bye."

DISCONNECT

SUNDAY, 4:14 P.M. CST (OUTGOING—OFFICE)

"Hello?"

"Hey. I'm at the office. Thought you might have tried to call me—"

"I was sleeping."

"Ha! Gotcha!"

"I'm glad you're able to get such joy out of the simple things in life, Phoebe. I really am."

"Did you try to call that cryo place?"

"On Sunday?"

"There has to be someone there all the time."

"Yeah, well, we tried. That was our thinking. But we only got a recording. Their business hours are Monday through Friday, 8 A.M. to 5 P.M."

"How un-high-tech of them."

"My feelings exactly."

"Y'all doing a show tonight?"

"Last one. I'm supposed to be out of here on a noon flight

to Tucson tomorrow. Hope I can get some answers before I have to leave."

"This could become an unsolved mystery, Kimmey."

"Hurry, call Robert Stack."

"Why?"

"Jeez. It's a joke. *Unsolved Mysteries*, Phoebs. It's a TV show."

"Oh. Another television reference."

"You realize you are missing out on a large part of Americana, don't you?"

"*Hee-Haw* and *My Mother the Car*? I'll live."

"Speaking of which, they're rerunning *Fantasy Island* here at 4:30. Gotta run."

"You realize your mind is a cesspool, don't you?"

"And a quagmire. Bye."

DISCONNECT

MONDAY, 1:00 A.M. EST (INCOMING—HOME)

"Hello?"

"Thought I'd call you early so we can witness it together. Marilyn's tired of the game."

"I'm with Marilyn."

"Surely you weren't sleeping? It's barely midnight there."

"When one must be at court at 9 A.M., necessitating that one be in one's office by 7 A.M. to confer with one's minions, one tries to get to bed at a reasonable hour, which precludes phone calls from bozos past midnight."

"Weirdest thing happened."

"You didn't hear a word I said."

"I heard it. I just decided not to acknowledge it."

"Your prerogative."

"Thank you. Anyway, Marilyn and the junkman and I

decided to stop on our way to the club to get a bite to eat at that Irish pub I was telling you about?"

"Uh huh."

"Anyway, Nancy, our next-door neighbor?"

"Right."

". . . was in there. And we told her about last night. And about finding the stuff written on the top of the door jamb, and I swear, Phoebs, she came unglued. Wanted to know what it said. If we'd written it down."

"What did you tell her?"

"Not a damn thing. She pissed me off. Grabbed my arm, for God's sake."

"The nerve."

"My sentiments exactly. Marilyn started to blab, but I kicked her and she shut up. Which is probably why she didn't come home with me tonight."

"Obviously wears her feelings on her sleeve."

"Exactly. Very touchy woman. Anyway, this Nancy person is number one on my Superglue list."

"Fingers or eyelids?"

"Definitely eyelids. Phoebe, she grabbed my arm. I may bruise."

"What time is it?"

"One oh five and a half."

"Where are you in the house?"

"Sitting on the stairs. Which is in the hallway where all the commotion was last night."

"Are the lights on?"

"Nope, I'm sitting in the dark."

"Should you be talking so loud?"

"Probably not—Shh. I hear something."

"Oh, God, Kimmey—"

"Shh."

THIRTY-SEVEN SECONDS OF SILENCE

"Aha!"

"Kimmey, what is it?"

"What are you doing here? You really don't need the gun. I really think you should put that down—"

DISCONNECT

MONDAY, 12:08 A.M. CST (OUTGOING—HOME)

"Third Precinct, Marshall."

"My friend is being held at gunpoint at this place she's staying in Fells Point!"

"What's the address, ma'am?"

"I don't know."

"How do you know she's being held at gunpoint, ma'am?"

"We were on the phone! Listen. Call the comedy club in Fells Point. Ah. God. What's the name? Giggles! Something like that! You know it?"

"Never heard of it, ma'am."

"That's the name of the club, I'm sure. Giggles or something like that. The owner of the club owns the house where my friend's being held at gunpoint. Kimmey Kruse. That's my friend. The owner can tell you the address of the house. She's being held at gunpoint, for God's sake!"

"Ma'am, you got a phone number I can look up the address in the City CrissCross Directory."

"Oh, God, yes. I never thought of that. 555-7348. The area code is—"

"Ma'am, I know the area code."

"Right. Okay. Just hurry, please?"

"Ma'am, I got somebody on their way there now. If you'll just stay on the line and let me get some information—"

"Don't have time. Sorry."

DISCONNECT

MONDAY, 12:15 A.M. CST (OUTGOING—HOME)

"Hello?"

"Kimmey?"

"She can't come to the phone right now."

"Marilyn?"

"She's not here right now. May I take a message?"

"Nancy?"

". . . Who's this?"

"Is this Nancy?"

"Who's calling?"

"Nancy, this is Phoebe, Kimmey's friend."

"Kimmey can't come to the phone right now."

"Nancy, is she all right?"

"She's sorta tied up at the moment. Ha, ha, ha."

"Nancy, I don't understand what's going on. Please tell me."

"Who did you say this was?"

"This is Phoebe. I'm Kimmey's friend. Her very close friend."

"Are you lovers?"

"No. More like sisters."

"Oh."

"We've been best friends since we were both thirteen, Nancy. Have you ever had a friend like that?"

"I need to hang up now—"

"No! Nancy, please. Don't hang up. Please."

"Why not?"

"How's Kimmey? Is she okay?"

"She's fine. Really. She just can't come to the phone right now."

"Why, Nancy?"

"Ha, ha, ha. Cause she's all tied up."

"Have you tied Kimmey up?"

"You're very quick."

"Why? Nancy, why did you tie Kimmey up?"

"Because she's in my way."

"Nancy. Listen to me. Kimmey's not in your way, I promise you—"

"Look, you don't know squat. Okay? Where are you anyway?"

"Texas."

"See? What do you know? You're in Texas. We're here. Kimmey and I. Right, Kimmey? We're here and she's there and never the twain shall meet. Ha, ha, ha."

"Could I speak to her, Nancy? Just to make sure she's all right?"

"You don't trust me?"

"I don't know you, Nancy."

"Oh. You have a point. Just a minute."

"Hello?"

"Kimmey?"

"Hey, Phoebs."

"Are you all right?"

"Depends on your definition—"

"Has she hurt you?"

"Not at the moment, but I'm not looking forward to this duct tape she has on my arms coming off. All those little hairs—"

"Kimmey! For crying out loud! What's going on?"

"I'm not totally sure."

"Well, I'll tell you."

"Nancy?"

"Right. Try to keep up."

"Right."

"You tell your friend Kimmey here that she gives me the

numbers for the Cryo Lab or I do terrible things to her. Got
that?"

"Let me talk to her."

"Okay."

"Hello?"

"Kimmey?"

"Yes!"

"Give her the numbers to the Cryo Lab."

"I'd love to, but I can't."

"Why can't you, for God's sake!!"

"Well, I showed her where they were, on top of the door
jamb, but when she climbed up there they were all smudged.
Must have happened when I was up there."

"Didn't you write them down?"

"No."

"Yes, you did."

"No, Phoebe, *I didn't*."

"Can she hear what I'm saying?"

"Probably."

"What's this all about?"

"I don't know."

"Let me talk to Nancy."

"Hello?"

"Nancy?"

"Yes!"

"I called the police."

"You what!?!"

"They're on their way now—"

"Jesus!"

LOUD SOUND AS IF PHONE IS DROPPED TO FLOOR

"Kimmey? Kimmey? Can you hear me?"

"Phoebe! Hold on! Wait! Ow! Hold on! Phoebe?"

"Are you okay?"

"My hands are tied behind me, my feet are bound, my

head and my knees are both on the floor and my butt's sticking up in the air. But, yeah, I'm just dandy!"

"Why is your head on the floor?"

"Because that's where the phone is. Duh."

"Where's Nancy?"

"She went into the closet under the stairs."

"What's she doing in there?"

"God knows."

"Kimmey, those are townhouses, right?"

"Yes, but I'm not up to discussing architecture at the moment—"

"With common walls?"

"Yes!"

"Are the stairs on a common wall?"

"Yes, but what the— Oh, my God. Nancy's the ghost."

"I'm thinking that."

"There's some sort of passage between this townhouse and hers next door."

"That's what I'm thinking."

"Wow. Ghosts, bondage, secret passages. *What* a fun weekend I'm having."

"Where are the police?"

"I'm wondering that myself. You *did* call them?"

"What? You think I'd make that up? Or maybe I'm not *sure* if I called them?"

"Wait! I hear them now!"

"You sure it's them?"

LOUD NOISES CAN BE HEARD

"Yeah. Gotta run. So to speak."

"Call me!"

"I will and, Phoebe—"

"What?"

"Thanks."

"No problem."

DISCONNECT

MONDAY, 3:07 A.M., EST (INCOMING—HOME)

"Kimmey?"

"You waited up."

"Are you all right?"

"You know what I said about those little hairs and the duct tape? I was absolutely right. Remember when we both went for those bikini wax jobs?"

"Kimmey—"

"It was sorta like that, but actually not as bad. I'm thinking childbirth wouldn't be as bad as *that* experience."

"Kimmey, for God's sake. What's going on?"

"There are cops running around everywhere. Marilyn's taken two Valium and still can't get to sleep. Cleve is following this female officer around everywhere she goes. And there's this one plainclothes guy who's really cute—"

"Where's Nancy!?!"

"No one knows. Her car's gone and they've got an APB out on her."

"An APB? Just for holding you at gunpoint?"

"Well, personally I think holding me at gunpoint is worth the chair, but that's not really the point. The point is Dan—he's the cute plainclothes guy—Dan says he's been suspicious from the start about the murder/suicide. He thinks Nancy did it."

"Why?"

"Well, there was talk in the neighborhood that she spent a *lot* of time in this townhouse. More than in her own."

"Ah hah. She and the husband—"

"Nope. She and the wife."

"Oh. Did you tell Dan about the cryo lab?"

"Yeah. They've got someone going out there to see if she could be there."

"What's it all about, Kimmey?"

"I don't know. But I'm thinking. You said mostly cryo labs work on reproductive stuff, right?"

"Yes."

"And those numbers I found. They've got to be an ID number or case number or something like that, right?"

"Makes sense. But why put them on top of the door jamb?"

"Whoa. Wait a minute. How's this? The wife steals her husband's sperm while he's sleeping—"

"How?"

"I don't know. Maybe she slips him a mickey. Anyway, she steals his sperm and has it frozen at the cryo lab so when she and Nancy run off together they can have a baby."

"So Nancy kills her lover and her lover's husband and now her deepest desire is to be a single mother carrying the child of her lover's husband? Really good, Kimmey."

"Well, you come up with something— Wait. Dan wants me. In more ways than one, I'm sure. Gotta run."

"You're leaving Baltimore in just a few hours, Kimmey. Try to remember that."

"Bye."

•

DISCONNECT

MONDAY, 11:15 A.M., EST (INCOMING—OFFICE)

"Phoebe Love."

"Hi."

"Where are you?"

"The airport. Dan brought me. He's here. Wanna say hi?"

"Hello?"

"Hi, Dan?"

"Yeah. Phoebe? Heard a lot about you."

"None of it's true."

"I was hoping not."

"May I speak to Kimmey?"

"Sure, hold on."

"Hey."

"Kimmey, I hate it when you do that."

"Do what?"

"Stick some strange man on the phone to talk to me."

"Like I do it a lot."

"Have they found Nancy?"

"Oh, yes. She was at the cryo lab."

"But she never got the numbers from you, right?"

"No. But when they found her she had a turkey baster in one hand and some frozen embryos in the other."

"TMI, Kimmey."

"Huh?"

"Too much information."

"Tell me about it. Anyway, she's been singing loud and long since about six this morning. She says it was more or less an accident that she killed the couple."

"An accident?"

"Yeah. She accidentally walked in on them while they were making love—this was after Wanda—the wife—told her she and Derek—the husband—hadn't made love in over a year. Anyway, Nancy accidentally got Derek's gun out of his bedside table and accidentally blew them both away."

"I can see that. Okay, but what about the sperm?"

"Not sperm. Embryos. Half a dozen of them. I didn't realize this myself, not being a DINK—dual income no kids—"

"I know what a DINK is. I used to be one."

"Right. Anyway, Wanda and Derek stored the embryos until such time as they might want to actually have a child. Storing them helped somehow with the blood line. For instance, if Derek were to die in a car wreck, Wanda would still be able to have his child, thus giving the horse breeders in Virginia a grandchild. Which is what Nancy decided to do."

"You lost me."

"Nancy knew about the embryos because—okay and here I was partially right—Wanda was going to leave Derek so she gave him a phony number for the embryos. According to Nancy, Wanda told her she hid the number in the house, but didn't tell her where. The plan was Wanda and Nancy were going to have Derek's baby and make a little something extra from the horse-breeding grandparents."

"Lovely people."

"Well, with Wanda dead, Nancy figured she'd impregnate herself with Derek's and Wanda's embryo and—with the proof in the records at the cryo lab, not to mention DNA—she could hold up not only the horse-breeding grandparents but Congressman Grandpa on the other side as well."

"That's disgusting."

"I thought so."

"*Did* you write down the numbers from the cryo lab?"

"What numbers?"

"Kimmey—"

"You know, with a little ketchup, even paper goes down easily."

"You didn't!"

"There's my plane. See you in ten days!"

"Kimmey! We have to talk! Don't you dare—"

DISCONNECT

If all the miles I've traveled while promoting my books were added up, I'm sure they would equal more than one trip around the world. Still, whether I'm in Los Angeles or London, there's always something to be said for manners and common courtesy when traveling. And occasionally something as simple as the lack of these can lead to the most terrible crimes.

Brodie and the Regrettable Incident of the French Ambassador

Anne Perry

"Really?" Colette raised her delicate eyebrows in an expression of surprise and implied contempt. "You allow the cook to do it for you? In France we always prefer to boil our own." She was referring to the rice, the water from which was used to stiffen linens and muslins. "One can get so much better a consistency," she continued, looking at Brodie with a very slight smile.

They were in the ironing room of Jamie Seaforth's country home. Colette was the young and very pretty lady's maid of Mrs. Violet Welch-Smith, house guest, and wife to General Bertrand Welch-Smith. Brodie was considerably older, of a comfortable rather than handsome appearance, although

she had possessed a considerable charm in her youth. Now
the first thing one noticed about her was intelligence and an
air of good sense and a sharp but suitably concealed hu-
mour. She was lady's maid to Hannah Peverell, Jamie
Seaforth's widowed sister. Since he was unmarried, he always invited Hannah to act as hostess when he had a house
party he felt of importance, or where he was concerned he
would be out of his depth. Violet Welch-Smith was a
woman to give any man such a feeling.

Colette was still regarding Brodie with an air of superiority, waiting for an answer.

"Yes I do," Brodie replied, referring to the cook and the
rice water. "Cooks, especially in other people's houses, prefer that visiting servants do not attempt to perform tasks in
the kitchen. They invariably get in the way and disrupt the
order of things, upset the scullery maids, boot boys and un-
dercooks."

"Perhaps that is what happened at the last house where we
stayed," Colette retorted, changing the flat iron she was
using on her mistress's petticoat for a warmer one from the
stove. "The food was certainly not of the quality we are accustomed to in France." She looked very directly at Brodie.
"I had not realized that that was the cause."

Brodie was furious. Normally she was of a very equable
temper, but Colette had been trumpeting the innate superiority of everything French, both in general and in particular,
ever since she had arrived nearly two days ago. This was
enough to try the patience of a saint . . . an English saint
anyway, most particularly a north country one, used to plain
ideas and plain speech. Unfortunately she could not at the
moment think of a crushing reply; she merely seethed inside
and kept a polite but somewhat chilly smile on her face.

Colette knew her advantage, but pushed it too far.

"Do you think your cook would be able to manage rice

water as well as preparing dinner for guests?" she said charmingly. "Would it be kinder not to ask it of her?"

Brodie opened her eyes very wide. "I had not realized you were attempting to be kind!" she said with exaggerated surprise. Then she smiled straight at Colette, this time quite naturally. "Perhaps a French cook would find it an embarrassment, but our cook is English, she is quite used to being helpful to the rest of the staff." And with that she picked up the enamel jug sitting on the bench and swept out with it. "I shall ask her immediately," she called back, before Colette could think of a response.

She made her request in the kitchen and was on her way towards the back stairs when she all but bumped into the imposing figure of Winchester, Jamie Seaforth's butler. He was a most dignified and correct person whose acquaintance she had made rather more closely the previous summer.

"Good afternoon, Mr Winchester," she said somewhat startled. He was eight inches taller than she, of magnificent stature. He had probably been a footman in his distant youth. Footmen were picked for their appearance. Height and good legs were especially required. A poor leg was most observable when a man was in livery.

"Good afternoon, Miss Brodie," Winchester replied stiffly. She disconcerted him, and he had not yet worked out why, although he had spent some time thinking about the matter. She was really quite agreeable, even if a trifle over-confident, and opinionated above her station. It was not becoming in a woman. But she had been of great assistance to him in that terrible business last July. A certain latitude was perhaps allowable. "A most pleasant day," he added. "I fancy the ladies will be enjoying the garden. Spring is one of the most attractive seasons, don't you think?"

"Most," she agreed.

He frowned. "Is something troubling you, Miss Brodie?

Is it a matter with which I could assist?" He owed her a certain consideration—a protection, if you like. She was a woman, and a visiting servant, and this was his house. Her welfare was his concern.

"I doubt it, Mr Winchester," she replied, her lips tight again at the thought of Colette. "I find Mrs Welch-Smith's maid very trying, that is all. She is convinced of the superiority of all things French, and she is at pains to say so."

"Ignorance," Winchester said immediately. "She is a foreigner, after all. She may not know any better."

"Stuff and nonsense!" Brodie snapped. "She is not in the least bit ignorant. She is simply . . ." She stopped abruptly. What she had been going to say was unbecoming to her. She closed her mouth.

Further down the corridor a maid went by with a dustpan in her hand.

"Fortunately the General's man, Harrison, is as English as we are," Winchester looked at her sympathetically. "In fact he seems to have very little liking for France or the French. Although naturally he is discreet about his remarks, merely an inflexion here or there which the sensitive ear may discern."

"I have barely seen him." Brodie thought about it for a moment. "Is he the rather portly young man with the brown eyes, or the fair haired man with the absentminded expression?"

"The fair haired man," Winchester answered. "The other is the coachman. But it is understandable you should be confused. Harrison spends at least as much time in the stable. I confess I don't think I have seen him in the laundry or the bootroom or the pantry. And the General looked rather as if he had dressed himself. I believe he shaves himself also."

"Then what is Harrison here for?" Brodie said curiously.

"That is a mystery which I have solved," Winchester

replied with satisfaction, a smile on his long-nosed, rather round-eyed face. "The General is an inventor, of sorts, and has brought with him his latest contraption, which is intended, so I believe, to clean and polish boots by means of electricity."

"Land sakes!" Brodie exclaimed. "Whatever for?"

"For something to do, I imagine," Winchester replied. "Gentlemen are largely at a loss for something to do."

"How does this concern Harrison?" Brodie asked.

"He is assembling it in the stables," Winchester answered. "Or at least he is assisting the General to do so, although I fancy he may be doing most of the work. However he seems to enjoy it, in fact to take a certain pride in it." A look of puzzlement crossed his rather complacent features. "There is no accounting for the difference in people's tastes, Miss Brodie."

"Indeed not," she said with feeling and proceeded up the stairs.

Dinner was an awkward meal, in spite of the unquestionable excellence of the food: a delicate consommé, fresh asparagus from the kitchen garden, picked at its tenderest, fresh trout grilled until it fell from the bone, a saddle of mutton, several kinds of vegetables, followed by apple pie and thick cream or trifle or fruit sorbet of choice. The awkwardness was caused largely by Violet Welch-Smith. Hannah Peverell could see very easily why her brother had wished assistance over the week. Violet was a difficult woman, and she believed in candour as a virtue, regardless of the discomfort it might cause. She was also an enthusiast.

"We had the most marvellous food in our recent trip to France." She looked at her husband who was sitting opposite her across the table. "Didn't we, Bertrand?"

Bertie Welch-Smith was unhappy. He thought the remark, just as they were finishing a meal provided by their host, to be unfortunate.

"Didn't care for it a lot, myself," he said with a frankness his wife should have admired. "Too many sauces. Like apple sauce with pork, or mint with lamb, or a spot of horse-radish now and again, that's about all. Oh, and a good custard to go with a pudding of course."

Hannah hid a smile. She liked Bertie Welch-Smith. He was in his middle fifties, retired from a career in the army which was brave rather than brilliant. He had reached the rank of General in the old system of his father having purchased a commission for him, and then his turn for promotion having come fortunately soon. A single escapade of extraordinary valour in the Ashanti wars had brought him to the favourable notice of his superiors. He was not a naturally belligerent man; in fact he was not unlike Jamie Seaforth himself: good natured, rather shy, something of a bumbler except in his particular enthusiasms. For Jamie it was his garden, a thing of extraordinary beauty with flowers and trees from all over the world. For Bertie Welch-Smith it was mechanical inventions."

"You need to cultivate your taste more," Violet said earnestly.

"What?" Bertie was already thinking of something else.

"Cultivate your taste," she repeated slowly, as if he were foolish rather than merely inattentive. "The French are the most cultured nation on earth, you know?" She turned to Hannah. "They really know how to live well. We have a great deal to learn from them."

Jamie stiffened and looked at Hannah with desperation.

"I think living well is rather a matter of personal preference," Hannah said with a smile. "Fortunately we do not all like the same things."

"But we could learn to!" Violet urged, leaning forward

across the table. The lights of the chandeliers winked in the crystal and the silver. The last of the dishes had been cleared away. Winchester came in with the port. The ladies did not retire, since there were only four people present altogether. They took a little Madeira instead and remained.

"Do tell Jamie and Hannah about our stay in France, Bertie," Violet commanded. "I am sure they would be most interested."

Bertie frowned. "I had rather thought of going for a stroll. Take Jamie to see my new machine, what?"

"Later, if you must," she dismissed his plea. "It is a harmless enough occupation, I suppose, but there is absolutely no requirement for such a thing, you know? There are valets and boot boys to polish one's shoes, should they require it. Which brings something to mind." She barely paused for breath, her Madeira ignored. "Do tell Jamie how you found poor Harrison and employed him. A French valet is a wonderful thing to have, Hannah; and a French lady's maid is even better. I cannot tell you the number and variety of skills that girl has." And she proceeded to tell her, detail after detail.

Bertie attempted to interrupt but it was doubtful in Hannah's mind if Violet even heard him. Her enthusiasm waxed strong, and Bertie's eyes took on a faraway look, although Hannah guessed they were really no greater distance than the stable and his beloved machine.

"So very modern," Violet gushed. "We really are old-fashioned here." Her hands gesticulated, describing some facet of French culture, her face intent.

"I say!" Jamie protested. "That's hardly fair. We are the best inventors in the world!"

She was not to be deterred. "Perhaps we used to be," she swept on. "But the French are now . . . endlessly inventive . . . and really useful things . . ."

Bertie opened his mouth, then closed it again. He looked vaguely crushed.

"You should tell them about finding Harrison," Violet glanced at him, then back to Jamie. "And French manservants are excellent too, not just capable of one skill, like ours, but of all manner of things. Bertie never ceases to sing Harrison's praises."

"Harrison is English!" Bertie said with umbrage. "Dammit Violet, he is as English as steak and kidney pudding!"

"But trained in France!" she retorted instantly. "That makes all the difference. His mind is French."

"Balderdash!" He was growing pink in the face. "He speaks the language because he spent time there. That was where we found him. But he was more than happy to return home again with us . . . his home. He made that very plain, at least to me."

"I never heard him say that!"

Hannah hid a smile behind her napkin, pretending to sneeze.

"You don't listen . . ." Bertie muttered.

"What did you say?" Violet looked at him sharply.

"He said you don't . . ." Jamie began.

Hannah kicked him under the table. He winced and opened his eyes very wide.

Hannah smiled charmingly. "He said he won't miss it," she lied without blinking. "I presume he meant that Harrison won't miss France, when he has been with you for a while. After all, you have adopted so many French ways, haven't you? And you have a French maid yourself, so he can always speak the language, if he chooses."

Violet looked confounded for a moment. She knew something had passed her by, but she was not quite sure what.

Hannah rose to her feet. "Shall we go for a stroll in the

garden?" she suggested. "There is a clear sky and a full moon. I think it would be very beautiful."

Jamie sighed with relief. Bertie's face broke into a smile. Violet was obliged to agree; mere civility demanded it.

The following morning Brodie woke Hannah with a hot cup of tea and drew the curtains to a brilliant spring day with light and shadow chasing each other across the land. A huge aspen, green with leaf, shivered in the breeze and the garden glistened from overnight rain. Hannah's clothes were ready, since she had decided the previous evening what she would wear. After a few exchanges of pleasantries Brodie left to draw the bath and came face to face with Colette on the landing, looking efficient and very pretty, and—to Brodie's eyes—a trifle smug.

She looked even more pleased with herself two hours later when Brodie encountered her in the kitchen. She had just come in from the back door and glancing towards it, Brodie saw a nice-looking, if rather foreign, young man in the yard, somewhere between the coal chute and the rubbish bins. He seemed to hesitate for a moment, as though undecided whether to leave or return, but Colette did not look back, and indeed she flushed with colour as she caught Brodie's eye. But there was no way to know if it was annoyance or embarrassment. Brodie thought the former.

A junior housemaid, a girl of about twelve, passed by with a bucket full of damp tea leaves for cleaning the carpet. They were excellent for picking up the dust. She nodded to Brodie respectfully and walked past Colette as if she had not seen her. Brodie assumed she was another victim of the superiority of all things French. What did the French clean their carpets with? She had heard they did not drink tea! Coffee grounds would hardly serve. The very thought of it was unpleasant.

The cook was giving orders for the day's menus. She was

a buxom woman with a face which at first glance seemed benign. But Brodie knew her well enough to be aware that a fierce temper lurked behind the wide, blue eyes and generous mouth. At the moment it was drawn tight as she caught Colette's smirk at the mention of custard for the suet pudding. "Yes?" she said challengingly.

Colette shrugged. "In France we 'ave more of the fruit and less of the suet," she said distinctly, but without looking at anyone. "It is lighter, you understand? Better for the digestion, and of course for the form." She was petite herself, beautifully curved, and moved almost like a dancer on a stage. Brodie felt a little squat and clumsy beside her. "Although you could be right," Colette went on with a delicate little shiver. "After all, the climate, it is so damp! Maybe you need all the suet fat to keep you warm." And without allowing time for anyone to think of a retaliation, she swept out, giving her skirts a little flick as she turned the corner.

"Oh!" the cook let out a snort of exasperation. "That girl! I swear if she comes in here one more time and tells me how good French cooking is, I'll . . I'll . . . I'll not be responsible!"

The kitchen maid muttered her agreement and heartfelt support.

Winchester arrived looking portentous. It was his job to keep the entire household in order, and domestic difficulties were his to deal with. He had anticipated trouble in his address to the servants in general in morning prayers before breakfast, but it appeared that might prove insufficient. He should have known the cook by now, but habit and duty were too strong. "I am sure you will always be responsible, Mrs Wimpole," he said smoothly. "You are the last person to let us down by behaving less than perfectly." He straightened his shoulders even further. "We must not allow other nationalities to think we do not know how to conduct ourselves . . . even if they do not."

Mrs Wimpole snorted again and banged her wooden spoon so hard on the kitchen table that she all but broke it. The scullery maid dropped a string of onions and gave a yelp.

"We all have our own difficulties to bear," Winchester said sententiously.

"Leastways Mr 'Arrison in't French," the boot boy said venomously, looking at Winchester as boldly as he dared. "And no visitin' General in't makin' a machine wot'll take away yer job from yer." He looked thoroughly unhappy and frightened, his blue eyes wide, his blond hair standing slightly on end. The housekeeper had cut it rather badly when Winchester had been absent, up in London with Jamie.

"It won't take your job, Willie," Brodie said comfortingly. "I don't suppose for a moment it works, and even if it did, do you imagine any gentleman would use it himself?"

"Mr Seaforth is all-fired keen on it, Miss," Willie said doubtfully. "'Im or Mr. 'Arrison and the General is out there in the stables playin' wif it every chance they gets."

"They are assembling it, Willie," Winchester broke in. "That is entirely different."

"I don't see no difference," Willie replied, but he did look rather more hopeful.

"Of course there is a difference," Brodie reassured him. "In fact there is no relation. Putting it together is invention, a very suitable occupation for a gentleman, keeping him out of the house and harmlessly busy. Operating it every day to clean shoes would be work, and entirely unsuitable. Whoever heard of a gentleman cleaning his own boots?"

Willie was almost mollified. There was only one last hurdle to clear.

"Wot if 'e 'specs Mr Winchester ter use it, seein' as it's a machine, an invention, like, and Mr Winchester's clever, as is 'is butler, an' 'e don't keep a separate valet?"

Winchester stiffened.

"Butlers don't clean boots," Brodie pronounced without hesitation. "Regardless of how clever they are."

"Oh . . . well I s'pose it's alright then."

"Of course it's alright," Brodie said briskly. "There is no reason whatever for you to worry."

After a late and excellent breakfast of the sort Bertie Welch-Smith most enjoyed—eggs, bacon, sausages, kidneys, crisp-fried potatoes and tomatoes, followed by toast and sharp, dark Dundee marmalade and several cups of strong Ceylon tea, all of which he had sorely missed in France—he and Jamie went out to the stables to tinker with the machine.

"Ah!" Bertie said with satisfaction, patting his stomach. "Can't tell you, old chap, how I missed a decent breakfast in France. Don't mistake me, food's very good, and all that, but I do like a proper cup of tea in the mornings. Don't care for coffee much, what? And I like a little real marmalade, some of the stuff you can taste, not all these damn pastries that fall to bits in your hand."

"Quite," Jamie agreed. He had never been to France, but he did not approve in principle. He did not dislike many people. One had to be either dishonest or unkind to offend Jamie, but he did dislike Violet Welch-Smith, although he would not have dreamed of letting Bertie see that. Bertie was both his guest and his friend, and therefore sacred on both counts.

They strolled side by side in the sun towards the stables and the marvellous machine.

"And then you must come and see my magnolias," Jamie

said hopefully. "I've got some purple ones which really are very fine, if I say so myself."

"Certainly, old boy," Bertie agreed. "Delighted!" He did not know what a magnolia was, but that was irrelevant. Jamie was a good fellow.

Brodie busied herself about her duties. There was delicate personal laundry to be done. There was a spot of candlewax on the gown Hannah had worn the previous evening, and she must take it to the ironing room and press it between blotting paper with a warm iron. She would have to remove the pink with a little colourless alcohol. Gin was best. It was a tedious job, but it was the only way. Then naturally there would be a great deal of other ironing to do. A lady's maid's accomplishments were many, but Hannah very seldom desired to be read to or otherwise entertained. She always found more than sufficient to occupy herself. Anyway, she was obliged to accompany Violet and listen continuously to her endless account of her sojourn in France and its sophisticated pleasures.

Just before midday Brodie was walking through the hall towards the conservatory to deliver a message when she saw the newspapers lying on the table near the umbrella stand. It was the local newspaper and had obviously been read and cast aside because it was open at the centre page. She glanced at it and her eye was caught by an advertisement for an exhibition of modern inventions, to be held in the town. Apparently it was most remarkable for the variety and ingeniousness of the machines. In fact in two days' time the French Ambassador himself was going to open the exhibition formally. In the meantime, it was possible for local people to take a preview on the following afternoon, if they should so wish.

Brodie was not interested in machines. On the whole she

considered them inferior to a mixture of industry and a little common sense. But perhaps she should keep abreast of ideas, even if only to know what they were and ease the minds of poor souls like the boot boy.

Tomorrow was her afternoon off. There was really very little for her to do here. All but the most urgent of jobs would wait until she returned home. It would be a pleasant diversion from having to be civil to Colette. The matter was decided. She made a mental note of the time and the place and continued with her errand to the conservatory.

Winchester also saw the newspaper, but the copy that caught his eye was the one that Jamie had read and cast away, folded where he had finished it. Winchester bent to tidy it quite automatically. Books and papers out of alignment, pictures crooked, odd socks, a smear on a glass, all scraped his sensibilities. As he folded the papers neatly his eye fell on the advertisement for an exhibition of the latest inventions to be held in the town hall, preview for local persons with a scientific interest possible tomorrow. Winchester most certainly had a scientific interest. He was eager to acquaint himself with all things modern and to keep up with the latest challenges and conquests of the intelligent man.

If Mr Seaforth would permit it, he would make a brief sortie into the town and observe what was on display. The household would take care of itself quite adequately between say two o'clock and half past four tomorrow afternoon. He wold be home again in plenty of time to make sure that everyone did their duty at dinner. There was no need to mention it to anyone except Mr Seaforth. Mrs Wimpole would be about her own skills in the kitchen, the footmen did not need to know anything except when he would return, and it was not a suitable matter to discuss with Miss Brodie. After all, scientific inventions were hardly woman's business.

• • •

The evening was long and punctuated with moments of definite unease. Violet Welch-Smith kept repeating recipes for food that was supposed to be remarkably good for the health, which embarrassed her husband, though not greatly. He was too rapt in his satisfaction with his boot polishing machine, which Harrison had assured him was now perfect. Jamie endeavoured not to listen, simply to make agreeable noises every time Violet stopped talking long enough. Hannah kept the peace as well as she could, and her temper as well as she thought possible.

Brodie had the curious experience of seeing Colette's admirer again. It was just after ten in the evening and she was coming back from fetching a petticoat she had inadvertently left in the ironing room, when she saw Colette standing in the passageway with her back to the light, and not a foot away from her was the man Brodie had seen her with before. This time he was facing the light and she saw his features quite distinctly. He was very dark with fine brows and a slightly aquiline nose. She judged he would normally be a very pleasant looking man, but at this moment his expression was one of earnestness bordering upon anger, and he was whispering fiercely to Colette something which seemed not to please her at all.

"Auguste, c'est impossible!" she said furiously.

Brodie did not speak French, but the meaning of that phrase was clear enough, as was Colette's defiant stance, hands on hips, chin raised, shoulders stiff.

Something must have distracted Auguste—perhaps the light reflecting on Brodie's face or the faintest of rustles as the fabric of her dress brushed against the wall. He turned and left so quickly, melting into the shadows of the passageway back to the door, that had she not seen the look on

Colette's face, she might have supposed he had been a fig-
ment of her imagination and not a real person at all.

Brodie disliked Colette profoundly, but to tell tales was a
contemptible thing to do, something she had never sunk to
since one dismal episode in her youth which she preferred
not to think of now. She contented herself with looking at
Colette meaningfully, to Colette's discomfort, and then with
a decided swing in her own step, she continued on her way.

The following afternoon Brodie, with Hannah's good
wishes, dressed in her best afternoon skirt and jacket, a
green which became her very well, and set out to walk
briskly into the town. It was only a matter of some two miles
or so, and she expected to accomplish it in half an hour. It
was an extremely agreeable day, mild and bright with a
steady breeze carrying the heady scents of hawthorn blos-
som. There were still primroses pale on the dark banks of
the ditches. Birds sang, and far away over the fields a dog
barked. Other than that there was no sound but the wind in
the trees and her own footsteps on the road.

The exhibition was very well signposted and she found it
immediately. There were few people attending, which was
fortunate. It would give her time to look for the General's
device without being hurried on.

The first machine which caught her attention was a travelling electric stairlamp, made by Monsieur Armand
Marat—obviously a Frenchman with a name like that. In
fact about everything she saw in the first room appeared to
be invented, designed or made by a Frenchman.

She passed to the second room, but before she could examine the machines in it, she saw the back of a very upright
man of robust physique, his clothes immaculate, his hair
greying and perfectly barbered, a completely unnecessary
furled umbrella in his hand. What was Winchester doing

here? She considered retreating, then was furious with herself. Why on earth should she allow Winchester's presence to dictate what she should do? She would not be driven out!

"Good afternoon, Mr Winchester," she said decisively.

He turned around very slowly, his face almost comical with surprise. "Miss Brodie! What on earth are you doing here? Has something happened?" Now he looked alarmed.

"Yes, something has happened!" she said disgustedly. "It appears that the French have stolen a march on us. All the inventions in this miserable place are French! There is barely a single exhibit that is English that I have seen! It is most disconcerting."

"I agree," he said unhappily. "It is most regrettable. However I can think of nothing whatever to do about it, except take defeat like gentlemen . . . and ladies. To concede defeat with grace at least has dignity, and that we must never lose, Miss Brodie. Stiff upper lip in times of hardship."

Brodie disliked conceding defeat at all, even if she were rigid to her eyebrows.

"Is there nothing British here at all?" she asked.

"Only the General's boot polishing machine," Winchester said grimly. "I fear it is hardly a great cultural step forward for mankind, nor will it be of particular benefit to anyone at all. As you quite reasonably pointed out to young William, it is merely a toy for gentlemen, until they tire of it and find a new one. Probably the best that can be said of it is that it is not dangerous. No one will cut off their fingers or set fire to the house with it."

Brodie sighed. "I suppose we had better have a look at it, since we are here anyway." She gazed around her. "Where is it?"

"It is in the next room, where the curator is. Although

what harm he imagines could come to any of these, I don't
know. I suppose someone might try to use one of them?"

Brodie gave him a withering look.

He shrugged.

Side by side, but not touching, they made their way to the
third room and its exhibits. The curator was standing in the
centre. On the wall by the door as one would leave was a
poster declaring proudly that the event would be opened of-
ficially by the French Ambassador to the Court of St James,
on April 12th: that is, the day after tomorrow.

"Well, which is it?" Brodie whispered, staring around her
at the extraordinary array of machines and contraptions of
every size and shape which were established against the
walls. Not one of them looked obviously useful. Some resembled clothes mangles, others tin boxes with wires, yet
others elaborate typewriters. One looked rather like a bicycle stood upside down on its saddle, with two rather small
wheels. Winchester pointed to it.

"That is it," he said very quietly, so the curator would not
hear him.

Brodie's heart sank. It really did look extraordinarily
cumbersome: more fun than a brush and cloth and a good jar
of polish, but a great deal less convenient. She was now
quite convinced that William's job was in no jeopardy.

"Oh dear," she murmured sadly.

They walked over with affected casualness and stared at
the contraption. It was even more like a bicycle viewed from
only a yard away. It was possible to see quite easily which
were the moving parts, where the brushes were, and where
one was intended to place one's foot in order to have one's
boots very highly polished. There was a metal tree with
many joints, and a ratchet to alter its size according to the
boot in question, but it would still be an awkward and rather
time-consuming task to place the boot accurately. It was so

much easier simply to put one's hand into a boot or shoe and polish with a brush in the other hand. Brodie refrained from comment.

"Ah . . ." Winchester said thoughtfully. "I believe I see the principle upon which it works. Simple, yet clever. It would obtain a most excellent shine."

"Yes," Brodie agreed loyally. After all, it was a British invention. The General was one of the household. "It certainly would. Unparalleled." She continued to look at it in the hope she could see something she could admire more genuinely. The longer she looked at it, the less hope did she entertain.

Winchester must now be feeling the same, from the despair in his face.

Brodie went over the mechanism in her mind once more, envisioning precisely how it would work, when switched on. There seemed to be a part whose function she could not see. In fact the more she considered it, the more convinced she was that it was not only redundant, but it would actually get in the way when the thing was set in motion. There were two parts of it, metal parts, which were bound to touch when they moved in the only way they could. She pointed it out to Winchester.

"You must be mistaken, Miss Brodie," he said quite kindly. After all, how could she be expected to understand how a machine would work?

"No, I'm not, Mr Winchester," she replied. She was very good at judging the length of a thing with her eye. Good heavens, she had sewed from exact measurements for enough years. She knew the length of a skirt, the size of a waist or the width of a hem to an exactness. "It will strike that piece there!"

"Really!" he said with decreasing patience. "Do you imagine Mr Seaforth and the General have not tried it out?"

Actually Brodie thought that must be very likely, since

she was more than ever convinced that the rising bar would catch against the angled cross bar, not violently, but sufficient to graze it, and since they were both apparently metal, to strike a spark. It also looked long enough to touch the bar immediately above, but perhaps that did not matter. That might be where it was meant to rest. However with the best will in the world, which she had, she could not admire it with any enthusiasm.

Winchester was still regarding her crossly, waiting for an answer.

"I suppose they must have," she conceded reluctantly and then with a parting shot, "I don't understand what that piece is for?" She pointed to the metal bar against which the moving part must rest when it completed its cycle.

Winchester's face took on a look of indulgent superiority.

"It is part of the structure, Miss Brodie, necessary for the strength of the machine when it is in motion."

"I don't see how." His tone troubled her. "Surely that piece above it is sufficient for that purpose? It is not going to bear either weight or stress."

His mouth compressed into a thinner line. "It must do, or it would not be there!"

"What stress? Surely the piece above it serves that purpose?"

"Do not concern yourself, Miss Brodie," he said coldly. "Machinery is not the natural talent of women. It is hardly to be expected that you should understand the principles of engineering. It reflects no discredit upon you."

She had not for an instant considered it might. It was discredit to the machine she had in mind. But she could see from the set of his face that he did not understand it either and therefore would brook no argument. However he added one word too many. "I am sure you can appreciate that, Miss Brodie!"

"No," she said abruptly. "It is not myself I am questioning, it is the machine. I am afraid it is not quite right and may let the General and Mr Seaforth down when the French Ambassador comes to test it."

"Balderdash!" Winchester retorted, pink in the face now and plainly discomfited. "I think, Miss Brodie, that we have looked at this exhibit long enough. I am going to have a cup of tea. I observed a very agreeable establishment a mere five minutes away. If you wish to join me, I do not mind."

It was an uncharacteristically ungracious invitation, made under duress, but Brodie accepted it, partly because she would not be dismissed like that, but mostly because she was extremely ready for a cup of tea. It had been a long, thirsty walk into the town and would be the same on the return, especially if she were to try to keep up with Winchester's pace.

"Thank you," she said stiffly in reply.

He looked a little surprised but after a moment's hesitation offered her his arm. He would never have dreamed of doing so in the house, but this was different. Here they were practically socially equal.

She accepted it as if it were her due.

They walked together across the street and along the pavement without speaking any further, but when the tea was ordered by Winchester, and poured by Brodie, he broke the silence at last, tentatively to begin with.

"Miss Brodie . . ."

"Yes, Mr Winchester?"

"I have observed a . . . person . . . around the house and grounds lately, a foreign-appearing person, who seems to be paying attention to Mrs. Welch-Smith's maid, Colette. Have you noticed anything?"

"Yes, I have," she said quickly. Mention of Colette thawed her annoyance with Winchester very rapidly. After all, it was a very secondary matter. "I have seen him twice now. I heard her address him as 'Auguste,' and say what I believe was 'it is impossible'."

He leaned forward. "You believe? Did you not hear clearly?"

"What I think she actually said was 'c'est impossible'."

"I see. No doubt you are correct about the meaning, but it could refer to anything, even another meeting between them. But let us be diligent, Miss Brodie, and be warned. It is not unknown for servants of a certain character to open the way for accomplices to rob a house. We must be ever aware of the possibility. I shall have the footmen be extra alert where locks are concerned . . ."

"That will be no use if she lets him in," Brodie warned. "And . . ."

"And what?" he said urgently. "There is something else? Strive to remember, Miss Brodie. Crimes are solved by deductive reasoning and prevented by acute observation beforehand." He blinked very slightly. "I am still reading the exploits of Mr Sherlock Holmes in the *Strand* magazine. I find him most satisfying in his logic and somewhat instructive as to the processes of detection. Please, inform me of all you recall of this person Auguste."

Brodie thought very carefully before she began. It was most important that she did not allow her feelings to colour her memory, for the sake both of truth and most particularly of honour, in front of Winchester, of all people.

"It is more a matter of impression," she said guardedly. "He was a good-looking man . . ."

"I have seen him," Winchester interrupted. "I have no difficulty in accepting that Colette may be enamoured of him. I wish to know something of use . . . relevant to . . . to detection! Perhaps I have not made myself clear . . ."

"You do not need to!" she said frostily. "If you had permitted me to finish, it would have been apparent."

He flushed faintly pink, and stared back at her. He was not going to go further than that. An apology was out of the question. He waited.

She cleared her throat. "He was very careful about his person: well-groomed, well-behaved, his shirt collar clean and pressed, his tie straight . . . that was as much of him as I observed. The shadows made it impossible to see the rest of his apparel clearly enough to describe. He gave me the impression of a senior clerk in some firm of business, or . . ." She hesitated. That was not quite right.

"Yes?" he prompted, curiosity gaining the better of pride.

"Yet he had rather more confidence than I would have expected in a man of such occupation. He left very quickly upon seeing me, as if he did not wish me to look at him closely; yet I had no feeling of alarm in him, and certainly not of guilt. When I look back on that, it is curious."

"It is indeed," he agreed, ignoring his tea. "Are you quite sure of that, Miss Brodie?"

"Yes, I believe so. And the odder thing is that rather than stop flirting with each other when they became aware of me, that was the moment they started. Before they saw me, or to be more accurate, before she saw me, they were talking earnestly, but as if about some matter of importance. There is a great deal of difference between a woman's attitude when she is talking to a man simply to play, and the subject matter is irrelevant, and when she means what she says."

"I am aware of that," he pursed his lips. "I have dealt in my daily profession with a large number of young housemaids and footmen. Then what you describe is most puzzling, if indeed it was as you say. We require to know a great deal more about Colette and her admirer, if that is what he is, although now I begin to believe he may be something else. The question is, is he deceiving her too, pretending to be enamoured of her, but in truth merely using her to gain access to the house, or is she a knowing accomplice? And what of the valet, Harrison? He is an unusual man." Winchester frowned, puzzlement marked deeply in his normally smooth, even complacent face.

"In what way?" she asked, sipping her tea, but not taking her eyes from his. "I have barely seen him. He is never in the laundry or ironing room . . . or the stillroom or bootroom either, for that matter."

"Quite," he agreed. "It seems to me that the General does the greater part of his own valeting, while Harrison is in the stables attending to that invention of theirs. Now it is safely installed, he is back in the house, but I still see little of him. However it was his remarks, his expression to which I refer."

"What remarks?" Tacitly she offered him more tea, and he accepted. She poured it while he answered, after she had disposed of the now cold dregs in the slop basin.

"He says very little about France. Thank you . . ." he referred to the tea. "But when anything French is mentioned a look of distaste crosses his face, almost of anger. I am not certain if it is his own personal feeling, or if he is merely embarrassed that Colette, and Mrs. Welch-Smith, should be so eager to praise everything French, while in the house of an Englishman. They do it to a degree which borders on offence."

"It is well across the border!" Brodie said tartly, helping herself to a fresh scone, butter, jam and clotted cream, a very English delicacy in which she would not normally indulge. She would have to abstain from pudding at supper.

"You are correct," Winchester agreed graciously. "I am afraid several of the staff are beginning to be ruffled by it. There is some peacemaking to be done."

Brodie sat in silence, thinking. There was indeed a mystery. Perhaps something genuinely unpleasant threatened. She and Winchester must join forces, as before.

"This time we must prevent any crime before it happens, Mr Winchester," she said very sincerely.

"I have every intention that we shall do so, Miss Brodie," he agreed with feeling. "We must be equal to the task. As before, I shall find your assistance invaluable. You shall be my Watson!"

"On the contrary," she thought to herself, "I shall be your Holmes!" But she had more tact than to say so.

The evening did not go smoothly. When Brodie returned to the house, more than a little footsore, Colette surveyed her tired face and wet feet with disdain and made a remark about the glamour and excitement of Paris, and the charm of the French countryside, where of course the climate was kinder. Sunshine was so very good for the spirits.

Brodie glared at her and went upstairs to change into dry shoes and her uniform dress. Even in the days of her youth she had never had a figure like Colette's or the art to tie a bow till it looked like a frill of lace for the occasions when an apron was required.

After dinner, quite by chance, as she was returning from the stillroom, Brodie again saw the mysterious Auguste. He was walking along the passage from Winchester's pantry towards the back door. He had not seen her, and she had time to study him quite carefully, making mental notes to observe with skill, not mere curiosity. To begin with he was quite tall, and he walked with an elegance. Certainly he did not sneak or cower. His jacket was well cut but as he passed under the lamp on the wall, she could see that it also was not new. She glanced very quickly at his feet. One could sometimes tell much about a person's station in life from their boots. His were very well worn indeed, and now wet.

"Good evening, Monsieur," she said briskly.

He froze, then very slowed turned and stared at her. He was obviously abashed at having been seen, but he did not look guilty, rather annoyed at himself.

"Good evening, Madame," he replied courteously. His voice was pleasant enough, but heavily accented.

"I assume you are looking for Colette?" Brodie continued.

For a moment he was taken aback. She thought he was even going to deny it. Then he made an awkward little movement, half a bow. "No thank you, I was just about to go." He indicated the way to the door.

She looked him up and down closely. His suit fitted him too well for him to conceal anything of size in his pockets. At least on this occasion he had not robbed the household.

"Good night, then," she answered pleasantly and resumed her way toward the kitchen. She was pleased to see Colette there, busy preparing a special egg and milk drink which Mrs. Welch-Smith liked before retiring. She was looking for the nutmeg.

"Second drawer in the spice rack," Brodie said tartly.

"Oh!" Colette spun around. "How do you know what I wanted, Miss Brodie?"

"Well that's black pepper you have in your hand! Or maybe you like pepper in your milk in France, even last thing at night?"

"Of course not!" Colette snapped. "Although if you know anything about cuisine, you would not need to ask! Really, such an idea! All the delicacy would be lost. But then, English cooking is hardly an art—is it!"

"Well it is obviously not one you know," Brodie returned. "Nor is a decent respect for the household of your host, or you could not make such an unseemly remark. But then French manners are hardly an art either!"

Colette drew in her breath to retaliate.

Brodie got there first. "And another thing, while we are discussing it, it is not done in England for a visiting maid to have her followers in the house without permission, which would not be granted. I dare say Monsieur Auguste is a perfectly respectable person, but it is a principle. Some maids can attract a very dubious class of follower . . ."

Colette was furious, but oddly she did not explode with outrage. She seemed on the verge of speech, and then to hesitate, as though undecided, even confused.

"Many houses have been robbed that way," Brodie added for good measure.

Extraordinarily, Colette started to laugh, a high-pitched giggle rising towards hysteria.

Winchester appeared at the door, his face dark with disapproval.

"What is going on here?" he demanded.

Brodie was annoyed at being caught in what was obviously a quarrel. It was undignified. And by Winchester, of all people.

She was prevented from replying by the arrival of Harrison, General Welch-Smith's valet. He was a pleasant featured man with fair hair and large, strong hands. At the moment there was a sneer on his lips.

"Saw that follower of yours going across the yard," he said to Colette. "You'd better make sure you don't get caught, my girl! French may have the morals of an alley cat, but English don't like their servants having strange men in off the streets. Imagine what the mistress'd have to say if I brought some dolly-mop into the house! Get caught having a quick fumble in the cupboard under the stairs, and the mistress won't be able to protect you, no matter how well you can use a curling tong . . . the General'll have you out!"

Colette looked at him with utter loathing, but she seemed to have nothing to say. She turned on her heel, but when she stopped at the door, the milk and nutmeg temporarily forgotten, the look in her face was not one of defeat, but of waiting malice, as if she knew she would triumph in the end.

Brodie went to bed unhappy and profoundly puzzled. There was too much which did not make sense, and yet when she examined each individual instance, there was nothing to grasp. Who was Auguste? He did not behave like a man in love. Why did Colette seem to think she had some peculiar victory waiting for her? Why had Harrison been living in France so long if he disliked the French as he seemed to? She realized in thinking about it that she had heard him make other disparaging remarks, and there had been a light in his eyes of far more than usual irritation or disapproval. There was some deep emotion involved.

How on earth was the General's machine going to work when one piece was going to strike another as soon as it was set in motion? And what about the extra cross bar? So far as she could see, it offered no additional strength, no purpose, and certainly no beauty.

She went to sleep with it all churning in her mind and woke in the middle of the night with the answer sharp and horribly clear, as if she had already seen it happen: the two pieces striking would ignite a spark . . . the extra piece had a hideous use . . . it was not metal but dynamite! It would explode, a mechanical bomb, killing the French Ambassador, or at the very least seriously injuring him.

General Welch-Smith would be blamed, naturally. He designed the machine. He made it, with Harrison's help. He had just returned from a long sojourn in France.

And Jamie Seaforth would also be blamed, by implication. The General was staying in his house; they had been friends for years; Jamie had assisted in the last-minute touches to the machine. It was all quite horrible.

Perhaps Colette knew of it? That could be why she had that look of secret triumph in her eyes. Then who was Auguste? An accomplice. He must be.

But an accomplice to whom? Surely the General had not really done this? Why? What had happened to him in France that he could even think of such an idea?

The reason hardly mattered. The thing now was to prevent it from happening. She must tell Winchester. He was the only person who would believe her. Then together they would tell . . . who? Not the General, certainly. And would Jamie give a moment's credence to such a tale?

She and Winchester must do it alone, and there would be no opportunity to speak in the morning. They would all be far too busy with their own duties. She needed time to persuade him of the inevitable logic of what she had deduced. He could be stubborn now and again. And he would be appalled at being woken in the middle of the night. It was conceivable there had never been a woman in his bedroom in his adult life except a housemaid to clean it. If he had ever had any personal relationships they would most assuredly have been conducted elsewhere, and with the utmost discretion.

She sat up and fumbled in the dark for matches to light the candle. There were gas lamps downstairs, of course, but on the servants' level, even the superior servants such as herself, it was candles. She succeeded, then reached for her shawl. There was no time to bother with the fuss of dressing, chemises and petticoats and stockings. Wrapped up with a shawl for decency more than warmth, she tiptoed along the corridor to the farther end where she knew Winchester's room was situated. There was a connecting door between the male servants' quarters and those of the female servants, as decorum required, but it was not locked.

She was watching ahead of her so carefully that she caught her toe against the foot of a side table where ewers of water were left. She almost cried out with the pain, and there was a distinct rattle as china touched china.

Good heavens! What on earth would anyone think if she were found here? She was right outside Winchester's door. How could she possibly explain herself? She couldn't! The General's invention was going to explode and kill the French Ambassador! She could hear the laughter now and see the total contempt in their eyes. It was almost enough to make her turn back. She had a blameless reputation! It would be a lifetime's good character gone—and for what?

To save one man's life and another man's reputation, that was what.

Dare she knock?

What if someone else were awake and heard and thought it was their own door?

They would answer it. They would see her standing here in her nightgown and shawl, her hair down her back and a candle in her hand, waiting at Winchester's bedroom. She would never be able to live it down! She could hear the young maids' comments now! They would never let her forget it! Silly old woman—absurd—at her age!

That was it. It was decided! She put her hand on the knob, turned it and went in. She closed it behind her very nearly without sound. Winchester was lying curled over on his side in the middle of the bed, blankets tucked up to his chin, nightcap on his head, a little askew. He looked very ordinary and very vulnerable. He would probably never ever forgive her for this.

"Mr Winchester . . ." she whispered.

He did not move.

"Mr Winchester . . ." she said a trifle more loudly.

He stirred and turned over.

Heavens alive! What if he saw her and cried out? That would be the worst of all possibilities. "Don't say anything!" she ordered desperately. "Please keep quiet!"

Winchester opened his eyes and sat up slowly, his face transfixed with horror. His nightcap slipped over one ear.

She could feel her face burning.

"I had to come!" she said defensively.

"Miss Brodie!" The words were forced between his lips. He was aghast. He opened his mouth to continue and could not.

"I know what is wrong!" she said urgently. "With the machine! With the General's machine! It is going to explode . . . and kill the French Ambassador . . . and General Welch-Smith will be blamed. I don't know . . . perhaps he should be. But Mr Seaforth will be blamed also, and he shouldn't. We must do something about it before that can happen!"

To do him justice, he did not ask her if she had been at the port, but his expression suggested it.

"Imagine it in your mind!" she urged. "Visualize how the contraption will work. The French Ambassador places his foot on the rest, presses the button and the polish cloth rubs his boot, then the second piece starts to move." She waved her hands to demonstrate. "It has to come down, in order to buff the leather. It strikes the cross bar, only very lightly, but sufficiently to cause a spark." She leaned forward a little. "Now—visualize the other piece: unnecessarily double, you recall. That is dynamite, Mr Winchester. It will ignite, and explode!" She jerked her hand and nearly threw the candle at him.

"Miss Brodie!" he cried.

"Be quiet!" she whispered in agony of embarrassment. "Think where we are! I had to come, because there will be no time in the morning. We may not even see each other till halfway through the day. We must do something to prevent this! No one else will. It lies with us."

"I . . . I shall speak to Mr Seaforth," he offered. "In the morning!"

"To do what?" she said exasperatedly. Really, Winchester was being very obtuse. Perhaps he was one of those people who woke only slowly?

"Well . . . to . . ." He looked uncomfortable. He could now see the pointlessness of expecting Jamie to do anything at all about it. He would only speak to the General, in his own innocence believing him to be equally innocent.

"If the General knows about it, he will deny it," she pointed out. "And if he doesn't know about it, of course he will deny it. Mr Seaforth will be immensely relieved and tell us we do not need to worry. All is well."

He frowned. He was obviously feeling at an acute disadvantage sitting up in bed, but he did not wish to rise with Brodie standing there. He felt very exposed in his striped nightshirt. There was something about being without trousers which was highly personal.

"Perhaps all is well?" he said with a thread of hope. "Surely it is more than possible the design is simply clumsy?"

The perfect answer was on her lips. "Do you imagine Sherlock Holmes would be content with a possibility, Mr Winchester?"

He straightened up visibly, forgetting his embarrassment and his doubts.

"I shall meet you at the stables at a quarter past eleven, Miss Brodie," he said with absolute decision. "We shall take the carriage, as if on an errand, and determine for ourselves the exact nature of this wretched machine. Be prompt. Whatever your duties, see they are completed by then. We must act."

She smiled back at him approvingly. "Assuredly, Mr Winchester. We shall prevent disaster . . . if indeed disaster is planned. Good night."

He clutched the sheet with both hands. "Goodnight, Miss Brodie."

It was a fine day and the ride to the town was swift and pleasant. Outside the exhibition hall were posters proclaiming the official visit of the French Ambassador the following morning. Inside there were rather more people than there had been yesterday. Brodie and Winchester were obliged to excuse themselves and pass several groups standing in front of various examples of French ingenuity and design. They heard exclamations of admiration and marvel at a race who could think of such things.

Brodie gritted her teeth and remembered why they were here. The French might be the most inventive race in Europe, but it would be English courage and foresight, English nerve and integrity which saved the Ambassador.

They found the boot polisher, looking more than ever like a bicycle upside down. Brodie was both relieved and offended that there was no one else in front of it, admiring the ingenuity which had thought of such a thing. That was the trouble with the British: they always admired something foreign!

She glanced at Winchester, looking utterly different this morning in his pin-striped trousers and dark jacket, his face immaculately shaved, if a little pink, his collar and tie crisp and exactly symmetrical. She thought she saw in his eye a reflection of the pride and the conviction she felt herself. It was most satisfying.

She turned her attention to the machine. It would not move without the electrical power, and that was to be turned on tomorrow, by the Ambassador, but the more she looked at it, the more certain she was that the parts would rub against each other with sufficient force to strike a spark. There was only one thing which remained to be done. She leaned forward to touch the redundant piece and feel its texture. Metal . . . or dynamite? She did not know what dynamite felt like, but she knew steel.

"Don't touch the exhibits, if you please, Madame!"

It was the voice of the curator, sharp and condescending, as if she had been a small child about to risk breaking some precious ornament. She flushed to the roots of her hair.

Winchester leaped into the fray with a boldness which surprised even himself.

"Yes, my dear, better not," he said calmly. He turned away from Brodie as if the order would be sufficient, his word would be obeyed, and engaged the curator in conversation. "Please tell me, sir, something about this remarkable piece of equipment over here." He all but led the man across the room to the farther side and a monstrous edifice of wires and pulleys. "I am sure you know how this works, the principle behind it, but I confess I fail to grasp it fully."

"Ah well, you see . . ." The curator was flattered by this upstanding gentleman's interest, and his perception in realizing that a curator was a man of knowledge himself, not merely a watchman who conducted people around. "It's like this . . ." He proceeded to explain at length.

"Well?" Winchester demanded when he and Brodie were outside again.

"You were magnificent," she said generously and quite sincerely.

He blushed with pleasure, but kept his face perfectly

straight. "Thank you. But I was referring to the redundant piece. Is it metal?"

"No," she said without hesitation. "It is soft to the fingernail, a trifle waxy. I was able to take off a flake of it with no difficulty. I believe it is dynamite."

"Oh . . . oh dear." He was caught between the deeper hope that it would not after all be necessary to do anything and the satisfaction of being right, and with it the taste for adventure. "I see. Then I am afraid it falls upon us to foil the plan, Miss Brodie. We shall have to act, and I fear it must be immediate. There is no time to lose."

She agreed wholeheartedly, but how to act was another thing altogether.

"Let us take a dish of tea and consider the matter," Winchester said firmly, touching her elbow to guide her towards the doorway, and at least temporary escape.

As soon as tea was brought to them, and poured, they addressed the subject.

"We have already discussed the possibility of informing the authorities," Winchester stated. He glanced at the tray of small savoury sandwiches on the table but did not touch them. "The only course open to us is to disarm the machine. We shall have to do it so that no one observes either our work or its result. Therefore we must replace the dynamite with something which looks exactly like it."

"I see," Brodie nodded and sipped her tea, which was delicious, but still rather hot. "Have you any ideas as to how we should accomplish that?"

"I have an excellent pocket knife," he replied with a slight frown. "I think I should have relatively little trouble in removing the dynamite. I believe it will cut without too much difficulty. I could also use the blade as a screwdriver, should one be necessary. However I have not yet hit upon any idea what we should put in place of that which we remove."

Brodie thought hard for several moments. She took one of the sandwiches and bit into it. It was very fresh and really most pleasant. She took another sip of tea. Then the idea came to her.

"Bread!" she said rather more loudly than she intended.

"I beg your pardon?" Winchester looked totally nonplussed.

"Bread," she replied more moderately. "Fresh bread, very fresh indeed, may be moulded into shapes and made hard, if you compress it. I have seen beads made of it. After all, it is in essence only flour and water paste. We still have to paint it black, of course, but that should not prove too difficult. Then we may put it in place of the dynamite, and we will have accomplished our task."

"Excellent, Miss Brodie!" Winchester said enthusiastically. "That will do most excellently well. But of course it is only a part of our task . . ."

"I realize making the exchange will not be easy," Brodie agreed. "In fact it may require all our ingenuity to succeed. The curator is not impressed with me as it is. He will not allow me near the machine again, I fear."

"Don't worry, I shall accomplish the exchange," he assured her. "If you will distract the curator's attention. But that is not what I meant. We cannot claim our task is completed until we know who placed the dynamite in the machine." He shook his head a little. "On considering the problem, it seems clear to me that it can only have been either the General himself, or Harrison. I have weighed the issue in my mind since you brought it to my attention, and I believe that the General has no reason for such a thing and would bring about his own ruin, since he will naturally be blamed. Whereas Harrison appears to dislike the French and may have some deeper cause for his feelings than we know. He has far less to lose, socially and professionally speaking.

And he would be able to disappear after the event, take the next train up to London, and never be seen again. We know nothing of him, whereas we know everything of the General. Mr Seaforth has had his acquaintance on and off for thirty years."

"I am sure you are right," Brodie nodded. "But as you point out, it remains to prove it—after we have removed the dynamite. I shall purchase some fresh bread at the bakery across the street. Can you obtain some black paint and a brush without returning to the house?"

"I am sure I can. Where shall we meet to do the work? It must be discreet."

Brodie thought hard, and no answer came to her.

"I have it!" Winchester said with pleasure. "There is a public bath house on the corner of Bedford Street. It has private changing places for both ladies and gentlemen. If you use the rooms for ladies, you can make the bread the requisite size. Do you know what that is?"

"I do. It is two inches less than the distance from my wrist to my elbow, and as thick as my thumb."

"Bravo! Then we shall begin. I think I may say 'the game's afoot.' Come, Miss Brodie. Let us advance to battle."

But distracting the attention of the curator was less easy than they had supposed. They returned some considerable time later, the long, black stick of bread, paint just dry, concealed up Winchester's sleeve. The curator regarded them with displeasure. Had it been anything but the utmost urgency, Brodie would have left and gone home. But that would be cowardice under fire, and Brodie had never been a coward. England's honour was at stake.

"Now, Miss Brodie," Winchester said gently and perhaps with a touch of new respect in his tone. "Charge!"

She gulped and sailed forward. There were only four other people in the room, a gentleman and two ladies, and of course the curator.

"How wonderful to see you again!" she said loudly, staring at one of the ladies, an elderly person in a shade of purple she should never have worn. "You look so well! I am delighted to see you so recovered."

The woman stared at her in perplexity.

"And your great-uncle," Brodie went on even more loudly. Now the others were staring at her also. "Is he recovered from that appalling affair in Devon? What a perfectly dreadful woman, and so much younger than he."

The woman now looked at her in considerable alarm and clutched at the hand of a gentleman next to her.

"I don't know you!" she said in a high-pitched voice. "I don't have a great-uncle in Devon, or anywhere else!"

"I'm not surprised you should disown him," Brodie said in a tone of great sympathy, but still as loudly as she could, as if she thought the woman in purple might be deaf, and shouting would make the meaning plainer. "But older men can be so easily beguiled, don't you think?"

Two more people had entered the room from one of the other halls, but they paid no attention to Winchester or the exhibits. They focused entirely upon Brodie and the scene of acute embarrassment being played out in the centre of the floor. The curator dithered from one foot to the other in uncertainty as to what to do, whether to intervene in what was obviously a very private matter or to pretend he had not even heard. Sometimes the latter was the only way to treat such a matter with kindness.

The woman in purple was still staring at Brodie as if she were an apparition risen out of the floor.

"Of course she was very attractive," Brodie resumed relentlessly. Winchester could not be finished yet. She must buy him time. "In an extraordinary sort of way. I've never seen so much hair! Have you? And such a colour, my dear! Like tomato soup!"

"I don't know you!" the woman repeated desperately, waving her hands in the air. "I have no great-uncles at all!"

"Really!" The man beside her came to her rescue at last. "I must protest, Mrs er . . . I mean . . ." He glared at Brodie. "Lady Dora has already explained to you, as kindly as possible, that you have made a mistake. Please accept that and do not pursue the matter."

"Oh!" Brodie let out a shriek of dismay. "Lady Dora? Are you sure?"

Lady Dora was very pink in the face, a most unbecoming colour.

"Of course I'm sure!" she shrieked.

"I do apologize." Brodie shouted back, still on the assumption she was hard of hearing. "I mistook you for Mrs Marshfield, who looks so like you, in a certain light, of course, when wearing just the right shade of . . . what would you say? Plum? Claret? I really should remember my spectacles. They make such a difference, don't you think? I am quite mortified. Whatever can I do?" She asked it not rhetorically, but as if she expected and required a reply.

Lady Dora looked not a whit comforted. She stared at Brodie with loathing. "Please don't distress yourself," she said icily. "Now that the issue is settled, there is no offence, I assure you."

"You are too generous," Brodie exclaimed. Where on earth was Winchester? Had he finished yet? She dared not glance around in case she drew anyone else's attention to him also. What on earth was there left for her to do? "I feel quite ill with confusion that I should have made such an error." She rolled her eyes as if she were about to faint.

"Water!" Lady Dora's companion said loudly.

The other woman moved forward to offer assistance, still looking sideways at Lady Dora as if she half believed Brodie's tale of the uncle. There was something of a smile about her lips.

"For heaven's sake fetch some water, man!" Lady Dora's companion commanded the curator, who at last moved to obey. With much assistance Brodie was led to a seat and plied with water, a fan, smelling salts, and good advice. It was a full five minutes before she could bring herself to leave. She staggered out into the fresh air and was overwhelmed with relief to see Winchester looking triumphant and pretending not to know her as the curator let go of her arm and suggested very forcefully that she did not return.

"The atmosphere is not good for you, Madame," he said between thin lips. "I think for your health, you should refrain from such enclosed spaces. Good day."

The following morning Hannah and Jamie went with Bertie and Violet Welch-Smith to see the formal opening of the exhibition. Both men were very excited about it, and Hannah felt she had to balance Violet's disinterest by feigning an enthusiasm herself. They were accompanied by Harrison, a just reward for his many hours of work in helping to construct the General's machine and for his care and maintenance of it.

When they got there, it was very difficult. Almost all the exhibits seemed to be French. There were electric jewels invented by Monsieur G. Trouvé of Paris, largely for use on stage. Next to that was an optical theatre designed by a Monsieur Reynaud. There were other French inventions: a portable shower bath, created by Monsieur Gaston Bozetian; a device to prevent snoring; a construction for reaching the North Pole by balloon; and an invention by Dr. Varlot, again of Paris, for electroplating the bodies of the dead so that they were covered with a millimetre-thick layer of metallic copper of a brilliant red colour. Then the remains of a beloved could be preserved indefinitely.

Violet became even more appreciative, praising them vociferously, and making Hannah feel more and more irritated.

At eleven o'clock the French Ambassador arrived, a neat and elegant man immaculately dressed and carrying a furled umbrella as if he did not trust the mild and delightful spring day. He declared the exhibition open, made several remarks about the service that inventors performed for humanity, and then proceeded to walk around the various exhibits and examine each in turn. He was followed by a small crowd of people.

He reached the boot polishing machine at about a quarter to twelve.

"Oh! And this is the English invention!" he said with as much enthusiasm as he could muster. He looked at it carefully, and it was apparent he was highly dubious about its value, but it would be a national insult if he did not try to use it.

Hannah watched, as gingerly he put his foot on the pedal and reached for the switch to turn it on. She saw Harrison, his face alight with jubilation, as if a great moment of triumph had at last arrived.

The Ambassador's finger was on the button.

"No! It is a bomb!" Someone yelled wildly, and a dark haired, dark faced man leaped from the crowd, waving his arms, and hurled himself on the Ambassador, carrying him forward onto the machine, and the whole edifice collapsed beneath them in a pile of fractured metalwork and flailing arms and legs.

There was an in-drawn breath of horror around the room. The women screamed. Someone had hysterics. One woman fainted and had to be dragged out. She was too big to carry.

"Send for the fire-brigade!" the curator shouted. "Bring water!"

A quick-witted man fetched a fire bucket of sand and threw it at the Ambassador and the other man on the floor, knocking them back again and sending them sprawling.

"A bomb! A bomb!" the shouts were going round.

Hannah stared at Jamie and saw the complete bewilderment in his face.

"What on earth is going on?" she demanded fiercely. Then she looked farther across and saw consternation in Harrison's face and thought perhaps she glimpsed an understanding.

Someone else arrived with a pail of water from the tearooms opposite. Without asking anyone, he also threw it over the Ambassador and the man who was even now attempting to rise to his feet. They were both drenched.

"I say, old fellow," Bertie moved forward in some concern. He put out his hand and hauled the Ambassador to his feet. He was sodden wet, covered with sand and mud, and purple in the face. "I say," Bertie repeated. "I can't imagine what this is all about, but it really won't do." He looked at the other man. "Who are you, sir, and what the devil are you playing at? This is a machine for polishing the boots of gentlemen, not dangerous in the least . . . and certainly not a bomb! You had better explain yourself, if you can!"

The man saluted smartly and addressed himself to the Ambassador, ignoring Bertie.

"Auguste Larrey, sir, of the French Sureté. I had every reason to believe that this device would explode the moment you pressed the switch, and that you would be killed . . . sir . . ."

"Balderdash!" Jamie said loudly.

The Ambassador tried to straighten his coat, but it was hardly worth the effort, and he gave up. He looked like a scarecrow that had barely weathered a storm, and he knew it.

"Monsieur Larrey," he said with freezing politeness. "As you may observe, I have met with great mischance, and in front of our neighbours and friends, the English, but the machine, it has not exploded. It has imploded, under the combined weight of your body and mine. It is wrecked! We owe the English a profound apology! You, sir, will offer it!"

"Yes, Monsieur," Auguste stammered wretchedly. "Indeed, Monsieur." He looked at the assembled company. "I am most deeply sorry, ladies and gentlemen—most deeply. I have made a terrible mistake. I regret it and beg your forgiveness."

"Really?" Brodie said with wide eyes when Hannah told her of the incident that evening when they were alone in the withdrawing room, the others having retired. Winchester was just leaving to see if the footmen had locked up. She looked at Winchester and caught his answering glance. "How very regrettable," she said with great sobriety.

Hannah looked at her narrowly but said nothing further.

Winchester cleared his throat. "Indeed," he said with shining eyes and a rather pink face. "Most regrettable, Madam."

I've been invited to several of those "murder-mystery week-ends." Can't say that I care for them too much. Besides the fact that I would have an unfair advantage, I've also had too much experience with the real thing. However, when the line between fantasy and reality becomes blurred, that's the time when a sharp mind and eye for detail will enable a sleuth to discern fact from fiction.

Beauty Is Only Skin Deep

Gallagher Gray

"Absolutely not." There was no way T.S. would relinquish the wheel to Auntie Lil. Fat flakes of snow whipped against the windshield and dark clouds above promised more. Besides, she never drove more than twenty-five miles an hour. At that rate, it would take them a week to get to Highland Lake Lodge.

"I'm an excellent driver," Auntie Lil protested. She crossed her arms firmly and glared out the window. The trouble with Auntie Lil was that, at age eighty-four, she was not only a horrible driver herself, but firmly convinced that everyone else was much worse.

"You owe me one for this weekend," T.S. said, ignoring her sulking.

She ignored him. "A mystery weekend jaunt will be fun for both of us. We can relive old glory."

"I don't see how a bunch of bad actors screaming lousy dialogue can ever approach solving the real thing." An unwelcome fantasy unfolded before him: suppose he was trapped in a blizzard with an entire houseful of Auntie Lils? It was enough to make him turn around and speed home to New York City.

"Besides," Auntie Lil added. "We had to come. I promised Clarabelle. I believe we are part of the draw. That's why we attend for free."

Oh Lord, it really had to be a low-rent crowd if they were the celebrities, T.S. thought grimly as he steered his way through the storm.

The snow was approaching blizzard proportions by the time they neared Highland Lake, making the steep ascent perilous and Auntie Lil's attempts at backseat driving all the more maddening. The town was no more than an intersection marking the final crest of a mountain overlooking the Delaware River. Following Clarabelle's directions, they passed a small community of deserted summer homes blanketed with snow, then turned left down a narrow road. They abruptly came upon a converted Victorian house that was splendid in its overgrown majesty. A porch wrapped around the entire structure, and snow-dusted bushes grew wildly over the carved wooden railings. Through a large bay window, a cozy sitting and smoking room could be seen, complete with crackling fire.

"I see my room," T.S. remarked cheerfully as he helped Auntie Lil up the steps. Ice made the going slippery, and he was forced to perform several heroic maneuvers in order to preserve his elderly aunt's dignity.

"I can't think why they don't have someone to help the

guests," Auntie Lil muttered as she grabbed a fence post to keep from tumbling ass over teakettle.

Before they could ring the bell, the door was opened by a small woman with impossibly orange hair. She was in her early fifties and dressed in a purple leotard topped by an elaborately embroidered blue vest. She collapsed into raptures at the sight of Auntie Lil. "You made it!" she squealed in a babyish voice that made Marilyn Monroe sound like a truck driver with congestion. "I knew you would come through for me."

"Neither rain nor sleet nor snow nor . . ." Auntie Lil began.

"I'm T. S. Hubbert, Lillian's nephew," T.S. interrupted, before Auntie Lil moved on to quoting Tennyson.

"I'm Clarabelle Clarke," their hostess replied, leading them into a huge hallway with the highest ceilings they had ever seen in their lives. A curving stairway led upward past a wide landing to a three-sided balcony area that served as the second floor hallway. Huge oil portraits of dour ancestors crowded the walls. Dozens of sour expressions caught the casual observer in a crossfire of ancient grumpiness.

"Are these all yours?" Auntie Lil inquired faintly.

"Of course not. But don't they just lend the place the most fabulously rich and exotic aura?" Clarabelle spread her arms wide and breathed deeply.

Uh-oh. Clarabelle was heavy into aura, T.S. deduced. He hoped her enthusiasms would not rub off on his aunt over the weekend. Auntie Lil didn't need anything remotely New Age in her life. A dose of Old Age would be far more appropriate. She was impossible to control as it was.

Their one tantalizing glimpse of a cheerful sitting room hurried both T.S. and Auntie Lil through the unpacking. Before long, they were ensconced in a cozy sitting room, warming themselves by a fire while they waited for other guests to arrive.

"Who else will be here? Where are the actors?" Auntie Lil looked about as if hoping a body might tumble from the cupboard.

"Unfortunately, we've had quite a few cancellations," Clarabelle explained. "Because of the weather. A few have already arrived, however. Technically, it's cheating to know in advance because that's part of the game—figuring out who's a guest and who's an actor. But just between us, the guests already here include two elderly sisters, Dotty and Agnes Baird; Mr. Charles Little, a retired gentleman; Donald and Marion Travers, he's the real estate mogul; and Dr. Sussman, a well-known Park Avenue dermatologist who is napping at the moment."

"Donald Travers?" T.S. asked, mystified. "That's a surprise." Travers was the last person T.S. had expected.

Clarabelle looked smug. "I know his wife. A lovely woman. He brought her here for the weekend as an anniversary gift. I better go see how they're doing." She scurried away so quickly that T.S. was left wondering if Clarabelle was angling for an infusion of capital into her bed-and-breakfast from the famed Donald Travers.

"There you are. Hiding from us, I see." This booming voice was followed into the room by a woman in her early sixties who looked like a domesticated Gertrude Stein. Her nose was prominent and shaped like a fat banana, her eyes were exceedingly large and somewhat protruding, and her cheeks hung down in pronounced pouches. She bore down on T.S. as inevitably as a steamer.

"T. S. Hubbert," he said quickly, extending his hand. It was crushed in a powerful grip.

"I'm Dotty Baird." The large woman laughed as if this were a tremendous joke.

"Is it safe, Dotty? Can I come in?" The second voice from the hall was soft and tentative.

"Oh, for God's sakes," Dotty broadcast in reply. "They aren't going to kill the paying guests. Of course it's safe." She dropped her voice and explained. "My sister Agnes has quite an imagination. She gets carried away."

Agnes had a headful of wiry gray curls springing about in every direction. Her general air of unconscious distraction was enhanced by the too large cardigan sagging about her shoulders. "Are you a guest or an actor?" she asked Auntie Lil excitedly. "You look a lot like a fat Lillian Gish."

Astonishingly enough, Auntie Lil took this as a compliment. "Me?" she said in a pleased voice. "Well, actually . . ."

"Now, now," Dotty interrupted. "You can't just ask if a person is a guest. You have to figure it out or you're cheating and you know it."

"I know one person who is not a guest," Agnes declared in small triumph.

"Who is that?" Auntie Lil asked politely.

"Maria Taylor. She's going to be here this weekend." Agnes beamed in awe. "She's famous for having the most beautiful skin on television. I can't wait to see it up close."

Auntie Lil's eyebrows raised briefly. She clearly had no earthly idea who Maria Taylor was. T.S. knew but could not admit it without also admitting that he watched soap operas. He wisely decided to keep silent.

Dotty grabbed Agnes by an elbow. "Come on, dear. We've got to get a jump on everyone. Let's look for clues." She led the way out of the sitting room, nearly bowling over Clarabelle, who had an expensive-looking couple in tow.

"May I present our honored guests for the weekend, Mr. and Mrs. Donald Travers," Clarabelle gushed, clearly in awe of their net worth, if not their aura.

Donald Travers ignored everyone. He ambled over to a window and stared morosely at the falling snow. He was trim as only a man with access to racquetball courts and a private gym can be, with a face so completely tanned that it looked as though it had been burnished with walnut oil. Marion Travers proved more gracious than her husband and nodded at Auntie Lil as she made her way to an empty seat by the fire. She was fashionably slim but possessed a sweet face, with kind eyes and gentle features. Her hair was a becoming silver gray and, whether or not it had been treated to produce that color, the overall effect was more in keeping with her age than could be said for her husband's suspiciously blond hue.

"We're off to a roaring start," T.S. whispered to Auntie Lil as he sipped his drink. "What have you gotten us into?"

Auntie Lil smacked his hand lightly. "You must admit that there are far worse places to be in the midst of a snowstorm."

She was right. The fire crackled merrily in the hearth, the bar was well stocked and, outside, a terrible blizzard raged. T.S. snagged a chair by the fire and dozed off in hopeful anticipation of, at the very least, a decent dinner. He awoke to find the sitting room full of occupants. The weekend had begun.

A bored-looking butler lounged against one wall without even a pretense at working. He took out a pocket watch and exclaimed, "What? What's this, I say?" in an utterly wretched British accent. Suddenly, a girl dressed as a French maid charged into the room with a tray of champagne and nearly plowed down Auntie Lil. She apologized profusely and went careening off in another direction.

T.S. removed himself to a safer spot behind the bar, but Auntie Lil dragged one of the armchairs into the middle of the room and sat down in the flow of traffic. She beamed at everyone and waited for the real action to begin.

An elderly gentleman with a head as oval and smooth as an egg grinned at Auntie Lil from the doorway. The reflection of flames danced over a backdrop of his slick pink scalp. A few tufts of white hair about the top of the ears gave evidence to earlier glory. His tie was wide and orange, with a hula dancer painted on it. He flipped it flirtatiously at Auntie Lil when she made the mistake of glancing his way.

Auntie Lil stood abruptly and joined T.S. at the bar. "Be a darling and make me a Bloody Mary, will you, Theodore? Champagne isn't nearly quick enough."

T.S. hid his smile and went to work. The old fellow was Charles Little, he remembered Clarabelle explaining. A retired gentleman. Well, Mr. Charles Little would just have to take a number and get in line behind the rest of Auntie Lil's unrequited suitors. Auntie Lil was so full of life that elderly men surrounded her like beggars at a temple, hoping some of her joie de vivre might rub off.

An imperceptible humming filled the room as the weekend's star arrived. In person, Maria Taylor was smaller than expected. But the familiar dark eyes were there, flashing in a catlike face. She had a mane of black hair, arched brows and thin red lips. She smiled, revealing a row of tiny teeth so feral and sharp that T.S. half expected her to drop to her knees, seize his trousers in her teeth, and shake him into submission.

It would have been entirely in character for her to have done so. Maria Taylor played a vixen, as the entertainment magazines so politely put it. Every day for an hour, in living rooms across America, she schemed, plotted, lied, cheated and killed. All the world loved to hate her and she reveled in her image. She surveyed the assembled guests and asked in a bored voice, "What must one do to get a drink around here?"

T.S. offered his services and was roped into making a complicated concoction involving milk and three kinds of liqueur. He was soon sorry he had asked.

"Let the games begin," Maria Taylor said, raising her frothy green drink in salute.

With impeccable timing, a thin and extraordinarily pale man appeared in the doorway. "How do you do," he announced, with a slight bow. "My name is Dr. Ronald Sussman."

His mannerisms were so flamboyant that, had Auntie Lil and T.S. not known he was the real thing, it would have been impossible to say whether Dr. Ronald Sussman was a guest or an actor. His voice fluttered as if a vocal cord had snapped loose. He mixed a drink, all the while darting his eyes around the room, toting up people like prices on a cash register. He sipped his drink speculatively, then raised his eyebrows in approval as he spotted a suitable conversational partner.

Marion Travers, wife of the Wall Street millionaire and an heiress in her own right, according to all press reports, was sitting by the fire, apart from the others. Dr. Sussman pulled a stool up by her feet. "You have incredible skin," he told her. "The skin of a goddess. I feel it's my duty to help you protect that gift." His enraptured expression focused on her face. "I can tell you take excellent care of your body."

"I eat no meat or dairy products," she said, returning to her book.

"Even the most perfect of complexions must be protected," the dermatologist declared. He leaned closer. She shifted her leg away from him and ignored his comment. "I have a fabulous skin care system," the doctor continued. "I developed it myself. Some of the most beautiful women in the world swear by it. Their wrinkles disappear virtually overnight."

"I believe in inner beauty, doctor," Marion Travers said brusquely. "I'm not ashamed of my wrinkles. God knows I've earned them."

"I would be happy to give you some free samples," Dr. Sussman persisted smoothly. "After all, someone of your social standing could do me a lot of good. Help me attract more clients."

"It doesn't appear to me that you need any more patients," Mrs. Travers said. "I understand you're responsible for Miss Taylor's skin and isn't it supposed to be the most beautiful on television?" The glare she sent the actress was quite out of character, as was the alarmed look that Maria Taylor returned.

"Then you've heard of me," the doctor insisted. "Perhaps some of your close friends rely on me to enhance their own inner beauty, shall we say?"

"Dr. Sussman—" Marion Travers put her book down. "I like the way I look. I have no intention of wasting three hours a day slathering overpriced oils and creams on my face. Please go away."

"Honestly," T.S. thought, inching toward the bar. "I'm not the only one around here who could use a drink."

Suddenly, a young girl dressed in a shimmering green evening gown dashed into the middle of the room. Her face was contorted in fury and she held a small pistol in her hand. She cast a murderous gaze at Maria Taylor. "I hate you, but I can't kill you!" she screamed at the star, collapsing in a heap on the rug. The gun flew across the carpet and the fake butler retrieved it, tossing it carelessly on top of a bookshelf. The young girl burst into enthusiastic sobs, her face buried in the folds of her green dress. T.S. wondered whether her shoulders were shaking from actual tears or from helpless laughter at how silly the guests were to watch this nonsense.

"She's ruined him for life," the young actress sobbed. "The only man I'll ever love! Now he'll never marry me!"

The assembled crowd watched the proceedings with expressions ranging from delight to suspicion. Auntie Lil looked confused, but the sisters quickly produced notebooks and feverishly scrawled information. The elderly man, Charles Little, placed his empty glass at his feet and clasped his hands, his face shining with excitement.

"I haven't a clue as to what the little snip is talking about," Maria Taylor said, rising majestically from her chair. But just as she started across the room, the young girl flung herself at the older actress, grabbing her around the ankles. It was a dangerous improvisation. Maria Taylor produced a hiss that could never have been faked, then unceremoniously dragged the girl toward the door. The green evening dress zigzagged across the blue rug like a trout being brought to shore.

The exit was further spoiled by the arrival of an enormous maid, who fixed the actresses with an uncomprehending stare that T.S. deeply understood. "Dinner is served," she announced, shaking her head in amazement, "If you can tear yourselves away from all this excitement, that is."

Despite the welcome arrival of personality in the form of the no-nonsense maid, dinner was a resumption of the tepid plot unfurled in the sitting room earlier. The assembled guests ate nervously, unsure if or when the plot might once again explode. All was quiet until just after the main course when the young actress, apparently deciding that the guests' digestive tracts had enjoyed enough of a headstart, gave a shriek and stood, swaying dramatically against her chair. She clutched her throat and screamed, "She's poisoned me! She's poisoned me!"

Maria Taylor rose from her chair, eyes flashing as she stared haughtily into the distance. "Rubbish." She dismissed the girl with a wave. "Simple indigestion. I'd never be so indiscreet. I won't listen to any more nonsense."

"Hear! Hear!" T.S. wanted to agree, but before he could follow this impulse, Maria Taylor swept from the room and headed upstairs, leaving the girl to swoon to the floor. Unsure of the protocol, guests crowded around and stared down at the inert body. Only Donald Travers remained at his seat, staring sourly at the dessert before him.

When no one stepped forward to take the lead, Clarabelle intervened. "That's it," she announced loudly, clapping her hands. "Murder most foul. And, if any of you can sleep tonight, we'll get started solving it tomorrow."

T.S. fled to his room as soon as was decently possible, noticing with amusement that Auntie Lil gave him a wide berth. She was in no mood for a round of "I told you so's." He dressed carefully in his favorite silk pajamas. He'd get his revenge on Auntie Lil, he vowed, then amused himself with several possible scenarios as he lay awake in the darkness, drifting off to sleep. Before long he was oblivious to anything but a delicious dream in which he lay beneath a pristine Caribbean sky, the hot sun baking his winter-weary bones as he sipped an endless supply of rum funnies.

His fantasy was shattered by a reverberating gunshot that echoed like deep thunder through the house. Within seconds a pounding threatened to lift his door from the hinges.

"Theodore!" Auntie Lil demanded. "Open up."

He stumbled to the doorway, groggy with sleep. "This is too much," he protested. "They should let the guests sleep."

"This can't be the play," Auntie Lil said sharply, drawing him into the hall. "I feared something like this might happen."

"Like what?" T.S. asked. He tried a light switch. It did not work. "Was that thunder and lightning? The power is off."

"It was murder," she said. "Real murder. Follow me." Doors opened as they passed, sleepy faces peeking out in bewilderment. They acquired a small parade of confused guests by the time they reached the far side of the staircase.

"What's going on?" Auntie Lil demanded.

"The power's out," Clarabelle wailed from the darkness. "And I heard a gunshot. A gunshot in my own home!" She was waving a small flashlight wildly in her nervousness. In front of her, a tall figure bent down in the shadows, fiddling at the lock of a closed door.

"It's locked," the figure announced. It was the fluttery voice of Dr. Ronald Sussman.

"The gunshot sounded like it was right outside my room," Clarabelle cried. "The doctor is on the other side of me, so it has to be this room."

"Whose room is it?" Auntie Lil demanded.

"Maria Taylor's," Clarabelle said, her cry escalating into a wail. "She won't answer our knocks."

"Open up!" Dr. Sussman shouted, pounding vigorously on the door. He stepped aside. "You try it," he ordered T.S.

T.S. took up the challenge, turning the knob, lifting and pushing, jiggling and shoving, all in vain.

"Oh, get out of the way," the doctor ordered again, and T.S. backed off. Dr. Sussman stepped back until he was pressed against the second-floor railing, then hurled himself against the door. It flew open with a wrenching crack as the lock plate gave way. The doctor dashed through a small sitting room into the back. He returned to the hallway within seconds. "Give me your flashlight!" he ordered Clarabelle, snatching it from her hands. "Keep everyone back," he told T.S. and Auntie Lil. "There's trouble. Call an ambulance. Now!"

The others shrank back and stared in horror as he shut the door in their faces.

"Call," Auntie Lil told T.S., pushing him gently toward the steps. "Pray the phone lines are still up. And call the police at the same time."

"What should we do?" Agnes asked, her voice breaking. "Dorothy, I'm scared."

"Do nothing," Auntie Lil ordered. "Stay here. I'm going in. I'll see if the doctor needs any help. And keep this door open. The poor woman may need air. Clarabelle, stop that crying! Take charge of the crowd."

Auntie Lil marched back into the darkness of the suite, determined not to let the doctor bully her. The smell of cordite hung heavy in the air, and it took her eyes a few seconds to adjust to the deeper darkness of the inner room. Dr. Sussman was bent over the bed, gazing down at the lifeless figure of Maria Taylor. His delicate fingers probed beneath her throat, searching for a pulse.

"What are you doing here?" he asked brusquely. "This is no place for amateurs."

"I came to see if you needed help," Auntie Lil explained. "I can hold the flashlight for you."

"It's no use," he told Auntie Lil abruptly. "She's beyond help. Gunshot through the temple."

Auntie Lil was not surprised. She went to work examining the room. Maria Taylor had occupied a spacious suite with windows opening onto the back lawn. Auntie Lil checked the frames for signs of forced entry. They were firmly locked from the inside with heavy old-fashioned brass half-moons. She stared into the backyard. The blizzard had stopped and a heavy blanket of snow coated the lawn in one unending and undisturbed blanket. No footprints at all. Above, the clouds had cleared and a nearly full moon shone down, reflecting off the snow. Auntie Lil drew open the curtains and enough moonlight entered the room to allow her to get a better look at the scene.

A huge canopied bed was sumptuously covered with a ruffled pink satin comforter that cascaded to the floor on one side. Across the sheets, sprawled so dramatically that she might have been styled by a photographer, lay Maria Taylor. Her famous black hair fanned out around her upturned face in luxuriant snakes of dark color. Her arms were outstretched, and her mouth was slightly open. She was clad in a luminescent white dressing gown that pooled around her in shimmering waves and revealed a matching slip.

Dr. Sussman opened one of her eyes with his thumb and forefinger, then gazed into her pupil. "It's just happened," he said confidently. He examined her face. "The wound goes right through the forehead. There's absolutely no question about it."

"Well, then, for God's sakes, get out of this room and stop contaminating the evidence," Auntie Lil answered briskly.

The doctor glanced at Auntie Lil. "I apologize, but I took an oath to save lives and fulfilling that oath is my first priority. I had an obligation to see if I could help. I assure you I touched nothing."

"Well, now that you know you can't help," Auntie Lil said sensibly, "get out and stop spoiling things for the police."

Dr. Sussman snapped his black bag shut, annoyed. "It's a suicide, you silly old bat. This isn't one of those dismal murder mystery games."

Auntie Lil looked him over quietly. "That's all the more reason to let the police take over," she said.

The doctor had been outflanked. He marched from the room, head held high, and slammed the door pointedly behind him.

This was just what Auntie Lil had hoped. Scurrying over

to the bedside, she examined the actress, gently stroking her face and noting that the skin was already cooling. Without makeup, Maria Taylor's celebrated beauty was decidedly pedestrian. Fine wrinkles spread out like miniature fans from the corner of each eye. Heavy lines traced from each side of her nose to the edges of her too-thin lips. Her famed complexion looked splotchy and reddened by death. And it was indeed a fresh bullet wound: small, deadly and perfectly placed in the center of the forehead like a Brahmin's mark. How odd that so precise and neat a hole could destroy a life. But where was the gun? Auntie Lil lifted the edge of the comforter where it had slipped to the floor. There, deep beneath the folds of satin, lay a flat gray gun. She touched it with the tip of her elbow. It was still warm. No sense leaving fingerprints, not with this crowd. They'd read clues into everything.

Which wasn't a bad idea at all. Auntie Lil hurriedly detoured into the closet, where she discovered a small box containing a spectacular jewelry assortment, including a costly diamond necklace and bracelet set. The actress had not been robbed. She quickly scanned the bathroom as well, where a collection of cold cream and beauty jars on the windowsill drew her attention. She examined the labels in the bright moonlight, chose two and slipped them into the enormous pockets of her housecoat.

T.S. was waiting for her by the door. "What were you doing?" he hissed. "The police and ambulance are on their way."

"Never mind what I was doing," she murmured, looking up at the crowd huddled in the darkness. "The doctor is right," Auntie Lil announced. "Maria Taylor is dead."

"Dead?" someone called out. "How?"

"Suicide," Dr. Sussman said sadly. "The graceless exit of yet another aging actress. The gun is right there by the bed where it slipped from her hand." He shook his head sadly. "Such a waste of talent and beauty."

"An actual death," Charles Little said with reverence.

"I've never seen a real dead body," Agnes ventured.

"Me either," Dotty agreed. "It would be so interesting to—"

"No," Auntie Lil said firmly. "Absolutely not. We must not disturb the scene."

"She's quite right," Dr. Sussman agreed. "Perhaps we should guard it against curiosity seekers. I am used to such things. I shall be glad to wait by her bedside until the police arrive."

"Theodore, go with him," Auntie Lil said. "Don't argue. Just do it."

T.S. knew better than to debate. He followed the doctor inside, taking a position by the window where he could gaze out at the clean snow and forget that a suddenly still life force was lying void on the bed before him.

After a moment, the doctor excused himself and almost ran to the bathroom. T.S. could hear the sounds of repeated flushing. Thank God he wasn't that squeamish himself. And Sussman was a doctor.

Outside in the hallway, the assembled guests waited anxiously. The maid had appeared with an electric Coleman lantern. Clarabelle hovered beside her, her bright orange hair bulging at odd angles where the pouf had been flattened on one side from a pillow. Mr. Little crept toward the beacon, blinking like a baby owl in the glare from the lamp. He had obviously fallen asleep in his clothes, and his vest had fallen open to reveal a large red wine stain spread across the breast of his white shirt like a pool of blood. The sisters stared at it with keen interest and exchanged glances that threatened to erupt into accusations.

A distraction averted such a disaster. The door opposite

the murder scene opened and Donald Travers, Wall Street mogul, appeared with suitcases clasped in each hand. He ignored the crowd and called back into his room. "I said, let's go. I didn't come here for the weekend to get tangled in this nonsense."

"I'm not leaving with you," a determined voice answered. Marion Travers appeared in the doorway of her room and stared at her husband.

"This place is dangerous," her husband said. "I forbid you to stay."

"No." Her voice grew in confidence as she surveyed the many onlookers. "I refuse to leave with you. If you pursue the matter, I will start screaming."

"What?" Travers stared down at his wife. So did everyone else. The thought of the proper Marion Travers screaming was startling indeed.

"If you so much as move one more step closer to me, I'm going to start screaming." She opened her mouth silently, as if practicing.

Auntie Lil butted in with little hesitation. "Could I be of assistance?" she asked Mrs. Travers.

"Yes, thank you. I would like someone to remove my things from the room I am currently sharing with my husband," she replied with quiet dignity. "You may put them in Clarabelle's room, if you like. I'll wait there for the police."

"Stop this nonsense at once, Marion. You're coming with me." Donald Travers looked around, challenging anyone to interfere.

Auntie Lil parked herself directly in front of Mrs. Travers. "We won't let you take her anywhere against her will," Auntie Lil declared firmly. "In fact, I don't think it's a good idea for anyone to leave until the police get here. Perhaps it would be best if we all gathered together in the dining room to wait."

The thrust of her strong jaw and the glint in her eye dared anyone to disagree. Slowly the group began to trudge down the stairs, exchanging theories in low voices. Auntie Lil followed behind them, peeking out each window as she passed, examining the snow for fresh tracks. When they passed the sitting room, she popped in for a few seconds, emerging with a satisfied look.

They gathered in silence in the dining room, taking their places around the large table and gratefully accepting mugs of hot tea from the maid. Sipping in silence, they eyed one another suspiciously until the doorbell finally rang. The maid hurried to answer it as tension in the room rose palpably.

A burly man in a heavy down jacket appeared in the doorway. A gold badge was pinned to the lapel of his coat, and he wore a sheriff's hat pushed back on a graying crew cut. Behind him, a small group of uniformed men stood holding battery-operated lanterns, as if they were a particularly mature group of Halloween trick-or-treaters.

"Who's in charge?" the sheriff asked in a growl

No one answered. "In that case, I am," he announced. "Everyone stay in their seats. Who was injured?"

"Not injured—dead!" Agnes cried out and other voices joined in.

The sheriff efficiently dispatched several officers and the ambulance crew to Maria Taylor's room. Soon T.S. and Dr. Sussman joined their fellow guests in the dining area. The sheriff nodded for them to be seated. As soon as everyone was still, he placed two lanterns in the center of the table, making them all look spectacularly guilty, their faces alternately shrouded in darkness or glare.

He waved an arm expectantly. "Who's the person who phoned me?"

"I am," T.S. admitted.

"Then start," the sheriff ordered.

"But I saw the body first," Dr. Sussman interrupted. "I was lying awake, unable to sleep, when I heard a gunshot. The sound was unmistakable. I met Miss Clarke here in the hallway,"—he nodded toward Clarabelle—"and together we ascertained where the shot had come from. As these people can attest, the outer door to Miss Taylor's room was locked and I was forced to break it down. She had clearly committed suicide. The gun is lying right by the bed."

The silence that descended on the room after this seemingly inarguable synopsis was interrupted when Auntie Lil rose from her chair and pointed to the doctor. "That man," she announced calmly, "is a murderer. And I can prove it."

The room erupted in murmurs and Dr. Sussman raised his hands in a gesture of friendly helplessness. "Officer, this is a murder mystery weekend," he explained. "Everyone's imagination is on overdrive, shall we say. I'm afraid you'll find your progress hampered by all kinds of theories. Please don't hold it against this nice woman." He smiled kindly at Auntie Lil.

"Wipe that smirk off your face, you cold-hearted killer," Auntie Lil retorted. "And don't you dare patronize me."

"This is ridiculous," Dr. Sussman said, looking to the sheriff for help. "I was in my room when the gunshot occurred. Everyone saw me. The door was locked. I can't possibly have killed her."

The sheriff stood mutely between them, content to watch the play unfold. Several officers entered the room and were directed to stand around the table.

"You most certainly did kill her," Auntie Lil snapped back. "But not with the gun." She took two round bottles of face cream from her pocket and slammed them down on the table. Everyone jumped. "You killed her with these."

The sheriff stared at the objects. "Please continue," he said calmly.

"Maria Taylor is supposed to have the finest skin on television," Auntie Lil explained. "Yet when I examined her right after her death, her skin was red and splotchy."

"Did you happen to notice the gunshot through her head?" the doctor interrupted, his voice tight with anger.

"There was a gunshot wound, all right," Auntie Lil agreed. "But Maria Taylor was dead well before she was shot. I touched her skin. She had started to cool. She'd been dead for at least an hour."

"So now you're a pathologist?" Dr. Sussman challenged.

"Let her continue," the sheriff ordered.

Auntie pointed toward the beauty jars. "These are the murder weapons," she insisted. "If you let me, I can explain."

"Continue," the sheriff said.

"I knew at once it had not been a suicide," Auntie Lil said. "Because of the body's temperature. But murder? Only by an outsider. It would have been impossible for anyone to shoot Maria Taylor and return to their room in time without being noticed by another guest. Yet when I checked the snow all around the house, it was undisturbed. No one had entered. So that left only one explanation: events had not happened as they seemed. A murder had been staged after all. I had to figure out how—and why—Maria Taylor had really been murdered."

"This is ridiculous." The doctor rolled his eyes and stood. "Is everyone going to get a chance to play this game?"

"Shut up and sit down," the sheriff ordered. Dr. Sussman quickly complied.

"There were plenty of oddities to consider," Auntie Lil went on. "For example, traveling here this weekend was quite difficult, yet everyone made an effort to get here. My nephew and I came simply because we had promised Clarabelle. But why had the others traveled through sleet and snow to get here? And why had Maria Taylor agreed to take the part in the first place? No offense, Clarabelle, dear. But what was the doctor doing here—he thought the whole idea 'dismal'? Or Mr. Travers, who clearly thought it beneath him?"

"I resent the insinuation," Donald Travers said.

Auntie Lil eyed him carefully and continued. "The staged mystery was really very silly. People drank too much, the acting was wretched and we all retired early in defense. The alcohol, the fatigue, the weather all combined to encourage heavy sleeping. No one heard a door opened here or there, no one heard footsteps in the hall. No one heard the murder being committed—because it all happened hours before the gunshot rang out." She stopped and glanced around the table. "The gunshot was merely to establish an alibi for Dr. Sussman here, who had decided to murder the wrong woman. And he's not the only murderer among us."

"What do you mean?" one of the sisters asked.

"I believe that Miss Taylor had recently started an affair," Auntie Lil answered. "An affair with a very rich man. I'm speaking, of course, of Donald Travers. There can be no other credible explanation for his presence here."

The millionaire rose from his chair and stared at Auntie Lil. She shrugged. "It will be quite easy to prove, you know. While searching Maria Taylor's room—you needn't look so shocked, I'm not bound by rules of search and seizure—I discovered a fabulously expensive bracelet and necklace set. You can trace its purchase back to Donald Travers. Or simply ask Marion Travers—Maria Taylor does not strike me as a very discreet woman."

"It's true," Marion Travers confirmed quietly, as her husband abruptly reclaimed his seat. "I never dreamed she would be here this weekend. I thought my husband wanted to get away together to repair our marriage."

"He wanted to destroy your life," Auntie Lil explained sadly. "You have a great deal of money on your own, do you not? Forgive me if I pry."

The woman nodded, not looking up.

"Money I believe your husband needed," Auntie Lil confirmed. "And this need coincided with Maria Taylor's own need to marry quickly and to marry well, before the bloom faded even more from her rose, shall we say. She and your husband conspired to have you killed, I am sure, and turned to Dr. Sussman for help. There was a very curious conversation earlier in the sitting room that helped me make the connection. Dr. Sussman attempted to force his beauty creams on Mrs. Travers." Auntie Lil pointed toward the graceful woman. "Her skin is flawless. Why in the world attempt to alter perfection? What Dr. Sussman was really trying to do was force his poison creams on her."

"How dare you!" Dr. Sussman shouted.

"Chemical analysis will confirm it," Auntie Lil said simply, sliding the jars toward the sheriff. "I suspect a topical poison capable of soaking through the skin. Some sort of insecticide, perhaps Parathion."

The sheriff took the jars without comment, storing them in a jacket pocket for safekeeping. He was not smiling.

"It had to be done that way," Auntie Lil said, "Marion Travers couldn't be poisoned any other way because she is very strict about what goes into her body. She eats only the purest of foods with the blandest of tastes. So Donald Travers came up with a plan worthy of a successful businessman when Marion Travers mentioned to her husband that she'd met a woman named Clarabelle at a New Age convention. Clarabelle owned a lodge, she told her husband, and staged mystery weekends. People paid a lot of money to participate. How much fun it all sounded." Auntie Lil nodded an apology toward Clarabelle. "It was terribly rude of them to involve you," she said.

"This is just too awful," Clarabelle choked out, her hand massaging the base of her throat.

"Because Donald Travers had always been vain himself—and had affairs with vain women—he assumed that his wife must be as well," Auntie Lil continued. "He based his plan on vanity and that was his undoing. He cultivated an acquaintance with Dr. Sussman at Maria Taylor's suggestion and offered him a significant sum of money, I suspect, to prepare a special set of face creams for his wife. Dr. Sussman appears quite vulnerable to offers of money." Auntie Lil shook her head in great distaste; this was a clear sign of poor breeding in her book. "Executing the plan was easy. Maria Taylor was part of it. She simply called up Clarabelle and asked to be in one of her weekend mysteries."

"It's true," Clarabelle confirmed. "I could not believe my good luck."

"Donald Travers then invited his wife up here that same weekend," Auntie Lil continued. "The plan was to compliment Maria on her skin, to make Mrs. Travers jealous enough to try Dr. Sussman's remedies. But Marion Travers would not accept the cream, and the doctor saw his payment slipping away."

"Then why was Maria Taylor killed instead?" Mr. Little asked.

"You'll have to ask Dr. Sussman," Auntie Lil said. "I think he had a deeper grudge against Maria Taylor in mind all along, despite the fact that he had offered to commit murder on her behalf. Perhaps Dr. Sussman had wanted more from Maria Taylor than she cared to give him, in terms of both money and affection. I noticed Miss Taylor snubbed him in the dining room. She pretended not to know him at all. Certainly her murder was premeditated."

"You have no proof of that!" the doctor cried.

"Don't I?" Auntie Lil said. "Last night, for whatever reason, you entered Maria Taylor's room and switched her regular creams for your poisons, making it look as if the jars were half-used. I am sure if these nice young officers search thoroughly enough, they'll find plastic gloves and poison residue in this house somewhere. Try the drains in Miss Taylor's bathroom first. Thanks to my nephew Theodore standing guard on the body, the doctor here was unable to remove the creams from Miss Taylor's room. But perhaps he tried to flush away other evidence."

The doctor's back stiffened and he looked away.

"But why the gunshot?" the sheriff asked, intrigued.

"To take attention away from her skin," Auntie Lil said. "And to give the doctor an alibi. I suspect that Maria Taylor had left her door open for late night visitors." She coughed discreetly and glanced away from the stricken Marion Travers. "That made it easy for Dr. Sussman to check on her later, to confirm that she was dead. When he saw the unexpected condition of her skin, his plan became all the more important. He stole a prop gun from the sitting room, where one of the actors had left it last evening. When the time was right, he shot off the blank gun in the upper floor stairwell. That was why it boomed so loudly. He has admitted he was the first to examine the body. In fact, no one else had a chance. He made sure that everyone knew the door was locked, even using my own nephew to establish that fact, then shut it in our faces and was alone with the body long enough to shoot her for real, using the gun you will find by the side of her bed and a silencer. His own words convict him. He told us all that the gun was right there by the bed; yet I had to lift up the covers before I spotted it—and he claimed not to have touched a thing. I am sure you'll find the silencer somewhere in this house." She looked at the doctor. "It proves premeditation, wouldn't you say? The fact that he brought the gun and a silencer along. He had agreed to kill Mrs. Travers, but his real victim had been Maria Taylor all along. Or perhaps he had intended to kill them both, earning a tidy sum and gaining revenge at the same time. If you decide to search for the silencer, I'd try Donald Travers's luggage first. He seemed extremely anxious to leave before the police arrived."

There was a thump as Donald Travers recrossed one of his legs.

"Travers had to agree to help Dr. Sussman cover up," Auntie Lil explained. "He could not say anything without implicating himself in another murder plot. I suspect blackmail would have been the doctor's next step."

Auntie Lil finished her story, and her bright eyes darted around the room.

The sheriff stared at Auntie Lil, his face an impassive mask that was threatening to crack. "What did you say your name was again, ma'am?" he asked, pushing his hat even further back and scratching at his hairline.

"My name is Lillian Hubbert," she told the sheriff crisply. "But you may call me Auntie Lil."

Love is a funny thing, not just sometimes, but all the time. It can make people you've known all your life do the strangest things. It can drive friends apart and family away. And of course, the crimes love can lead to, well, those are innumerable. Our next story is set in the South, where emotions often run hot, and some feelings, especially love, can take years to cool off.

In Memory of Jack

Elizabeth Daniels Squire

Because I bought a dozen candy bars from Billy Read, I was able to fulfill my Uncle Jack's last wishes.

It's hard to say no to Billy. He came in the kitchen door, gave me a hero-worship smile, and put some Mars Bars and Reese's Cups on the table. He said, "What I like best about that book you wrote is the part about how you can remember something better if you see a real shocker of a picture in your head."

It's nice to have an avid admirer thirteen years old. It's different.

"That system really works with names," he said. "I have a new teacher. Miss McCarson. McCarson is like My Car's On. So I see her under the front wheels. That's neat."

Billy is our neighbor who likes books and wears thick

glasses. He was all dressed up in good slacks and tie. "I'm selling candy," he said, "to raise money for our eighth-grade trip."

In this awestruck tone, he added, "and I think it's wonderful you write books *and* you solve murders." My book, I hasten to add, is not about murders. It's called *How to Survive Without a Memory*, by me, Peaches Dann. It's a subject I know well.

Billy squirmed with admiration. Kind of sweet. "And I read in the paper how you saved that girl who was tied up and locked up, and you found out who killed her sister." He beamed. "And she wasn't much older than me."

I *have* solved murders, though not on purpose, exactly. My mountain relatives and friends are just plain accident-prone. They get killed and accused like you wouldn't believe. Maybe because I'm related to half the population. At least on my father's side.

"I'm reading a book about famous murders too," he said, ignoring his mission with the candy bars. "I just see shocking stuff in my head and I can remember all the ways there are to get killed."

Good grief, was I that ghoulish as a kid? Well, I did like blood and thunder.

". . . Like plain old hanging. . . ."—he grabbed his necktie and held the loose end up above his head to imitate that and picked up the bread knife from the kitchen table—". . . and stabbing." He pretended to plunge the knife into his chest.

"And fancy kinds, like strychnine poisoning. Where the person thrashes around"—he arched his body back and forward—"and then they die with this 'rictus sardonicus'—I like those words, which mean a hideous smile. And their eyeballs are rolled up in their head and bulging, too." He made a face that was hideous and grinning worse than death. It was an image to remember, all right.

"But didn't you want to sell me candy?" I asked, so I bought a dozen Mars Bars quick to end the conversation before he cut himself or his eyes got stuck. I figured I could take some candy to my Uncle Jack, who needed spice in his life. He loved chocolate.

The following Thursday I went to visit Uncle Jack. I just had a feeling that was the right day. Maybe he told me something and I forgot it and it just hung around in my mind like intuition. I knew I should go then.

Jack was my only nearby relative on my mother's side. I told you I have a million kin on Pop's side. But my mother's folks have moved away from here. Only Uncle Jack stayed near Asheville, living in a shack out in the country. He grew a small garden and called himself an old hermit. Like Thoreau without philosophy or a pond, my husband said, sounding like a college professor, which he is. Still, Jack didn't have a single enemy that I knew of.

I went by Uncle Jack's whenever I was down his way, off the road to Paint Fork, not far from Asheville. He had the gift of making you feel like there was nobody he would rather see in the whole world. I was sure he was lonely, in spite of the million birds that flocked around his house because he fed them even in summer.

As I drove onto the dirt drive that leads to his weathered wood cabin, the sun was shining. The birds were calling back and forth in the trees, an irregular symphony. I got out of my car and paused to hear.

Then those birds flew up in a flutter and streamed away as a woman banged my uncle's back screen door. She came running out, screaming, "Oh, God, he's gone." I stood still in surprise. She ran right over to me, past a white Cadillac— of all things!—parked in the drive. She stopped, gulped a

couple of times, looked me straight in the eye and cried,
"This is terrible. I loved him. I loved them both." A red bird,
confused, flew right across in front of her. I felt his wind. I
was confused too. "But I couldn't marry either one," she
cried. "I couldn't do it. And now he's gone!" That part is
etched on my mind because it seemed so absolutely strange.
"Strange" is a memory aid, par excellence.

Now, I may be bad at names, and also faces, but I was
sure I had never seen this woman with the triangular face,
small mouth and large lustrous eyes before in my life. And
how could Uncle Jack be gone? I was alarmed. He never
went anywhere.

You see, something went wrong for Jack. My mother said
it began back in school, where Jack had almost flunked out.
But he wasn't stupid, he just couldn't fit a mold. One of his
brothers became a lawyer and the other became a doctor,
which made that even harder. But he was seventy years old
now. He could relax.

Jack had found a place for himself. He'd looked after an
aunt. She'd had nurses, but he did errands. She died and left
him enough to manage in his shack in the woods.

Still, he hadn't had a girlfriend in years that I knew of.
And here was this hysterical woman in rich-city-folks country clothes. Designer-type denim, a huge leather bag,
Birkenstocks, southwestern silver and turquoise dripping
from her neck and ears. Her body was shaking but it still
looked like a work of art—composed, painted, curled, manicured, massaged, whatever. She was also petite and pretty,
though she must have been at least sixty-five.

This woman threw her arms around me, engulfed me in
heady perfume, and wept on my shoulder as if I was her
mother. I'm not old enough, for goodness sakes. I'm only
fifty-six.

"You expected him to be there and now he's not?" I asked. "He knew you were coming?"

"Yes, yes, I wrote. And he wrote back. He expected me at two o'clock." She and I both looked at our watches. It was two-twenty.

"And now he's dead," she cried.

Dead! I couldn't move. She had me in a going-down-for-the-third-time hug. "He was my friend," she sobbed on my shoulder, "even when I wouldn't marry him—even when I never saw him. I knew he was there. He couldn't keep a job, and I need looking after. Well, I do! But now he's dead."

Dead! I managed to pull loose and started to run and see what had happened to Uncle Jack.

"No!" she cried. "Don't look! It's terrible!" She clasped her silvered throat as if she might choke. But I had to go. I ran down the dirt drive past blooming daisies and tall grasses, pulled the screen door open and looked inside. And there, next to the worn couch where he often slept without even bothering to remove his jeans and shirt, was Uncle Jack, contorted on the gray wooden floor as if he died writhing. He had such a terrible grimace on his face that right away I saw Billy Read, the candy-bar boy with his whatever-sardonicus, his horrible smile. My uncle's eyes were rolled up in his head just like Billy said, and bulging too. Strychnine! I felt sick.

I knelt down and felt. No pulse. I couldn't believe this. Uncle Jack never hurt a soul. So who could want to hurt him? Why?

But wait, I told myself. Suppose this was a heart attack? I didn't believe it. Suppose he killed himself? He wasn't the type. He was spartan, but in his way he enjoyed life. He certainly enjoyed his birds.

So call the sheriff, I told myself, choking back tears—but Jack didn't have a phone. Besides, I needed to look around.

By the reclining chair where he always sat, and where one contorted hand now pointed, the small glass-topped table that had been his mother's lay on its side on the floor. The glass had cracked. The Paris ashtray he'd brought back from the war always sat on the table, but it was on the floor, too. With cigarette butts scattered all over. Somehow, Jack had done OK in the army. He used to tell me how he meant to look up his old army buddies after the war, but then he never did.

Had something from that time come back to haunt him? Why so many cigarette butts? Had he been nervous and smoked double-time? Or had someone else smoked too? I looked closely. All were his cork-tipped kind of butts.

In the corner near his chair stood the big brass-bound black trunk that had belonged to his father. I couldn't open that without touching—never corrupt a crime scene—so I took a chance that the undisturbed dust on top meant it hadn't been opened lately. I knew the trunk held a German gun he'd managed to bring back from World War II which probably didn't work. "I could have gotten in trouble for bringing that back," he used to say and shake his head and chuckle. His photograph albums were in there, too, showing how good-looking he was as a young man, with that widow's peak and rebellious dark eyes with long lashes. A heartbreaker.

Was that why this carefully made-up woman had come back to find him? She said she'd loved him! But she didn't fit.

Out the window, I saw his big bird feeder, a tray on a pole. A lone black bird had ventured back and pecked at seed.

My eye fell on his rock collection on one windowsill. Oh, he loved to tell about that. As a kid he hiked a lot and collected quartz and such. And he loved to tell how he'd almost stepped on snakes a couple of times. "I should have looked where I stepped more carefully, but I never did." Always a storyteller, Uncle Jack. He liked to laugh at himself. About how he wasn't clever at looking out for number one.

The champagne-bottle lamp on the table at the end of the couch looked out of place in his rustic room. He'd said he'd given a party for his best girl and some friends right after the war and they drank the champagne. "And at that party I introduced her to the rich good-looking guy that she upped and married. I wasn't very smart, was I?" And yet, as I say, my Uncle Jack wasn't exactly dumb. He had an open library book cover-up on the arm of his chair. A new life of Robert E. Lee.

I heard a sniff and saw the city woman standing in the door, quietly crying and watching me. Her makeup was smeared now, distorting her face. Reminding me of his. I had to stand close to him, the room was so small. I shuddered. And I suddenly had the oddest feeling that this woman was sad and shocked—but not surprised.

So had Jack done something careless that enraged someone to the point of poison? What did this woman know? Why didn't I go right over and ask her? But I wanted to look around first. I let my eyes go back to his poor contorted body. Who could my uncle have infuriated to the point of murder? Uncle Jack never went anywhere. Not except with a neighbor to the grocery store or sometimes the laundromat, or to the bookmobile that parked just down the road.

I looked at the old brown throw-blanket on the end of the couch. Jack never wanted anything new. He said the throw belonged to his grandmother. It was full of holes but "I like what I'm used to." That's what he said when I tried to get him a new one for his birthday. He didn't ask for much.

The bathroom door was open, so I stepped in. A brown

bath towel hung on a rack at the end of the claw-foot enamel tub. By now, that tub must be a valuable antique. But he wouldn't have sold it. He was used to it. A couple of tissues and a wrapper from some Tums lay in the bottom of the dented metal wastebasket. The medicine cabinet hung open. His few bottles of medicine sat on the shelf. Not that he ever used them. Like I said, he was a spartan. He ignored pain.

Once, a few years back, when I dropped by, he was down with flu. I said I'd get him something for his upset stomach, but all he'd let me get him was a cup of tea. "And put the Tums on the table and if I don't feel better in a while I'll take one." I noticed he had an ancient-looking bottle of Pepto-Bismol and an antique-looking tin that said baking soda. I remembered the soda tin. When I was a kid I saw him put two spoonfuls from that tin in a glass of water and drink it down, and I asked if it was instant orange soda or some other kind. And he just laughed and said baking soda helped an acid stomach and wasn't sweet soda at all.

Later, on the day when he had flu, I said his medicines looked kind of old and I'd get him some new ones. "I don't waste things," he said. He sounded angry. "You leave those there." And now the antique Pepto-Bismol was still there, but no Tums or baking soda. There was some rubbing alcohol, some aftershave lotion Ted and I had given him the Christmas before, and a box of Band-Aids.

I came back to the living room and the woman was no longer in the door. I looked out and saw her down the drive a little way, sitting on a log, still crying. I decided she wasn't going to run away.

I cased the small lean-to kitchen—nothing out of place there. I went in Uncle Jack's bedroom. A sweater for our cool mountain evenings hung over a chair. A few holes in that too. On the table under the window, I saw a box of letters, maybe about twenty. My fingers itched. But I knew I should leave the crime scene as it was. Still, one letter was open on the table. The second page was on top. I could read that.

Don't say you're almost scared to see me again, Jack. You've been my friend all these years. And now that I am alone I need my friends. I'm glad that you remember me when you feed the birds, that you think how I love birds. I'll be by at two on Thursday, and we'll reminisce.

It was signed *With Love, L.*

How long had it lain there? Why was he almost afraid to see her? And did it matter if anyone but my uncle knew the woman was coming at two o'clock?

Now I was afraid the woman might leave. I ran out, but she was still sitting on the log.

"Nothing looks disturbed inside," I said. "Except near his body. Did you touch anything?"

The woman seemed to relax a little and raised her blotched face and I thought: Why, she's relieved at what I just asked. That's odd.

She said, "No."

Then I remembered myself and said, "I'm Peaches Dann, Jack Harrison's niece."

"We have to call the police, don't we," she said. "And they have to talk to me because . . ." She choked up again. She's afraid, I thought. Could she have done this?

"We have to call the sheriff, not police," I said. "We're out in the county. I'll call from the house down the hill. You'd better come with me."

She got in my Toyota, leaving her white Cadillac. Perhaps she didn't trust herself to drive. "Where are you staying?" I asked as we headed toward a neighbor's house. "You may have to stay over."

"I was only passing through."

Next I did something which may prove I'm nuts. "You

cared about my uncle," I said. "Why don't you stay with us?" I said that to this woman about whom I knew nothing at all, not even her name, this woman I'd have never met if I hadn't brought my uncle candy bars. She might perfectly well be the one who killed my mother's brother. But I felt no woman who loved birds could be all bad.

Of course she told me her name then: Lulu Girder. Lulu. Yes, that matched the L. on the letter.

Lulu! The girl who went with the bottle of champagne! Suddenly that came back to me. My uncle used to say "Her name was Lulu, and she was a real Lulu!" To him that obviously meant a real winner. Maybe a hot babe. I wished her last name—Girder—didn't rhyme with murder, but that did mean I wasn't likely to forget it. Billy would have been pleased.

The county sheriff I had known well had been defeated for office several months back, which was just as well because he didn't like me. The sheriff's men who arrived were new to me. I told them everything I'd noticed and that my uncle had no enemies at all that I knew of. They agreed that, yes, as the next of kin, they'd keep in touch with me. Good.

They questioned Lulu and asked her to stick around. And so my invitation was accepted.

Lulu was no trouble as a houseguest, I'll say that. She knew how to pitch in and help snap the beans or pick the blueberries in the yard. Oh, she appreciated nice things. She spotted the Persian rug Ted's great-aunt left him. The great-aunt whose husband owned the largest brickyard in South Carolina. And Lulu seemed to be a nurturer. She pulled a thorn from my cat Silk's paw. But mostly she sat on our terrace, listened to the birds sing, and retreated into a book. Whatever was around: *The Kitchen God's Wife* by Amy Tan or a mystery by Margaret Maron. She sat and read for hours, like someone recuperating from an illness. She could have been recuperating from committing a murder. But I didn't want to think so. I liked her. Still, I had an odd feeling she was waiting for something. Was it something she expected from me? From the sheriff? What?

She told me the basics of her life. She'd grown up in Asheville, met Uncle Jack as one of the boys coming back from World War II. Left Asheville when she married and lived in Atlanta. No children. Now her husband had died. She was wandering, not sure what next.

"Jack and I were so young when we met," she said, as she and Ted and I had breakfast on the terrace. "Twenty-three didn't seem young then, but it certainly does now. Jack was kind," she said, sipping her coffee. "I never heard him say one mean word. A rebel, yes, impractical, but never mean. He was terribly good-looking. And he worshiped me. That may sound vain," she said, fluttering eyelashes, "but it's true." She smiled a dreamy smile at the clematis vine with white star flowers at the edge of the terrace.

Ted excused himself. He said he had to finish digging the hole and plant the two-foot-high quince tree he'd bought at Penland's nursery the day before. He winked at me. "I like your quince jelly."

After he left, Lulu reached out and touched my hand and said, "You have to understand that I loved your Uncle Jack," she frowned. "But I also loved Martin Heller."

What? "Martin Heller? Who was that?"

"I don't know how you can love two men at once." she sighed. "But I did. Martin wasn't like Jack. He was trouble. He couldn't control his temper. If you hurt Martin Heller, he had to get even. He actually went to jail for breaking a friend's nose."

I'd remember that name: He was a real hell-raiser, a *Heller*.

"I was a crazy kid," she said. "I had to fix people. I had to

love the ones who needed to be loved. We actually hung out
together, Jack and Martin and me. But I couldn't marry either one. So then I met Harold, and he was kind, and he was
practical, and he was rich and he asked me to marry him.
And I didn't love him, so I knew he must be OK."

Suddenly this all fit together. "Jack introduced you to
Harold," I said. "At a champagne party."

"Yes," she said. "Poor Jack. He took it hard." Tears glistened in her eyes. She dabbed them with her napkin. "But
we stayed friends. We wrote now and then. My husband was
a little dull. And I cheated on him. I'm not proud I cheated,"
she said. "Harold was important to me. He took care of me.
And I disappointed him. So it was nice to have a friend like
Jack, who still thought that I was wonderful."

But he was "almost scared" to see you again, I thought—
that's what it said in the letter. Because Uncle Jack still
loved her? Or why?

"Was your husband jealous of Jack?" I asked.

"He was a very jealous man, but why of Jack? Jack became a friend. I needed a friend."

"And this other man you said you loved? This Heller?"

She sighed deeply. She plucked a daisy by the edge of the
deck and began to pull off the petals. "I've always believed
Martin killed himself." She threw the daisy down as if she
was angry at it. "Martin drove his car into a tree right after I
married Hal." She waited for me to react, but I outwaited
her. "He was so damned angry to learn I'd picked another
man that he killed himself," she said. "I sure have my regrets."

Killed himself! Both of the men she loved died violent
deaths. Poor Lulu. Or was this woman by my side the kiss
of death? There were people, I'd heard, who needed to kill
what they loved. People who looked as friendly as Lulu.

She was silent for a long time, staring into the heart of the clematis as if it had an answer for her. I finished my pancakes. I watched my husband digging a deep hole for the quince tree. He believes it's important to put in fertilizer below the plant. To prepare the soil just right. I thought how lucky to have a husband who likes to make things grow instead of two dead lovers and a husband who died disappointed.

I glanced at Lulu. She must have been a lovely young girl with those lustrous blue eyes and small gentle mouth. Wide-browed like a kitten. She was toying with her pancakes, not eating much.

Finally Lulu spoke again, eyes sorrowful but hopeful. "Jack believed that Martin hit that tree because he was drunk."

That would be less painful for Lulu. Yes. "How would Jack know?"

She began to twist and shred her paper napkin. "Jack wrote me about it," she said. "Martin came to see Jack right after I married Hal and brought some bottles of red wine in a grocery bag. Brought the whole bag inside because it was hot outside in his car and he didn't want the milk to sour." She sighed. "Jack was so funny he wrote me all the details. Lord, that was fifty years ago! He said Martin told him they'd both lost me, so they should be friends—they should get drunk together. Jack was touched. So Martin drank a lot of red wine, but Jack couldn't drink much. Red wine upset his stomach, always had. But he wanted to be friends, so he drank a little. Then he couldn't find bicarbonate of soda to settle his stomach. Just the empty tin. But Martin had soda in his groceries. He gave the box to Jack. 'Which proved he really was my friend.' That's what Jack wrote me. Little things touched Jack. And he was horrified that Martin went out from his house drunk and drove into a tree." Her napkin was now in shreds. "Jack felt he should have stopped Martin. But no one ever could stop Martin from what he meant to do."

"And that is why the soda, which he put in his old tried-and-true baking soda tin, was one of my uncle's mementos," I said. I laughed. "A very odd memento. The one he never talked about. But he wouldn't let me throw it out."

Later that day as I washed lettuce and Lulu cut up chicken for salad, Deputy Frank Robb from the sheriff's office called to tell me that the lab report showed strychnine had killed my Uncle Jack. So I was right. I shuddered. "There was not a bit of strychnine anywhere in the house. Not even a glass that had had some in it," he reported. "No clear fingerprints but his and yours. Frankly, we're baffled."

I came back and sat down at the kitchen table. I told Lulu the news. She went dead pale.

And I realized I knew who killed my uncle.

I jumped up and went to call Chuck Sprinkle at the Weaverville Pharmacy, who knows about such things, and ask him a few questions about strychnine. Yes, he said strychnine would keep potent for years and years mixed with baking soda in a tin.

Then I confronted Lulu. "You stole my uncle's soda," I said . "He never threw it away. He never threw anything away."

She began to tremble, so she put the knife down. She put her small, plump hands flat on the table to steady herself.

"Strychnine was mixed into the soda," I said. "You removed it for that reason."

She blinked several times. Blue eyes furtive in their mascara rings. Desperately trying to think of a good lie, I thought. I was disappointed.

Then her shoulders slumped. She seemed to fade. Blonde hair washed out, skin shriveled beneath her make up, eyes watery blue, hands clasped as if each was afraid to be alone.

"I killed him," she whispered. Then she sat straighter and said it out loud. "I killed him."

"Why?" I asked.

"I killed them both." Her voice cracked like a teen's. "It was my fault. I could have prevented what happened. With Martin, I should have known."

She rocked back and forth in her chair. She swallowed. "Martin called me and began to yell that he would never forgive me for 'leading him on' and then marrying another man. I should have known he would do something wild. I knew what he was like and I loved him anyway. I felt weak when he kissed me. I can still remember." She pursed her lips. She sighed. "But I never felt safe with him. I felt safe with Jack." She cried a little. To get my sympathy? No, I felt her tears were real.

"And when Martin said that he was going to go get drunk with Jack because I'd done them both in, I should have known. 'That fool, Jack,' Martin screamed at me. 'It was just like that fool to introduce you to the perfect man to marry. Stinking rich. And stinking respectable. Good-bye!' He hung up in my face."

Her eyes looked straight through me, back to the past. I knew she didn't hear the two finches calling to each other across the lawn or see the small green inchworm that had landed on one of her hands. Those hands were holding the table again as if it might run away. "Martin," she said, as if the word was a curse.

"And so, what happened?" I asked.

She blinked and came back to the present. She brushed away the inchworm. "Martin knew red wine gave Jack a stomachache," Lulu said unhappily. "We all knew that. Red wine or nerves. Either one. So Martin gave Jack red wine and soda."

"Wine and soda?"

"Martin brought the red wine and also the poison mixed into the baking soda, and I'm sure he told Jack he needed to take some soda when his stomach hurt. He was so damn clever. If Jack already had soda in the bathroom, Martin probably threw it out. And Martin was persuasive, he really was. He meant to poison Jack and kill himself. I'm sure of that. To get even with Jack and make me feel bad."

"But he didn't wait and watch Uncle Jack take the strychnine and soda," I said, "because Uncle Jack didn't take it. Thank God. He had the habit of trying first to sleep off whatever hurt. And then he got to taking Tums instead of soda. He liked the flavor."

She shook her head amazed. "So why . . . ?"

"And when, after all these years, he expected you—when he was so nervous about this meeting that he smoked a whole pack of cigarettes—he got a stomachache. And he wanted to be his best with you. He had no time to sleep it off. And he was out of Tums. The empty container was in the trash. So he took some soda and he died."

"Yes," she sobbed, "and as soon as I found him dead, it all slipped into place. And I knew. And it was my fault because I should have known sooner. I should have known when Martin said good-bye he meant the big good-bye. I should have written Jack to throw away that soda Martin gave him. What Martin gave my Jack was death. And Martin killed himself because of me." She shook: a child-woman in her rich woman clothes. I felt a surge of fury at this Martin, but not at Lulu.

I squeezed her hand tight. "No," I said. "He killed himself because he couldn't live with himself. Anymore than you could live with him. He killed himself because he was angry at the whole world. That's not your fault. And you don't need to keep protecting him. He's dead. He can't be tried for murder. You didn't need to steal that poison to protect his name."

"And Jack—" she sobbed.

"He died expecting you," I said. "And maybe hoping for more than was really possible. He had a few minutes of pain. But, basically, he died happy."

She stared at me, wide-eyed, incredulous. "You're generous, like Jack."

I felt like crying myself. "I'd like to do what he would have wanted me to do," I said. "He would have wished for you to be happy."

And then I did something that wasn't like me at all. It *was* like Uncle Jack. Generous and a little bit reckless.

Lulu was crying so hard, I didn't think she could hear me. "Stop that!" I called out. She almost choked, but she stopped.

"Now, if you take that soda tin to the police," I said, "you may be charged with withholding information. You could even be a prime suspect for murder, since you were the last one to see Uncle Jack alive. And you certainly had the means."

She nodded unhappily.

"If you don't take that soda tin to the police, and if you dispose of it forever—in an incinerator, for example—then if by some chance an innocent person should be accused of the murder, we have no way to prove otherwise. So I want you to write down the story of Jack's letter to you about Martin's visit and the red wine. Just that part, no admission of anything, and sign it. I'll put it in my safety deposit box in case of need. And then," I said, "you might take that soda tin from where ever it's hidden, and the glass and spoon— you must have those—and put them in one of those plastic bags that are a problem because they don't biodegrade in the dump," I said. "And when Ted comes in to lunch, you could drop the poison in that hole that Ted has dug for the quince tree and put a little dirt on top so Ted won't notice.

"And then you need to forgive yourself, because you never meant to hurt." I gave her a big hug for Uncle Jack.

Later, when Ted finished planting the quince and tamped the dirt around the bush, I admired the lovely job. "It looks so at home, you'd think it had been there forever," I said. A red bird perched on top and began to sing.

I almost cried. But then at the same time I almost laughed. Because I thought how bug-eyed Billy Read would be to know that murder can lie in wait for almost fifty years. And that an accessory to hiding evidence lived right down his street in my house. I must never tell Ted. He'd be shocked.

"It's always a fine thing," Ted said, "to plant a fruit tree because it's useful as well as ornamental."

"Yes," I said. "Let's say we planted it in memory of Uncle Jack."

Although I pride myself on my professionalism, I have to admit that there have been times when I finished some of my novels a little too close to deadline. As much as I hate to admit it, there's something almost enjoyable about racing against the clock. I don't think, however, that I've ever had the problems the author in the following story encounters.

A Surfeit of Deadlines

Susan Dunlap

I'm not that kind of writer. Really.

Not that my agent or my editor believes that. Okay, so I've missed a few deadlines. Well, every deadline. But I have had excuses. Well, not great excuses. But what kind of tyrants would demand that I come up with a great excuse when I'm madly trying to finish a book?

I used to have great excuses, but I've gone through them by now; that's what makes my position so difficult. "When you said September, naturally I assumed you meant the *end* of September, not the first." My editor and my agent had both heard that one before. (Actually, it was my virgin offering to the sacrificial pyre of publishing deadlines.) A real daughter's wedding, that would be a lock for a month's extension. For the first time I was sorry I didn't have children.

Earthquake? Great for eliciting sympathy, but hard to fake. The flu? Too temporary. Broken arm? Too much hassle, and besides I'd already used that twice. Dying grandmother, lover, Labrador retriever?

I sighed. I had fabricated so often, nothing short of death was going to get me an extension from my editor. But suicide seemed a bit extreme, and it was too late to fly to New York and do him in.

I sighed again and contemplated the remaining eighty—that's eight-oh—pages necessary to complete my contractual obligation. Necessary in order for me to get paid. Knowing how close to the financial edge I live, my editor and agent cooked up a Machiavellian deal to "encourage me to deliver the manuscript in a timely manner." My "payment upon delivery" sat in a checking account. As soon as my agent authorized its release I could write a check for it—and cover my expenses for the trip to Paris I'd arranged to reward myself (not to mention the house payment and my tab with the grocer, the dentist, and six credit card companies).

So, I had to get the book done.

September 1 was Friday. Friday evening I would be on a plane to Paris. And my manuscript had to be on its own UPS plane to New York. Perhaps I would even pass it in the jet stream. Five hundred fifty pages of magnificently plotted prose, sporting devilishly clever characters, diabolical deeds, and a beats-the-devil denouement. The threads of those misdeeds would be winding in and out, creating a Gordian knot of danger, deception, doubt, and dubiety, until my detective, the suave and prescient Cerai, skillfully unraveled it, thread by slick, colorful thread. By page four hundred he'd be chasing after danger, by four seventy-five he'd stare death in the face, till, around five four-three, give or take a page, he'd skewer the murderer on his own sword.

Well, clever characters had done their job. They had tied

the plot in knots tighter than I had managed in any novel before. Cerai appeared stumped.

Cerai *was* stumped. He couldn't pick out the murderer or his sword, much less impale him on same.

It was now Monday, August 27. In the next five days I had to write those eighty pages, pack for Paris, figure out who the killer was, and how he or she did the dastardly deed. Even then my editor would ask "How come Cerai, so flummoxed for five hundred pages, suddenly, out of nowhere, cottons to the truth?" But his question was weeks away. I wouldn't have to deal with that till after I got back from Paris. By then I would have found the answer. (Answers, like fine wine, love, and inspiration flow more freely in Paris. All writers know that.) For now it was just a question of fingers flying and nose to the computer, a tortured posture at the best of times. I had turned off the phone, canceled the newspaper, and wouldn't have answered the door had it not been for the handyman who needed to redo the tiles on one wall in my studio shower which he had botched in the remodel last week. Hassling with Fred, the handyman, was the last thing I had time for, but I knew Fred. If I let that repair go till after Paris, it would never happen. When he was on the job, it had taken all my carrot-and-stick abilities to get him through his allotted work each day before he settled on my step outside for his afternoon break, which invariably meant a couple of beers and cigarettes and the denouement of the workday.

I have only myself to blame, of course—not that that makes any situation better. The same Fred patched my still-leaking roof, installed a used stove on which the burner flames go out after two minutes heating, thus threatening me with carbon monoxide poisoning every time I brewed a cup of tea, and constructed a deer fence low enough so it wouldn't block my view, or, as it soon became obvious, deer. He had promised to rectify all those mistakes. I was still waiting.

Those problems I had decided to live with. After all, it was the dry season, and I could be careful with the stove, and deer really were preferable to gardens anyway. But the tiles were a different issue—row upon row of eyesores. If they stayed on the wall a week they'd be there forever. I knew Fred.

"Fred," I had said Friday afternoon when I saw the 'champagne' colored tiles, "those tiles are green!"

"Champagne."

"Fred, champagne is golden. Those are seaweed."

"Champagne." He pointed to the tile box.

"I know champagne when I see it. I've drunk it, not as often as I'd like, but I've held a fluted glass or two in my time. I've watched the bubbles bustle to the surface and dance into the air. I've felt the frisson of liquid excitement as I lifted the glass to my lips. I've—"

He jabbed a stubby finger at the box. "Champagne."

"Bilge water green."

"Champagne."

"Pus."

"Champagne."

"Cash."

"Cham—" Fred stared, confounded.

Perhaps he thought I had merely raised the vulgar level of my replies to one more ladylike, if less aptly descriptive. I have not been a writer for years for nothing.

I was still sitting at my desk out here in my garden studio. I looked past the beige computer monitor, across the ersatz pine desk, past the stove and the tiny refrigerator that turned milk to white bricks, through the never-quite-closed French doors at the slate step on which Fred stood, like an oversized plaid shirted garden gnome. Smoking a cigarette.

Smoking was why he was not inside the studio here, planted on the other side of my desk, poking his paw into the tile box as he chanted chorus after squeaky chorus of "champagne." He wasn't standing outside from courtesy, or due to concern that the stench of smoke would linger in my rug and chair cushions, much less my own clothes and hair. He had no conception of that; he'd long since burnt out his olfactory mechanisms, which may have explained why he now assumed showering to be an unnecessary indulgence. No, it was not the danger to my lungs that touched him. It was our contract. I had written into the contract an escalating penalty for each time he crossed my threshold with a lighted cigarette. He had already accrued the five dollar fee, and the twenty-five two days last week. (I could tell by the telltale stench that he trotted in here smoking every time I was gone, but evidence of those breaches was too circumstantial to fine him.) Even so, he knew that one more step forward now would cost him $625.

So he kept himself outside.

And in doing so, he reminded me of the power of the contract. My editor and agent had taught me only too well the tyranny of contractual agreement. Like my publishers, I had paid Fred a third of his fee in advance, with two thirds due upon completion on the job. I said, "Until those *green* tiles are replaced, Fred, the job is not complete."

He grumbled. He muttered. He waved cigarette in air. But in the end there was nothing for him to do but accede.

It was a moment so sweet, I would almost have put up with the green tiles for it. Sweeter yet that I got to have my cake and watch him eat my green tiles too, so to speak.

"I got to get more tiles from the store. Store'll be closed by the time I could get there. I can't get to this here till after."

I nodded, willing to be magnanimous after so grand a victory. "So, I can expect you Monday morning, then."

Fred stubbed out his cigarette on the sole of his work boot.

"Monday, the twenty-seventh," I reiterated.

"Yeah. No problem."

"Good, it's settled then," I said, suddenly panicked that I would have to write Fred a check Monday, long enough for it to bounce before Friday, when I got paid.

That only showed how unused am I to being on the "proprietor" side of the contract. I have good reason. I've only owned this house for a year. Before then I never had the money to even think of buying a house. And, in fact, I should never have taken the leap then. The payments took every penny of my advance. And this studio, which clinched the deal for me that bright hopeful day last August had proven to be icy in winter, clammy in summer, leaky in rain, and a curse every time I needed coffee or toilet (major hobbies in the writer's day). And when my book was done, my money in the bank, I would replace . . .

When the book was done.

But at least now, I'd have my lovely bathroom. As I pondered Cerai's escalating dilemma, I could stare lovingly through the bathroom door into the depths of the muted golden tiles. By noon next Monday, I thought then, I could stare lovingly.

Monday morning as I sat in my studio watching the fog unroll, exposing the land (and my studio) to the August sun, I waited for Fred. Had it not been for the problems with my book, probably I would have overlooked his tardiness (after all, we hadn't specified an hour. I had just assumed he understood that first thing Monday morning meant eight A.M.). Had it not been for the plodding plot, I wouldn't have been sitting here to contemplate Fred at all. I'd have been out at brunch celebrating with crêpe suzettes and, of course, champagne.

Instead my eyes were making a circuit from the computer on which Cerai was slowly, painstakingly interrogating the murdered woman's adulterous husband, to the clock on which the minutes till my Friday, September 1 deadline ticked away, to the tiles that grew ever greener.

"You say, Mr. Montgomery, that you were out sailing on your yacht the afternoon when your wife was murdered. Alone?" Cerai raised a bushy eyebrow.

9:45.

Lime green.

"I wasn't alone."

"Really?"

"Really."

Cerai pulled a pen and pad out of the pocket of his plaid shirt. "Then you must let me speak to the person who can vouch for you."

"No."

9:48.

Algae green.

"This is a matter of life and death."

"No!"

"Mr. Montgomery, save us both time here. You got a mistress. You spent that afternoon with her there on your yacht, right?"

9:51.

Pond scum green.

Montgomery's lips tightened. He was avoiding Cerai's stare.

Cerai stepped forward, jabbing his finger in the adulterer's fa—

Damn! I was so caught up in the time and the tiles, I had

turned my suave and clever detective into Fred, the handy-man!

This had to stop. I barely had time to finish the book, much less go back and correct this kind of mistake. I had to deal with this problem now.

I picked up the phone and dialed Fred.

It rang. And rang. And rang and rang. I was just about to put down the receiver when the message tape activated. "Fred D'Amato. I'm out on a job. Leave me your number and I'll call you as soon as I get back. No problem."

Out on a job! A job for someone else! The tiles pulsed slime green. It embarrasses me to admit how long it took me to realize that Fred, the handyman, was not out working for someone else. Fred, the handyman, was still in bed.

I turned the phone on and called back. "Fred. You were supposed to be here at my studio this morning replacing those green tiles. I'm waiting. Call me right away." I resisted the urge to slam down the receiver. But I couldn't keep myself from staring at the offending instrument as it sat, blithely not ringing.

The phone rang. I grabbed it. Too quickly.

"Good morning, Jeffrey Hammond here." *My agent!* "So, how's that manuscript of ours coming?"

"Just putting the final touches on it," I croaked out.

"It's going to be the full five hundred fifty pages?" There was a touch of wariness in his smarmy voice, as if he hadn't quite believed me about those final touches.

"Easily."

"You're sure that—"

"Jeff, Jeff. No problem." Jeez, now *I* was talking like Fred, the handyman. "But if you expect me to finish up, you've got to let me get back to work."

"Uh . . . huh."

I knew better than to question what exactly that *uh huh*

meant. "Okay, bye now." I hung up, guiltily turned back to the computer and began to type.

Cerai stepped forward, pointing his slender, elegant finger in the adulterer's face.

10:01.

Bile green.

"It is past the time when lying will help you, Mr. Montgomery. It's already ten oh two and the tiles behind you are the color of school room walls."

Damn! This was ridiculous. What I needed was tea. A nice soothing cup of Assam tea.

But the tea was all the way across the courtyard in the house. I didn't want to miss Fred's call. This phone line rang only out here. But it was audible that far away. Surely if I ran I would be back here before it stopped ringing.

I headed over the lawn. It was still wet from the nighttime sprinklers. By the time I reached the kitchen door my shoes were muddy. No time to scrape them off. I'd deal with the muddy footprints later. I pulled open the cabinet door. I'd always meant to straighten up the jumble of tea boxes in there. People give them to me—peppermint, chamomile, Morning Thunder, Evening Slumber. Now the Assam was nowhere in sight. I could take another, I reminded myself. But when you're already grumpy the wrong tea will not make things better. I reached behind the Pleasing Peach, pushed aside a box I'd gotten to accompany an ill-fated diet—Rose Hips for Large Hips—dug under two boxes of Lemon Spice, balancing them on my arm to keep the entire wall of tea boxes from collapsing and forcing me to excavate again to unearth the Assam.

The phone rang.

I spotted the Assam.

The ringing stopped.

I tunneled.

The phone rang again.

I grabbed the Assam.

The second ring stopped.

I yanked the box free, sending rejected boxes hang gliding onto the kitchen floor. I spotted one as it landed in a blotch of mud. Leaping over it I ran for the door as the third ring commenced. I raced across the wet lawn like a hare. Well, more like a bear. As I neared the slate step to the studio my feet slipped on the slick grass. I could "see" my head striking the sharp edge of the stone, my skull splitting open, my brains spewing onto the lawn. The *green* lawn.

I scrambled mightily to keep my balance, feet racing in place, arms circling fast enough to qualify me for a helicopter license. My hand squeezed the Assam box. Tea flew like confetti. But I succeeded: my head was uncracked, my brain still an *in*terior organ. I slumped down on the doorstep and sighed loud enough to be heard at the airport.

That's when I realized the phone had stopped ringing.

I sprang up, raced across the room, grabbed up the receiver.

No one there.

No beep indicating a message.

Didn't matter. Fred couldn't have gotten more than a couple feet from the phone. I dialed.

It rang. And rang. And rang and rang. "Fred D'Amato. I'm out on a job—"

"Fred," I yelled over the message, "I know you're still there. Fred! Fred?"

The message ended. Silence continued. I glared at the clock. 10:12. "Fred, it's now nearly ten-thirty. I don't have all day. Call me."

Fred didn't. He didn't call; he didn't come. Not Monday morning, nor Monday afternoon. Nor Tuesday, Wednesday,

Thursday. Tuesday my agent called; I had finished the manuscript itself and was merely redoing the dedication page, I
reassured him. Wednesday my editor called and I swore that
I had just this minute recalled a possibly libelous comment
and I was going through the manuscript to exorcize it lest
the publisher be sued. Thursday when my agent caught me
again I was so depressed with the sixty remaining unwritten
pages I went blank on excuses and almost 'fessed up. But
years of experience in fiction rushed to clamp the hand of ra-
tionality over my mouth. When I had regained my senses, I
said, "I just need to go out and get a mailing envelope. The
book will be ready for the UPS pickup in the morning. No
problem." But from Fred, the handyman, I heard zilch. He
might have forgotten our appointment for first thing Monday morning, but he couldn't have overlooked his need to
call me. I had left him two more messages Monday, another
Tuesday, four Wednesday, one every hour on Thursday.

I had a business card with his address, but he didn't live
close to me, and with my deadline looming tighter every
day, I hardly had time to go searching for a workman's cottage in some town across the hills. What was the matter with
the man? Was he so irresponsible that he had forgotten not
only about my tiles and his promise to replace them, but
about the payment he wouldn't get until he did?

If we writers comported ourselves like workmen, there
would be no literature at all.

I was stumped. Just as Cerai was stumped. Here it was a
dank, gray, fog-covered Friday morning, September 1. I
hadn't packed. I still had fifty pages to create and Fred, the
handyman, had shoved Cerai and his petty fictional problems out of my mind. How could I concern myself with Mr.
Montgomery's mistress's admission that while she was on
the yacht she couldn't corroborate Montgomery's alibi be-

cause they had a kinky affair and she had been blindfolded?
How, indeed, when the bile green tiles were glaring at me?

What I needed was a miracle. Two miracles, actually, one
for Fred and the other for Cerai.

Miracles are not highly thought of in detective fiction.
But in life they are quite fine. And just as I was about to give
up entirely, I got my miracle. It was 10:06 Friday morning.
I was dialing Fred for the who-knows-how-many-th time. I
pushed in the final number. I could hear the phone mechanism connecting me.

Then nothing.

Then "Hello?"

It was Fred.

There, at home.

In that instant I knew he would never have answered my
call. But by chance—by miracle—before the ring started he
had picked up the phone to dial out. I could "see" him standing by a mortar-scarred phone, wiping his hands on his plaid
shirt, cigarette poking out of his mouth.

"Fred, it's me. I want those tiles changed and I want it
now."

"Oh, hi. I've been trying to reach you."

"I've been here all day, every day."

"There must be som't'ing the matter with your phone."

For a moment I almost believed him. Later I would wonder if he had this conversation so often, with so many different clients that it began to take on a certain truth for him,
the way we give validity to a religious chant in a foreign
tongue even though we really have no idea what the words
mean. But for now, I recognized the smokescreen. "You
were supposed to be here Monday morning."

"Oh yeah. But, you know, I was down at the shop trying
to get the tiles you wanted. But they were out. They said
they'd have them in the next morning, so, see, I figured I'd

just pick them up then and come on out to your house right after like. But when I got to the store Tuesday—"

"Fred, do you have the tiles now?"

"Oh, yeah."

"Then come on out now."

"That's what I was planning. I was halfway to my truck when you called."

"So you'll be here when?"

"In an hour. No problem."

"By eleven o'clock then."

"What? Yeah, sure. No problem."

I sighed in triumphant relief as I put down the receiver. So Fred had told a few lies? So he hadn't tried to call me, he probably hadn't called the tile store, and he certainly hadn't been halfway to his truck when the phone rang, *because* the phone had never rung on his end. In two hours he'd have been here and gone. My tiles would no longer be compost green, but sparkling gold. Cerai would no longer be digging himself deeper in the bilge of Montgomery's yacht but pulling together all the clues, muttering "Aha" and charging on to his penultimate danger.

Fred didn't come in an hour, nor at eleven.

Not at noon.

Cerai was still on Montgomery's yacht trying to coerce a confession from Montgomery's mistress's accountant's incestuous sister's dachshund trainer.

I stared at the computer.

I scowled at the tiles.

I glared at the computer screen, not the words but the page number.

I glowered at the tiles, the phone, the computer, the crisp new mailing envelope that was clearly not going to get filled with my manuscript by the end of the day. I slumped back in my chair. I had to admit it, I was defeated. The only fiction I had been creating this week was telling my agent, my editor, and myself that I would meet the deadline. No way would I be able to do it. I couldn't even *type* fifty pages in an afternoon, much less create them. There was no more chance of my doing that than there was of Fred, the handyman, turning up with my champagne tiles. Even for the remainder of my publisher's payment I couldn't do it. Even for double the payment. Or triple. And no excuse I could create would be good enough. From me they'd heard them all. With them I had milked dry the cow of sympathy.

Depression had relaxed my face so that I wasn't glowering anymore, just staring dully at the tiles. I would simply have to get used to that awful green. It didn't matter about Fred anymore. It was only a matter of time till the bank called him to announce that the initial check I gave him last week, postdated to yesterday, had bounced. Then I would have to promise him double his fee just so he didn't sue me. Fred was nothing if not greedy. He'd told me often enough about the other much better-paying jobs he normally worked. I hadn't believed him, of course. Why would anyone willing to pay more put up with unreliable, dishonest, smelly Fred? But I did believe in his greed. Double his fee? Even he would haul himself over here for that.

Suddenly the curtains of fog split and bright golden sunshine poured through onto my studio, onto me, onto the phone, which I picked up and dialed. I waited till I heard Fred's message ending—"I'll get back to you. No problem"—and said, "Fred, I've been thinking. This tile job is really important to me. I absolutely have to get it done today. I know you've got other, better-paying jobs, but if you can finish mine today I'll"—I started to say *double*. But in for a kid, in for a goat—"triple your fee if you can do it today. I'll be home for half an hour, then I'll be in and out, so if you can call me—"

"Hey, Fred here. I just walked in from the tile store and heard your voice. I got tied up in the tile store or I would have called you sooner, see. When I asked them about the tile—"

Another time, just out of professional curiosity, I would have let him go on so I could see where his story line ended up. But now there was no time. "No problem, Fred. How long will the job take you?"

"Half an hour max. If you're in that big a rush I could probably get the green tiles out and the champagne ones up in . . ."

He was still talking, but I wasn't listening. It didn't matter what lie he was giving me. I knew he'd never take the old tiles down nor put the new ones up. What mattered was that he'd known all along he'd installed the wrong tiles! It made me feel better.

Still he was talking. "So, like I said, I can be at your place in an hour, as soon as I go by the tile shop. The thing is those champagne tiles are going to cost you more than the green ones."

I didn't say *so that's why you installed the cheap green ones to begin with.* Or shout *on top of your triple fee?* "No problem, Fred."

"But see, the tile shop—"

"I said it was no problem. Listen, Fred, I'm going to be straight with you, and I expect you'll be straight with me." Fat chance. "I know you've got other jobs and you're not going to get here this afternoon. And in fact I've got too much work to do here this afternoon to be interrupted for the tiles. So here's the deal. I'm leaving for the airport at seven this evening. I will put the check on my desk then. You can do the work any time this evening. But my house sitter"— house sitter, that was a laugh. If I'd been organized enough to find a housesitter, I'd have been organized enough to finish the damn book—"my housesitter is coming in late, around midnight, and I'm leaving him a note telling him to go to the studio and if he finds an envelope with a check in it, tear it up. Clear?"

"Yeah. I'll be there this evening."

"After you've had a couple of beers, huh?"

"Hey, listen—"

I sighed a mite too loudly. "You're right, what business is it of mine if you arrive half-sotted as long as you do the work? So you will be here this evening?"

"Yeah, no problem."

I hadn't lied to him about needing all the time I had before my seven P.M. pickup. There were clothes to wash, clothes to iron, a quick trip to the store for ointments and potions to fill all those essential little jars in the travel cosmetic bag. And there was the manuscript to print out. Those last fifty pages stumped me for a while until it occurred to me to print out the first fifty again and simply change the page numbers. I was being overcautious, of course, but I have had years of training in planting all the clues and tieing up all the loose ends.

It was a bit after four when I plucked the last page out of the printer and pushed the manuscript into the mailing envelope. I called UPS and arranged for a morning pickup tomorrow. Then I dialed my agent.

"Jeffrey, it's done! It's in the envelope. UPS is coming tomorrow morning."

"Great, my dear. I'll release the money as soon as it gets here."

I had expected that, of course. This wasn't the first time I'd told him the manuscript was in the mail. Once I'd even said I had just gotten back from the airport after dropping off a friend who was hand carrying it on the red-eye. "Jeffrey,

I'm leaving for Paris tonight. Do you expect me to sleep on the street there, Rue de la Pennyless?"

"My dear, we have a deal."

"I know, I know. But Jeffrey, what good would it do me to lie to you now? If the manuscript isn't in your office by noon the day after tomorrow, you'll know it. You've got my address in Paris; if I lied to you about this—oh, yes, Jeff, I know you think I would lie about it—you would simply make my vacation hell. So what would I gain by lying? If I hadn't finished the manuscript, which, of course, I have, wouldn't it be easier for me to beg for a day or two's indulgence rather than give you a lie you're bound to see through?"

"My dear, your past record—"

"I know, Jeffrey. I am ashamed. What can I do to convince you? My plane leaves in a few hours. There's no way—No, wait, I could fax it to you. Do you have a fresh box of fax paper?"

I could picture Jeffrey picturing himself canceling his Friday night dinner reservations so he could stand by the fax as five hundred fifty pages chugged out. Maybe he would have to race to an all-night supply store for more paper or blacken his hands changing the ink cartridge. All for a commodity that would be redundant when the UPS man arrived.

"Well, my dear, I don't—"

"Would you like to call UPS to confirm the pickup? You can do that; I'm sending the package as a bill-to."

He was silent for what seemed eternity. Finally he gave one of those little chuckles of his. "Well, my dear, what you say does make sense. All right. I'm releasing your money. Have a great vacation. We'll talk about the book when you get back."

"Right, Jeffrey, I'm sure we will."

I heated water for my last cup of tea here in the studio,

poured it, shut the door with relief, and walked across the lawn to the house. Then I really had to scurry to get to the bank before it closed, to get back home, do all the last-minute things you have to for a long trip, culminating with dragging my suitcases down to the end of the driveway so the van driver didn't have to come up here knocking on doors for me.

At the last minute, I left the luggage and ran back to the studio, smacked a Don't Smoke in Here sign on the French door where Fred couldn't miss it, and raced back down the drive.

There were three other passengers in the van, a couple headed for Detroit, and a woman who had been out here on business now going back to Houston. The driver grumbled when I asked him to turn off the radio, but it was an hour's ride to the airport and you can't be too careful. If there was one thing I trusted it was that Fred, the handyman, wouldn't get to my house right away. But, like I said, you can't be too careful, and so we rode in a silence broken only by those snippets of pretravel conversation. The others were intrigued that I was a writer, that I had just finished a manuscript this very day. Wasn't I nervous, one of them asked, leaving it home awaiting the UPS man? No, I assured them, everything was taken care of.

I was in my pension on Rue de La Guerre when my hometown police called transatlantic to notify me of the explosion in my studio and the unfortunate fatality. Fred they had identified as much from his truck in my driveway as his remains. "Guy's a mess, Ma'am. Everything was blown to smithereens, pardon me for saying so. But just scraps all over." Even an ocean away, I could see the cop shaking his head. "Can't imagine what would possess a guy to light a cigarette and open the door to a place filled with gas. Had to've been drunk."

"Officer, I told him time and again not to smoke in there. The stove has a gas leak, but he knew that, he's the one who installed it. I don't know what more I could have done, Officer, I even left a sign on the door."

"Terrible shame. Must be awful for you, Ma'am. If there's anything we can do, you just ask."

In any other circumstances a woman who had killed a man the day before would be uneasy talking with the police, but I had not one twinge of worry. I had plotted well, laid in a school of red herrings and left the police to follow them. But that was not what gave me such ease of mind. No. Suppose the worst did happen and I was arrested. Suppose I came to trial before a jury of my peers. Suppose the wiliest district attorney in the state presented his most compelling evidence that I had premeditated and murdered. Upon hearing of Fred's unanswered calls, all the times he did not show up, hearing that the gas-leaking stove Fred himself had installed and never repaired had ignited from his own cigarette, which of those twelve of my peers would not sympathize with me? I defy anyone to find twelve American citizens who would not declare my act justifiable homicide.

So, it was with calm heart and a clear conscience that I said. "This is going to sound strange, Officer, but would you do me a favor and call my literary agent and tell him about the explosion? I wouldn't want him to hear about it and worry. Would you call him and tell him that the studio and its contents were destroyed, but everything else is okay? He'll be concerned about my manuscript—agents are so venal—so tell him that I've got a back-up disk in the house that has all but the last fifty pages on it."

About the Contributors

ADAMS, Deborah. "The Cadaver Waltzed at Noon." In this story, Deborah Adams pays an affectionate tribute to the J. B. Fletcher tradition. Watch for references to certain familiar movies and novels in the text. Adams writes the Jesus Creek, Tennessee, series—*All the Great Pretenders, All the Hungry Mothers, All the Dark Disguises, All the Deadly Beloved*, and *All the Blood Relations*.

BLACK, Veronica. "Daughter of Compassion." In this story, the indefatigable Sister Joan finds skullduggery while shopping for ecclesiastical underwear. Sister Joan appears in *A Vow of Silence, A Vow of Sanctity, A Vow of Obedience, A Vow of Penance, A Vow of Devotion, A Vow of Fidelity, A Vow of Chastity,* and *A Vow of Poverty*. Black lives in England.

CARLSON, P. M. "The Uncrowned King of Ireland; or, a Most Toad-Spotted Traitor." With this story in which the Irish politician Charles Parnell appears, P. M. Carlson continues her entertaining short stories featuring the enterprising nineteenth-century actress Bridget Mooney. The versatile Carlson also writes two series of mysteries with Indiana deputy sheriff Marty Hopkins and amateur sleuth Maggie Ryan.

CHRISTMAS, Joyce. "Up the Garden Path." In this story Christmas's retired businesswoman Betty Trenka finds more trouble in the garden than the original serpent. Trenka appears in *This Business Is Murder* and *Death at Face Value*. Christmas's other mystery series features elegant British expatriate Lady Margaret Priam.

COOPER, Susan Rogers. "Ghost Busted." In this story, Cooper's stand-up comic Kimmey Kruse and roommate Phoebe Love investigate strange bumps in the night with the help of AT&T. Kruse and the long-suffering Love appear in *Funny as a Dead Comic* and *Funny as a Dead Relative*. Texas resident Cooper's other mysteries feature romance novelist E. J. Pugh and Oklahoma deputy Milt Kovak.

DAMS, Jeanne M. "The Miser of Michely Hall." Chicagoan Jeanne M. Dams writes mysteries featuring Dorothy Martin, an older sleuth like J. B. Fletcher. The expatriate American Dorothy, who is fond of unusual hats like her author, appears in this story and in *The Body in the Transept* (winner of the 1995 Agatha Award for Best First Novel), *The Trouble in the Town Hall*, and *Felony in Fingal's Cave*.

DUNLAP, Susan. "A Surfeit of Deadlines." Susan Dunlap provides a humorous look at that ubiquitous of all writers' dilemmas: The Approaching Deadline. Dunlap is the author of three series featuring Berkeley homicide detective Jill Smith, meter reader Vejay Haskell, and private investigator Kiernan O'Shaughnessy. Dunlap, who lives in California, won the Anthony Award for her short story "Checkout."

GRANGER, Ann. "A Lady Should Avoid Murder." British author Ann Granger gives an etiquette lesson in murder in this tale. Granger's mysteries feature former diplomatic envoy Meredith Mitchell and chief inspector Alan Markby, including *A Touch of Mortality, Candle for a Corpse, Flowers for His Funeral, A Fine Place for Death,* and *Where Old Bones Lie.*

GRAY, Gallagher. "Beauty Is Only Skin Deep." Like the capable Jessica Fletcher, Gallagher Gray's forthright octogenarian Auntie Lil uncovers nefarious doings at an appalling mystery weekend. Auntie Lil, with her nephew T. S. Hubbert, also appears in *Hubbert & Lil: Partners in Crime, A Cast of Killers, Death of a Dream Maker,* and *A Motive for Murder.* Gray also writes the Casey Jones series under her real name, Katy Munger.

HOLBROOK, Teri. "Both Feet." In this tale, Atlanta native Teri Holbrook pits two old Southern rivals against each other. Holbrook is the author of the Anthony-, Agatha- and Macavity-nominated *A Far and Deadly Cry* and *The Grass Widow.*

LAWRENCE, Margaret. "The Ghost Who Died Dancing." In this story, Margaret Lawrence waltzes with death and explores the unexpected reappearance of a corpse in the 1920s. Lawrence's mysteries include *Hearts and Bones,* featuring Revolutionary War midwife Hannah Trevor.

MARON, Margaret. "The Stupid Pet Trick." North Carolina native Margaret Maron writes about a cat with more on her mind than conventional cat toys in this story. Maron's two series feature New York police lieutenant Sigrid Harald (including *Fugitive Colors*), and judge Deborah Knott (including *Up Jumps the Devil*). Maron's first Knott book, *Bootlegger's*

Daughter, swept all the mystery awards in 1992: the Agatha, Anthony, Edgar, and Macavity.

O'KANE, Leslie. "Tipping the Scales." Colorado resident Leslie O'Kane looks into the cold heart of a murderer in this story. O'Kane's books include the witty *Death and Faxes* and *Just the Fax, Ma'am*, featuring cartoonist and reluctant sleuth Molly Masters.

PERRY, Anne. "Brodie and the Regrettable Incident of the French Ambassador." A clever lady's maid and unflappable butler team up to investigate mysterious doings at an exhibition in this latest of Anne Perry's Victorian tales. Perry is the author of the Charlotte & Thomas Pitt and William Monk series and has been nominated twice for the Agatha Award for Best Novel, for *The Face of a Stranger* (1990) and *Defend and Betray* (1992). Perry's most recent novels include *Ashworth Hall* and *The Silent Cry*.

ROBERTS, Gillian. "Murder, She Did." Gillian Roberts provides some sly references to J. B. Fletcher's presence in this story of a delayed reckoning. Roberts is the author of the Philadelphia-based Amanda Pepper series, including the Anthony-winning *Caught Dead in Philadelphia*, the Agatha-nominated *Philly Stakes* and more recently *The Mummer's Curse* (1996).

SQUIRE, Elizabeth Daniels. "In Memory of Jack." Peaches Dann, Elizabeth Daniels Squire's absent-minded heroine, uses her mnemonic tricks to solve an old crime in this story. Peaches appears in *Who Killed What's-Her-Name?, Remember the Alibi,* and *Memory Can Be Murder*. Squire, a former reporter who lives in North Carolina, won an Agatha Award for her Peaches short story "The Dog Who Remembered Too Much."